Up Close and Personal

FERN MICHAELS

Up Close and Personal

DOUBLEDAY LARGE PRINT HOME LIBRARY EDITION

KENSINGTON BOOKS
http://www.kensingtonbooks.com

KENSINGTON BOOKS are published by

Kensington Publishing Corp.
850 Third Avenue
New York, NY 10022

ISBN-13: 978-0-7394-8519-4

Printed in the United States of America

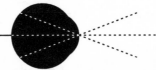

This Large Print Book carries the
Seal of Approval of N.A.V.H.

I would like to dedicate this book to four wise and wonderful, not to mention witty, people who on a daily basis make my life easier. In alphabetical order, of course, Audrey and Michael Bernstein, Martin Friedman, and Peter Rubollota. Thank you for your wise counsel and your expertise that allows me to sleep peacefully. Thank you and know that I respect and love you all.

Prologue

The hour was late, the middle of the night to be precise, and the silence was so total it was ominous. The woman standing at the window stared out at the dark night. Here and there she could see tiny pinpricks of light, but she had no idea what they were. She could also see her reflection in the dark window as well as the entire room behind her.

The woman closed her eyes and wondered if she would ever sleep again. How long could a person go without sleeping? She should know the answer. Why didn't she know? When she opened her eyes she could see the reflection of a woman standing in the middle of the open doorway. She was still as a statue.

The woman knew that the figure in the

open doorway wasn't going to speak until she was spoken to. Strange how she knew that and yet didn't know how long a person could go without sleep. "Did you do as I asked?"

The woman waited for a response. None came. "Grace, I'm speaking to you. Did you do what I asked you to do?"

Five seconds passed, then five more seconds before Grace said, "Yes."

The woman at the window turned. She peered at Grace, and said, "You sound unsure. You can't lie to me, Grace. I gave you enough money to put your four boys through Ivy League colleges. When you told me your husband had medical problems I gave you enough money to buy a small lake house so you could both retire. With the additional money you demanded, you can both live quite comfortably for the rest of your lives. Now, I am going to ask you again. Did you do what I asked you to do?"

The woman turned back to the window. She stiffened when she heard the single word, "Yes."

"Thank you, Grace. I'll be leaving in a few hours. Thanks to you, I'll be able to leave with a lighter heart. I don't ever want to see you again. I don't want our paths to cross again. It will be best if you never return to this state again. When you leave you will follow all my instructions to the letter. Do we understand each other, Grace?"

"Yes, ma'am, we understand each other."

The woman watched Grace Finnegan's reflection in the window as she left the room, closing the door behind her. Long ago she had committed Grace's face to memory; not that she had any intention of remembering her in the days to come. There was no need to say good-bye. After all, they weren't friends. Business associates, if you will. She banished the picture of Grace Finnegan from her mind as she continued to stare out at the tiny dots of light. Soon the sun would rise, and she'd walk away from this place and never look back.

Chapter 1

It was a beautiful summer day, but the agitated woman pacing and kneading her hands barely noticed. Warm, golden sunshine flooded the sunroom where she was pacing, doing its best to warm the trembling woman. As hard as she tried, she couldn't avoid the gallery of pictures that lined one wall. She knew she shouldn't have come here this morning, of all days. Yet she'd carried her coffee cup in with the intention of sitting on one of the rattan chairs. Not to think. Never to think. She knew it was impossible, but she'd come anyway. The sunroom had been Emily's favorite room in the whole house.

Once this room had held a life-size giraffe, easels, paints, brushes, a blackboard and pastel chalks, a television, a pink polka-dotted sleeping bag with the name EMILY embroidered across the front in huge, white silky letters. An oversize toy box, also with the name EMILY stenciled on it, was stuffed with animals and assorted toys. Deep, comfortable furniture suitable for a sickly little girl had been covered in all the colors of the rainbow, just waiting for her to sit or lie down with her storybooks.

Once, a long time ago, a hundred years ago, a lifetime ago, this had been Emily's favorite room. Before she had become bedridden.

Tears puddled up in Sarabess Windsor's eyes. Why had she come in here? She looked around for her coffee cup. She reached for it and sipped the cold brew. Okay, she'd had some coffee. Now it was time to leave. But could she walk out of this room today? Of course she could. She had to.

Sarabess looked at herself in the mirror that hung on the back of the door leading into a small lavatory. She'd taken exceptional pains with her dress. She was wearing her grandmother's pearls, her mother's pearl earrings, and a mint-green linen dress that so far was unwrinkled. If she sat down, it would wrinkle. She wanted to look put together when Rifkin Forrest arrived, and part of that put-together look did not include tears. Every silky gray hair was in place. Her makeup was flawless; her unshed tears hadn't destroyed her mascara. Just because she was sixty didn't mean she had to *look* sixty. The last time he'd been to the house, Rif had told her she didn't look a day over fifty. Rif always said kind things. Rif said kind things because he'd loved her forever.

Sarabess turned around at the door, seeing the sunroom as it was. Other than the gallery of pictures, all traces of Emily were gone. Now the room held rattan furniture covered with a bright-colored fabric. Dozens of green plants and young trees could be seen through the wall-to-wall windows. Overhead, two paddle fans whirred softly. A wet bar sat in one corner. She was the only one who ever came into this room. Once a year on this date she unlocked the door, walked into the room, and allowed herself ten minutes to grieve. Most times she cried for the rest of the day. For weeks afterward she wasn't herself. Still, she put herself through it because she didn't want to forget. As if a mother could ever forget the death of her child.

Sarabess closed and locked the door. Maybe she would never go into the room again. Maybe she should think about moving away. But she did not see how she could. Emily was buried here in the family mausoleum. She could never leave her first-born. Why did she even think it was a possibility? Then there was Mitzi Granger lurking on the fringe of her life. Even Rif couldn't do anything about *squirrelly* Mitzi. Something had to be done about Mitzi.

The Windsors had lived on Windsor Hill in Crestwood, South Carolina, for hundreds of years. She was the last of the Windsors, though only by marriage. Then again, maybe she wasn't the last of the Windsors. She would have to wait for time to give her an answer.

As the mistress of Windsor Hill walked down the hallway toward the heavy beveled-glass front door, she realized she'd left her coffee cup in the sunroom. Well, it would have to stay there for another year. Or, until she felt brave enough to unlock the door and enter the room that was simply too full of memories. At the end of the hallway, she opened the door and walked out onto the verandah. She looked around as though seeing it for the very first time. She was surprised to see that the gardener had hung the giant ferns, cleaned the wicker furniture, laid down new fiber rugs, and arranged the clay pots of colorful petunias and geraniums. Even the six paddle fans had been cleaned and waxed.

How was it possible she hadn't noticed? Because she was so wrapped up in herself, that was why. She tried to remember the last time she'd sat out here with a glass of lemonade. When she couldn't come up with any answer, she started to pace the long verandah, which wrapped around the entire house. Where was Rifkin? She looked down at her diamond-studded watch. He was ten minutes late. Rif was never late. Never. She wondered if his lateness was an omen of things to come.

For the first time since getting up, she was aware of the golden June day as she stared out at the Windsor grounds. Once the endless fields had produced cotton and tobacco. Now, they produced watermelons, pumpkins, and tomatoes that were shipped coast to coast. The acres of pecan trees went on as far as the eye could see. The pecans, too, were shipped all over the country. On the lowest plateau of the hill, cows grazed, hence the Windsor Dairy. Horses trotted in their paddock. There was a time when she'd been an accomplished horsewoman. Once there had been a pony named Beauty and a little red cart that carried Emily around the yard. Just like Emily, they were gone, too.

Sarabess heard the powerful engine then. She looked down at her watch once more. Twenty-three minutes late. What would be Rif's excuse this fine Monday morning? Did it even matter? He was here now.

When the Mercedes stopped in front of the steps leading to the verandah, Sarabess waved a greeting before she rang the little bell on one of the tables next to a wicker chair—Martha's signal that she should serve coffee on the verandah. Sarabess walked back to the top of the steps to wait for Rif's light kiss on her cheek. She smiled when she realized there was to be no explanation as to why he was late. Rif hated to make explanations. It was the lawyer in him. She motioned to one of the chairs and sat down across from the attorney.

He was tall and tanned from the golf course. His hair was gunmetal gray. His eyes were sharp and summer blue and crinkled at the corners when he smiled. She loved it when he smiled at her. An intimate smile, she thought. Because he was semiretired, Rif felt no need for a three-piece suit on his days off. He was dressed in creased khakis and a bright yellow T-shirt. His only concession to his profession was the briefcase he was never without. He dropped it next to his chair before sitting down. His voice was deep and pleasant when he said, "You're looking particularly fine this morning, Sarabess."

"Why thank you, counselor. You look rather fit yourself this fine morning. Are you playing golf today?"

"Unless you have something important you need taken care of. You sounded . . . urgent when you called."

"It's time, Rif."

The attorney didn't bother to pretend he didn't know what she was talking about. He knew his old friend was waiting for him to say something, but he opted for silence. Sarabess raised an eyebrow in question. Instead, he reached for the cup of coffee the old housekeeper poured for him. He sipped appreciatively.

Sarabess set her own cup on the table. "I want you to hire someone to find her. It's time. And it's also time to do something about Mitzi. I . . . I want her taken care of once and for all. Do we understand each other, Rifkin?"

Rifkin. Using his full name meant Sarabess *was* serious.

Rifkin watched as a tiny brown bird flew into one of the ferns. He knew the little bird was preparing her nest. "Let it be, Sarabess. You need to stop obsessing about . . . about Mitzi. There's nothing I can do legally, and we both know it."

Sarabess leaned forward. "How can you say that to me?"

"I can say it because I'm your friend. Mitzi aside, you should have called me fifteen years ago to ask me to find her. I warned you this would happen. Now, it's too late."

Sarabess stood up. "It's never too late. You hounded me daily for years to do what I'm asking you to do now, and suddenly you're telling me it's too late! I don't believe that. If you won't do it, I'll find someone who will. Mitzi may have me on a short leash financially, but I am not without influence in this town. As you well know, Rifkin."

Suddenly he felt sick to his stomach. "You waited fifteen years too long. If you think for one minute that that girl is going to forgive you, you are wrong." Rif brought the coffee cup to his lips. He didn't think he'd ever tasted anything so bitter.

"She's my daughter. I'm her mother."

Rif sighed and closed his eyes. His voice was so low Sarabess had to strain to hear it. "You gave birth to her. You were never her mother. You were Emily's mother. As your attorney, I'm advising you to let matters rest. As your friend and lover, I'm asking you to let matters rest. Please, Sarabess, listen to me."

"I have no intention of following your advice, Rifkin. It's time."

"For you, perhaps. Not for Trinity. If she wanted to see you, she knows where you are. She could have come home anytime. The fact that she hasn't called or written in fifteen years means she doesn't have any interest in seeing you."

"She doesn't even know Harold died. She should know that," Sarabess said coldly. "Mitzi knows. If you could just get inside that . . . that *squirrelly* head of hers, we could find Trinity in a heartbeat."

"Now, almost fifteen years after the fact, you think Trinity should know her father died! I can't believe I'm hearing what I'm hearing. I advise you to think seriously about what you are contemplating, Sarabess. You gave birth to Trinity so you could use her bone marrow so that Emily would live. Then you gave that child to your foreman and his wife to raise. You hauled her up here one day a year on Princess Emily's birthday. You had the Hendersons dress her up like a poor relation; then you sent her away after the party. Not to mention the humiliation of those countless other command performances— whenever Emily pitched a fit. You're delusional if you think Trinity will want to see you."

"I had no other choice. Emily would have died. Because of . . . of that . . . procedure, I had thirteen more years with my darling daughter. Thirteen years! I wouldn't trade those thirteen years for anything in the world. When . . . When I explain things to Trinity, I'm sure she will understand. She is my daughter, after all. She has only one mother. We all have only one mother." Despite Sarabess's efforts, her voice was colder than chipped ice, her eyes colder still.

Is he buying into my explanation? At first blush, it doesn't seem like it. Well, that will have to change quickly.

"I don't care how much it hurts, Sarabess, but you were never that girl's mother. You didn't sit with her at night when she was sick. You didn't take her to church, you never took her shopping. You never once looked at her report card, never went to a school meeting. You never read her a bedtime story or tucked her into bed. Half the time you couldn't remember what her name was. Emily didn't like her, either, thanks to you. Guilt is what took Harold to an early grave, and we both know it. I guess you're just a lot tougher.

"Trinity has never touched the trust fund your husband, her father, set up for her. I believe that Harold told her about it when she was quite young. I cannot even begin to imagine what that young girl thought at the time if, indeed, he did tell her. Maybe the knowledge of that monstrous trust fund was what made her run away. At least that's

Mitzi's theory. If so, apparently Trinity didn't want any part of it, you, or Harold. Let it be."

Sarabess fingered the pearls at her neck. She felt choked up at her lover's words. "When did you get so ugly, Rifkin Forrest?"

"Ten minutes ago, when I saw what you were about this morning. Today of all days. Why didn't you make the decision a week ago, a month ago, yesterday? Today is the anniversary of Emily's death. In seven months Trinity will be thirty and will come into the trust," Rif said, his voice sounding ominous.

Sarabess didn't think Rif's voice could get any colder, but it did. She actually shivered in the humid June air.

"You went in that room, you looked at the pictures, you relived the thirteen years that Trinity gave your daughter. You probably cried, and then you decided maybe this was a good time to find your other daughter. The thought probably crossed your mind that you might have grandchildren somewhere. That's the part I want to believe.

"The other part, having to do with the trust fund that will revert to you if Trinity dies or isn't found in time to take possession of her trust, is not something I want to think about today. I'm sorry, but I have to leave. I have a tee time in thirty minutes."

Sarabess was speechless. "You're leaving?"

"Yes, I'm leaving. I don't want any part of upsetting that young woman's life for your own selfish desires."

Sarabess started to cry. "Please, Rif, don't leave. I . . . I'm not doing this for me. You may be right—it may too late—but I won't know if I don't try. I just want to find her. I won't invade her life if it looks like I . . . if . . . she isn't interested. I thought that Jake," she said, referring to Rif's son and law partner, "might do the search. He used to play with Trinity when they were little children. Emily used to watch them from the sunroom. She was so envious."

A linen handkerchief found its way to her eyes. It all sounded good to her ears. It should—she'd rehearsed this little speech for hours in front of the mirror.

Rifkin sighed wearily. "It always comes back to Emily, doesn't it?"

"Yes, it always comes back to Emily. You can't expect me to turn thirty years off and on like you'd turn off a light switch. I made a mistake. I want to try and make it right."

That sounds good, too, Sarabess thought smugly.

"Jesus, Sarabess, you didn't just make a mistake, you made the Queen Mother of all mistakes. Now you want the child you threw away back. I'm sorry, it just doesn't work that way. On top of that, it's too late."

"Stop saying that. I didn't throw Trinity away. I . . . What I did was pay the Hendersons to take care of her. I couldn't do it. I was fighting for Emily's life. Trinity had a roof over her head, good food, adequate medical care. If she was neglected, as you say, it was only by me and my husband. I will concede the point that the child needed a mother, and that's where I failed her. If she . . . If I had brought her here to the big house, she would have been raised by servants. At least with the Hendersons she had a normal life. She wanted for nothing, and don't try to tell me otherwise."

Sarabess had said these words so often, they sounded truthful to her ears. She struggled to cry. She whipped the handkerchief past her eyelashes as she watched Rifkin carefully. She needed him.

"Too bad you couldn't pay the Hendersons to love her. When are you going to factor in Trinity's trust fund?"

"The fund has nothing to do with this. The Hendersons did love Trinity in their own way. They are plain, hardworking people. They're not demonstrative. That doesn't mean they didn't love Trinity. They raised her for fifteen years. There was feeling there. Even as sick as he was, and living with *that woman,* Harold told me they were heartbroken when Trinity ran away. Harold would never have lied about something like that."

Rifkin watched the little brown bird as she dived into the fern with a piece of string in her beak. Preparing her nest for her young. *That's how it's supposed to be,* he thought. *Even the birds know about motherhood.* "Were you brokenhearted, Sarabess? Did Trinity's running away affect you in any way?"

He was just saying words, words he'd said hundreds of times. It was a game, pure and simple.

Sarabess drew a deep breath as she fingered her pearls. "No. It barely registered. I was still mourning Emily. Nothing registered. Nothing." *Such a lie,* she thought.

"I have to leave now, or I'll miss my tee time."

"Well, a tee time is certainly important. Even I understand that. Run along, Rifkin. Enjoy your golf game," Sarabess said, in an icy voice.

Rifkin refused to be baited. He waved as he descended the steps. "Thanks for the coffee."

Sarabess wanted to tell him to go to hell, but she bit down on her bottom lip instead. Her eyes filled again. Everything Rif had said was true. Tomorrow she would think about everything he'd just said. Everything she'd been thinking about for the past fifteen years. Tomorrow. Then again, maybe she wouldn't.

Today was Emily's day. Today she had to go to the cemetery to talk to Emily.

Tomorrow was another day. Rif would come around; he always did.

Chapter 2

Crestwood, South Carolina, population 27,855, was a pretty little town with sidewalks, tree-lined streets, cozy shops with colorful awnings, homey window displays, white benches underneath the ancient trees that shaded the streets like giant umbrellas, and old-fashioned lampposts. There was a town square with a bandstand where the town fathers stood at attention to view the seven yearly parades.

On the Fourth of July, the picnic kicked off at the bandstand, covered with flags and banners. The children of Crestwood decorated the entire square for Halloween in the hopes of winning the grand prize, which was a double-decker ice-cream cone from Elmo Mitchell's drug store every Saturday afternoon for a full year. Santa Claus and his elves came to town in a horse-drawn sleigh on wheels the day after Thanksgiving. It was said in the *Crestwood Record* that every resident in town turned out for the event.

Just about every citizen of Crestwood said their town was the prettiest in the whole state. As far as anyone knew, no one had ever disputed the claim.

The main street in Crestwood really was named Main Street. Parson's Bakery had the best croissants and peanut butter cookies. Elmo Mitchell served the creamiest ice cream, which came from the Windsor Dairy. John Little of Little's Hardware had every garden tool and gadget known to man. John even kept a barrel of peanuts sitting by the white bench outside his store for those who wanted a handful to munch on as they did their daily shopping. Eva's Tea Shop sported double tubs of bright pink petunias at each side of the pristine white Dutch door. It was hard to pass Eva's and not stop for a frosty glass of sweet tea and a cucumber sandwich on fluffy white bread made by Eva herself at the crack of dawn.

Visitors to Crestwood, and there were many, said that the nicest thing about the little town was how everyone knew everyone else and that they felt a real sense of place when visiting. When the visitors left the sleepy little town, most, if not all, agreed that Crestwood was more small-town America than the fictional Mayberry of television fame.

Jacob Forrest, "Jake" to everyone in town, walked down the tree-lined street to the end of the block, turned right on Richardson Avenue and continued on to the offices of Forrest & Forrest & Granger. There was no Granger these days, just the elder Forrest and Jake.

Jake hadn't always practiced law with his father here in Crestwood. Fresh out of law school, he hadn't wanted to return to Crestwood, where, according to him, they rolled up the sidewalks at eight o'clock in the evening. He wanted some nightlife, some razzle-dazzle inside and outside the courtroom. So, he'd headed for Atlanta, Georgia, and had done a three-year stint working as an assistant district attorney before the nightlife and the razzle-dazzle lost their allure. After leaving the DA's office, he joined a small criminal defense law firm in Albany, Georgia, where he spent five years before deciding to return to Crestwood.

With little or no crime in Crestwood, both senior and junior Forrests mostly dealt in real estate closings, deed filings, speeding tickets, wills, and the like, which left time for fishing and golf in the summer and skiing in the mountains in the winter.

Jake walked up a flower-lined walkway to a one-story building constructed of old Charleston brick. Every morning Jocelyn, the receptionist, polished the brass plaque at the entrance. The high shine allowed Jake to see his reflection. He grinned the way he always grinned. He grinned now as he opened the door and walked into the cool reception area. He waved to Jocelyn, and said, "It's getting hot out there."

"It's only June, Jake, it's going to get hotter. Your father has called four times. He said to call him. He should be on the ninth hole by now."

"Did he say what he wanted?" Jake called over his shoulder. Like he really cared what his father wanted.

"Now, Jake, you know better than to ask me that. But if it will make you feel better, no, he didn't say what he wanted. Your twelve thirty is due any second now. Stacy," she said, referring to Jake's secretary, "went to

Eva's. She said everything you need is on your desk. Call her if you need anything." The plump, grandmotherly receptionist winked at Jake.

Jake tossed his briefcase on one of the client chairs as he shrugged out of his light-weight suit jacket. He jerked at his tie and rolled up the sleeves of his white dress shirt. Seventy-seven-year-old Clara Ashwood, his twelve thirty appointment, didn't stand on formality. He looked down at his appointment book. Clara wanted to change her will. Again. She'd changed her will the week after Christmas, then again in April. He wondered what happened this time. At Christmas she hadn't liked the presents her children had given her. In April, two of her six children hadn't shown up for Easter dinner, so she'd changed it again. As far as he could tell, Clara was on schedule. Clara was his favorite client.

Jake looked at his watch. He had five minutes before she was due. Did he have time to call his father? His father was always succinct, especially if he was on the golf course. He pressed in the numbers, waited, then his father's voice came on.

"Jocelyn said you called," Jake said by way of greeting.

Instead of responding to his son's statement, Rifkin asked a question. "Can you have dinner with me this evening? I have something I need to discuss with you. It's important, Jacob."

Jacob. When his father called him Jacob, Jake knew that whatever he wanted to talk about was serious—to him. "Hey, you're the boss. Your name is first on the plaque," he said, bitterness ringing in his voice. "Back-bay at six thirty. I have to eat and run, so don't try throwing any guilt trips in my direction."

"It sounds fine, Jake. I'll see you at six thirty."

Jake's hand was shaking when he broke the connection. He took deep breaths to stop his internal shaking. He was on his last one when he heard her cane before he saw her. He got up and walked over to the door. For some reason he felt like he always had to escort Clara Ashwood to her chair. "Miss Clara, how are you on this fine June day?"

"Don't ask me that, Jake. I wouldn't be here unless something was wrong. Here," she said, reaching into the huge straw bag she was never without, "I brought you some brownies. I made them early this morning." The brownies were his payment.

"Well, I appreciate it, Miss Clara. Would you like some sweet tea?"

"I would. I told Jocelyn to fetch it when I came in. Such a darling lady. You're lucky to have her. She's always so pleasant. I wish I could be pleasant all the time the way she is. I get so damn cranky sometimes. I made up my mind this morning that I want to change my will and leave everything to the SPCA."

Jake blinked. *Everything* wasn't all that much. "Okay, if you're sure. I'll get right on it. You can stop in tomorrow and sign the new will. Are you sure, Miss Clara?"

"Damn straight I'm sure. I'm not even going to bore you with the details. I stopped by the cemetery to visit with Arnold, and who do you think I saw? Sarabess Windsor, that's who. She was sitting there on that green grass with a huge bouquet of summer flowers, and she was all gussied up in fine linen and those pearls of hers. She was wailing up a storm. That mausoleum is so ostentatious." She sniffed. "I wanted to go over and tell her to give it up already. Fifteen years is too long to be railing on like that.

"I'd give up my porch rocker—and you know how I like my porch rocker—to know where little Trinity is," she said, changing the subject. "Every time I think about Sarabess Windsor I think about Trinity Henderson. She arrived *a little too conveniently* after Sarabess's return from New York." Clara sniffed, then said, "Emily now, she was a mean-spirited little girl. I know, I know, she was ill, and Sarabess didn't help matters any the way she coddled her."

This was all said in one long breath. Clara was Crestwood's town crier, but Ardeth Gamble was snapping at her heels for the honor.

Jocelyn tapped on the door and came in with Clara's sweet tea. After thanking Jocelyn, Clara took a sip and put the tea glass on the little table next to her chair. After Jocelyn had left, Clara said, "Do you know, Jake, Sarabess hasn't invited any of us to the Hill in years? I find that peculiar. I think she's *tetched* in the head these days. Not that I care. I did get a little sick and tired hearing about Princess Emily for two hours every week. I couldn't concentrate on my cards.

"Now, where was I? Yes, yes, the SPCA. Call me when the changes are ready, and I'll come by and sign it. That's my business for the day. You need to tell Jocelyn the tea is a tad too weak. Not that I care, but someone else might. Too many ice cubes water it down. You need to make a tray of ice cubes out of the tea so that doesn't happen. You might want to pass that on to her. Good-bye, Jake. It was nice seeing you again. No need to walk me out. I can still do that myself."

Jake knew the drill. He smiled and waved. He waited until he could no longer hear the sounds of Clara's tapping cane before he propped his feet on the desk. A frown built itself between his eyebrows. Trinity Henderson. Now that was a name from the past. A name that made his heart pound in his chest. He didn't want to think about Trinity Henderson because then he'd have to look at his own conscience.

Stacy Messina knocked on the edge of the door and poked her head in. She gurgled with laughter when she said, "Who is

Miss Clara's new beneficiary this time? Hey, I'll fight you for those brownies."

Jake grinned as he looked at his secretary. Stacy made coming to work easy. She was a short, buxom young woman with shoulder-length red hair that was so curly it looked like a mass of corkscrews. She was always early for work and the last one out of the office at night. Jake knew he was going to miss her when she left at the end of the summer to get married. "The SPCA this time. You can have *one* brownie. You don't want to lose that girlish figure and not fit into your gown, now, do you?"

Stacy was also defiant. She helped herself to two brownies. "Why so pensive, Jake? You looked like you were a million miles away. Is anything wrong?"

"No, nothing's wrong. Miss Clara was talking about Trinity Henderson. I used to play with her. I was five years older, but they had horses out at the farm and I liked to ride and so did she. When you're kids, age doesn't matter. She could climb a tree better than me. I always fell out. She never did. She was a nice little kid. I had a really serious crush on her back then." *Even now I can't think about her without my heart quickening.*

Stacy looked at her handsome boss. Six-two, curly black hair, eyes that were the color of cobalt and two of the most adorable dimples she'd ever seen. When he smiled he looked like a movie star. She'd told him that once, and he'd laughed his head off. "*Was* a nice little kid? Did something happen to her?"

"I was in college at the time but Dad said she ran away on her fifteenth birthday. As far as I know, she's never come back. If she had, this town would have buzzed like a beehive. I don't think anyone talks about it anymore. You were probably five or six at the time, so I can understand why you didn't know her."

"So, why was Miss Clara talking about her? Are they related or something?"

"No, nothing like that. Miss Clara said she went to the cemetery the way she always does and saw Sarabess Windsor there. It's not important, Stacy. Get me the Merrill file. I need to do some work for Mr. Merrill. Type up the new will and make sure it's ready tomorrow. Oh, Miss Clara said to tell Jocelyn that the tea was a tad too weak. You might want to correct that the next time you make it. She also said that making a tray of sweet tea ice cubes will prevent watering down the tea. How come you didn't think of that?" Jake teased.

"Uh-huh," Stacy said as she left the office, closing the door behind her. A second later the door opened again. "There's a story about the runaway girl, isn't there? You're supposed to keep me apprised of everything. I am your secretary."

"Go! There's no story!"

The door closed.

Like hell there was no story, but he couldn't dwell on it right now. He reached for the Merrill file and got to work.

Rifkin Forrest was early, so he settled himself down outside the restaurant on a weathered bench festooned with an old fishing net to wait for his son and to do a little people watching. He packed his pipe and fired it up. A fragrant puff of smoke circled upward. From time to time a customer would stop for a few seconds, and greetings were exchanged. Others would clap him on the shoulder, ask about his golf game, while still others would comment on the weather.

Sometimes it was nice, Rifkin thought, to live in a town where everyone knew everyone else. Other times it wasn't so nice. No matter, he would never leave Crestwood.

As Rifkin puffed on his pipe he did his best to concentrate on his golf performance earlier in the day, but his thoughts took him elsewhere. He didn't want to think about the reason he was meeting his son for an early dinner. He also didn't want to think about Sarabess Windsor, but he couldn't clear his mind. He heaved a mighty sigh when he finally saw Jake cross the parking lot and head in his direction. How handsome he was. He was fit and trim because he worked out religiously. Right now he was mopping at the perspiration on his forehead. He had his mother's finely chiseled features, her dark hair, her ready smile. He also had his mother's gentleness, which wasn't to say he didn't get angry or belligerent; he did, but it never lasted more than a few seconds. With other people. Never with him. Jake hated his guts and made no secret of that hatred.

Rifkin gently knocked the tobacco from his pipe on the edge of the bench as he stood up to greet his son. He smiled. Jake grimaced.

"I'm here, let's get out of this heat. I don't have much time."

"Excellent idea. How are you?"

"Miss Clara changed her will again today."

"That's hardly news. You busy?"

"Semi. June is always slow, you know that. I hope this impromptu dinner isn't because you're going to tell me you're going away for the entire summer and leaving me with all your cases the way you usually do. We're supposed to be a partnership. That means we share the load."

Rifkin clapped his son on the back. He felt Jake flinch. "Now, Son, would I do that to you?"

Jake reared back. When his father used that particular tone of voice, he knew he wasn't going to like whatever he was about to say. And, when he referred to him as *Son* as opposed to *Jake,* then Jake knew that whatever his father wanted to discuss was serious. Shit, he had his whole summer planned out. His lady of the moment, one Amanda Pettijohn, was not going to like this one little bit.

"Yeah, Rif, you *would* do that to me. You did it last year and the year before. So, you're saying you aren't going away for the summer, is that it?"

"No, Son, I am not going away for the summer. You are."

Jake was saved from a reply as the hostess appeared and led them to a booth with a view of the canal. Rifkin waved away the menus. Both he and Jake always ordered the same thing when they dined at Backbay: pecan-crusted salmon, shoestring sweet potatoes, Miss Eva's sweet pepper relish, and Backbay's house salad with a pecan-grape vinaigrette dressing. Today would be no different. When the waiter appeared, Rifkin ordered their dinners and two bottles of Heineken.

Jake leaned across the table. "What? Where? We don't have any pending business that requires travel. Do you have a new client? Look, I have plans for the summer. Send one of the paralegals to handle whatever it is that requires travel."

"I would if I could . . . *Son*."

There it was again, that tone, and the term *Son*. Jake clenched his teeth. "But you can't, is that it? Or is it that you won't?"

"My client specifically asked for you to handle this matter. You're the logical person, Jake. I think you'll agree when I explain it all to you."

Jake was pissed now. He reached for the bottle of beer the waiter handed him. He didn't bother with a glass but started slugging from the longneck. That in itself should have been warning enough to the elder Forrest that his son probably wouldn't be happy with what was coming. His father always made a toast to something or other when they dined together.

Jake let his eyes wander around the nautical décor of the restaurant. Suddenly he didn't like the place. He made a mental note not to return anytime soon. "Who is this mysterious client of yours that thinks I'm the only one who can handle whatever it is that needs handling?"

Rifkin made a production of pouring his beer into a glass. He looked everywhere but at his son, instead concentrating on making sure the suds from the beer didn't slosh down the side of the glass. "Sarabess Windsor!"

Jake's face closed tight. "The answer is no, and further discussion is not negotiable, *Pop*. I refuse to discuss anything that has to do with Sarabess Windsor. If that's what this dinner is all about, I'll leave now and go to Burger King."

"The least you could do, Jake, is show me the courtesy of listening to me. Let's not create a scene. I'd also like it if you'd lower your voice."

"Personally, Pop, I don't give a good rat's ass what you'd like. If you're worried about how loud I'm talking, let's not talk about it at all, and there won't be a scene. Look, Pop, I understand you have feelings for Mrs. Windsor, have always had feelings for *that woman* even when Mom was still alive. I didn't like it back then, and I still don't like it. You really don't want to go there with me. Maybe she can jerk *your* strings, but she sure as hell isn't going to jerk mine. If you promised her my help, rescind that offer right now. I wouldn't tell *that woman* what time it was if she was standing in a dark room. I think I'm going to go to Burger King after all. See ya, Mister Forrest." Jake was greased lightning as he bolted from the chair and left the dining room.

Rifkin stared at his son's back as he weaved his way through the tables to the exit. He'd known an explosion was going to happen, so why had he arranged the dinner? Because Jake was right—Rifkin had always been in love with Sarabess Windsor and could deny her nothing.

Now he had to concentrate on eating the dinner that was about to be put in front of him. Food that he knew would stick in his throat. Still, he couldn't give the other diners something to speculate about. He looked up and smiled at the waiter as he set his food in front of him. "Jake had to leave. I'll take his dinner to go and drop it off later."

"No problem, Mr. Forrest."

"I'll have another beer if you don't mind."

"That's not a problem, either, Mr. Forrest."

Somehow or other, Rifkin managed to chew his way through his dinner. He wasted no time with dessert or after-dinner coffee. He stuck some bills under the saltshaker, picked up the to-go bag, and left the restaurant. His next stop: Sarabess and Windsor Hill. To report his failure—a word that wasn't in Sarabess's vocabulary.

Chapter 3

Jake did precisely what he had told his father he would: headed straight for Burger King on Bacon Ridge Road. He ordered two Whoppers, a Big Double Fish, fries, a milk shake, and a Coke before he headed to a parking space where he chewed his way through his fast-food dinner. He really had to stop eating this crap even though they said the burgers were flame-broiled, he thought, continuing to chow down on the fast food.

Now he had two things to think about tonight (three, if you counted Amanda Pettijohn): Trinity Henderson, the little girl from his past; and Sarabess Windsor, the woman his mother and his aunt Mitzi had hated with a passion.

As Jake munched his way through one of

the two Whoppers he thought about his mother, who had died during his senior year in high school. Nola Forrest had been the sweetest, gentlest, kindest woman in the world. To his knowledge, his mother had never said an unkind word to or about another living soul. She'd loved all children and animals. He knew for a fact that she'd loved him with all her heart.

Their gardens, which his mother had planted and tended, had been written up in every Southern magazine in print. She'd taken him and his friends camping and didn't mind sleeping in a tent, and she'd laughed about the creepy-crawly things that abounded in all campgrounds. She'd taught him to drive, taught him how to swing a baseball bat. She'd played tennis with him at least twice a week. Even though they'd had a cook and a housekeeper, his mother had cooked all his favorite foods one night a week. They'd laugh and giggle over the food that wasn't good for them, but she'd justify it by saying they would double up on vegetables the rest of the week. The brownies that she made every Saturday morning were the best.

But she knew. How could she not have

known? Everyone in town knew that Rifkin Forrest had *a thing* going on with Sarabess Windsor. However, no one in town, and that included his mother, knew if *that thing* had ever been acted upon. Jake thought it had, but he couldn't prove it. Once, during his sophomore year, he'd gotten the courage to actually discuss with his mother what he considered his father's indiscretion. She hadn't put him off. Instead, she'd said rumors should never be repeated. Her eyes had been so sad when she said it. *Oh, yes, she knew*.

When she'd gotten sick, she'd changed her will, leaving the entire Granger fortune, except the mansion, to him, in a trust that he couldn't tap until he was thirty-five years of age. The mansion had come to him when he turned thirty. The remainder of the robust trust would be available to him in ten months. His father had been stunned and actually started proceedings to contest the will, but he hadn't followed through once he read a letter his mother's attorney handed him hours after the reading of the will. His father had never divulged the contents of the letter, nor had Jake asked. Things had changed after that, though. There was less

spending money, his first car had been secondhand. He'd gone to a second-tier college, and his allowance had been meager.
He'd worked to have extra spending money.

To say he and his father had a close,
warm relationship would be a lie. They
worked in the same office, had dinner occa-
sionally, but they didn't really socialize. They
never called one another just to chat—there
was nothing to chat about. As far as Jake
knew, his father never went to the cemetery
to visit or leave flowers on his mother's
grave.

His father still lived in the stately historical
mansion that had once belonged to the
Grangers of Crestwood. He himself had
never gone back to the mansion after he
graduated from law school. Instead, after his
time in Albany, he found a three-bedroom
apartment on the outskirts of Crestwood
that suited him just fine because the owner
of the complex said they accepted dogs.
Not that he had a dog, but he was going to
get one. Plus, he liked the window boxes
and the colorful striped awnings over the
windows. The window boxes and the flowers reminded him of his mother. Each renter
was responsible for the flowers, something

he took seriously. His window boxes were the prettiest, he thought smugly. When he was finally settled, he was going to go to the SPCA and adopt a dog.

He'd furnished the entire apartment with secondhand furniture and a few antiques he'd picked up at garage sales. If he had anything to say about it, he would never set foot in his mother's old home even though it now belonged to him.

Jake jammed the napkins and the leftovers from the Whoppers into the bag his food had come in. He slipped his car into gear, drove over to the trash can, and dumped the bag. "You can just kiss my ass, Sarabess Windsor," he muttered as he waited for a break in traffic before swinging out onto South Main Street.

So much for Sarabess Windsor. Short and succinct. On to Amanda Pettijohn. No doubt she was ticked off big-time. He had to decide if ticking off the lovely beauty was important or not. In two seconds flat he decided that in the scheme of things it wasn't important.

Jake buzzed on down the road, stopped for the light at Five Points, continuing on until he came to Tea Farm Road, where he made a left. He made several more turns before he brought his Mustang to a complete stop. He climbed out, briefcase in one hand, the fish fillet and milk shake in the other. He whistled for Elway, the resident cat that he and the others fed and took care of. Elway was disdainful and had no loyalty to any of the tenants. He went where the food was, the main reason he was so fat. No amount of enticing or cajoling could tempt the cat to come indoors. He would follow the tenants up the steps to their individual decks, where he would wait patiently for his food to be put onto a plate and his milk or water into a bowl. Battle-scarred Elway, one part of his ear missing, his tail limp and bedraggled, had six such arrangements.

Jake whistled for the cat, who came on the run and followed Jake up the steps to his second-floor apartment. Jake opened the door and waited like he always did to see if Elway would follow him. He always left the door open in the hope the fat cat would venture indoors, but he never did. Today, however, Elway trotted indoors, looked around, then leaped up onto the tweedy-looking sofa that held a thousand different smells. Stunned, Jake made no move to close the door but reached for a dish and a little bowl in the cabinet. He crumbled up the fish fillet and poured the milk shake into the bowl. He set them on the floor and waited to see what the cat would do. What a coup this was! He could hardly wait to tell his neighbors.

Elway hopped off the sofa and marched to the kitchen. He gobbled down his food, licked his whiskers, then inhaled the milk shake. Jake felt pleased with himself. When the fat cat finished his dinner, he meandered back to the sofa where he hopped back on, stretched out, and went to sleep.

"Son of a gun! Looks like I got myself a cat!" Jake walked outside to bring in the box he had placed on his deck, hoping this day would come, and filled it with litter from the plastic container he kept in his pantry. He closed and locked the door.

Jake was so pleased seeing the cat sleeping on his couch, he forgot the anger he felt toward his father. He didn't care about Amanda, either. How weird that a mangy cat could take the place of the luscious Amanda Pettijohn.

As Jake started to get changed he had

one leg in his jeans when he thought about Trinity Henderson. He'd promised himself to think about little Trinny. In his bare feet, he walked out to the kitchen, popped a beer, and carried it back to the couch of a thousand smells. He was extra careful not to wake Elway. He made a mental note to take Elway's picture so he could prove to the other tenants that Elway had indeed come indoors and actually climbed onto the couch and gone to sleep. He propped his feet on the scarred coffee table, fired up a cigarette—his one bad vice, which he had no intention of giving up—and puffed contentedly. He told himself two cigarettes a day weren't going to harm him. Settled on the couch, he leaned back, closed his eyes, and traveled back in time to the last time he'd seen Trinity Henderson. . . .

The back tire of the bike he was riding skidded on the shale road. A heartbeat later he was flat on his back staring up at Trinity Henderson, who was laughing her head off. *Girls are so stupid,* was his first thought. Then he decided to cut the girl a little slack because she was great fun. "Anyone else make it out here today?" he grumbled as he got to his feet. He picked up his bike and straddled it.

Trinity brushed at her curly blonde hair that was always full of straw. She was picking at it. She shrugged.

Jake immediately knew what the shrug meant. Sarabess Windsor had corralled the others and invited them to the house to spend time with Emily, which meant there would be no ball game today. "I told them to come in the back way. Miz Windsor can't see us on the back road," Jake said.

"Then how do you explain the fact that she was waiting for them on the back road? They didn't want to go, but you know how Miz Windsor is. She would have called their parents and told them about their bad manners. They're probably playing Parcheesi, drinking lemonade, and eating those sticky little cakes Emily likes so much. It's pretty hard to say no to Miz Windsor," Trinny said sourly.

"That means the guys will be up there for two hours, and I have to get home to mow the lawn. I hate that woman, and I hate Emily even more," Jake grumbled.

"Yeah, I know. It could be worse, Jake. She could have corralled you, too."

"Nah. I told my father how much I don't like her and Emily. I told him I wasn't going up to the big house anymore. I told my mother, too. My mother told my father I didn't have to go there if I didn't want to go. My father tried to tell me it was a charitable thing to do. He meant keeping Emily company. All she does is whine and cry. You have to let her win every game or Miz Windsor gets mad. I'm seventeen, and I think I'm a little old to be playing Parcheesi. I can't stand that girl. She isn't even nice to Miz Windsor. My parents would ground me for a month if I sassed them the way Emily sasses her mother."

"When you're sick you can do whatever you want." Trinity gave Jake such a push he sailed forward on his bike. "I heard Emily is sweet on you. Like in *really* sweet. Marie told me the last time they were up there all Emily wanted to do was talk about you until Miz Windsor made her stop and told her you were too busy with your paper route and all that kind of stuff. Marie said Emily kicked and screamed and said she wanted you there NOW. You must be hot stuff, Jake Forrest. I don't know how she can think that.

You're so homely, with all those freckles and that hair of yours that stands straight up."

Jake flushed. "You're only twelve years old. You shouldn't be talking about stuff like that. If I'm homely, then you're downright ugly, with those spaces between your teeth and that pigtail. You have freckles on your nose, too. Look how skinny you are! You look like a stick of spaghetti."

Trinity stopped in her tracks, hands on her hips. "I can *whup* your ass with one hand tied behind me. You take that back, Jake Forrest."

"Not in this lifetime, Trinny Ninny." Jake pedaled as fast as he could on the shale road because he knew she was going to make good on her threat. "Okay, okay, I didn't mean it. You're beautiful even if you do have spaces between your teeth. I'm getting a haircut tomorrow. Truce, Trinny." He was looking over his shoulder and knew his words weren't getting through to the skinny girl. From the determined look on her face, he knew she *was* going to *whup* his ass. How was that going to look to the others when they found out? And they *would* find out because Trinny Ninny would make sure she told them. Not good, that was for sure. He slid on the shale and once again was on the ground, Trinity standing over him. He looked up and was stunned to see Trinny's eyes glistening with tears. Ah, shit! He rolled over and got to his feet. "Okay, take your best shot," he said cavalierly.

Trinny strode past him. "You aren't worth it, you jerk!"

"Aw, c'mon, Trinny, give it up. I'm sorry. Maybe I am homely. Who cares? Let's go riding, or we can hit balls. I'll pitch to you."

Trinny pounced and was in his face within seconds. "Are you really sorry, or did you just say that?"

"Yeah, I'm sorry, but you are skinny. I guess you can't help that. Neither one of us can do anything about our freckles. Sooner or later your teeth will grow together. If they don't, you can always get braces. So, do you want to go riding, or do you want to hit some balls?"

Trinity thought about the question. What she really wanted to do was go swimming in the pond, but there was no way she was going to let Jake Forrest see her skinny body in a bathing suit. He'd laugh himself silly, and she'd cry all night long. "Why don't you just go home and build your character some more by mowing the grass."

"If that's the way you feel about it, I will. Not that my character needs building, either. Who's being a jerk now?" With that, Jake turned his bike around and headed down the shale road. He pedaled slowly to make sure he didn't slip again. Trinny would be laughing into next week if that happened. He stopped once, turned around, and waved at his young friend. He felt a lump form in his throat when she didn't wave back.

When Jake arrived home ahead of schedule, he walked around to the back of the house, where his mother was working in one of the flowerbeds.

"Was the ball game canceled, Jake? You're home early."

Jake sat down on the grass and hugged his knees. "Things didn't work out. The witch got to the guys first. There was just me and Trinny. We got into . . . a thing, and we both said some things to each other. I hurt her feelings, and she hurt mine."

"Jake, please don't call Mrs. Windsor a witch. Why in the world would you say anything unkind to Trinity? I know she's younger than you are, but that's no excuse. Little girls have feelings. On top of that, I do believe she has a bit of a crush on you. That's not like you. Well, Jake?"

Jake plucked at a blade of grass and put it between his fingers and whistled. His mother did her best to hide her smile. "She said I was homely and my hair stuck up or something like that."

Nola Forrest's smile blossomed as she plunged the trowel into the soft, loamy earth. "Your hair does stand up on end. You were supposed to get a haircut a week ago. You aren't homely, you're rather cute. I think that's what Trinity was trying to say."

"Jeez, Mom, you didn't hear her. That's not what she was trying to say. I was there, and she was mad."

"Did you apologize?"

"Yeah, up one side and down the other. She wasn't buying it, so I came home. How come I have to mow the lawn when we have a gardener?"

Nola smiled again. "Because I said so." Jake rolled his eyes as he made his way to the toolshed to pull out the lawn mower.

As hard as he tried, Jake couldn't get Trinny's tear-filled eyes out of his mind. He pushed the mower with a vengeance. He looked over at his mother several times. She waved and smiled.

Seven months later he was standing at the cemetery saying good-bye to his mother. Trinny, wearing a dress and a hat, was there with the Hendersons. She looked so silly he almost laughed, but it was hard to laugh when you were grieving for your mother. He raised his eyes to look across at his aunt Mitzi, his mother's younger sister. He wished he could leap over the yawning hole in the ground and fall into her arms. Mitzi could always make things better. Suddenly he felt his father's hand on his arm. He jerked it away. His eyes were still on Mitzi, who had lifted her black veil and shook her head slightly. That look meant he was to cool it.

When it was all over, and he could no longer stem the flow of tears, he made his way to Mitzi's side. "Can I go home with you, Mitzi? I don't want . . . I can't . . ."

"No problem, kiddo. You better tell your father, though."

"I'm not telling him anything. In case you haven't noticed, he isn't exactly grieving.

And what in the damn hell is *she* doing here?"

Six different answers tickled Mitzi Granger's lips, but she didn't utter any of them. It wasn't the day to stir up a hornet's nest. "The whole town is here, Jake. Everyone loved your mother. It's called paying your respects."

Jake came out of his reverie and carried his beer bottle out to the kitchen. It was fully dark now. He walked around, turning lights on throughout the apartment. He craned his neck to see if Elway was still on the couch. He was. Before he forgot, he rummaged in a drawer for his digital camera and proceeded to take pictures of the old tomcat from every angle.

Sometimes things worked out really well. Other times, no matter what you did, things just went to hell.

"Where are you, Trinity Henderson? I wonder if you ever knew about the crush I had on you," Jake muttered as he headed off to the shower.

Chapter 4

Jake Forrest groaned in his sleep and rolled over. Was that burned bacon and coffee he smelled? Since he lived alone with the exception of Elway's temporary visit, he must be dreaming. He rolled back over when he realized he wasn't dreaming. He groaned again, louder this time. Finally, he opened his eyes to see Elway sitting up on the bottom of the bed, staring at him. He supposed he was seeing some kind of miracle. Unless . . . Mitzi Granger was in the kitchen cooking breakfast. At four thirty in the morning! Mitzi Granger, coupon clipper extraordinaire, square dance queen of the South, fourth-richest woman in the country, thanks to her prescient investing during and after the dot-com boom and bust, matchmaker to the geriatric population of Crestwood, and the world's worst cook. *That* Mitzi Granger. Feisty, opinionated, tell-it-like-it-is Mitzi, lover of all four-legged creatures, and his beloved aunt.

"Mitzi!" he roared.

"Yes, darlin'." The ninety-pound, skinny stick of a woman wearing bib overalls and a flowered shirt, holding a spatula, appeared in the doorway.

"It's four thirty in the morning, Mitzi!"

"I've been here since three. Your cat kept me company. I didn't know you had a cat, Jacob. You should have told me you had a cat. I would have brought some catnip and a scratching post. By the time you brush your teeth, your breakfast will be ready."

"Is the bacon burned, and will the eggs be rubbery? Is the coffee weak?"

"Yes to all of your questions. You know I can't cook. Your mama was the cook in the family. Since I was the baby in the family, your grandmother understood my lust for life and let me do what I wanted. Cooking was not one of those things. Food is sustenance. That's how you have to look at it. Someone has to look out for you, darlin'. I do wish you'd get married. Your cat likes me." It was all said in one long *swoosh* of breath while the spatula waved back and forth.

"All right! All right! It's four thirty! Why couldn't you wait till six o'clock, when decent people get up to make breakfast?" Jake muttered on his way to the bathroom.

"Because I never sleep. I consider sleeping a waste of time. I have worlds to conquer, and as you can see, I'm not getting any younger. I like to get an early start on the day, unlike some people I know," she said, jabbing the spatula in Jake's direction. "For your information, I have an aerobics class at six thirty. Then I have my martial arts class at eight, and I do my yoga for an hour. No decent person eats breakfast at ten thirty. Ten thirty is time to start thinking about lunch," Mitzi insisted as she made her way back to the kitchen, Elway hot on her trail.

"How stupid of me," Jake continued to mutter as he stepped under the spray. Maybe if he stayed there long enough, Elway would eat the shitty breakfast his aunt was making. Had made. It sounded like it was just waiting for him to choke down.

When Jake trundled into the kitchen ten minutes later, he promised himself he would make a valiant effort to eat everything Mitzi made him, even if it killed him, because he adored his aunt and didn't want to hurt her feelings.

Jake settled himself at the table but not before he looked around. Newspapers were everywhere. He raised a questioning eyebrow even though he already knew the answer.

"I was cutting out coupons to make the time go faster until it was time to wake you. I have eighteen dollars' worth. You don't mind, do you, darlin'?"

"Hell no! Just don't buy me any more bargains. I have two hundred rolls of toilet paper jammed in my linen closet, sixty-four rolls of paper towels under the bed, forty-four cans of string beans sitting on top of my dishes, and sixteen tubes of Colgate toothpaste in my medicine cabinet. There's no room for my aspirin bottle, and I don't even like Colgate, I like Crest."

"Get over it, darlin'. A bargain is a bargain. A penny saved is a penny earned."

Why did he think he could win with Mitzi? "What's on sale?"

"All kinds of good stuff. I heard about your dinner, or lack of it, with your father."

Jake slapped at his forehead. "How *do* you do that, Mitzi? It was last night. Do you have some kind of pipeline that automatically feeds you information?" Jake asked as he picked up a piece of dry, burned toast.

Mitzi ignored the question. "He had a bad time on the golf course. That means something's brewing with that . . . *that woman*. Tell me I'm wrong, darlin'."

Jake jabbed his fork into the mound of rubbery eggs. There had to be at least six scrambled eggs on his plate. He shrugged. "I didn't give him a chance to tell me whatever it was he wanted to talk about. I left and went to Burger King. He did say Sarabess Windsor wanted me to do some traveling for her. Yesterday was the anniversary of her daughter's death. Miss Clara came in to change her will again and told me she saw Sarabess at the cemetery. Maybe there's some kind of significance to the two things. That's all I know, Mitzi. Do I really have to eat these eggs?"

"Of course not, just dump them in the disposal. I heard *she* was at the cemetery. I guess we can assume your father's golf game had something to do with that visit."

Jake dumped his breakfast into the sink

before he slid his plate into the dishwasher. "Mitzi, do you remember Trinity Henderson?"

Mitzi's cheeks puffed out. Jake thought she looked like a squirrel with flaming red hair. "Of course I remember her. I loved that girl as if she were my own. Time or her absence will never change my feelings for that young woman even though we don't talk about her these days. You should know that. Why are we talking about Trinny? She ran away when she was fifteen. I remember it clear as if it was yesterday. I was the only one alarmed, but no one cared if I was concerned or not. They just let her go. I could never understand that. The Hendersons work for *that woman,* so what do you expect? As far as I know, the police weren't even called in. I had the feeling back then that it was something like good riddance. The child never came back here as far as I know. I even hired private detectives to try to find her, but they didn't. Why do you ask, darlin'?"

"Her name came up yesterday during my conversation with Miss Clara. Clara went on to say Sarabess was doing the weeping-and-wailing thing. Then I got to thinking about Trinity last night when I got home. She was a tough little cookie. I was wondering what happened to her, that's all."

"Your mama thought Trinity had a crush on you. I thought so, too. I *know* you had a crush on *her*. Oh, well, that was then, this is now. She's probably married with little babies. I have to go now, darlin'. You don't mind cleaning up this mess, do you?" Mitzi asked, waving her arm about to indicate the mutilated newspapers and the countertops.

Jake shook his head, dismayed at her words. "Thanks for the breakfast. How come you didn't eat any?"

"Are you crazy? I only eat legumes, Jell-O, and greens. Your cat really likes me."

Elway hissed as the door opened, then closed.

Jake sat down, exhausted. He looked at the clock. It read 5:15. He waited until he heard the roar of the racy Jaguar his aunt drove before he opened the door for Elway. The cat looked at him, then trotted off toward the living room. Jake didn't know if he should laugh or cry. Actually, at that precise moment he felt meaner than a snake for some reason.

With nothing else to do until it was time to

dress and head into the office, Jake made fresh coffee and toast. While he waited for the coffee to drip, he cleaned up his aunt's mess. A wry smile tugged at the corners of his mouth. He loved Mitzi, and he knew she loved him.

He wasn't sure if the term *misfit* applied to Mitzi or not. She was certainly her own person and marched to a different drummer. Everyone in town loved Mitzi except his father and Sarabess Windsor. Mitzi could always be counted on to lend her name to any worthy endeavor, give generously to causes, and work tirelessly for children's and animals' rights. It was true, she never slept; well, hardly ever. He'd seen her take what she called power naps. She had more stamina and energy than he had on his best day, even though she puffed on cigarettes all day long, to everyone's disgust. The truth was, he couldn't keep up with her.

Once he'd asked his mother why Mitzi wasn't married and her response was that Mitzi had had her heart broken and didn't trust another man to mend it. His mother seemed to approve of her sister's wild and wicked lifestyle. In later years, he thought his mother would have liked to cut loose, but her upbringing wouldn't allow it. His father made no pretense of liking Mitzi. He called her a disgrace to the family, a rebel who chased rainbows. Mitzi retaliated by saying he was a shitty lawyer with his brains in his ass. After she thumbed her nose at him, she attacked Sarabess Windsor and hinted at secrets she would divulge when she wrote her memoirs. Jake was a kid at the time, and it was the first time he saw fear on anyone's face. It wasn't until years later that he wondered why his aunt's words would make his father so fearful.

From that day forward, Mitzi had taunted his father with her dark secrets. His father had made it his business not to respond to her taunts, Southern gentleman that he was, and never to be in Mitzi's company if he could help it.

One of these days I'll have to ferret out those secrets. One of these days . . .

Jake was tying the knot in his tie when his doorbell rang. He looked at his watch. He was almost certain it wasn't Mitzi, who at the moment was probably exercising, turning herself into a pretzel. Amanda Pettijohn? He laughed at that ridiculous thought. Then, who?

Jake didn't bother to look through the little peephole. He yanked open the door and found his father. "I know it's early, Jake, but I thought I would stop by before you left for the office. I have court all morning, so I won't be in the office till after lunch."

What happened to, "Hello, Son"? Jake wondered as he motioned for his father to enter the apartment. Elway skirted his father's ankles, his back arched and the fur standing on end. *What does that mean?* Jake wondered. *Mitzi would probably say it meant the cat didn't like Rifkin Forrest.*

"What's up, Pop?" Jake asked coolly. If his father came for an apology, he was going to grow a beard before that happened. "Coffee?"

"No thanks. I had some earlier. Look, I'm sorry about last night. I'm here to ask you if you'll go up to Windsor Hill to talk to Mrs. Windsor. She wants to hire you. You, Jake, not me."

"I'm not taking on any new clients. What part of 'I don't want anything to do with Miz Sarabess Windsor' didn't you understand? There are two other lawyers in this town, let her hire them. I'm not interested, and you know what else? I resent you trying to coerce me into it. Maybe you make house calls, but I don't."

"Jake, I think you know I wouldn't ask you to do this if it wasn't important. Can't you do it for me? If Mrs. Windsor is agreeable to an office visit, will you at least talk with her?"

Jake snorted. "I don't *think* so. For the second time, what part of 'I want nothing to do with Sarabess Windsor' don't you understand? How many times do I have to say it? I never made a secret about my feelings where Sarabess Windsor was concerned. Mom might have closed her eyes to it all, but mine were wide-open. You put that in your pipe and smoke it, *Pop*. By the way, Mitzi stopped by earlier to make breakfast for me. Did you know she's writing her memoirs? I'm going to represent her," he lied, with a straight face.

Rifkin's eyes narrowed. "Your aunt has supposedly been writing her memoirs for twenty-five years. I'm sure she hasn't written a word, and there's no reason to think she'll actually sit down on that bony ass of hers to do it now, either. My guess would be that she's bored and wants to stir up trouble. She excels at stirring up trouble."

Jake turned belligerent. He hated such

discussions with his father. He really hated it when his father turned on Mitzi. For some reason, the old man always made him feel like an errant schoolboy whose punishment he was debating. "Oh, yeah, well, how do you explain the fact that she's on chapter six? She's doing it!" he lied again. "What do you think of *that?*"

"What I think, young man, is, you're acting like a petulant schoolboy and lying about Mitzi. I wish you'd reconsider and talk with Mrs. Windsor."

"You do have a one-track mind, don't you? You're the one on retainer with the Windsor family, not me. I'm way past the age when you can tell me what to do, *Pop.* I gotta go now."

Elway scurried around his ankles. Jake bent down and picked him up. He was stunned when the mangy old cat started to purr. For some reason, Jake felt a lump form in his throat. Mitzi always said every single person in the world needed someone at one point in their lives. He wasn't sure, but it looked like Elway needed him right now. And he suddenly needed Elway to hold on to, for some strange reason. He made a move to open the door for his father to leave.

Rifkin's narrowed eyes were now mean-looking slits. "Jacob, would it make a difference to you if I told you the reason Mrs. Windsor wants to see you has to do with your old childhood friend Trinity Henderson?"

There was that name from his past again. Elway was purring so loudly, Jake felt light-headed as he struggled with his father's words and the cat's uncharacteristic behavior. He needed to say something and he needed to say it *now.* "No, it wouldn't."

The door was wide-open. Elway could leap out of his arms at any second and be lost to him. He wished his father would leave. He stepped forward, Elway secure in his arms. As Rifkin walked through the door, he said, "You're turning into a jackass, Jacob."

Jake knew his mother would be appalled at his response. Mitzi would clap him on the back and say something witty. "Takes one to know one," Jake muttered under his breath. An instant later, he was sorry. The man was his father, and he owed him a modicum of respect. Just a modicum.

When the door closed tightly, Jake locked

it. Only then did Elway leap out of his arms to head for the couch, where he settled down in the mound of pillows and started to groom himself. Jake walked back to the kitchen for a second cup of coffee. If it hadn't been so early, he would have poured a jolt of Southern Comfort into the coffee. Instead, he added three sugars and some heavy cream.

As he sipped at the coffee, Jake's mind raced. What the hell was going on that involved Trinity Henderson? More to the point, why was Sarabess Windsor interested in Trinity? Sarabess had to be aware of his feelings where she was concerned. Over the years he'd never made a secret of those feelings, to his father's chagrin. Yet, Sarabess had sent his father to plead her case. "Well, lady, you can plead till the proverbial cows come home, and I still won't give you the time of day."

Jake rinsed his coffee cup, set out some food and water for Elway, and left the apartment. The minute he reached the office he was going to do an Internet search to see if he could locate his old playmate. Something was going on, and he wanted to know what it was.

Chapter 5

Sarabess Windsor, dressed in beige linen and sensible heels, walked through her garden's early-summer flowers. While she appeared to be admiring the colorful blooms, her thoughts were far away. Then she looked down at the begonias, which were huge and healthy-looking. There were no yellow leaves on the geraniums. The borders of impatiens were more vibrant than in any other year in her memory. Maybe she should think about giving the gardener a raise. She realized the improbability of that. She sniffed as she strolled along the cobbled garden path. She loved the sweet scent of the Confederate jasmine that was carried throughout the garden by the warm June breeze. Emily had always loved the scent of jasmine.

Sarabess plucked one of the small white blooms and brought it to her nose. She threw it on the ground immediately because it brought back too many memories of Emily. As she hurried down the old path, the sweet scent chased her relentlessly.

Sarabess stood at the split rail fencing that afforded her a spectacular view of the entire town of Crestwood. From where she was standing she could see the gravel road that led uphill to her front door. She took a deep breath when she saw Rifkin's car. She stomped her foot in irritation when she saw there was only one person in the vehicle. Yet, in truth, she wasn't all that surprised that Rifkin's son wasn't with him. Perhaps he would come to the Hill later in the day. If not, she'd just have to go into town to his office. He wouldn't dare refuse to see her. Then again, he might just do that because he was just like his crazy Aunt Mitzi, who marched to some unseen drummer, according to Rifkin. Only God and Rifkin Forrest knew how much she hated Mitzi Granger.

Sarabess's heartbeat quickened as she watched Rifkin get out of his car. For some reason her pulse always quickened at the first sight of the man walking toward her.

He looked incredibly handsome in his business suit, pristine white shirt, and power tie, a tie she'd given him not too long ago. She adored his tallness, his long-legged stride, and the smile that was just for her. She smiled in return even though she knew he wasn't bringing good news.

"It's all right, Rif. I think we both knew he wouldn't come up here. I appreciate your coming to the Hill to tell me as opposed to calling me. I can always go into town. Don't look so stricken, it's all right."

Rifkin reached for Sarabess's hand. She gave a gentle squeeze in return. No one but servants were there to see, and they couldn't care less what the mistress of Windsor Hill did or didn't do.

"I did my best, but my best wasn't good enough. Jake is . . . he's incredibly stubborn. He's also bitter where I'm concerned. It eats at me, but there's nothing I can do about that, either."

"What you wanted, Rif, was a chip off the old block. Your son is his own person, and that's admirable. I'll think on the matter and go into town when it's time. I know you're running late, so go along. Dinner this evening?"

"Absolutely." Rifkin exerted some of his own gentle pressure on Sarabess's hand before he turned to go back to his car. The car door open, Rifkin looked over his shoulder, and said, "Jake has a cat!"

Sarabess laughed. "Really!"

Rifkin grinned as he climbed into the car and turned on the engine. He laughed all the way downhill and into town. He had no idea why he was laughing.

Sarabess waited until she could no longer see Rifkin's car before she walked back into the mansion. She walked through the rooms, touching this, looking at that. She was upset. For the first time since Rifkin Forrest came into her life, he hadn't been able to give her what she asked for. No one had ever said no to her before. She didn't like the feeling. Not one little bit. She corrected the thought. Mitzi Granger said no to her on a regular basis.

Sarabess continued to walk through her impeccably decorated house. She'd lost count of how many times she'd redone the entire house. Just to have something to do so she wouldn't think. Choosing fabrics, looking at paint swatches required one's undivided attention. She'd striven for hominess, but it was an impossible task. The house simply didn't allow for a home-and-hearth décor. Once she'd gone the antique route, and Rifkin had laughed his head off. The next day everything had been carted off. She rarely made a mistake, but when she did, it was what Rifkin called a doozy.

Always, when she got upset like this, Sarabess wished she had a hobby instead of the obsession that haunted her day and night. If you believed what you read in the slick magazines, everyone had a hobby of some kind, but she imagined few people were obsessed. Maybe there was something wrong with her. Nothing in the world interested her except Rifkin, and she lived for his visits. How in the world had her life come to this?

She was at *the door* with no memory of walking down the hall to get here. She never just opened the door. Oh, no, that was too easy. She had to go through the painful ritual of casting her mind back in time, back to when her beautiful little girl inhabited the fairy princess room.

Sarabess squeezed her eyes shut so the burning tears wouldn't roll down her cheeks. She inserted the little gold key she wore around her neck. She turned the knob, her eyes open now. For some reason she always gasped at the beautiful room. It truly was fit for a princess. Her little princess. The canopy bed had sheer pink netting gathered at each of the four posts with sparkling white ribbon. The bedspread was pale pink, with appliquéd ballerinas dancing across it. Even the pillows were covered with miniature ballerinas. A crystal lamp with a frilly pink shade stood on each night table.

Sarabess sat down on the edge of the bed. She wasn't sure, but she thought she could detect the faint scent of Confederate jasmine, or maybe it was a gardenia scent. Emily had loved having her bedding sprayed with the scent. When the delicate little flowers were in bloom there was always a vase of them on the nightstand. She got up and looked around the enormous room—which was part bedroom, part playroom, part schoolroom—surprised that after all these years the carpet was just as white as the day when it was installed.

So many books. Books that hadn't interested Emily. Every toy known to a child sat in the playroom. And yet, Emily had rarely played with anything. The schoolroom section of the room was relatively bare except for the white desk, the white chair with a pink cushion, the blackboard with pink chalk, the pink Princess telephone. A pity there had been no friends to call. The rambunctious youngsters Emily's age, even those younger or older, had no time for a semi-invalid. They wanted to play ball, climb trees, chase each other, go swimming in the pond, ride their bikes. All Emily could do was watch from her window on the Hill. The princess in the tower.

Sarabess walked over to one of the diamond-pane windows and opened it. The warm summer air *swooshed* inward, the sheer organza curtains billowing in the breeze. She closed her eyes, remembering other times she'd done the same thing. The scent of jasmine invading the room was almost overpowering. With shaking hands, Sarabess closed the window and straightened out the crisp white curtain.

She took one last look around. Did she have the guts to dismantle this room? Could she donate all these things to some worthy cause? What would she do then? Just paint the room, change the carpeting and curtains, then walk out and lock the door?

Sarabess walked down the hall to her own bedroom and picked up the phone. She punched in the numbers she knew from memory. "This is Julia Barrows, and I'd like to make an appointment with Mr. Forrest. The young Mr. Forrest." Five minutes later, Sarabess hung up the phone. She had an appointment for eleven o'clock the next morning with Jacob Forrest.

It was midafternoon when Jake Forrest turned away from his computer. He'd searched for hours for something that would lead him to Trinity Henderson, with no results. It was as though she'd dropped off the face of the earth the day she'd run away. LexisNexis offered nothing, no Social Security number, no driver's license in her name. Mitzi might be right. The girl could be married with a new name. Still, he should have been able to come up with a Social Security number. Maybe she had been smart enough to get herself a new identity. For all he knew, his old playmate could live on the other side of the country or maybe in another country altogether. He wondered if there was any point in hiring a private detective. He'd read in an article not too long ago that modern-day private eyes never left their offices. They had the ways and the means to do everything by computer.

Jake looked at the pile of work on his desk. Nothing that couldn't wait for a day or so. Clara Ashwood's updated will was complete, all she had to do was sign it. He looked down at his watch before reaching for his jacket. He waved good-bye to Stacy, waved again to the receptionist, and was out of the building in three minutes. His destination: Trinity Henderson's family. *Why the hell not,* he thought as he climbed behind the wheel. He pressed the power button to lower the windows. The car was stifling with the early-summer heat.

Jake didn't see his father watching him from his office window. Even if he had, he would have ignored him.

The ride out to the Henderson farm took barely ten minutes. He used to make it on his bike in five minutes, with all the bike paths he'd taken. There were no traffic lights on bike paths. He smiled to himself as he recalled those long-ago days when he'd pedaled out to the farm like a bat out of hell, trying to beat his own time.

The Henderson farm wasn't really the

Hendersons' farm. It belonged to Windsor Hill and Sarabess Windsor. John Henderson managed the farm, and Mrs. Henderson cooked for all the farmhands. Back then, he'd just assumed Trinity's parents owned the farm. Mrs. Henderson had on more than one occasion looked the other way when he and the other kids tried to outwit Sarabess so they wouldn't have to play with or entertain Emily. It was Trinity who knew the best hiding places, places where Sarabess Windsor would not trample in her high-heeled shoes and fancy dresses.

Jake parked his car and waited for the golden retriever to sniff him before he made his way to the back door where Mrs. Henderson was shelling peas. "It's Jake Forrest, Mrs. Henderson. May I come in?"

"Lord have mercy, is it really you, Jake? I haven't seen you in a coon's age. What in the world are you doing out here? Would you like some sweet tea? Mercy, that was three questions."

Jake laughed. "It's okay. I'd love a glass of tea. It's going to be a hot summer, I think."

Lillian Henderson was what his mother would have called a plain lady. She wore a simple cotton dress with a sparkling white apron. He'd never seen her without an apron. Her hair was as white as the apron she wore and was pulled back into a knot at the nape of her neck. She wore wire-rimmed glasses that appeared to be trifocals. She handed him the glass of iced tea. Jake couldn't help but notice that her hands were rough and red, the nails clipped short.

"Sit down, Jake. Imagine you being a lawyer! John and I were talking not too long ago about coming to see you about making out a will. I don't know why we keep putting it off. For the same reason we haven't bought cemetery plots, I guess. Would you like some gingerbread? I just made it this morning."

"No thanks, the tea is fine. I guess you're wondering why I came out here."

Lillian Henderson smiled. "I figured you'd get around to telling me."

Jake decided to make it up as he went along. "I've been delegated to get in touch with all the kids we used to pal around with. We want to hold a reunion of sorts over . . . over the Fourth of July. We want to include Trinity. Do you know how we can reach her?"

Lillian's head jerked upright. The emerald

green pea pod she was shelling fell to the floor. It was obvious to Jake that whatever she had thought he was here for, Trinity was not it.

"I'm sorry, Jake, John and I never . . . Trinity never . . . What I mean is when she lit out, she didn't look back. We've never heard a word from her. I'm afraid she won't be attending your reunion."

"Do you have any idea where she might have gone? Did she have cousins, friends of yours, anyone she might have gone to? What did the police say?"

Lillian looked away. She folded her hands in her lap. "There was no one that we knew of. She helped herself to the grocery money and left an IOU for the three hundred dollars. She might have had about sixty dollars of her own money. She took a few of her clothes and her gym bag. She made her bed and tidied her room before she left."

"Did she leave a note?" Jake asked.

"No, she didn't. Unless you count the IOU. She sent a money order for the three hundred about two years later. The envelope had a Pennsylvania postmark. You couldn't make out the town, it was kind of pink and blurry."

"Do you know anyone in Pennsylvania?"

"Not a soul."

"What did the police say?"

Lillian bit down on her bottom lip. "Mrs. Windsor said we weren't to call the police. She said Trinity was going on sixteen and capable of taking care of herself. She said she wouldn't have run away without a reason, and she didn't want the police crawling all over Windsor Hill. John said we should do what she said since we worked for her. I didn't want to do it, but . . . John can be very convincing, as can Mrs. Windsor. I cried for months. Every time the phone rang I'd get so nervous I could hardly talk."

Jake didn't know what to say. He knew his mother would have been out beating the bushes with her bare hands to find him if he'd run away. She wouldn't have stopped crying after a few months, either. "Did Trinity have a Social Security number?"

"What a strange question. Not that I know of. You being a lawyer and all, do you think you could find her? I have a little money saved up. It's not much, and I don't know how much something like that would cost."

"I can't take your money, Mrs. Henderson. I will keep trying to find her, though. Is there anything you can tell me that might help in the search?"

The shock over, Lillian went back to shelling the peas into the bowl in her lap. "Trinity was a good girl. She was a hard worker. Anything she did, she did well. She was an honor student, but then you know that. She wasn't into fancy things or frilly dresses. Sometimes when she'd come back down the hill after visiting Miss Emily, she'd tell me about all the fancy things that little girl had. Now, don't you be telling Mrs. Windsor I said this, but Trinity always called Miss Emily 'the mean little princess who had evil eyes.'"

Jake laughed. "I grant you that wasn't very nice, but we all called Emily the mean little princess. She was a spiteful, whiny little girl. We probably didn't understand back then that she was as ill as she was. If we had, maybe we would have been kinder. At least I hope we would have. I've thought about those days over the years, and I think it was Mrs. Windsor we didn't like. As kids we resented being told we had to entertain Emily."

Lillian's mouth straightened out to a thin, tight line. "Miss Emily was very unkind to

Trinity. She would taunt her and say unkind things. One time she called her ugly. Poor Trinity kept staring in the mirror for hours hoping she'd magically change into a beautiful swan. I did my best to explain that Miss Emily was jealous, but Trinity didn't believe it for a minute. She really changed after that. But before that happened she told John and me one night at supper that she would never *ever* go up to the Hill again, and she wanted us to tell Mrs. Windsor why. No amount of punishment could make that girl change her mind, either."

Jake sucked in his breath. "Did you?"

Lillian shook her head. "John wouldn't do it. He told me to mind my own business, it was a child thing, kids being kids. I don't think Trinity ever forgave either of us. She simply endured her punishments. I'm sorry, Jake. I know I haven't been much help. Will you let me know if you have any luck finding Trinity? Tell her . . . Tell her we miss her terribly."

Jake wondered. For some reason Lillian's statement didn't ring true to his ears. "Yes, of course. Well, Mrs. Henderson, thanks for the tea. I'll stay in touch."

Jake's only thought as he drove home was how bizarre the whole thing was.

What kind of parents would listen to someone else tell them what to do where their only child was concerned? Then again, Sarabess Windsor wasn't exactly *someone* else.

Chapter 6

Jake looked at the little light blinking on his phone console. "Yes?" It was Stacy telling him his new client was in the waiting room. He shook down the cuffs of his shirtsleeves, shrugged into his lightweight jacket, and jerked at his tie before he got up to walk over to the door to greet Miss Julia Barrows, his brand-new client.

To his credit, Jake didn't even blink. The urge to slam the door in Sarabess Windsor's face was very strong, but he turned on his heel, his back ramrod stiff, and walked back to his desk.

"Don't be tiresome, Jacob. This is business. I'm not an ogre. View this appointment as the mountain coming to Mohammed."

Jake leaned as far back in his chair as he could. Sarabess leaned forward. Jake was aware of how charismatic she was, how elegant, how forceful. It didn't change his feelings one iota. "I told my father to tell you I have no free time, and I'm not taking on any new clients. There's nothing you can say or do, Mrs. Windsor, to make me change my mind. I think it's safe to say it's carved in stone."

Sarabess leaned back in the comfortable client chair and crossed her legs. She had nice legs, Jake noted. He clarified the thought. For someone her age.

"The only thing I'm guilty of, Jacob, is . . . was a mother's love for her child and wanting that child to have some kind of normal childhood. Your father warned me that I was stepping over the line of doting mother by forcing you and other youngsters to come up to the Hill to entertain my daughter. I'm sorry to say I didn't listen to him. I did not steal your father's affections. Your father and I were friends, but nothing, I repeat, nothing, happened while your mother and my husband were alive. In plain English, Jacob, there were no intimacies, no trysts, contrary to what you might have been led to believe. Neither your father nor I would permit something like that. We were married to other people. Two years after your mother's death, that all changed, and I don't deny it."

"I'm really not interested in your love life, Mrs. Windsor, nor am I interested in my father's. The two of you broke my mother's heart. I resent your coming here under false pretenses. I can't help you, and I don't know why you're so insistent on my doing so. I was quite clear with my father. And just to keep the record straight," Jake said, as he remembered Lillian Henderson's words of yesterday, "I resented the hell out of those command performances all us kids had to endure in regard to Emily. Your daughter was a mean, selfish, hateful little girl who lashed out at us, knowing it was what you did to others in your own way. Trinity Henderson used to get punished because she wouldn't tolerate your daughter's hatred. My mother and father had a verbal knock-down, drag-out fight when he tried to force me to go up to the Hill. I'm delighted to say, my mother finally won that argument."

"Emily was a sick little girl."

"Yes, she was. But you condoned every-thing she did. You allowed her to raise her hand to you. Billy Osborne told us all how

Emily would spit on you when she threw one of her tantrums. You allowed that."

Sarabess licked at her lips. "Guilty as charged," she whispered. "Emily just wanted to be like all of you."

"Well, she wasn't like all of us. Had we known, I'm sure we would have been kinder and more tolerant. We were kids. If Emily had been a little nicer, a little less demanding, less spiteful, we would have welcomed her into our circle of playmates. I blame *you,* Mrs. Windsor."

"And I accept that blame. I made mistakes. Perhaps one day your father will share some of those mistakes with you. I'm simply not up to it right now. I want you to find someone for me. I have no desire to broadcast my business, and I thought that you would be a little kinder and accommodate me. I want to . . . I want to make things right for this person I want you to find. Her name is Grace Finnegan. She's roughly my age. I would like to make her last years more comfortable."

"You're a little late out of the gate, aren't you, Mrs. Windsor? You want to make things right after a lifetime of wrongs. At least I think that's what you're saying. It doesn't work that way for me. I can recommend an excellent private investigator. He works out of Columbia, so you won't have to worry about his broadcasting your personal business."

Sarabess knew she was beaten. She'd been so certain she could convince Jacob Forrest to help her. She didn't need or want a private investigator, she needed the attorney-client privilege. She couldn't afford to make a mistake at this point in time. She stood up and looked down at Jake. "I hope you can let go of your hatred, Jacob."

Jake stood up. "*Hatred* is a strong word. Until yesterday I would have said I didn't like you. I never would have used the word *hatred*. Who are you, and what right did you have to tell the Hendersons not to try to find Trinity Henderson? Who gave you the right to hold that man's job over his head so he would obey your decree? The arrogance of you. Tell me that, Mrs. Windsor. It's easy to see where Emily came by her own arrogance. Now, I do hate you. For all you know, Trinity Henderson could have been picked up by some pervert and abused or killed. My God, Mrs. Windsor, she was only fifteen years old. What you did was unforgivable.

Yes, you made some mistakes, but you have to live with them, don't you?"

"Yes, I do have to live with them. Good-bye, Jacob."

"Good-bye, Mrs. Windsor." Professional that he was, Jake escorted Sarabess Windsor to the door. The minute she was clear of the door, he kicked it shut. He was so angry, he wanted to smash something.

Stacy poked her head in the door. "Wasn't that . . . ?"

"Yes. Close the door, Stacy. Wait a minute. Is my father in his office?"

"He just arrived. He came in the back door. If your next question is, Did he see Mrs. Windsor?—the answer is no." The door closed softly.

Jake stood rooted to the floor. He'd always been a responsible person. He never did foolish things. He was dedicated to his profession. He considered himself a man who cared. All thanks to his wonderful mother. He took a deep breath, walked over to the wall where his law degree hung. He removed it, packed up his briefcase, then wrote out an outrageous check to Stacy. His possessions under his arm, he walked out to his secretary's desk, handed her the check, and said,

"As of this moment, you are unemployed. Don't say anything. Go home and plan your wedding."

Jake strode down the hall to his father's office. He didn't bother to knock. He opened the door, and yelled, "I quit. It's all yours, *Pop!* I want you out of my mother's house, my house, by the close of business today. Move in with that bitch up at the Hill."

"Jake! What the hell! What's wrong with you?"

Jake lost it then. "You're what's wrong with me! You and that arrogant woman!" he shouted. He yanked the door closed and proceeded to gallop down the hall to the EXIT door. Outside in the bright summer sunshine, he looked around. There wasn't a soul in sight in the parking lot. He didn't have to look back at the building he'd just exited to know there were faces at the window watching him. Only God knew what they were thinking or saying. He sat in his car for a full minute trying to decide if he cared or not. He decided he didn't care at all. The ignition caught and he barreled out of the lot. His destination: Mitzi's house.

As he drove down Dorchester Road, Jake wondered what the hell was happening to him. He'd never done an irrational thing in his life. Well, he'd sure as hell gone for the brass ring this time.

Fifteen minutes later, Jake careened onto Mitzi's driveway, at which point he slowed down to admire the landscaping, or lack of it. Everything looked au naturel, viny and overgrown, just the way Mitzi liked it. The vibrant purple wisteria was everywhere. Because of the exceptionally cold winter, the wisteria had been late to bloom. His mother had loved wisteria and had it climbing all over the pillars on the front porch, but she'd kept it pruned. She'd likened the beautiful flowers to bunches of grapes. Jake knew that the reason Mitzi let the flowers go wild was because of his mother. Sometimes he thought Mitzi had never gotten over his mother's death.

The closer he got to the old house that had been his grandparents', which had gone to Mitzi on their death, the better he could see that the Confederate jasmine was at war with the wisteria. He knew the jasmine would win out. Mitzi said it was an insidious plant. She claimed to have mutants.

He knew little about plants, but he did know that he loved the scent.

Jake stopped the car before he got to the house, and a herd of animals raced toward him. He counted six dogs and five streaking cats that were hissing and snarling. A small goat named Annabelle brought up the rear. The only creature missing was Jezebel, the forty-five-year-old red and green parrot. He got out and let everyone sniff him before walking the rest of the way up to the house. Mitzi was standing on the verandah.

She waved and called a greeting. "Darlin', it's nice to see you again. You look terrible."

"Yeah, well, there's a reason for that," Jake said as he hugged his aunt. "What's that smell?"

Mitzi laughed. "Sesame oil. I rubbed it all over to soften my wrinkles. I don't think it works, but I'll try anything once. Can I get you a beer?"

Jake looked around the verandah. The rockers were old, the fiber carpet just as old. Clay pots of summer flowers were everywhere. He liked coming here, sitting on the ratty rockers and talking to Mitzi with all the animals parading around, even the little goat who thought she was an indoor pet—which, in fact, she was. "What you can do is get me two beers and have three more standing by," Jake said as he flopped down on his favorite rocker.

"That bad, huh?"

Jake sighed as one of the cats leaped onto his lap. Jezebel appeared out of nowhere and swooped across the porch to settle herself on his shoulder. He reached up to stroke the bird's silky back as he looked up at the three paddle fans twirling overhead. "One of these days you're going to get those tail feathers of yours singed, Jezzie."

"Good boy, Jake," the parrot squawked. "Jake is a good boy."

"Damn straight on that, Jezzie."

"Damn straight Jake is a good boy," the parrot squawked again.

The screen door banged, and Mitzi appeared with a tray holding four bottles of beer. "Bottoms up, darlin'."

Aunt and nephew chugged until the first bottle was empty. "Jezebel knows a hundred fifty words. Isn't that amazing?"

"Yeah, amazing."

"So you quit, eh? Told your father off in the bargain and kicked his butt out of Nola's house. Guess the Wicked Witch of the Hill thought you'd kowtow to her. Now, you want to talk about amazing . . . *that's* amazing!"

"How *do* you *do* that? Who called you? I know it wasn't Pop, so it must have been Stacy or Jocelyn. Well?"

"Does it matter? No, it doesn't. *Now* what are you going to do?"

"Damn good question, Mitzi. I don't have a clue. Yes, I kicked my father's ass out of Mom's house. I can't believe I did that."

"You should have done it four years ago. It will be interesting to see if he moves up to the Hill. Tongues will certainly wag if that happens." Mitzi held out one of her skinny legs to display the new tattoo on the bottom of her big toe. "What do you think? I got it last week. Now there's a career if you care to branch out. So, Sarabess wanted you to find someone named Grace Finnegan. Imagine that."

"You have to stop marking up your body, Mitzi. You can get a disease from a dirty needle. I knew it! You bugged my office. Who the hell is Grace Finnegan?"

"For your information, darlin', the needle was clean. I made sure. I like the idea of a bumblebee on the bottom of my big toe. I have no idea who Grace Finnegan is. Maybe she's one of Sarabess's relatives." Mitzi shrugged her bony shoulders, an indication she couldn't care less who Grace Finnegan was.

"I know you have an opinion on everything, Mitzi, so tell me, why do you think Sarabess Windsor wants to find some strange woman? She said she wanted to make sure this Grace Finnegan was taken care of in her old age or something like that. I find it odd that she doesn't want anyone to know she's looking for her. That fact alone tells me the woman is up to something, and that something is not good. I offered to get her a private detective in Columbia, but she didn't want any part of that. My guess is that she wants the attorney-client privilege. Why isn't she using my father?"

Mitzi turned contortionist so she could better view the bumblebee on her toe. "I have no idea. Nary a clue, darlin'. Sounds to me like you're going to look into it on your own, would be my guess. Are you going to move into the house?"

Mitzi's abrupt changes of thought and verbiage made Jake nuts. He should be used to it by now, but he wasn't. "At some point I might. I was trying to make a point. Maybe I'll move in here with you. Can I bring Elway?"

Mitzi roared with laughter. "Don't push it, nephew. You'd go out of your mind in three days. Maybe two. But you're more than welcome to take a shot at it."

"I'm just talking to hear myself." Jake thumped his empty beer bottle down on the table next to his chair.

"More beer! More beer!" Jezebel squawked.

"Is she smart or what?" Mitzi asked, getting up from the rocker. "How many, darlin', to numb your pain?"

"Just keep bringing them till I tell you to stop. What the hell is going on, Mitzi? I think you know. Pop said you didn't have the guts to write your memoirs. Because he pissed me off, I told him you were on chapter six. How come you didn't mention anything about my visit to the Hendersons yesterday?"

Mitzi turned around in the doorway. "You went out to the Henderson farm? Why?"

"Hell, I don't know why, I just did. I didn't learn anything if that's your next question. Sarabess didn't want the Hendersons to report Trinity's running away to the police. I guess she threatened Mr. Henderson with his job if he did. They buckled the way most people buckle when Sarabess issues an edict."

The screen door slammed shut. One of the dogs nosed it open and held it so the other animals could scurry through, even the miniature goat. Jake wondered if Mitzi had taught the golden dog how to open the door. He looked up when Mitzi plopped an entire six-pack down in an ice bucket. "Go for it, nephew."

"Are you telling me you didn't know I went to the Hendersons?"

"No, Jake, I didn't know. What did you hope to learn?"

"I wanted to know if Trinity has been in touch with them. Mrs. Henderson said Trinity sent a money order for the three hundred dollars she took when she ran away. There was no note, no message of any kind, but the envelope had a Pennsylvania postmark. I don't know why I say this, but I don't think Mrs. Henderson or her husband ever told Sarabess about that. I wish I had asked, but I didn't, so it's just a feeling I have.

"You know what, Mitzi? Mrs. Henderson

didn't act like any mother I've ever met. C'mon, Mitzi, tell me what you know."

Mitzi stared across the balcony at the profusion of wisteria blooms. She looked to be in another place. Almost like she had the weight of the world on her shoulders.

Jake jerked upright in the rocker. "What, Mitzi? Tell me."

Mitzi turned around, tears in her eyes. "Trinity is Sarabess Windsor's daughter. Lillian and John Henderson are not her real parents. Emily had aplastic anemia. The doctors here said there was nothing they could do for her. Sarabess wouldn't accept that. She found out that if she had Harold's baby, the bone marrow could be used to save Emily. That's exactly what happened.

"The only thing I didn't know at first was the identity of the father. When Sarabess left for New York and took Emily with her, with virtually no one knowing that she was pregnant, I thought . . . your mother thought . . . it was Rifkin. Of course he denied it. Your parents drifted further apart after that. Ironically, had we known what was really going on, she would never have accused Rifkin of being the father, since even Harold's child had only a one-in-four chance of being a compatible donor. And as Trinity grew, it became obvious she was Harold's daughter.

"Sarabess had the baby's bone marrow stored the minute Trinity was born, then Emily went through chemotherapy and radiotherapy. Sarabess spent money on the best heme/oncologists in the country. I looked into the procedure, and it's relatively simple. A transfusion done by a transplant team. The baby, Trinity, was brought back here and given to the Hendersons to raise. Those of us who knew that Sarabess had been pregnant never said a word. We certainly did not want Trinity to be raised by someone like Sarabess, who devoted every waking moment to Emily. She had no time for little Trinity, who had been born only so Emily could live. She didn't even exist as far as Sarabess was concerned and was better off away from that house.

"That little girl deserved to be loved, and I'm sure the Hendersons did their best, but they were hired hands. They would dude Trinity up in fine clothes and Mary Jane slippers and take her up to the Hill for holidays. Then they'd take her back to the farm when Emily got cranky and the party was over. Trinity was everything Emily wasn't. She was healthy, happy, always laughing and smiling. The children all liked her. God only knows what that child thought when she was forced to go up to the Hill. That's when I stepped in, and Lillian and I covered for each other where Trinny was concerned. There, now you know. What are you going to do about it, Jake?"

Jake was so stunned he could barely get his tongue to work. "How long did Emily live after the procedure?" he asked in a choked voice.

"Thirteen very long years. I think Trinity somehow found out, and that's why she ran away. That's strictly my opinion, Jake."

"How did you find out about Sarabess's pregnancy?"

"You don't need to know that, Jake."

"Yeah, Mitzi, I do need to know."

"Harold told me. Harold and I had been . . . friends . . . for a long time. Before he ever married Sarabess. He came out here the day before Sarabess was due to return from New York. He needed to talk to someone, and that someone turned out to be me. He told me everything but swore me to secrecy. I've kept that secret for the most part. I did share it with your mother because I knew she'd never tell anyone, and I didn't want her continuing to think her husband had done something he hadn't done. As much as I don't like your father, I could not allow your mother to torture herself over it. Harold was a regular visitor here after Sarabess returned. I doubt she even missed him. Now *you* know."

"Yes, now I know."

Chapter 7

Mitzi Granger stared at her inebriated nephew for a full five minutes before she made the decision to load him into her SUV. It wasn't easy with Annabelle and Jezebel getting in the way. She knew, just the way she knew everything, that Jake would be mortified to wake up at her place with a king-size hangover. He was like a Gumby figure as she pushed and shoved to get him into the backseat, where he went limp. Annabelle leaped over him as Jezebel swooped through the open door. "Jake's sick, Jake's sick!" the parrot squawked.

"Jezebel, get your feathered ass out of this truck right now. Jake's not sick, he's drunk. Get your facts straight, Jezzie."

"Jake's drunk, Jake's drunk!" the parrot continued to squawk as Solomon, the golden retriever, hopped into the truck and settled on Jake's chest. Annabelle, who was no bigger than Solomon, settled herself next to the golden dog and started to make funny noises. At least Jake thought they were funny. He started to laugh and couldn't stop.

"Okay, everybody out!" Mitzi shouted. The animals ignored her. Jake continued to laugh. Mitzi grinned as she slipped behind the wheel in her bare feet. "Well, this will certainly give the town something to chew on for a few days."

"Where're we going, Mitz?" Jake bellowed as he tried to sit upright.

"Over the rainbow!" Jezebel squawked.

"Is there a pot of gold there?" Jake demanded as he stared glassy-eyed at the colorful parrot. "Huh?"

"That response is not in Jezzie's vocabulary, Jacob."

Her eyes on the road, the cars, and the scenery, Mitzi put the pedal to the metal and drove like a maniac. She knew that none of the cops would pull her over because she was the one who paid for the Policeman's Ball, the PBA carnival, donated heavily to whatever the department needed, and could always be counted on. What would Crestwood's finest do?—they would escort her home with sirens wailing, hoping to embarrass her. That word wasn't in *her* vocabulary. Twice she offered up a single-digit salute to sedans going a sedate seventy miles an hour. She was rewarded by the irate motorists with blasts of sound that she totally ignored. Not so Jezebel, who fluttered and cussed with gay abandonment.

"Here we are, darlin'! Safe and sound. Do I have to help you out? If I do, my other passengers are going to bolt. C'mon, c'mon, darlin', shake it. I have things to do and places to go."

Jake did his best to untangle himself as he literally slid out of the SUV. He landed with a loud thump on his rear end.

"Oh, oh!" Jezebel squawked.

"You okay, darlin'?"

"Hell no, I'm not okay," Jake said, struggling to his feet. "I'll live, though. Thanks for bringing me home, Mitzi."

Mitzi waited until Jake climbed the steps, slipping and sliding, and opened the door. The minute the apartment door closed, Mitzi slammed the SUV into REVERSE and peeled out of the parking lot. "Hang on, boys and girls, we're going for a ride." The animals settled down immediately, even Jezebel, who perched on the dashboard, her wings fluttering at the high rate of speed and the breeze coming in the half-open window.

Mitzi swirled into the Hendersons' driveway, gravel spurting in all directions. She was glad dusk was settling. She was almost certain Sarabess Windsor wouldn't see her from the Hill. If she did, oh, well, that was the way the cookie crumbled sometimes.

Mitzi hopped out of the car, looked around, then marched, still in her bare feet, to the front door of the small house. She rapped sharply on the screen door. Lillian Henderson gasped when she saw who her visitor was.

Mitzi wasted no time in amenities. "Why didn't you ever tell me about Trinity returning the money she borrowed? You better hope you still have that envelope, Lillian."

Lillian held the screen door open and motioned for Mitzi to come in. "Come into the kitchen, Mitzi. John is down at the barn. We can talk. Can I get you anything to drink, and perhaps a piece of cake?"

"Just the envelope. After all I've done for

you and Trinity, you owed me that at least," Mitzi said.

Lillian wiped at her eyes with the hem of her apron. "I wanted to, Mitzi, I really did. John wouldn't allow it. You know how he is . . . was back then. He told me to burn the envelope. I don't know how I did it but I substituted another envelope. I guess I knew this day was going to come sooner or later. I didn't want *her* to find Trinity. I figured, sooner or later, as I told John, Her Highness would want to find her. Especially with Emily passing and all. I just didn't think it would take her so long to get around to it. Your nephew was here, and I told him about Trinity returning the money but I didn't tell him I still had the envelope. I told him . . . because Trinity was so fond of him. What are you going to do, Mitzi?"

Mitzi looked down at her bare feet. "Would you look at that? I forgot my shoes. Where's the envelope?"

Lillian walked over to one of the kitchen cabinets and opened it. She pulled out a battered old cookbook that was thicker than the New York telephone directory. "I wrapped it in tinfoil to protect it. The postmark isn't legible, Mitzi."

"Maybe not to the naked eye, but there are tests that can be done to bring the name to the surface. I wish you had given me this a long time ago. I could have helped her. God knows what she had to endure out there on her own. If there's anything else you haven't told me, now is the time to get it off your chest. Is it possible she found out she was Sarabess's daughter? The truth, Lillian. There has to be a reason for her to have bolted like that in the middle of the night."

Lillian bunched the bottom of her apron in her hands. Tears rolled down her cheeks. "I don't know. I suppose she might have heard me and John arguing. You know what a curmudgeon he can be. This is the only life we've ever known. You know how Sarabess is; she could boot us both out of here on any kind of a wild whim. We both know she is not a kind person. Where would we go, how would we survive? Our savings wouldn't last long. I'm sorry, Mitzi, so very sorry."

"Well, for starters, you could have come to work for me. I would have paid you decently and put a roof over your head. That husband of yours is more stubborn than a mule. This is the result."

"For God's sake, Mitzi, the girl wasn't ours. We just took care of her. I did my best not to love her because in my heart I knew one day she'd go up there to that Hill, and I'd eat my heart out. John . . . John wouldn't allow himself to get close to her for the same reason. Sometimes, late at night, Mitzi, when John thought I was asleep, he'd go to her room and just stare at her. Curmudgeon that he can be, he always had tears in his eyes. Despite all that, our hearts were broken when Trinity ran away. John wasn't himself for years."

Mitzi leaned across the table and patted Lillian's hand. "I know, I know. It's my own guilt, Lillian. I promised Harold I would . . . Let's just say I promised him nothing bad would ever happen to Trinity. I have to leave now. I'll call you if anything turns up."

Lillian walked with Mitzi to the door. Both women stood on the small front porch and looked up at the Hill. It was lit up like a Christmas tree.

"I think *she's* afraid of the dark," Lillian said.

"Miss Sarabess Windsor is afraid of a lot more than the dark, Lillian. Don't tell John I was here. He might get upset."

Five minutes later, Mitzi was barreling down the highway, her eyes filled with tears.

Mitzi marched into the police station like she owned the place. She wrinkled her nose as she moved over to the desk sergeant. "Good morning, William. I know it's early, and you just came on duty, but I wanted to beat the rush. I need a favor, and I need it right away. I want your crime laboratory people to tell me what this postmark is." She slid the small square she'd cut off the envelope Lillian had given her (so that no one would know who the addressee was) across the sergeant's desk.

"What exactly does 'right away' mean, Miss Mitzi?"

"One hour, William. I'm going to class now, and I'll be back. You need to get some deodorizers in here. Maybe some bleach or . . . something."

"I'll pass that along. You're looking a bit *peekid,* Miss Mitzi," William said.

Mitzi grimaced. Of course she looked *peekid.* She hadn't slept a wink. Then she remembered she never really slept. Maybe she would double up on her vitamins.

The desk sergeant winked at Mitzi. "Go

on and bend yourself in two. I'll have the information by the time you get back."

Mitzi waved airily as she sprinted out the door, holding her nose to make a point.

Mitzi felt her heart skip a beat when she entered the station an hour later.

William was smiling from ear to ear. "Got it for you, Miss Mitzi."

"Oh, you dear, sweet soul, I owe you for this. This is really important, William, and I can't thank you enough."

"You know, Miss Mitzi, fifteen years ago when this letter was sent, the lab might not have been able to clear this up but with all the modern technology we have, thanks to you, we got you the name of the town. The town is called Spangler. Look, I'm not going to ask you what this is all about, but if you need our help, just let us know. We can go where you can't go, that kind of thing. Cop to cop, we might be able to help you. Just tuck that into the back of your mind, okay?"

"Okay, William. Thanks again."

"Anytime, Miss Mitzi. You drive slow now. We pulled you over seven times this month. You have to stop taking that goat and parrot with you when you skedaddle around, too."

"Yeah, yeah, yeah," Mitzi mumbled as she danced her way out of the station. She called a greeting to this one, asked another one about the kids, agreed with others about the beautiful June weather.

Back in her SUV, Mitzi looked down at the lab report and the little square with the faded postmark in the clear plastic envelope. Spangler, Pennsylvania. All she had to do now was go on the Internet, do a search, print out her findings, and dump it all in Jake's lap. *Woohoo,* she thought, things were starting to pick up, and if there was one thing she loved in this life, it was a good skirmish, especially if said skirmish might lead to knocking Miss Sarabess Windsor on her elegant, haughty ass.

Thirty minutes later Mitzi was surfing the web. Far from being a computer wizard, she had to go to several sites before she found what she wanted. She printed out the zip code, which was 15775. She searched for the weather and population.

Small town, way smaller than Crestwood. A perfect place to get lost in for a young girl on the run. Small coal-mining town a long time ago. On the other hand, wouldn't a runaway stick out like the proverbial sore thumb? How did Trinity get there? Did she hitchhike? Probably. Mitzi shuddered at the thought. Gory headlines of missing children pricked at her closed eyelids. Still, fifteen years ago things weren't as bad as they were today.

Mitzi sat patiently as the skimpy information printed out. She used the time to remember how many detective agencies she'd hired to find Trinity, all to no avail. All of them said the same thing: Trinity Henderson had disappeared off the face of the earth. And those agencies were supposed to be the best of the best.

Mitzi's housekeeper, who was as quirky as her mistress, appeared in the doorway. "I fed the animals. I made you a soybean loaf, a baked potato, and some tofu and some kind of green stuff that's going to make you poop green. Call me on my cell if you think you're dying from eating that crap. I'm going to the movies."

"What did you have for dinner, Celeste?" The housekeeper's name wasn't really Celeste. It was Myrna Wojouski. Mitzi thought the name Celeste sounded more ethereal, more in tune with the stars and the universe.

"I had a small T-bone that was very pink, French fries with lots of ketchup, some fresh string beans, and a brownie with ice cream."

Mitzi snorted. "Then you better call me on the house phone in case you keel over. I thought I heard your arteries snapping shut a while ago. What are you going to see?"

"A Brad Pitt movie. You know how I lust after him."

"Are you still writing fan letters to him that he doesn't answer?"

"He's busy, Mitzi. I never expect an answer."

"That's your problem, Celeste, you have no expectations. Why do you spend money to fatten his bank account if he doesn't have time to answer your letters?"

"I don't want to talk about it. I should be back by ten thirty. I might stop for a banana split before coming home."

Mitzi waved good-bye and went back to sorting through the papers she'd printed out. It certainly wasn't much in the way of information but if Jake actually went to Spangler, Pennsylvania, he could ask questions, show off his charm. Few women could resist her nephew's pleasing personality. Everyone who met Jake liked him. He was a guy's guy, too.

Should she go over to Jake's now or wait till morning? Never one to let grass grow under her feet, Mitzi slipped on a pair of sandals and beelined out the door before the animals got wind that she was going cruising.

As she whizzed down the highway, Mitzi wondered where the day had gone. Hours these days just seemed to fly by. She'd read an article that said as a person grew older, time went faster. Maybe the writer of that particular article wasn't an idiot after all.

Jake was standing in the open doorway of his apartment when his aunt screeched to a stop in her SUV. He wondered where her fancy Jaguar was. She'd probably burned off the rubber on the tires. She was up to something. He could tell. And, she had a sheaf of papers in her hand. He felt a quiver of apprehension as he waited for Mitzi to climb the steps. Sometimes she reminded him of a gazelle.

"I come bearing news, darlin'. I have here

in my hand the possible location of one Trinity Henderson. Now that you're unemployed, I was wondering if you might be interested in checking this out. Of course, if you aren't interested, I can always turn it over to an investigative agency. If you decide to check it out yourself, no one needs to know. I know how to keep my lips zipped."

Jake stared at his aunt as he reached for the papers. "You want me to do this, don't you, Mitzi? Do you mind telling me why?"

Mitzi turned on her heel. "What a silly question. Trinity was Harold's daughter. Does that answer your question?"

"Guess so. I'll let you know what I decide."

"That works for me, darlin'."

Chapter 8

The sun was creeping over the horizon when Jake pulled out of the Subway drive-thru, a cup of steaming-hot coffee in hand. Elway sat on his lap purring contentedly. He settled the coffee, which was too hot to drink, into the cup holder. Then he stroked the mangy cat with one hand, his other hand gripping the steering wheel tightly. For some reason he suddenly felt a tremendous responsibility to the old cat on his lap. He wondered if he'd ever understand his new charge. Suddenly, Elway was his new best friend. A horrible thought struck him. Was the cat sick? Maybe he should have taken it to a vet. He would ask Mitzi. Mitzi was an authority on animals. Mitzi was an authority on *everything*.

Jake slowed, turning on his signal light as

he coasted toward the antebellum mansion that Mitzi called home. He crawled up the long driveway, surprised at how quiet it was. Today, there was no raucous greeting, not necessarily a bad thing, he told himself.

Jake sat quietly after he cut off the engine, and sipped at the cooling coffee. Elway was still sound asleep in his lap. The early-morning dew glistened and sparkled on the wide expanse of green lawn. To Jake's eye it looked like a meadow of sparkling diamonds. As he sipped, he was aware of the faint scent of jasmine that would turn cloying once the sun rose in the sky. For the moment it was just pleasant. Overhead, the birds chirped their morning song. The whole setting was beyond peaceful. He wished he felt peaceful.

Today was a new day. Jake couldn't help but wonder what it would bring in the way of happiness and sorrow. Why, he wondered, was he thinking like this? What was happening to him? He made a mental note to ask Mitzi, who knew him better than anyone else on Earth. Even his father didn't know him.

Jake climbed out of the car, Elway in his arms. The cat made no move to jump out of

Jake's arms or even wriggle, for that matter. He had a pang of guilt at the thought of leaving his new best friend with Mitzi. He stopped long enough at the bottom of the steps to pluck a cluster of wisteria.

At the top of the steps leading to the verandah, Jake was stunned to see Mitzi rocking in an old Charleston rocker. "Mornin', darlin'."

Jake grimaced. "Now why did I know you'd be awake? I know, I know, you never sleep. I don't suppose Celeste has coffee going, does she?"

The screen door opened before Mitzi could get her tongue to work. The housekeeper was carrying a heavy tray with fancy cups and a sterling silver pot of coffee. Jake heard her muttering about crazy people who got up with the roosters. He waited till the housekeeper stomped off, the screen door banging behind her.

Jake poured coffee and picked up his cup. "Let's cut to the chase, Mitzi. I'm not driving for sixteen hours on a whim to satisfy . . . whatever it is you're trying to satisfy. I want the *whole* story. That means the good, the bad, and the rumors."

The rocking chair seemed to pick up speed.

For the first time, Jake noticed his aunt's attire. Her hair was done up in giant yellowish-orange curlers that almost matched the long orange gown. Slippers with huge orange pom-poms graced her feet. The way Elway was eyeing them, Jake knew that sooner or later he'd pounce.

"I told you everything there is to know. If you have blanks, fill them in."

"Oh, no, it doesn't work like that. Is Harold Windsor the man who broke your heart?"

"Now where did you get an idea like that?" Mitzi asked, firing up a cigarette.

Jake thought she sounded pissed. "Mom told me. She said you never got married because someone broke your heart, and it never mended."

"Oh. Well, something like that might have happened. It's really none of your business, *Jacob,* unless you want to tell me about the long string of young ladies suffering from the same malady at your hands."

Jake winced. "I want to discuss you, not me. We can pick me apart some other time. Details, Mitz, and I'll know if you're not telling the truth."

"You young people are all such smart-asses. Fine, fine, I'll tell you. Here it is in a nutshell: I was engaged to Harold Windsor. We were to be married in June. It was to be a double wedding: your mama and Rifkin, and Harold and me. I had my gown, the invitations were ready to be sent out. Sarabess Jenkins came to town to visit. Harold and your father took one look at her, and they both fell in love. There we all were at the Memorial Day parade and there's Sarabess in her lacy hat and her flowered linen dress. I looked like a frump, and your very own mama didn't look much better. Flash forward, Harold got the girl and Rifkin got your mother. I . . . I . . . I ran away. I stayed away for six long years. I swear to God I don't know why I came back. Maybe I had a premonition or something. Then my father died. I was still reeling from that when Harold showed up on my doorstep telling me what a mistake he'd made. He told me how sick Emily was but not what they were doing about it. Sarabess had just left for New York. And, as I told you earlier, the day before Sarabess and Emily returned, Harold finally told me about Trinity and why she was born.

"After Sarabess returned, Harold practically lived at my house for the next fifteen years. No, that's not true, he did live at my house, moved in with most of his belong-ings. Sarabess didn't care. She had Emily and Rifkin. Trinity used to come here, and the two of them would sit for hours, talking.

"Anyway, Harold made me promise to look out for Trinity. I did the best I could. It was hard because Lillian Henderson was petrified of Sarabess. I had to sneak in to see the child. Lillian would bring her into town. Trinity knew it was all a secret. I loved her, Jake, like she was my own daughter. It wasn't until Harold died, not that long after Trinity had run away, that I found out he had made me executrix of his will. If he had not been so sick when she ran away, Sarabess would never have gotten away with keeping the Hendersons from looking for her and notifying the authorities.

"The day Harold found out about his ill-ness he started to liquidate his holdings, and they were considerable. Windsor Steel. He did it slowly, one by one. He transferred everything into a trust for Trinity, whom he identified in the will as his and Sarabess's daughter, and appointed me to oversee it. By now that trust is incredibly robust. It was to go to her on the day she turned thirty. He had the finest lawyers in the state go over everything to make sure it was all legal.

"All he left Sarabess was a summerhouse on Hilton Head Island. There's an account I monitor for household expenses and an allowance for Sarabess. That's why she hates me. I was torn between wanting nothing to do with it and trying to do what Harold wanted. I let my jealousy—and, yes, I was jealous of Sarabess—win out and decided to do what Harold wanted. Just so you know, Sarabess was as poor as the proverbial church mouse when she arrived in Crestwood. Her main goal was to find a rich husband, which, of course, she did."

Elway took that moment to jump off Jake's lap. He pounced on one of the orange pom-poms with a vengeance.

"Now, here's the clinker. If Trinity died before her thirtieth birthday, or did not return by then, I was supposed to inherit the money. Of course, I would see that the money went to Trinity whenever she showed up, and Harold knew that.

"But two years ago, when Rifkin was here pleading on behalf of Sarabess, he was half in his cups, and a little beer was enough to loosen his tongue. When I taunted him about my getting the money if Trinity died or didn't return, he let slip that there was a second will, one, if I understood him, that was made just two weeks before Harold died, and it said that if for any reason, including her death, their daughter Trinity didn't return by the age of thirty, it reverted to Sarabess. Then Rifkin passed out, and to this day I don't think he remembers telling me.

"Of course, I was in shock. I had no idea why Harold would have done such a thing. I've given it a lot of thought, and I hope that Rifkin is not involved, but I've reached the conclusion that the second will is a fake. I think I can prove it, since Harold lived here and for the last month was in no shape to make a will, doped up as he was. Still, I hope that it never comes to having to go to court to prove it.

"I spent thousands and thousands of dollars trying to find her. I never gave up. I followed up on everything and anything. I never, ever, thought that Lillian would hold something like that envelope out on me. I just might go back there today and kick her ass all the way to the Georgia border.

"Your father has no money except what

he earns from the law firm. Your mother left him nothing but the right to live in the house until it came to you and funds from a separate trust to maintain it. There was a letter her lawyer gave him informing him that if he contested the will, the house and the maintenance trust would go to you immediately, and his right to live in it would be canceled.

"In the beginning, your father visited me weekly, asking that I release monies so Sarabess could do this or do that. I always refused. That's why he hates me. I was being spiteful back then, but all I had to do was remember how Rifkin treated your mother, his indifference, his arrogance, and it made my job easier."

"Damn," was all Jake could think to say.

"The clock is ticking where Trinity is concerned. She'll turn thirty January fifteenth. So you have until then to find her. I've done my best to guard her fortune, and I've been almost as lucky with her investments as I was with my own. Of course I had some expert help along the way. She will be a very wealthy young lady if we can find her."

Jake watched Mitzi pick apart the wisteria bloom as Elway chewed and played with the pom-pom on her slipper. She appeared to be oblivious of both. "Are you sure Trinity doesn't know?"

"How could she know, Jake? Although anything is possible, I suppose. But I think that Sarabess, your father, and I are the only ones who know. Trinity ran away when she was fifteen. The Hendersons didn't know, at least I don't think they knew. No, I don't think she knew about the trust fund. But she might know . . . you know . . . the other stuff. All of this . . . is the reason I don't sleep."

Jake looked over at his aunt to see tears rolling down her cheeks. "I'm sorry, Mitzi." He was off the chair and had his aunt in his arms in the time it took his heart to beat twice. "I'm sorry I made you go through that. I want to help, but I just couldn't do it without knowing the whole story. I'll do my best to find her. That's a promise."

"I know you will, dear." Mitzi wiped her eyes on the sleeve of the orange gown. "The last time I cried was at Harold's funeral. Well, that isn't exactly true. His funeral was by invitation only, and I wasn't invited, so I went to the cemetery later."

Jake decided right then that he really and truly hated Sarabess Windsor.

"Listen, Mitzi, can you take care of Elway while I'm gone?"

"Oh, Jake, no. That cat for some reason has singled you out to be his owner. He's been a stray long enough. He's old, and he's tired. You should be honored and flattered that he chose you over the other tenants. Animals go through traumas just the way people do. You have to take him with you. Just take a litter box and a pet carryall. I have one I can give you. If you desert him now, he'll die." Mitzi wondered if what she had just said was true. "He can take my slipper with him. By the way, that town in Pennsylvania is now called Northern Cambria."

"I can remember that. I want you to do something for me while I'm gone. See what you can find out about Grace Finnegan. Hire some of those investigators who couldn't find Trinity. We can check in with each other every night."

"I can do that, Jake. When do you plan on leaving?"

"As soon as you get me that cat carryall and pack me up a travel kit for Elway, I'm hitting the road."

Mitzi stood in the doorway, her eyes full of tears. "Find her, Jake."

"I will. Listen, Mitzi, promise me you won't go out to the farm and kick Lillian's ass all the way to the Georgia border."

Hands on her bony hips, Mitzi blinked away her tears. "I never make a promise I can't possibly keep."

Jake shrugged. "Maybe you should kick her husband's ass instead."

"You know what, Jake, I'll give them both a good swift kick."

Jake scooped up Elway and the slipper and made his way down the steps to where Mitzi's Jaguar sat. *Damn, I forgot to tell Mitzi I need her car. Oh, well, she'll figure it out when she sees me transfer my gear to the Jaguar trunk.*

He certainly would have plenty to think about on his long road trip.

The old couple parked their car on the wide shoulder of the road because the parking lot surrounding the small bakery was jammed full. It was, after all, June. The month for warm golden sunshine, blue skies, weddings, and wedding cakes.

Inga's Bakery had been at the same location on Bigler Street almost forever. The truth was, the shop had been leased one month after Inga and Sven Kolina arrived on American soil. Customers were loyal and devoted, their children and grandchildren just as loyal and devoted. No one could bake a wedding cake like Inga Kolina. With the arrival of their niece, Lisa, years ago, and Inga's worsening arthritis, Lisa and three assistants now followed the old recipes. It was now said a wedding wasn't a wedding without a one-of-a-kind cake *created,* not baked, by Inga.

"The girls are busy, Mama," Sven said to his wife. "Maybe we should come back later. We don't want to get in the way. It is the busiest time of the year for wedding cakes."

"Nonsense," the rotund little woman said. "Lisa loves it when we stop by. At least I think she does. She's been acting peculiar of late, though. I know business is off, but I think it's more than that. She doesn't confide in us the way she used to. I just bet you a quarter that she shares all her business with that woman's daughter. We aren't going to lose the shop, are we, Sven? What will you do if you can't make the deliveries?"

Inga asked, referring to Sven's thirty years as a long-distance truck driver.

Inga patted her husband's arm with one gnarled hand. That day the pain wasn't so bad, and she thanked God every day that the crippling disease that had attacked her hands had not invaded her legs. Twinges in her knees, yes, but Advil helped. She tried not to think about it and did what she could by walking and doing mild exercises. "Lisa likes it when we stop by because she takes a coffee break with us." Inga looked up at her six-foot-four husband. She smiled. He was as dear to her today as he had been when she married him fifty years ago. "The best day of our lives was the night you picked up that child on the highway and brought her home to me."

The big Swede said, "Shhh, Inga. We agreed not to talk about that time outside the house. Lisa is our niece from Mobile, Alabama, who arrived here and decided to stay and help you in the shop."

"I do tend to babble at times, don't I? I think it has something to do with the shop. I was always so happy here and when Lisa . . . arrived, I was even happier. All right, all right, not another word. Let's go in and see what creation our niece is working on today. Six weddings tomorrow. If only every week was this busy. I hope we can make the bills this month."

Sven wanted to tell his wife that the six weddings tomorrow were for children who had come home from other places to get married. They weren't going to live in town, so they wouldn't become customers. But he didn't have the heart to tell his wife that financial problems loomed on the horizon. He stopped, his hand on the doorknob of the kitchen leading into the bakery. "I can remember the first day you asked me to hang those red-checkered curtains because you weren't tall enough to reach the top of the windows. You said they were a welcome sign, an invitation to come into the shop. How many different sets have we hung since you opened this shop?"

"Seven. Lisa made the last set. I wish she'd find herself a nice young man."

Sven laughed as he opened the door to allow his wife to enter the kitchen first. Warm, tantalizing smells were everywhere. "Ah, smell the vanilla. I just love it! I think I love the scent of vanilla more than I like to smell bread baking."

"Hello, everyone!" the Kolinas said as one.

The young woman wrapped in a humongous white apron and a white hat looked up, her expression blank. There was no smile in her voice when she said, "Ah, just in time for coffee. We just made a fresh pot. Sit, sit," she ordered. "I'll fetch it."

The Kolinas chattered with the three assistants as they continued to work while Lisa filled two cups. "It's hot, Inga, so be very careful. What brings you over here so early in the morning? I thought you were going to work in the garden today."

She was beautiful, tall and slim, with a waterfall of blonde hair that she kept tied back in a knot. She had soft brown eyes, the same color as her Sunrise Chocolate Cake. Double-fringed thick eyelashes covered those glorious eyes and turned more than one head.

Her smile was radiant, and she smiled a lot. Or she used to, but the smiles had stopped a long time ago. Sven had said she learned to smile the day her hated braces came off. To say that Lisa Summers was a workaholic would be an understatement.

There was no one to say if it was by choice or not.

"We're going to do that the moment we get home," Sven said. "Those dang weeds grow so fast I can't keep up with them. What time do you want me to start delivering your cakes, Little Miss?" he asked.

Lisa knew that the name Little Miss was supposed to make her feel special. At one time it had. Now, though, it was an irritant. "Five in the morning," she replied. She perched on a stool and sipped her own coffee.

Inga's voice was wistful when she said, "Guess you won't be home for dinner . . . again."

"I'll just call for a pizza. I'll be working through the night. One of the ovens isn't working as well as it should. Betty, Angie, and Carol have cakes baking in their own ovens. I also think we need to raise our prices. Every single ingredient you need to bake a cake has gone up in price. In some cases, it's doubled. I called several bakeries in Harrisburg, and they charge twice what we charge for a wedding cake. The shop is losing money, Inga, even with all the business we have. Then again, it's June, a time for wedding cakes. Mr. Holtz, the real estate manager, stopped by last week and said he was raising the rent sixty dollars a month. That's sixty dollars extra we don't have. I'm thinking we should move this operation to the house. Your kitchen is certainly big enough. If you don't want to raise the price of the cakes, we can save on the rent. Will you at least think about it?"

"I'll think about it, dear. You have to remember, we're just a little-bitty town. Our people can't afford to pay city prices. When you throw your wedding at the Polish Legion, it's because you're watching your pennies. Think about making the cakes smaller, don't be so decorative."

Lisa sighed. "Then the cakes won't be Inga Kolina cakes. It'll be just another cake. You might as well go to the supermarket and buy one. If we move our operation to the house, your customers will still be your customers. If we downsize the cakes, they won't come back for their baby's first cake, the first communion cake, the other birthday cakes, the holiday cakes. You know I'm right, Inga," she said wearily. She lost track of the times they'd had this same exact conversation.

Inga's good mood was shattered. "I'll think about it. Sven and I will talk about it while we work in the garden. I mean while he works in the garden and I watch."

"Think hard, Inga, because there's just enough money to pay the help this week. I owe two hundred dollars for flour. There isn't enough money in the account to pay for it. I haven't taken a check in three weeks. I'm not complaining, I just want you to be aware."

"I think we should be going so you can get back to work," Sven said coolly. He reached for Inga's coffee cup and set it on the counter. "We'll talk later, Little Miss. If you need me, call."

The brown eyes showed worry. "All right, Sven. I'm sorry, Inga, but facts are facts. We can't hide from them anymore, and I know what this little shop means to you. I really do."

In the car, Sven patted Inga's arm. "She's right, Inga. Think of it this way: if we move the business to the house, you'll be in the thick of things every day."

"No. I'll just be in the way. I'm totally useless these days. Sven, do you think God is punishing me because we never tried to . . . ?"

"Hush now, Inga. I don't want to hear any more talk like that. You had a touch of arthritis before the Little Miss came to live with us, and we both know it. You're just upset that we'll have to close the shop after fifty years. We knew this was coming because we talked it to death a hundred times. Unfortunately, we live in a depressed area, and there's nothing we can do about it. I don't want to see you sulking, either. I think the radishes are ready to be picked," Sven said, hoping to divert his wife's thoughts.

It didn't work. "Did you know Lisa didn't take a salary for three weeks?"

"Yes, I knew. I was waiting for her to say something. I can go to the bank later and put some money into the business account. Our balance is getting lower and lower. We need to do something, Inga, and we can't let our emotions get in the way of those decisions. If we move the bakery to the house, I can make whatever changes need to be made in the kitchen. We can spread out to the dining room if we have to. And I can close in the porch. It's all workable, and it won't cost that much. All you have to do is make the decision. I can hang red-checkered curtains if you want."

Inga forced a smile she didn't feel.

"Would you look at that fancy car!" Sven said as he pulled out onto the road. "Don't see too many Jag-u-ars in these parts. Wonder who that good-looking fella is visiting? A car like that costs more than I ever earned in any given year."

"That's not our business, Sven."

"No, I guess it isn't. Whoever it is probably is just passing through, or else he's lost."

"Can we just go home, Sven? I need to do some hard thinking."

Chapter 9

Jake woke with a start, his gaze going everywhere as he tried to figure out where he was and what had woken him. Elway sat on his chest, staring at him with burning intensity as if to say, "The sun's up, let's get going." He groaned as he took in the spartan hotel room, which smelled of mold and dust. He really had to get some better accommodations. Surely there was a motel somewhere close to Northern Cambria. All in due time, he decided as he shooed Elway off the bed.

Jake pointed out the portable litter box to Elway, who had already found it. Yawning, he made his way to the ancient bathroom and stood under a shower that was little more than a trickle. The water was hot, though.

Fifteen minutes later he was in Mitzi's Jaguar on the hunt for some breakfast. As he cruised up and down the streets he went over his game plan. His MO was that he was a journalist doing an article on small-town America. Everyone, he told himself, wanted their fifteen minutes of fame. His plan was to stop first at local businesses and talk to the owners, who would hopefully pave the way for an introduction to people who were adults when Trinity disappeared.

Jake turned into a roadside fast-food joint and pulled up to the drive-thru window. He ordered bacon and eggs on a croissant, which proved to be so good he went back and ordered a second one and a coffee to go. He broke off a part of his sandwich and fed it to Elway, who gobbled it down.

Ten minutes later he was back to cruising. He drove down Philadelphia Avenue. He passed Huether's Restaurant and Bar, the First National Bank, Paul's Shoes, and the Northern Cambria Public Library. He turned the corner and drove up Crawford Avenue. He mentally noted Valeria's Market where he could buy some fresh fruit later on. He made a right turn, and according to the map on his lap, he would drive through Allport, then a little town called Hastings. From time to time he stopped, whipped out his digital camera and took pictures.

People were friendly, Jake thought, or else they were admiring Mitzi's Jaguar. They waved or gave an airy salute as he walked around snapping his pictures. He was a little surprised that no one approached him to ask questions. He was, after all, a stranger in their midst.

Midmorning found Jake back in Northern Cambria on Bigler Street. He stopped to take a picture of Rouse's Flower Shop, the Polish Legion, the Mobil gas station, and a shop called Inga's Bakery. Finally, he headed for the Giant Eagle supermarket and parked his car. He shrugged into a backpack that contained his camera, a minirecorder, a legal pad, and a bunch of pens and pencils. Elway hopped into the pet carryall and Jake was ready to go on the hunt. He walked across the street, down an alley, and emerged on Crawford Avenue. He looked to his left and walked over to Valeria's Market and bought two apples, which he stuck in the backpack. He struck up a conversation with the owner.

He rattled off his bogus credentials and waited.

"A magazine article on our little town! Well, we certainly are small-town America. What's left of it, anyway. The young people today want to shop in malls. We only stay in business because of the old-timers. And there aren't that many of us left, either. So many shops have closed up. I've been here forever, just the way the others have been. Oh, there are a few novelty discount stores that opened up in the latter years, but that's about it. I just heard yesterday that Inga's Bakery might be closing. She's been here for fifty years like most of us old-timers. She might continue doing the baking out of her house. That's just small-town gossip."

"Why's that?" Jake asked curiously.

"Chester, the landlord, passed away. Chet's kids live in Philadelphia and don't want that ramshackle building, so they raised the rent and put it up for sale. They never come back here, either. It's sad that such a pretty little town like ours has come to this."

Jake nodded as he accepted his change for the apples. He snapped the woman's picture and another of the boxes of beautiful fruits and vegetables under the outside awning.

Jake walked around town until midday, when he stopped at Huether's and got the best hamburger he'd ever eaten. Conversation was plentiful but didn't yield a thing of importance. He moved on, Elway still in his carryall and sound asleep. So far no one had asked about the bag or the cat. He found that a little strange. He continued to snap pictures.

It wasn't until Jake made his way to Dumm Lumber that he casually asked about newcomers to the area. The man loading lumber into a customer's pickup truck laughed. "Not likely, young man."

"How about in the last fifteen years? Maybe some of the people who left came back here to retire, a youngster who couldn't make it in the big city who came home, something like that?" Jake asked, unwilling to give up. He wished Mitzi was within arm's length so he could strangle her. He had the feeling the whole thing was going to be a big bust.

"Lots of people come back around Memorial Day. There's a parade, and they all go to the cemetery. Like the Ferensic boy and his wife, Doris. Parents lived on Chestnut. They always come back."

"Do more guys come back or is it a mix of men and women?" Jake asked, trying to be clever.

"A good mix. Not more of one than the other," the old-timer said as he filled his pipe.

He leaned back against a stack of two-by-fours and puffed away. Jake thought the man looked ripe to have his brain picked.

"I'm hoping to slant this article toward women. Women are more of the *nesting* type. For some reason I thought more women would return than men. I can tell there isn't much employment in the area, so I just assumed men with families wouldn't come back. Too hard to earn a living."

"You're right about that, young feller. Ruth Ann Stitt's daughter came back some time ago and does alterations out of her little house, over near Cherry Tree. Then there was Inga's niece who showed up one day. She works in the bakery. Now, young feller, if you ain't tied up, she's a looker, she is."

Jake's heart kicked up a beat. "She is, huh? What's her name?"

"Lisa Summers. She's Inga's niece. Inga

used to make wedding cakes. Made the cakes for my two daughters' weddings. Inga and Sven are from Sweden. Real nice people. The niece is real nice, too. She bakes the cakes now because Inga came down with real bad arthritis."

"The lady at the market said the bakery was going to close."

"I heard that myself last night. It's a shame. Another scab of a building on the landscape. How long do you plan on staying in our little town, Mr., uh, Mr. . . . ?"

"Franklin. Call me Jonah. Until I get a story, I guess."

"You should stop by the library right there on Philadelphia Avenue and talk to Beatrice Carmody. She knows everything about our town. We weren't always called Northern Cambria. Town used to be called Barnesboro but they changed all that in 2000. Beats, as we call her, can tell you more than you probably want to know. You might need her to pave the way for interviews. Some of the older people don't take kindly to strangers asking questions."

"I'll do that. Thanks for the heads-up. Mind if I take your picture?"

"Will it be in the magazine?"

"I hope so. Say cheese," Jake said, snapping away. "Thanks for the information."

"Anytime. 'Bout to close up now. Be raining before long. Pleasure meeting and talking to you, young feller."

Jake looked up at the blue sky with puffy white clouds. It didn't look to him like it was going to rain anytime soon. "Likewise," Jake said, trotting off.

It was a pleasant jog to the library, the pet carryall bouncing against his side. Elway continued to sleep peacefully.

Jake stopped at Huether's to ask for a fishcake and some milk for Elway, who drank, gobbled, did his business at the curb, and waited for Jake to put him back into his cozy nest.

The Northern Cambria Library was like every other library he'd toiled in—cool, dim, and so very quiet. The woman behind the desk had to be in her eighties, Jake surmised. He rattled off his fake credentials as he stared at the primped and rouged old lady. She wore two hearing aids and seven strings of colored beads around her skinny neck. She looked him over, scrutinized his fake credentials, and pursed her lips. The request to take the woman's picture turned things around. She smiled, showing a glorious set of sparkling dentures capable of lighting up a dark night. They clicked and clacked when she talked.

Jake snapped six pictures, to the woman's delight. He got right to it the minute he stuffed his camera into his backpack. "The man over at Dumm Lumber said you were the only one in town who could really help me."

"Well now, that depends on what you plan on asking me, young man. I absolutely will not divulge any secrets that have been entrusted to me."

Jake chewed on that statement for a minute. "And that's the way it should be, Miss Carmody. I'm just looking for general information, human interest, small-town stuff." He made a pretense of looking over his shoulder to see if anyone was listening. No one was. "Are you telling me Northern Cambria is a Peyton Place?"

"It could be, but you didn't hear that from me. Every town has its secrets. Now, don't ask me any more questions about secrets."

"Fair enough," Jake said smartly, "but secrets would really spice up my article."

The dentures flashed and clicked. A bony

finger waved back and forth. "Ask your questions," Beatrice said as she wiggled to get more comfortable on the stool she was sitting on.

"Well, Miss Carmody, I don't really have any questions. I'd just like you to tell me about this town, going back fifteen years. I'll put it all together when I'm ready to write my article. I'm not sure how I'm going to slant it yet. Can we sit over there at one of the tables? I want to use my tape recorder to ensure I don't make any mistakes. I know how people hate being called up later on to clarify something or other or, God forbid, being misquoted. If you're needed at the desk, I can always stop the recorder."

The librarian pondered the question for a full minute before she slid off the stool and led the way to a round table with four chairs. Jake set up the recorder, settled himself as comfortably as he could. He nodded for the librarian to start talking.

It was all so boring, Jake's mind wandered as he looked around the library. It smelled like all libraries, a pleasant smell of old books, floor wax, and furniture polish that he associated with his early school years and, later, his college years. A place to study in peace and quiet. A place to whisper to your girlfriend, who sat beside you, your knees touching. And then the walk home from the library, hand in hand, when it closed. That long walk home was always special in the summertime . . .

Jake jerked his mind back to the situation at hand. He tried to look interested, but it was hard. How could one be interested in Jack Hunter's root cellar collapsing or Bill Kelly's garage door blowing off for no reason?

"The year Mamie Stewart won the blue ribbon at the state fair for her strawberry-rhubarb pie was a banner year for the town," Beats droned on. "Sadie Prescott won the handmade quilt the Sodality ladies made the previous winter. Bill Kline broke his leg in three places, and Stanislas Quimby died and left all his money to the church. Let's see, what else happened that year? Oh, yes, some film company drove through here filming footage for a Burt Reynolds movie. Of course we never saw the movie it was supposed to be in, but it was exciting while it was going on. And Inga Kolina's niece came to live with them. Now, if ever a couple deserved to have children, it was Inga and

Sven Kolina. The whole town was so happy for them. I don't know what Inga would have done without that girl."

Jake sat upright. "How old was the niece?" he asked casually.

"Inga said she had just turned sixteen. The very next week, Inga had the girl outfitted with braces by Doc Peters. She had some spaces between her teeth, as I recall. She has a lovely smile now. Sweet girl."

Jake grew light-headed. Spaces between her teeth. Bingo!

"The Kolinas sound like wonderful people," Jake said. He frowned as he heard a bolt of thunder followed by a streak of lightning that ripped across the sky. Rain suddenly battered the windows. The lumberman had been right.

"Very nice people. Everyone in this town is nice. Now, where was I?"

"The niece," Jake volunteered. "Did she come from Sweden?"

"By way of Alabama, I think. The girl came from Sweden to a distant cousin in Mobile. The couple were elderly and not up to dealing with a teenager, so they sent her to the Kolinas. Lisa loved America, and she loves our little town. I for one can see why she would want to stay. She takes care of her aunt and uncle better than some people take care of their parents. Something else happened that year, too. Oh, yes, Tom Yahner married a young woman from England. They have seven children. Lovely, lovely children."

Jake shifted into neutral, his thoughts everywhere but on what the librarian was saying. Was Lisa Summers really Trinity Henderson? He was jolted from his thoughts when Beatrice snapped her fingers.

"Lord have mercy, I almost forgot about Joyce Patrewski! She blew into our little town like a whirlwind with her two kids, Betty Lou and Donny. She claimed to be a seer of some kind. She had a crystal ball and did tarot card readings. She rented a little house between Barnesboro, only now it's called Northern Cambria, and Hastings. The townspeople just flocked to her for readings. I went myself, and everything she said came true. Betty Lou has the same calling but doesn't exercise it. By the way, Lisa Summers and Betty Lou are best friends. Anyway, after the novelty wore off, Joyce had to find another job to pay the rent. As I said earlier, job opportunities are sparse around here, so when Deke Logan passed on she took over the job of maintaining the cemetery grounds. She does a wonderful job, too. She ended up buying the little house she rented. Betty Lou teaches school now, and Donny lives and works in Pittsburgh. I really don't remember where they came from originally. Maybe Pittsburgh, since that's where Donny went after he finished college. Not too many of our youngsters go off to college around here."

"And Betty Lou is the same age as Lisa Summers?" Beatrice nodded. "Well, I can certainly agree with you that that year was a banner one. Are you sure now you don't want to confide just a few of the town's secrets?" Jake teased.

The old librarian pursed her lips tighter than a zipper. "No, I don't."

So that was that.

It was five thirty when Jake clicked off the recorder and thanked the librarian for all her help. She'd talked basically nonstop for close to five hours, with only three interruptions to check books out for patrons.

It was still raining when Jake headed to the corner outside the library to cross the street. He jogged to his car, but he was soaking wet by the time he slid behind the wheel of the Jaguar. Elway poked his head out of the carryall just long enough to look around. Like a turtle, he pulled his head back in and settled down to enjoy the ride.

Jake's thoughts were everywhere as he headed back to his hotel room. He stopped and bought a pizza and three bottles of beer. He stopped one more time for some cat food for Elway. He could hardly wait to call Mitzi to hear what she thought about the information he'd garnered so far. Two possibilities were more than he'd hoped for. He rather thought Lady Luck was riding on the roof of the Jaguar.

Chapter 10

Lisa Summers carried her coffee cup with her as she walked outside and sat down on the back steps of the bakery. She was beyond tired and worried out of her mind. The coffee she'd been drinking for the past thirty-six hours was having an effect on her. With only catnaps, she'd become a basket case and was twanging like the strings on a steel guitar. But there was no help for it. Just two hours ago when she removed the eight layers of cake from the oven for the Loysen wedding, she realized she'd forgotten to add vanilla to the mix. She'd cried buckets over her mistake.

Lisa stared across the small parking area, seeing it but not seeing it. When the small green Saturn invaded her eyesight she blinked. She waved listlessly as her best friend ran across the lot. She did her best to work up a weary smile for Betty Lou, or, as she called her, BL. Her friend looked fresh and rested, her curly hair still damp from the shower.

"I'm here to help. Tell me what I can do. I'm all yours. Is the coffee hot and fresh?" BL asked cheerfully.

"Yep, just made it," Lisa said as she listened to her banging around in the kitchen. For some reason BL always made noise no matter what she did. Her mother called her a heifer in a china shop.

When BL returned and sat down next to Lisa on the step, she said, "You need to hire some more help. This is the busiest time of year for weddings. Why didn't you think of that?"

Lisa eyed her friend. "What would you suggest I pay them with? I can't ask people to work for me and say, *'Maybe I'll pay you at some point.'* I'm at my wits' end. I finally had to tell Inga we have to close the shop. The two of them have no conception of money. Well, they do but they don't. Look, I don't want to talk about this today. All I want is to get these cakes baked and delivered so I can go home and sleep around the clock. How are you doing with summer school?"

"Two more weeks. Then I have to help Mom at the cemetery. I do like riding that mower. I feel so powerful when I'm driving it. Hey, did you hear about that good-looking guy who's in town? Some kind of journalist doing an article on small-town America. I saw Beats at Giant Eagle last night, and she said she talked to him for five hours at the library. She said he is mouthwatering good-looking. He carries his cat around in a bag. I'll fight you for him," BL teased, hoping to get a smile out of her tired friend.

"You can have him. The man hasn't been born that's worth fighting over. How'd he pick this town?"

"Don't know. Beats said he drives a Jaguar. His name is Jonah Franklin, in case you're interested."

"Well, I'm not interested. I forgot to put the vanilla in the last cake. Do you believe that?"

"Sure. Guess what, Lisa? No one will even notice. It's a wedding cake. People just pretend to eat it. It's a beautiful day, isn't it?" she asked, waving her arm about to indicate the rising sun, the gentle breeze rustling the trees that lined the small parking lot at the back of the shop, and the early-morning birds chirping their greeting for the day.

Lisa struggled to her feet. She was so tired she could barely stand. BL held the door open for her.

"When are you going to stop killing yourself like this? When was the last time you looked in the mirror? You can't be all things to the Kolinas, Lisa. Get out of this business. Let's go to Philadelphia or Pittsburgh and get real jobs that will pay us decent money. You can send money home and even pay someone to help out. We can drive home on the weekends."

Lisa reached for a white hairnet and pulled it over her hair. "Let's not get into this again. I can't leave Inga and Sven, and that's all there is to it. I owe them too much. It would kill them if I left. The main reason they don't have any money is because of me. They used up a chunk of their savings to send me to college, not to mention those damn braces they insisted I get. Sven is having problems now, too. Medicine is expensive. I stopped taking a full salary two years ago. I just take out enough for toiletries and such. I don't want to talk about this, BL. Don't bring it up again. I mean it."

"Okay, I won't. I guess this might be a good time to tell you I am going to Philly at the end of August. I applied for a teaching job that pays me more than I make here. They called two days ago and hired me. I saved up some money, and I'm going to go back for my master's. I didn't do it years ago because I thought Mom needed me. Guess what? She doesn't. I know this is a shock, but you would have found out sooner or later. I wanted you to hear it from me first."

Lisa heard the words and wanted to cry all over again. Everything was going to hell. First the business, then the vanilla, and now BL was leaving. Her world was falling apart. Angrily, she swiped at her eyes. This wasn't supposed to happen. Never, ever. She struggled for the words that would signal her approval. The best she could come up with was, "It's right for you. I'll miss you. We can talk about this tomorrow. Let's get through today and get all these cakes frosted and delivered. Sven is due any minute for the early deliveries. If I ever get married, I am not having a wedding cake!" she announced, frost ringing in her voice.

BL burst out laughing. "At least you gave me my laugh for the day. You, an old maid! In high school every boy in town had the hots for you. In college you had to beat them off with a stick."

Lisa's eyes narrowed. "Do you see anyone knocking down my door? No, you do not. I haven't been kissed in three years."

BL was still laughing as she tied an apron over her pale yellow sundress. "And whose fault is that? All those boys from high school are now married with kids. You even made their wedding cakes. You missed the bus, old girl."

Lisa slapped her pastry trowel into a bucket of creamy white frosting. She slathered the cake by rote, her thoughts far away.

Maybe someday things would change for her. Maybe.

Three days later Jake sat in his car in the Giant Eagle supermarket's parking lot reviewing his notes. His legal reasoning and the resulting scribbles would mean nothing to anyone other than himself. He perused page after page, satisfied that his memory was every bit as good as the notes he'd taken. It was time to do some real interviews.

His two leads he considered solid were
Betty Lou Patrewski and Lisa Summers.
Betty Lou was at school, so he couldn't talk
with her until after three o'clock. The bakery
was closed on Mondays, perhaps even per-
manently. That meant he had to amble over
to Chestnut Avenue and talk with the Kolinas
and their *niece*.

Today Jake was dressed in khaki shorts
and a yellow polo shirt. He wore sneakers
because of all the walking he was doing.
Since arriving in Northern Cambria there
had been no need for a workout at a gym.
That was probably a good thing since he
hadn't seen one around. He estimated that
he'd hoofed a good ten miles each day
since he'd arrived. At the moment he felt
knowledgeable enough about the town to
pass for a resident.

What really amazed him were the people.
No one approached him wanting to be in his
article or to give him an interview. However,
when he went up to them, they talked willingly. He now knew more about the residents of Northern Cambria than he did
about the people in Crestwood. He wondered if that was a good or a bad thing.

His backpack in place, Elway in his nest,

Jake climbed out of the Jaguar and looked around. He saw the slender legs first, then the rest of a tall, gorgeous young woman with flyaway hair that she was impatiently brushing aside. He could see her butt, and a nice butt it was, as she leaned into a dark maroon Honda for her purse.

Some long-ago memory tugged at him. Without knowing why, he opened the car door and climbed back inside as he continued to watch the young woman as she waved to someone. Then a woman approached her, and they started to talk animatedly. Obviously the two women were friends. Both leaned against the Honda and carried on what looked to Jake to be an intense conversation. The one with the nice rear end turned slightly, offering Jake a better view of her profile. He did a double take, swallowing hard as he continued to watch the two women.

Without taking his eyes off them, he managed to shrug out of the backpack, unzip it, and fumble around until, by touch, he found the photograph of Trinity Henderson he'd brought with him. He looked down at the photo Mitzi had given him that was taken when his childhood friend was around fourteen or so. He mentally added fifteen years to the picture as he closed his eyes. Could it be? Seconds ago something had tugged at his memory. The flyaway hair Trinity had never been able to control. The nice derriere.

The young woman turned completely around as she waved good-bye to her friend. Jake's heart stopped for a nanosecond. If this young woman wasn't Trinity Henderson, then she damn well had a clone. He panicked. What should he do? Should he get out of the car and follow her into the supermarket? Should he stay in the car and wait till she came out and follow her? He waited for his fine legal mind to kick in. When nothing happened, he let loose with an unlikely snort and got out of the car. He heard Elway hiss his disapproval at these strange goings-on.

Jake turned slightly and pressed the remote that locked his car. The young woman with the melting brown eyes and the delectable derriere swept past him without even looking at him. Elway hissed again.

It was her! Trinity Henderson! He was sure of it. Well, almost sure. Jake decided his ego was bruised. How could she have passed his six-foot-two frame and not even looked at him? He told himself she looked like her thoughts were a million miles away.

Jake opened the car again and sat down, then got back out. He took two steps forward, intending to head toward a row of shopping carts. He did a whirlwind turn-around when he saw his quarry exit the supermarket, a gallon of milk in each hand. He beelined for his car and opened it. Again. His options had just expired. Now he was going to have to follow the young woman. Elway kicked up a fuss, hissing and snarling as he clawed at the canvas bag. "Cool it, Elway, I've got a problem here, and I don't need a temperamental cat screwing things up."

The maroon Honda backed up and crawled past him. Jake ducked his head at just the right moment. He waited a minute, then peeled out, two cars behind the maroon car. He craned his neck to see which way she was going. One of the two cars in front of him turned left and the other stayed behind the Honda. Ten minutes later all three cars were on Chestnut. He should know who it was that lived on Chestnut, but he couldn't remember. The car in front of him waited while the Honda made a left and parked behind the house. Jake kept on going. A mile down the road he pulled over to the shoulder and opened his folder. He flipped through his notes. *Ha! The Kolinas and the niece live on Chestnut.* He felt like beating his chest in victory.

It would be a really good time to call Mitzi. Elway had settled down so it was quiet in the car. His cell phone in hand, Jake punched in the numbers. Mitzi answered on the third ring. "Where the hell have you been, Mitzi? I've been calling you all morning. I have news, and I need some advice."

"Class, then I was meditating. What is your news, darlin'?"

"I think I found her, Mitzi. If it isn't her, she has a twin. There's a whole story that goes with that, but I'll call you later and fill you in. Should I approach her or do you think I should carry on this charade that I'm a free-lance writer doing a story on small-town America?"

"My advice would be to stick with your story. Is that the advice you wanted?"

"Pretty much so." Jake's voice lowered. "She's beautiful, Mitzi. It's Trinity, just an older version. She bakes wedding cakes."

Mitzi laughed. "That's pretty funny, darlin'. Lillian tried to teach her to cook, but she was allergic to the stove. And now you say she makes wedding cakes. Are you going to talk to the aunt and uncle? I don't want to get my hopes up. I knew she was going to turn into a real beauty. I can't wait to tell Harold tonight when I say my prayers."

Jake didn't know what to say to that declaration. "At some point I'll talk to them, but today I am going to get my cards read by a tarot reader at four o'clock. With luck I'll get to meet my other possibility, which is Betty Lou, the tarot card reader's daughter, when she gets out of school. She's teaching summer school and lives with the mother. By the way, she charges sixty bucks for a reading."

Mitzi laughed. "Put it on your expense account. Call me this evening, darlin', and let me know how the reading goes. I'm really proud of you, Jake. Thank you."

Jake promised to call and clicked off. With nothing else to do, he headed back to the Giant Eagle parking lot and walked up the street to the library. He had a game plan. Well, he sort of, kind of, had a game plan. While he was the first to admit he was no authority on women, he did know one thing:

women hated to be ignored. He hoped that applied to Beatrice Carmody.

Jake sailed into the library, waved airily to the librarian, and headed to the back of the room. He placed his backpack and Elway on the table while he scanned the current newspapers on the rack. He helped himself and started to read, his gaze going to Beatrice from time to time. He flipped the pages of the paper as a woman with two toddlers in tow checked out a stack of romance novels and an elderly gentleman with two books about world affairs checked out behind the romance reader. And then the library was empty except for him and Beatrice.

Jake pretended to be engrossed in a day-old issue of the *Wall Street Journal* as the librarian walked up and down the aisles checking the books. Finally, she stopped by Jake's table and asked if there was anything she could help him with. He knew it, just knew he'd been right. Women really did hate to be ignored, no matter their age.

"No, not really. I'm just passing time until four o'clock. I made an appointment to have my fortune read by Mrs. Patrewski. I think that's going to add to the human interest when I do the article. I don't have much human interest," he said pointedly.

Beats sniffed, her lips a thin, tight line. "When I had my second reading, Joyce told me there was a brilliant scholar who would be seeking me out and that we would have so much in common, we would probably end up marrying. Well, that didn't happen."

"I thought you said everything came true."

"The first time, yes, but that was just to suck you in so you'd keep going back for more readings at fifty dollars a visit. The first time it was all general stuff. I heard Joyce charges sixty dollars a reading these days."

"That's what she said on the phone," Jake agreed.

"What exactly are you looking for as human interest?" Beats queried.

Jake shrugged. "Things like Joyce working at the cemetery doing maintenance work and doing the tarot card readings to supplement her income. This is a depressed area, where money is not plentiful, so Joyce will be of interest to the readers. Things like that. Do you have anything you want me to include?"

Beats wagged her finger under Jake's nose. "I see where you're going with this, young man. You want me to talk about the town secrets. Well, I won't do that because those secrets are nobody's business. Besides, they aren't really titillating secrets."

Jake nodded. "I understand. I thought I would start my article on the first day of the year, fifteen years ago. New Year's Day, and what the year would bring for a small core of people. I thought I'd work Joyce in, and the Kolinas, since I heard they were going to close their bakery. If you could tell me something about yourself that year, I'd consider including it in my article."

The sparkling dentures clicked and clacked. "I'm sorry, young man, my life is an open book but not very interesting. No pun intended. I live in a world of books. I do a little gardening, donate one day of every weekend at Miners Medical Center. I go to church on Sunday and play bingo on Wednesday night. That's my life."

Jake looked at his watch. He had an hour to go until it was time to head for Joyce Patrewski's house for his reading. He looked over the top of the paper to see Beats was still sitting in the chair opposite him.

"I heard last night something that saddened me. Betty Lou is resigning. She's going to

Philadelphia to teach. She'll make more money, of course, so she can't be blamed for deserting us. She's a fine teacher, and the children love her. She plans on going back for her master's. Poor Lisa, what will she do when she loses her best friend? If the Health Department won't allow Inga to bake in her kitchen, that means the end of Inga's Wedding Cakes. It also means Lisa will have no other choice but to leave, too, to earn a decent living. Like I said, it's a sad state of affairs. You should write about that, young man." Beats sniffed as she got up and made her way back to her desk.

"I hope I don't have to do that," Jake muttered to himself.

Chapter 11

Lisa Summers brushed the hair back from her forehead as she settled herself on the front porch swing. It was past time for a haircut, but time had gotten away from her. She made a mental note to call Curl and Cut. She closed her eyes and brought the cold glass of lemonade up to her cheeks. It wasn't really her hair that was bothering her, or that she was hot and uncomfortable, more that she was frustrated with the way things were going in her life. If she had to sum it up, she'd say her life was out of control, with no immediate fix on the horizon.

What was a person supposed to do when she ran out of options? How much longer could she keep doing what she was doing and not cave in to the pressures that surrounded her? A long-ago expression invaded her thoughts, but she couldn't remember where or under what circumstances she'd heard it. *You made your bed, now you have to lie in it.*

Eyes still closed, she gave herself up to the warm summer afternoon. Somewhere down the street she could hear the sound of a lawn mower. It was probably Mr. Paterno mowing the grass, since the sun was now in front of the houses instead of behind. Sven had mowed the grass as soon as he'd gotten up that morning. Now he was weeding the luscious tomato plants. She sniffed, appreciating the scent of the newly mown grass. She opened her eyes when she heard a hissing sound. The sprinklers came to life. Just another summer day. She recalled other summer days when she had no worries or problems except maybe Jake Forrest. Now that seemed like a lifetime ago.

Lisa jerked upright on the swing. For some reason she'd been thinking about the old days a lot. Was it because she was so unhappy, so pressured to keep the family together? Didn't they understand she wasn't a magician? She hopped off the swing and walked around back to the garden. She stood for a moment watching Sven as he bent over to pick at the weeds that grew faster than the tomato plants. "Sven, Inga is taking a nap. I'm going over to BL's for a little while. I'll be home in time to make dinner."

Sven straightened up and rubbed at his back. "Are we having hamburgers again?"

Lisa chewed on her lip. "Take your pick, meat loaf or scrambled eggs." She hated the look she read in his weathered face, but there was nothing she could do about it.

"Meat loaf is fine. It's easy for Inga to manage. Did you give her her pills? Did you rub her hands and arms with the Bengay?"

"Yes, Sven. I'll see you later." Ah, escape! Three hours of freedom. Immediately, Lisa felt guilty. She tried to shake the feeling as she headed for her car. Three hours to prattle on with BL. Three hours when she didn't have to smell the sickening scent of Bengay. Just three hours to do nothing.

"Did any orders come in this morning?"

"No, Sven. The phone didn't ring at all."

In the car, Lisa's eyes filled with tears. She had to get a grip on herself. She drove slowly, savoring being alone, with the radio playing softly. Again, a reminder of another time, another place. She smiled when she heard a car horn behind her. She looked in the rearview mirror. BL. She waved.

Five minutes later both women pulled into the gravel driveway and parked.

"Surprise! Surprise!" BL said, climbing out of the car. "How'd you get loose?" It was a joke between the two of them, with BL insisting Lisa was a prisoner of the Kolinas, something she usually denied. Not today, though.

"I just walked out. Inga doesn't like to use the air-conditioning. It was so damn hot in the house I was starting to get dizzy. The Bengay got to me today for some reason. She was sleeping, and Sven was in the garden. Older people fixate on things. Sven was upset when I told him no orders came in today. I have nine orders for this weekend, nine for next week, then zip."

BL tugged at her light summer jacket as she followed Lisa up the driveway to the house. "What I hate is seeing you so depressed. You used to laugh and be the life of the party. Now you're this . . . this curmudgeon. You need to get back on track, and you know what you have to do. The Kolinas qualify for aid, but as long as you continue to kill yourself for them, they aren't going to avail themselves of what's out there. You need to get a life before you become an old maid. As much as I hate to say this, I'm going to say it anyway. You should think about going back to Sweden. That's all I'm going to say on the subject."

Lisa forced a laugh she didn't feel. "You know what Thomas Wolfe said, "You can't go home again." Hey, how about cutting my hair? We can sit out back in the sun. You'll save me twenty-five bucks."

"Sure. Just let me change my clothes. Talk to Mom while I change. She's got someone coming at four o'clock for a tarot card reading. You might think about asking her to tell your fortune, too, since you're in such a funk. She never charges you."

"I just might do that," Lisa said, heading for the kitchen, which was neat as a pin. She saw a chocolate cake cooling on the counter. She sniffed at the delicious scent of roasting chicken.

"Lisa, how nice to see you. It's been a while since you were out here. Will you be staying for dinner?" Joyce Patrewski asked. She clucked her tongue when she commented on the dark circles under Lisa's eyes.

"I wish I could, because it smells delicious, but I can't. Things will level off after next week. You know, June weddings and all. It's been hectic. Well, I'll let you get ready for your client. BL's going to cut my hair down by the pond."

"How are your folks, Lisa?"

"The same. Nothing much changes. I'm sure BL told you we're going to have to close the shop. Inga just cries. Sven refuses . . . He just doesn't want to believe things are as bad as they are. No matter what I say, they have a comeback. I really think they think a fairy godmother is going to show up with a pot of gold. I'm not trying to be disrespectful. It's the way it is."

"You stop that right now, Lisa. Inga is a whiner. Sven coddles her, and we both know it. I know for a fact that Bob Binder asked Sven to work at the hardware store a couple of days a week, and he turned him down. It wasn't hard work, either, just running the cash register and waiting on people. Both of them are in a time warp. Look, we all have to do what we have to do to survive. Do you think I like working at the cemetery? I had children to support. I had to pay for college, so I did it. I didn't ask anyone to help me, either. I'll probably be doing tarot card readings and taking care of the cemetery until the day I die, and I'm not complaining like some people I know."

Lisa blinked. She hadn't known about the hardware store. The small-town grapevine. She hated how everyone in town knew everyone's business.

Lisa looked so stricken, Joyce wrapped her in her arms. "Oh, dear, you didn't know that, did you? I wonder if you know that Inga is a prime candidate for hand surgery. Mimi, Dr. Palmer's nurse, told me that a year ago. She also said Medicare would pay for the surgery but Inga said no. She said no because she said you and Sven take care of her. By your expression, I guess you didn't know that, either. Well, you should know. Now, scoot. If you change your mind, dinner's at seven. I have to get ready for my reading now."

BL blew into the kitchen with her haircutting kit and led a befuddled Lisa out to the back porch and down the steps to the lawn. BL was in no way a beautician, but she did have a knack for cutting hair. Like BL said, you couldn't screw up a curly haircut.

Lisa flopped down on the lawn chair and

looked up at her friend. "Do you know what your mother just told me? You do, don't you? Why didn't you tell me, BL?"

"Because you think the Kolinas are Mr. and Mrs. Santa Claus, and they aren't. They're selfish and inconsiderate. You're their slave. Why should they put themselves out when you shoulder all the responsibility and wait on them hand and foot? You just think about it, Miz Lisa.

"The day you came to live with them was the best day of their lives. I'm not saying they don't love you because they do, but it's the wrong kind of love. They smother you. They trade on your loyalty. Ask yourself what's going to happen when Sven has to have his hip and knee replaced. I know this is going to sound terrible, and I don't mean it that way. Those two have hearty constitutions and are going to live forever, and you're going to be taking care of them because of that loyal streak in you. The two of them have a lot of good years left in them, but they have to help themselves and stop depending on you.

"You should have closed that damn bakery years ago. It's time for you to leave. Make them take some responsibility for themselves. You can send money home. Let them be independent again. Every woman in this town will pitch in to help them. And, by the way, it was Mom's idea for me to leave, not mine. I'm going, too. Now, you think about all that while I cut your hair."

"You don't understand . . ."

"The hell I don't. You're the one who doesn't understand. You have two options, Lisa. You can stay here and play the martyr and wither on the vine, or you can get some guts and leave. Between Mom, me, and you, we can get the ball rolling. It's all up to you. Oh, wow! Look at *that!*"

Tears brimming in her eyes, Lisa turned around. All she could see was a tall figure walking to Joyce's front door.

"Lordy, Lordy, that man looks good enough to eat. It's that new guy in town, the one doing an article on small-town living. A reading takes an hour, so let's synchronize our watches and head for the house five minutes before Mom finishes. Ohhh, is he good-looking or what?"

Lisa didn't want to admit that she couldn't see the man. "If you say so. Will you just cut my hair? I have to go home to make dinner."

"See! See! You have no life. I know Mom

invited you to dinner. Call home and tell them to make do."

Lisa's thoughts whirled and twirled as BL snipped at her hair. She wondered if there would be hell to pay if she did as BL suggested. Of course there would. They'd throw the old guilt trip at her. Then they'd pout all evening. Her shoulders sagged. "Yeah, okay. That chicken did smell good."

"Attagirl! Did Mom tell you she baked sweet potato bread? She did. And, get this, she has a batch of early peas she picked from the garden. You're gonna stay, then? We can talk after dinner and make a plan. Please, Lisa."

A plan. She was going to need more than a plan. "Okay. How's it looking?"

"Beautiful. It's curling right up. It will be a lot easier to care for. I can highlight it for you tomorrow if you want. Mom always says when your hair looks nice, you feel good. She also says never pick a fight with anyone if you aren't looking your best. I think she's right."

"I *know* she's right. Thanks, BL," Lisa whispered.

Ten minutes later, BL provided Lisa with a handheld mirror. "Ta da!"

Lisa ran her hands through her newly cropped hair. "I like it! I think you're right about highlighting it. Absolutely. Okay, I'm ready to fight you for that new guy in there. How much longer?"

BL looked at her watch. "We have to wait eight minutes. Should we meander out front or go through the house? I have a great idea. Let's get Mom to invite him to dinner. I bet he'd like a home-cooked meal, and he's new in town. With all those delectable smells in the house, he'll be hard-pressed to say no. Whatcha think?"

"What I think is you are shameless. Let's do it!"

BL felt light-headed. Was it her imagination or had she just seen a spark of the old Lisa? Whatever it was, BL decided it was a good thing. A really good thing.

The two women spent the eight-minute wait picking up the mound of fallen hair and stuffing it into a bag for the trash. BL packed up her scissors and combs, zipped the bag shut, and winked. "Let's go," she said, giggling.

There was a lightness in Lisa's steps that hadn't been noticeable for a long time. BL felt encouraged all over again.

"Oh, oh, wait a minute. They just came out on the back porch. It looks like the guy is going to take pictures of Mom. Let's go around the side and go in the front door so we don't look so obvious. The man is a hunk! A gorgeous hunk! Lisa Summers, you are definitely going to have to fight me for this guy. Hey, girl, say something!"

Lisa stood frozen behind the lilac bush as she stared at the man snapping pictures of Joyce Patrewski. Her face drained of all color as she started to shake. Panic written all over her, she whispered, "I have to get out of here. Right now!"

"What . . . ? Hey . . . ! Lisa, come back here!"

Chapter 12

Lisa eased up on the gas pedal as she turned onto Philadelphia Avenue. Her head felt like it was going to spin right off her shoulders. What to do? Where to go? The last thing she wanted to do was go home to the Kolinas. She slowed to a full stop as two young boys on bicycles crossed the road. Once she had been that young. Such a long time ago.

Jake Forrest, aka Jonah Franklin. A lifetime ago she'd adored the rugged young man who had promised to marry her when she grew up. Over the years the adoration had turned to out-and-out hero worship and then . . . And then she'd fallen in love with the tall, good-looking young man with the unruly dark hair and those incredible dark, melting eyes. Emotions that Jake was totally unaware of. Now, here he was! Right here in her current hometown. What were the chances of that ever happening?

When she'd hit the highway fifteen years ago, Jake was her only regret. *What is he doing here? How did he find me? Journalist, my butt.* She pulled into the Dairy Queen lot and parked. She didn't realize how badly she was trembling until she had to try three times before she was able to turn off the ignition.

Lisa had no idea how long she sat in the parking lot watching cars come and go through the drive-thru. Her thoughts were all over the map, until one of the young men behind the ice-cream machine came over to her car with a cone and held it out. "Is something wrong, Miss Summers? You've been sitting here for over two hours. Here, I brought you a cone. I know you like banana parfait. On the house."

Lisa jerked to reality. "Have I really been here for over two hours?" She reached for the cone. She licked at it.

"Guess you're bummin' about the bakery, huh? I heard Mom and Dad talking yesterday, and they said it would be closing."

It was as good an excuse as any she

could come up with for why she'd been in the parking lot so long. "You could say that, Tommy. What time is it?"

Tommy looked down at his skinny wrist and the watch that was as big as a head-light. "It's seven thirty."

An hour and a half past the Kolinas' din-ner hour. Inga liked to eat promptly at six. If Sven had his way, they'd eat at five. Usually she prepared as much as she could before she left for the bakery in the morning. She hadn't done that today because the bakery was closed. What had they eaten? She felt a painful stab of guilt when she realized she didn't care what they ate or if they had eaten at all. The thought stunned her. She bit down on the wafer cone. She couldn't remember ever eating anything that tasted as good as this ice-cream cone.

Tomorrow, everyone in town would know she'd sat in the Dairy Queen parking lot for more than two hours. Time to leave. Where to go now? Finally, she turned the key in the engine and headed for Miners Medical Cen-ter and its parking lot. She would be barely noticed because people were always in a hurry to see their loved ones. She wished she had a cell phone, but there was no

money for such things. When she'd
broached the subject, Inga had stared at
her and called it foolishness. She'd dropped
the subject right then and there and never
brought it up again.

Lisa parked, leaving the windows open as
she walked across the lot to the main doors.
Inside, she headed for the phone booth and
called BL.

"Where the hell are you, Lisa? You scared
the daylights out of me. Sven called here
five times. I told him you left a long time
ago."

"I'm in the hospital parking lot. Can you
come here right now, BL? Please, don't ask
questions. Just do as I ask. I'll explain when
you get here. I need some money and
clothes. Pack me a bag. We're the same
size. Don't say anything to your mother.
What she doesn't know . . . It's just better
that you don't say anything. I'll wait for
you."

"My God, Lisa . . ." Lisa broke the connection before BL could ask any more
questions.

Now she had to think about the Kolinas. If
she just disappeared, they'd call the police.
Damn, they might call them anyway. Either

she had to call them or write them a letter making everything crystal clear. She was glad now she had never told either one of them about her background. Not that they hadn't tried to find out, they had. She'd made it clear that her background was hers and hers alone, and they weren't to ask any questions if they wanted her to stay. She'd been tough back then. Now she was penniless and exhausted. When was the last time she'd made a decision? The decision to close the bakery had been a no-brainer.

Lisa almost jumped out of her skin thirty minutes later when she saw BL pull into the lot and park six cars away. She hopped out of the car and headed straight for Lisa. Breathless, she got in the car, and said, "This better be damn good, my friend. Now, spill your guts, and I'll know if you're lying to me."

Lisa turned in her seat. "I never lied to you, BL. I just didn't . . . I never . . . I couldn't say anything."

"Yeah, why is that? I thought we told each other everything. I sure as hell told you all *my* secrets."

"I know and I'm sorry. I'm going to tell you now. Don't say anything until I'm finished."

"I don't like sitting here in your car. Let's go for a pizza but in my car because you don't look in any condition to drive. Close the windows and lock your car. In case Sven comes looking for you. I'm not going to like what you tell me, am I?"

"Probably not," Lisa said, getting out of the car.

It was dusk, everything appearing in stark shadows under the sodium vapor lights. People were starting to leave the hospital, visiting hours over. BL pressed her remote. Lisa slipped into the passenger side and buckled up.

Curb service at Dominic's Pizza produced a pepperoni pizza and two root beer slushes. BL ate one slice, Lisa ate four. She hadn't realized how hungry she was.

"Now, talk," BL said, when Lisa wadded up the last paper napkin.

Lisa talked for a full hour, never taking her eyes off her best friend. "And now, here I am. I have to leave. I don't have any other choice."

"Oh, God, Lisa, why didn't you ever tell me? Now it all makes sense. You're right, you have to leave. Are you going to go back to the Kolinas' first?"

"I can't. I haven't called them, either. What does that make me, BL?"

"Smart! Listen to me. You've done more than a biological daughter would have done for those people. So what if they paid for your education and bought you this car. By God, you earned every penny of it and then some. Slavery doesn't come cheap these days. You have nothing to feel guilty about. You haven't taken a salary in . . . forever. I'm going to tell you something that's going to anger you. I hate to repeat gossip but I'm going to tell you anyway. Mom told me a few months ago.

"The day Mrs. Elder was buried, Mr. Elder came back to the cemetery later and was just sitting there by himself. Mom felt sorry for him, so she stayed with him for a while and in the end had to drive him home. Somehow or other Mr. Elder got around to talking about his finances and said he was at the bank one day and Dottie gave him the wrong deposit ticket with the current account balance written on the bottom. He said the only way it could have happened was because Sven went through the drive-thru at the same time he was making a deposit inside. He took the deposit ticket back the next day and gave it to Dottie. For whatever it's worth, Sven didn't return Mr. Elder's. Mom said the Kolinas have over four hundred thousand dollars in the bank. They lied to you when they said Sven doesn't get Social Security; he does, seventeen hundred a month. Inga gets twelve hundred. That's what Sven was depositing that day because Mr. Elder was depositing his Social Security check, too. For some reason they don't believe in electronic banking like most people."

"And you didn't tell me? My God, why?"

"I wanted to but promised Mom I wouldn't say anything. She's hell on wheels about gossip in little towns. She remembers how it was when we first moved here. I tried in every way I knew to tell you in other ways. You wouldn't listen. You were the Kolinas' personal slave. It was you who got up at three in the morning so you could start baking at four. You cleaned that house, did the laundry, the shopping, the cooking. 'Slave,' Lisa. Say the word out loud until you believe it. Tell me you're listening and understanding everything I've just told you," BL said, cold anger ringing in her voice.

"Well, I'm listening now, and I sure as hell

do understand," Lisa said, her voice dripping ice. "Is there more, or are you finished?"

"Mom said Inga didn't have a bit of trouble praying the rosary using all her fingers at services for James Bryson. I'm not saying Inga doesn't have arthritis; she does. Half the people in this town have arthritis, including my mom. But Inga's is selective.

"Guess what else. She only takes over-the-counter medication. Even before the Medicare prescription drug benefit, there was no high prescription bill every month. Like I told you earlier, Dr. Palmer said she was a good candidate for the hand and finger surgery. I know because Mom asked Dr. Palmer what kind of medicine everyone in town took, and he told her that only a few of the older residents take prescription meds. The others, like Mom and Inga, take over-the-counter stuff," BL said flatly.

"Damn."

Cars of young people suddenly invaded the pizza-parlor parking lot, their stereo systems blasting. "Time to go," BL said.

They rode in silence, each young woman busy with her personal thoughts. Finally, BL broke the silence. "Are you pissed off yet?"

Lisa clenched her teeth. "You could say that. I'm going to leave from here. I want you to stop by the house. Did you bring some money and the bag?"

"Of course. I stopped at three ATM machines and cleaned out Mom's cookie jar. That's why I was late getting here. I have eleven hundred dollars. I filled the suitcase, and I want you to take my car. I had it serviced two weeks ago. It's newer than yours and a lot safer on the highway than the Honda. Look, don't even think about arguing with me. There is one condition, though."

"What?"

"That you let me know where you are and how you are. I mean it, Lisa. I'm not worried about the clothes, the money, or the car. We're friends, and I know you'd do it for me. I'll just use your car. School will be out in another week, and I'll just be hanging out at home. God, I wish I could go with you."

"I wish you could, too."

The hospital parking lot was almost empty when BL parked next to Lisa's maroon Honda. BL left the engine running as she got out and opened the trunk. "I packed a big bag because I wasn't sure where you were going or what you would need. I put in a hair dryer and a makeup bag. Here's the registration and insurance card. I'll need yours, and your keys." BL reached in her purse and handed over a wad of bills.

Tough, hard-as-nails BL broke down and cried. "I am going to miss you so much."

Arms around each other, both women continued to cry and wail softly.

"Say good-bye to your mom for me," Lisa said, wiping her eyes on the sleeve of her shirt. "I'll call your cell phone number at least once a week. I don't know if I should take your car or not."

"Well, I'm sure, and that's all that counts. I want you to take my cell phone, too. You're going to be alone traveling to God knows where. I'll get another one and I'll call you to give you the number. Don't look at me like that. I insist. When do you want me to stop by the Kolinas'?"

"Give me a couple of hours' head start. Park a few blocks away. I don't want them to know we switched cars. They're usually up till midnight sitting on the front porch."

"Where are you going to go? I swear to God, I won't tell anyone. Please tell me so I won't worry," BL said in a choked voice.

"You know on those crime shows you and your mom are addicted to? They always hide the loot in an obvious place. Then there's that old saying, keep your friends close, your enemies closer. It's so obvious, Jake will never think I'd go back to Crestwood, so that's where I'm going. *I'm going home, BL.* That's the last place Jake will think I'd go. I can lose myself in Crestwood until I decide what I want to do. I'll figure out a game plan as I drive. Don't worry about me. My eyes are open now. Hey, BL, I've survived this long. I'll be fine."

"Okay," BL said, giving Lisa one last hug. "Lisa, did you really love that guy?"

"As much as a fifteen-year-old is capable of loving someone. I thought my heart was going to jump right out of my chest when I saw Jake on your front porch."

"Too much, too little, too late. Take care of yourself. Don't forget to call."

"BL, I don't . . ."

"Go on, get out of here before we start blubbering all over again. Just drive carefully."

Lisa waved as she backed the Saturn out of the parking lot. She continued to wave, tears streaming down her cheeks. BL swiped at her own tears and cried all the way home.

Their eyes blurred by tears, neither young woman noticed the silver Jaguar parked at the far end of the hospital parking lot.

Jake's intention, after he got over the shock of seeing the women switch cars, hug, and cry, was to follow Lisa Summers. He peeled out of his parking space immediately just as Lisa, in the switched car, raced by him. He heard the wail of an approaching ambulance and froze, maneuvering the Jaguar to the side of the Emergency Room entrance to allow the ambulance to pass. By the time he reached the bottom of the hill, the Saturn was out of sight. "Son of a bitch!" he seethed. He looked into the rearview mirror to see Betty Lou Patrewski two cars behind him. He turned right, Betty Lou turned left. Jake crawled down the road and made a U-turn. He stepped on the gas and raced after her. When he realized she was going home, he made another U-turn and headed back the way he'd come. What the hell was going on?

Maybe he should take a chance and drive over to the Kolinas' on Chestnut Avenue.

Just to satisfy his curiosity. He told himself the car switch could be something as simple as Lisa's taking the car in for servicing because Betty Lou had to teach school. Or . . . the Saturn, three years newer than the Honda, was better for a long trip. It was a mind stretch, but Jake couldn't ignore it.

It was almost eleven thirty when Jake, after three drive-bys on Chestnut Avenue, decided Lisa Summers had indeed cut and run. That would account for the tears and the switch in cars. Jake cursed again and again until Elway protested by hissing and snarling before he climbed out of his nest to leap onto the headrest of the driver's seat and draped himself around Jake's neck.

"I screwed up, Elway. Time to go home. Tomorrow we'll pay the Kolinas a visit and see if we can learn anything."

He saw Betty Lou on foot as she turned into the alley behind the house on Chestnut Avenue. He slammed on the brakes, grateful there were no cars behind him. Why was the teacher paying a house call at eleven thirty at night? She wasn't returning Lisa's Honda, so his original theory that they'd switched up for some reason was confirmed. No, she was here to break the bad news to the Kolinas. Whatever the bad news was. He should have been a detective.

This whole scenario was definitely reason enough to call Mitzi.

Chapter 13

Mitzi Granger stared out at the star-filled
night, her thoughts on her nephew, on Trinity Henderson, on everything in her life.
Even though her thoughts were chaotic, she
felt peaceful and calm. She loved this time
of night, when she was alone on her verandah, except for the animals she adored,
dozing on the fiber carpet. From the rocker
she was sitting on she could see the fine
sprinkling of fireflies dotting the front yard,
while the tree frogs sang to her in a cadence
she found mesmerizing. The luscious ferns
hanging on chains from the rafters moved
lazily, either from the warm night breeze or
from the fans overhead. She sniffed, the
cloying scent of the Confederate jasmine invading her surroundings. The only thing

missing was someone to share these moments with.

Every night during her time with Harold, they'd sat out here talking about everything and nothing. Just sitting close had been more than enough.

The long night loomed ahead of her. She saw the headlights then, off at the entrance to her driveway. The tree frogs went silent, the fireflies moving away from the headlights. Visitors this late at night? How strange. She reached under the cushion to see if her little .22 was still there. It was. She pulled it out and sat on it. She was pretty fast on the draw, so she wasn't concerned. The animals got up and moved to the railing. Friend or foe? Foe, of course. Mitzi narrowed her eyes and waited for the car to come to a complete stop in front of the steps.

"Isn't this a little late for a social visit, Rifkin?" Mitzi drawled, when the car door opened and her brother-in-law stepped out onto the gravel driveway.

"You said you never sleep. I wanted to see if that was true or not. Do you mind if I come up on the verandah?"

"Make yourself at home, Rif. If you're here

to beg for more money for your paramour, you can stop right where you are. The answer is no."

Rifkin had one foot on the step, the other on the ground. "Why do you have to be so nasty about this, Mitzi? Is it a power thing with you? Do you like to see Sarabess grovel?"

"Now *that* I would love to see. Actually, I think I would pay money to see Sarabess Windsor grovel. That won't happen because she sends you to grovel for her. How unmanly. That makes you a fool in my eyes. The answer is still no."

"Then you leave me no other choice but to file papers with the court. You are being unreasonable, and you know it. You're doing this for spite."

"I'm simply obeying Harold's instructions. Nothing you can say or do will make me change my mind. Don't ever make the mistake of threatening me again, Rifkin. If you do, I might find the need to go public. Harold provided for Her Royal Highness so she could live out her days on Hilton Head Island. I should have evicted her a long time ago. If you push me, I just might exercise that right. I'm simply doing what Harold wanted, no more and no less."

"Sarabess wants to sell Windsor Hill and the farm."

Mitzi laughed until she choked. "I'd like to see her try. That property belongs to Trinity."

"Yes, but there is no Trinity. I've filed motions with the court to declare her deceased. It's been fifteen years. Everything, including the girl's trust fund, goes to Sarabess."

"No, it doesn't, Rifkin. It goes to me."

"Now you see, that's where you're wrong. Harold made a later will. No, Mitzi, not with me. He used a firm in Columbia. He made it two weeks before he died."

Mitzi pretended she was hearing the news for the first time. "Harold wasn't of sound mind two weeks before he died. He was drugged the whole time to ease his pain. I should know, I took care of him, along with round-the-clock nurses. Don't try this, Rifkin, because you will rue the day you aligned yourself with that bitch. If you have a will, it's a forgery. I'll hire the best in the land to prove it. I will tie you up in the courts till you both have one foot in the grave. I thought you were smarter than that."

Rifkin laughed. "And I thought you were

smarter than you are. I hoped it wouldn't come to this, Mitzi. You're leaving me no other choice but to go ahead and file those papers."

Mitzi's mind raced as she fired up a cigarette. "You will certainly waste a lot of man-hours then, Rifkin. Trinity is alive and well and will be home shortly. Jake found her."

"What?" The single word exploded from Rifkin's mouth like a gunshot.

"I thought that might get your attention. You heard me the first time. The girl is coming home. Tell Her Royal Highness to book a room at the Comfort Inn because the moment Trinity gets back here an eviction notice will be served on one Sarabess Windsor. You put that in your pipe and smoke it, Mr. Attorney. Now, get the hell off my property and don't come back."

"You're lying!" Rifkin sputtered as he removed his foot from the bottom step.

"Now, would I lie about something so important and make a fool out of myself? I think you know me better than that. I hate your guts, Rifkin, for what you did to my sister and my nephew, and all over that twit up there on the Hill. You backed the wrong horse. Go up to the Hill now and report your failure to Her Royal Nastiness."

The car door open, the fireflies swarming, Rifkin turned, and shouted, "You really expect me to believe that Jake, rather than the best detectives in the country, found Trinity when they couldn't? That's hogwash, Mitzi!"

"Yessireee, that's what I'm telling you! Is that fear I hear in your voice, Rifkin? Get used to the idea that this is not going to turn out pretty. Better book *two* rooms at the motel."

Mitzi didn't expect a response to her last salvo and wasn't disappointed when Rifkin slammed the car door shut and shot down the driveway.

"Bastard!" Mitzi muttered under her breath just as her cell phone rang.

"Darlin', you are just the person I want to talk with. But first, tell me your news, then I'll tell you mine."

BL walked through the backyard and around the side of the house to the front porch. Lisa was right. The Kolinas were sitting on a wicker swing. It was as quiet as church on a Sunday morning. Smoke from Sven's pipe eddied up and over the banister of the porch. BL called out a greeting but received nothing in response. The fifteen-watt bulb on the porch light cast a waxy yellow glow on the old couple. BL called out a second greeting. If they had been normal people, they would have asked what she was doing here at this hour of the night. They should be concerned that such a late visit might indicate an accident or something equally bad. BL could feel her insides start to shake as she climbed the steps, then leaned against one of the pillars supporting the porch. How menacing they looked.

BL took a deep breath and plunged into her rehearsed speech. "Lisa asked me to come by and tell you . . . to tell you she won't be coming back." There, she'd said it. When there was no reaction, she leaned closer, and said, "Mr. and Mrs. Kolina, did you hear what I said?"

A puff of smoke from Sven's pipe sailed upward. "When she didn't come home to make supper we figured something was wrong. We had peanut butter and jelly sandwiches. That ground meat that was supposed to be for meat loaf has to get thrown out."

BL didn't know what to say to that, so she

remained quiet. All she wanted to do was leave and go home so she could cry some more.

BL was halfway down the steps when Inga spoke. "We always knew she'd up and leave us one of these days. You young people are so ungrateful. We spent a fortune on her braces, sent her to college, and bought her a car. This is how she repays us. Sven said it would happen this way," Inga said, anger ringing in her voice.

BL bit down on her lower lip. A flood of words rushed to her tongue. "She, she! She has a name, and it's Lisa. You got your money's worth, Mrs. Kolina. You worked Lisa like a slave. Everyone in town knew it but Lisa. She would never tolerate a bad word where you or your husband were concerned. She won't be coming back."

"You young people are so callous. The bakery is going to close. What are we supposed to do now? How are we supposed to live? We did everything for that girl, and she didn't even have the decency to say good-bye," Inga whined.

"You have that all wrong, Mrs. Kolina. It was Lisa who did everything. She doesn't owe you a thing. Maybe you should think about spending that four hundred thousand you have in the bank. With all that Social Security you receive, I'm sure you'll survive."

"Well, I never . . ." Inga sputtered.

"I think the people in this town talk too much," Sven said.

"Good night," BL said as she ran across the lawn and out to the road. She jogged the rest of the way home, tears streaming down her cheeks. She kept brushing at her eyes with the back of her hand. She moved to the side of the road when a pair of headlights shone ahead of her.

The sleek silver Jaguar came to a stop alongside her. BL moved farther to the side. She jammed her hands into the pockets of her shorts. She wondered what would happen if she screamed at the top of her lungs. She started to run again when she heard the car door open and heard pounding feet behind her.

"Wait! Please, wait just a minute. I need to talk to you, Miss Patrewski."

"I don't want to talk to you. It's late, and I'm tired," BL called over her shoulder.

"Please, I need you to listen to me. Just give me five minutes. It's about Lisa."

"Then you should be talking to Lisa, not

me. If you don't leave, I'm going to scream as loud as I can. I'll say you attacked me. You're a stranger in town. Who do you think they'll believe, Mr. Journalist? I don't even think you're a journalist. I think you're some kind of . . ."

Oh, shit! Was his cover blown? "Some kind of what, Miss Patrewski?"

"Some kind of pervert." BL ran the rest of the way down the street and up the driveway that led to her mother's house. She blasted through the door and locked it. Shaking, she parted the curtain on the side window to see where her night visitor was. Getting into his car and backing up. God, she had to call Lisa, and she had to do it immediately if not sooner.

Jake let his breath out in a long *swoosh* of sound. His shoulders slumped. Tomorrow was another day. Then it would be time to head for home. Right now, though, he had to think about his phone call to Mitzi and what she'd blurted out to his father. He realized suddenly that he was homesick. He reached over to Elway's carryall and stroked the cat's head. Elway purred before he leaped out to settle himself on Jake's lap.

Jake sat in the parking lot of the motel for

a long time. He'd heard something in Mitzi's voice that he had never heard before. Panic. It unnerved him. He had to go home. With Lisa Summers gone, there was no reason to stay here, but he was going to take one more crack at Betty Lou Patrewski. If he could just get her to listen to him, maybe she'd help him find her friend Lisa, who, he was convinced, was Trinity Henderson.

Elway continued to purr on his lap. For some strange reason, the contented cat's purring calmed him down. Now that he had a plan of sorts—meeting Patrewski on her lunch hour—he would have to fill up his morning, and what better way than to pay a visit to the Kolinas. He wished he had taken the time to visit them earlier. If he had, maybe he would understand tonight's events a little better.

Jake opened the door of the Jaguar and walked across the parking lot to his motel room, Elway draped over his shoulder. He sighed heavily as he set Elway on the bed and pulled down the covers. He stripped down and was asleep within minutes.

Since Huether's, home of the best hamburger he'd ever eaten, was on his way to the Kolinas', Jake stopped for coffee and two fried-egg sandwiches. He wolfed down his food, asked for a coffee to go and a fish fillet for Elway.

Fifteen minutes later he was knocking on the Kolinas' screen door, where he dropped into his Jonah Franklin journalist mode. He introduced himself, was invited in, and sat down at the kitchen table with the couple. The kitchen was a mess, their breakfast hadn't been cleared away, and, if he was any judge, last night's dinner remains were still on the table. He tried not to look at the mess: crumbs, jelly globs on the table, peanut butter knives, spilled Cheerios, half-filled coffee cups, and milky-looking glasses—and all over the floor, wadded-up paper napkins. There were no apologies for the mess, no attempt to clear the table. Jake returned the Kolinas' intense scrutiny and smiled.

"I was hoping to get a picture of you both at the bakery along with your niece. Is that possible?"

"No. We aren't going to be opening the bakery again," Sven replied. "We made the decision over the weekend. Inga and I decided it's finally time to retire. Our niece isn't here right now, anyway."

"Oh. When will she be back? I'll be in town for a few more days. Maybe we could just do a shot of the two of you by the bakery. The shop, from what I'm told, has been an institution. Fifty years in business deserves some recognition. I understand your wedding cakes are famous in these parts. I'm sorry you're closing the shop."

"We're sorry, too, young man. Inga isn't up to going to the shop."

"Retirement can be a good thing," Jake said. "I understand you used to be a long-distance truck driver. I bet you could write a book about that time in your life. And you, Mrs. Kolina, what could be better than making wedding cakes for happy couples? Do you want to share some of your thoughts on those years?"

"No, son, we don't. We're private people."

"Well, what about your niece? What's she going to do now that you're closing the bakery? Someone told me a few of her wedding cakes, along with the recipes, were featured in some prominent magazines. Since she isn't here, could you provide me with a picture of her that I can put alongside yours?"

"We aren't a picture-taking family, young man. Is there anything else?"

Jake was getting the picture loud and clear. "Well, no, I guess not. I suppose I can find a picture of your niece at the library, or perhaps her friend Betty Lou can provide one. Young girls always take pictures. If you like, I'll send you a copy of the article when it's published."

"Don't bother," Sven said. "Inga and I have cataracts, and it's hard for us to read, so we get our news from the television and the neighbors tell us if something is going on in town."

As yet, Inga hadn't contributed a word to the conversation. Jake got up and stuck his notebook in his backpack. "Is it a yes or no on the picture? The sun is on the back porch. It would be a nice shot. You didn't say when your niece would be back." He let the statement hang in the air. Neither of the Kolinas responded, so Jake jammed his digital camera into his pocket. "Thank you for talking to me. I can see myself out."

On his way across the backyard, Jake turned around to see the couple watching him through the screen door. He had the feeling he'd just stepped into a hornets' nest. He drove away without looking back. As hard as he tried, he could not picture

Trinity Henderson living with that weird couple. Not the Trinity of his childhood.

Jake parked his car in the school parking lot forty-five minutes later. Joyce Patrewski had told him during his interview with her that Betty Lou's school lunch hour was at eleven thirty. Joyce had said that in nice weather, Betty Lou ate her lunch outside while she caught up on her reading.

Bearing that in mind, Jake walked to the back of the building, where picnic tables were set up under huge maple trees that were in full leaf. He saw her at the same time she saw him. It looked to Jake like she was getting ready to bolt, so he sprinted over to the picnic table.

"Wait! I want you to listen to me. It is imperative that you hear me out, Miss Patrewski. I understand your loyalty to your friend, and I applaud you for it. I don't want you to betray a confidence. I just want you to get a message to Lisa Summers. Will you do that for me?"

"Why? Who are you, anyway?" As if she didn't know who he was.

"My name isn't Jonah Franklin. I'm not a journalist. I came here under false pretenses to find a young woman named Trinity Henderson. In truth, that isn't even her name although it's the name she's gone by for a long time. My name is Jake Forrest and I'm a lawyer. I live in Crestwood, South Carolina."

Her appetite gone, BL broke her sandwich into pieces and tossed them onto the grass. Blue jays swooped down to gobble up the food. "What does this Trinity Henderson have to do with Lisa Summers?"

Jake sat down and propped his chin into his cupped hands as he stared across the table at the teacher. "They're one and the same. I think you know it, too. I'm going to be honest with you and tell you a rather sad story. I'm hoping you'll believe me and somehow get word to your friend. Look, I know you two switched cars. I have to assume that when I was at your home interviewing your mother, Lisa saw me, and she ran because she recognized me. Will you at least listen to me?"

BL nodded. "Make it quick, I only have twelve minutes left on my lunch hour. I won't make any promises."

"Okay, that's fair."

Chapter 14

The sun was creeping over the horizon when Lisa slowed the Saturn, turned on her signal light, and left the interstate to fill up the gas tank and get some coffee. She was bone-tired, and her eyes were full of grit. The long drive had been grueling even with the four stops she'd made for coffee. In addition, a detour because of heavy road construction had taken her two hours out of her way. According to the map on the seat next to her, she had less than an hour to go before she hit Crestwood. Her plan was to stop at the first motel she came to and sleep around the clock, if that was even possible. With no demands on her time, she could sleep for days if she wanted to.

Ten minutes later, the gas tank full, Lisa headed for the fast-food restaurant attached to the gas station. She washed her face, brushed her teeth, and combed her hair before she headed to the take-out counter, where she ordered two egg sandwiches, home fries, and two coffees. The coffee looked so black and strong, she knew it would shore up her eyelids until she could get to a motel and a comfortable bed.

As she chewed her food, Lisa wondered if she was making a mistake in returning to Crestwood. She had missed her hometown. A day hadn't gone by when she didn't think of someone or something having to do with the little town she'd lived in for the first fifteen years of her life. She'd been so young back then, a tomboy, with a heart-stopping crush on Jake Forrest. Until the day that her world turned upside down.

She'd made the best of the following fifteen years. The first fifteen years, the past . . . the second fifteen years, the present that she'd just left behind . . . Was this the third part, the final part of her life? Possibly, if you divided the pie of life into three parts. A beginning. A middle. And the end. Lisa shivered. The end of what?

Jake Forrest. Lisa's heart kicked up a beat. Jake. So many memories. Each time she thought about Crestwood, Jake was in the memory. Was what she felt for Jake back then puppy love? How had he found her and, more important, why was he looking for her in the first place? Something must have happened back in Crestwood for Jake to come looking for her now. As far as she knew, no one had searched for her before. She would give anything to know why they were now. She wished for a crystal ball that would give her the answers.

By now, those involved in her early life should have forgotten about her. With each passing year she had hoped that that was the case, but with Jake Forrest on the prowl, she knew she had to fall back and regroup. Why, after fifteen years? Why, why, why? When no answers popped into her mind, Lisa sighed, rolled up her trash, and stuffed it in the bag on her lap, but not before she took the lid off the second coffee she'd ordered. She opened the car door, looked around for a trash can. She left the door hanging open as she sprinted across the parking lot to toss the bag into the receptacle. Out of the corner of her eye she saw a flash of black. Half-expecting to see Jake Forrest on her trail, she whirled around. Twice she looked over her shoulder and around the parking lot, but nothing seemed out of the ordinary.

Lisa was about to slide into the driver's seat when she looked over at the passenger's side and gasped, her hands going to her chest. A big black dog, his tail wagging furiously, barked happily. "Hey!" Lisa squealed. "What are you doing here? C'mon, c'mon, you don't belong here. Where's your owner?"

Like the dog was really going to tell her. The dog tilted his huge head to the side and stared at her. He offered up his paw to shake hands. In spite of herself, Lisa laughed. A dog with manners. Lisa reached for the paw and shook it. The dog took that to mean he could lie down and go to sleep, which was exactly what he did.

Nonplussed, Lisa got back out of the car and walked around, asking each person she encountered if they'd lost a dog or if they had seen a big black dog. No one had. She entered the fast-food restaurant, which was jammed with travelers, and asked for the manager to make an announcement over the loudspeaker. When no one stepped forward to claim the dog, Lisa sighed.

She loved dogs and had had many while

growing up, but the Kolinas didn't like animals with their "nasty shedding," "dirty paw
prints" and the money they cost to feed and
take care of. A jitter of anxiety ran down
Lisa's arms as she marched over to the
take-out line and ordered three cheeseburg-
ers and a bottle of water.

The huge black dog was still sound asleep,
his head on his paws, but he was now in the
backseat, stretched out like a human. It was
obvious to Lisa that the animal thought he
had found a new owner. She smiled as she
climbed behind the wheel and turned the key
in the ignition. She drove down the road and
back out to the interstate.

Suddenly, Lisa felt less stressed, more in
control of herself. As she sailed down the
road, the smile was still on her face. "Crestwood, here we come!"

The only thing missing at the moment was
a game plan.

Lisa looked over at the digital clock on the
console as she slowed and drove off the interstate. Twelve o'clock. High noon. She
wondered if it was some kind of omen.

BL's eyes almost popped out of her head.
"You're a *lawyer!*" she screeched.

Jake winced. She made the term sound like he was the Devil Incarnate. He nodded as Elway hissed and snarled in his nest.

"I hate lawyers. They're the scum of the earth. On top of that, you came here under false pretenses, which just goes to prove my point. I'm not telling you a thing, and don't try to pry it out of me, either." BL was like a runaway train as she blasted on. "What's in it for you, *Mister Lawyer?* You aren't here to make nice, and don't deny it. I'm glad Lisa's gone, and I don't believe for a minute that Lisa Summers is this . . . this . . . Trinity Henderson person. Lisa would have told me something like that. We're friends. Friends tell each other secrets." BL hoped that what she was saying sounded sincere and honest, but one look at Jake's eyes told her he wasn't buying her indignation. He was simply waiting for her to run out of steam.

"You didn't answer my question, Mister Lawyer: What's in it for you?"

"For me personally? Nothing. I would like, however, to renew mine and Trinity's friendship if that's possible. You might not believe this but there are people in Crestwood who would love to have Trinity back in their lives."

"I guess that means you're saying Lisa, aka this Trinity person, left a void in someone's life. Aren't those people going to be surprised when she turns out not to be the person you and they think she is? Obviously Lisa doesn't feel the same way. If she did, and if she's Trinity Henderson, and not Lisa Summers, she would have gone back a long time ago to fill that void. Furthermore, you have absolutely no proof my friend is who you say she is. If you had proof, you would have produced it." BL's voice turned sarcastic when she said, "You're breaking my heart, Mister Lawyer." She started to gather up her sandwich wrapper and the apple core to stuff into the brown bag. A few seconds later she had her book bag, her purse, and her trash in hand.

Somewhere close to the building a bell rang. Jake recognized the sound from his own school days. The lunch period was over. He had to do something. He reached inside his back pocket for one of his business cards. He held it out to BL. "Please, take it. If you change your mind about your friend's whereabouts, give me a call. All I want to do is help her."

BL grimaced, but she did accept the card. She dropped it into her purse before she gave him a long, searching look. She shook her head as she raced across the playground to the open door, where the lunch monitors were clustered in a tight little knot.

Jake continued to sit at the picnic table long after the school doors closed as he tried to plan his next move. It took him five minutes to realize there was no next move to be made. He'd covered all the bases and struck out. The only thing left for him to do was head for home. He felt like he was a hundred-year-old failure when he reached for Elway's bag and left the school playground.

Jake settled Elway in the passenger side of the car, drove away from the school, gassed up, called Mitzi to alert her to his departure time, and headed straight for the interstate. If he made good time, he should be home in thirteen hours.

The minute school let out for the day, BL raced home and confided in her mother. Then she called Lisa on the cell phone that she'd given her. BL babbled nonstop, ending with, "I'm going to fly down to Charleston first thing in the morning. I booked my ticket online at school. I'm not going to allow you to face all those people without me at your side. That story was so bizarre, Lisa. I got Sandy Atherton to finish up my classes. I can stay with you for the whole summer. Don't tell me no, Lisa, because I won't listen. Mom agrees with me. Where are you right now?"

"I'm at a vet's office. I found a dog on the way. Actually, the dog found me. I was at a rest stop, and he hopped into my car and wouldn't get out. I'm here in Crestwood getting him checked out. The vet told me the dog has a microchip, so they're trying to track down his owner. Cross your fingers that I get to keep him. He seems to like me, too." She laughed then, a sound of pure delight.

BL found herself smiling. It had been years since she'd heard Lisa laugh like that. Maybe going home and finding a dog were the best things in the world for her friend. Maybe. "Where are you going to stay? Can you pick me up at the airport tomorrow?"

"Obviously I have to find a place to stay that will accept the dog if he stays with me.

I'm going to ask the vet, who, by the way, is very nice. I will gladly pick you up tomorrow if you're sure you really want to give up your summer to join me. Call me later to tell me what time your flight gets in. I'm going to have to get a job right away just to survive."

"I'll borrow some more money from Mom. Let's not worry about that right now. By the way, didn't you hear what I said earlier? You're an heiress. According to *that lawyer,* you will have money blowing out your ears if you claim it."

"That's not possible. Jake just wanted you to tell him where I am. As a kid he was always good at making up stories. I'm glad you didn't tell him. I'll get to the bottom of all of this on my own. There is one person in this town that I trust, but I don't want to go there unless I have to. I have to go now; the technician is motioning to me. That means the vet wants to see me. Call me later."

Exiting the clinic an hour later, Lisa knew the dog at her side was hers. After tracking the microchip, the vet had found the name of the huge dog's owner, but she had passed away a week ago. The woman's daughter was on her way to Ohio, taking the dog to live with her, when he got away from her at the rest stop. She was more than willing to allow Lisa to keep the dog, whose name was Lucky, and promised to send the dog's papers to the vet's office.

Happy with the news, Lisa's next question was to ask where there was a motel that allowed dogs. The vet said there were none, but that his sister had a furnished cottage she rented out to exchange students, and it was empty for the summer months. The rent was so reasonable, Lisa was stunned. She smiled when the vet told her there was even a small fenced-in yard so Lucky could run and dig.

Address in hand after a phone call to the vet's sister, Lisa had a temporary home. She was anxious to get there and get settled in.

As she drove down Old Trolley Road, Lucky sitting upright in the backseat, she felt like Lady Luck herself was smiling down on her. Twice she burst out laughing at her sudden good fortune. Lucky joined in by barking and pawing her shoulder.

Maybe life will be good from here on in. I can hardly wait for BL to get here.

A small, plump lady was waiting for Lisa when she turned off West Carolina Avenue onto the dirt road that led to a small white cottage nestled in a grove of pine trees. A front porch with window boxes full of bright red petunias beckoned her. Lucky barked his pleasure as Lisa opened the car door. The precocious dog raced up to the woman, who was wearing bib overalls and clogs. She tussled with the dog, a huge smile on her face before she waddled over to Lisa and held out her hand, introducing herself as Ardeth Gamble.

The tour of the little cottage and the back-yard was over before Lisa knew it. Everything was small but cozy. There were twin beds, a dresser, and a nightstand in the bed-room. The eat-in kitchen was old, but every-thing worked. The living room had a working fireplace, a couch, and four comfortable chairs. She smiled at the old claw-foot bath-tub in the one bathroom. She was a shower person, but suddenly the thought of taking a bubble bath appealed to her. The backyard was a rainbow of flowers. The small back porch held two yellow canvas chairs and a small table. "To watch the sunset," Ardeth said. But it was the front porch that thrilled and delighted Lisa. Two red rockers with a table between held a pitcher of lemonade and two glasses. Lisa just knew the lemonade would be tart but sweet.

Both women smiled when Lucky hopped up on one of the rockers, then hopped down and set off to explore. "There's a grocery store a few blocks over, and it will be your job to tend the flowers and keep them watered. All the bedding is in the linen closet. The refrigerator is turned on. The TV works, and so does the DVD player. If there's anything you need, my number is by the phone in the kitchen. It's not one of those newfangled phones. It hangs on the wall, but the cord stretches for *miles.*" Lisa smiled at the cherub of a lady and nodded. She counted out the rent money, with Ardeth promising to drop off the receipt in the coming days.

She had a home. The thought stunned Lisa to the point that she felt light-headed. She sat down on one of the rockers and poured herself a glass of lemonade, which she gulped. Tart but sweet. Perfect.

Lisa propped her feet on the railing of the little porch and looked out into the distance. All she could see were shrubbery and colorful flowers. Her eyelids drooped. They popped open the moment she felt the air stir around her ankles. Lucky had finished exploring and was ready to take a nap. She wondered if the big dog felt that he was home.

Not only did she have a home, albeit a temporary one, she *was* home.

At last.

Chapter 15

It was midafternoon when Mitzi turned off her computer. The last two hours she'd spent on her Mix & Match Web site had been a waste of time because her heart wasn't into matchmaking. Her mind had been on other things: Rifkin's visit and Jake's report. Where in the name of God was it all going to end? Maybe she needed to crack open one of her own fortune cookies to find out the answer.

The quiet old house suddenly took on a life of sound. The cats screeched, the dogs barked, and Jezebel was squawking her head off. The reverberating sound could only mean that someone was on the property. A stranger. More likely an unwelcome intruder.

Mitzi felt older than God when she heaved

herself to her feet to head for the front door. The decibel level increased to an all-time high as she pushed open the screen door, a weary sigh escaping her lips before she whistled for silence. The animals grew quiet immediately.

How splendid she looked. How regal. Her Royal Highness, Sarabess Windsor. *Widow* Sarabess Windsor. Harold's widow. Dressed in summer linen, wearing hose despite the humidity, in high heels, and perfectly made up. Smelling like a flower garden. In contrast, Mitzi knew she looked like she was getting ready to slop the pigs. If she had pigs to slop.

She took the initiative. "I appreciate the mountain coming to Mohammed, *Miz* Windsor, but the answer is no."

The two women were suddenly eyeball to eyeball. How green her eyes were, how creamy her skin, how silky her hair. The makeup she wore was so flawless it looked like she wasn't wearing any.

Mitzi stood her ground, forcing Sarabess to take a step backward.

"I understand Rifkin paid you a visit last evening. Just so you know, I didn't tell him to come here, *Miz Granger*."

Mitzi bristled at the woman's audacity. "Do you really expect me to believe that? He delivered your message. You try any of those shenanigans, and you'll be sorry, Miz Sarabess Windsor. Harold did not make a second will two weeks before he died. If you had cared enough to visit, you would know he was so frail, so sedated, he couldn't get out of bed. If you want to make a fool of yourself in the courts, be my guest. I'll fight you, Sarabess. This is not what your husband wanted."

Sarabess's head jerked backward. She sniffed. "I'm so glad you finally acknowledge that Harold was *my* husband and not yours." She sniffed again. "Even though you both pretended otherwise."

Mitzi slammed her hands on her bony hips. "Hell, Sarabess, we didn't pretend. We said it out loud to anyone who would listen. Everyone in this damn town knows what you've been all about your entire life. I loved Harold. Harold loved me. He trusted me to carry out his dying wishes, and that's what I'm doing. Everything goes to Trinity—your daughter, whatever you would like people to believe. You have no claim. Trinity will be arriving shortly, and on January fifteenth the trust will be turned over to her." Mitzi hoped she was telling the truth, and that Jake would somehow pull off a miracle and bring Trinity home. For now, the little white lie, maybe a big white lie, just hung there in the silence and the humidity.

Sarabess turned, grimacing as she advanced to step over a sleeping dog. "That's impossible. We both know it. But I'll demand a DNA sample. Rifkin is going to file the will. Get used to the idea. By the way, Mitzi, I never said the will was *made* two weeks before Harold died. I *found* the will two weeks before he died. He made the second will while he was . . . carrying on with you. Harold did come home from time to time, as you well know. Harold had many sides. I seriously doubt you were privy to them all, but I was. Harold was also loyal to me in his own strange way. Meaning, of course, that he realized he made a mistake where you were concerned, and he did the right thing as soon as he could. I anticipate a bit of a battle with you, but I'm up for it. I wonder if you are up for it, dear Mitzi. I need ten thousand dollars. Please write me a check."

Mitzi could feel her insides start to crumble. It couldn't be true. It wasn't true. She had to believe that. Harold would never have betrayed her. Never. But proving the second will a fake had just become much more difficult. Of course, if Trinity came back, the difference between the wills didn't matter, since both left the money in the trust to Trinity. Leave it to Rifkin to get things wrong.

She squared her shoulders and stared Sarabess down. Harold had always said that in the business world the first rule was: Never let them see you sweat because if you do, it is all over.

"I'm fresh out. Of checks, that is. Don't waste your time getting your panties in a wad. I'm definitely up for whatever battle you want to wage. The first thing I'm going to do when Trinity gets here is convince her to boot your ass off that Hill. You can live in that ramshackle house you allowed her to grow up in or that place in Hilton Head. The Hendersons will be pensioned off and move to a very nice retirement community, one of those fancy gated ones, in Florida. I suspect it won't take much convincing on my part to make Trinity agree. That girl dearly loved me, and I loved her."

"Damn you, Mitzi Granger, why don't you just die already and make me happy?" Sarabess screeched.

Annabelle, the little goat, sensitive to shrill tones, suddenly barreled through the half-open screen door. Sarabess gripped one of the white pillars that held up the verandah as she continued to screech. Jezebel let loose with every word in her vocabulary as she whizzed around the porch, fighting the downdraft from the paddle fans. Dogs barked, cats snarled and hissed. Mitzi laughed.

"You're an ugly, evil old woman. I'll see that you pay for this . . . this indignity!" Sarabess cried. "Enjoy what you perceive to be your authority because it's about to come to an end. Trinity Henderson isn't coming here, and we both know it."

With a cigarette hanging out of the corner of her mouth in defiance, arms akimbo, Mitzi watched as Sarabess untangled herself from the pillar to scurry down the steps to her car. The animals swooped through the door and followed her. Mitzi knew their intention was to paw and shred the elegant yellow linen dress as they chased the unwanted visitor.

Mitzi removed the cigarette, which she didn't even want, from the corner of her mouth and whistled sharply. The menagerie stopped in their tracks and returned to the porch. "Ladies and gentlemen," she said to the animals, "the lady isn't worth wasting your time or your energy. Come along now, it's time for dinner."

Mitzi did everything by rote, her mind on what had just transpired with Sarabess Windsor. The moment she finished feeding the animals she was going to head back to her office and go over the old calendars that she'd kept during her time with Harold. "You are a liar, Sarabess," she muttered again and again under her breath. "Harold would never do what you said he did. Never, never."

Jake reached up to the visor for his sunglasses. He blinked several times to ward off the blinding sun as he tooled down the interstate. The solid yellow line was mesmerizing, making him sleepy. Talking to Elway wasn't working. All the big cat did was purr from his perch on the headrest behind Jake. In desperation, Jake cranked up the

Jaguar's stereo system, hoping the sound would keep him awake.

Even though he felt coffeed out, Jake managed to work at the top of the container he'd purchased at the last rest stop. It wasn't too hot now, so he gulped at it, hoping it would prop up his eyelids. He had seventy more miles to go before he called it a day. He'd catch a few hours' sleep, then get on the road again. All he wanted was to go home and listen to Mitzi rant and rave about how he'd been stupid enough to lose Trinity Henderson.

Jake found himself grinning. Back when he and Trinity were kids, she could always outthink and outperform him. It had ticked him off at the time that a mere slip of a girl could get the best of him. Mitzi had explained it to him when she thought he was old enough to understand. Actually, it was the day of his college graduation. She'd looked him in the eye and said it was because his hormones had been raging back then, and he was thinking with his dick and not his head. He'd been amused by his aunt's blunt assessment. He wished he could still see the humor in it.

He *had* been thinking with his dick. All

he'd wanted then was to get Trinity into the barn to cop a feel, but Trinity knew what he was all about. Once he'd told her he loved her to see what she'd say. He'd expected her to laugh her head off. Instead, she had burst into tears and run to the barn. He remembered how he'd stood there in such total shock he couldn't make his feet move. Trinity Henderson crying! It was so bizarre he didn't know what to do. Mitzi would skin him alive when she found out he'd made a girl cry. Not just any girl, but Trinity Henderson. Mitzi thought the sun rose and set on Trinity Henderson.

Finally, feeling like ten kinds of a jerk, he'd gone to the barn, and there she was, huddled in a pile of hay. He'd sat down next to her trying to think of something to say. He couldn't remember now for sure, but he rather thought he'd promised everything under the sun if she would stop crying and not tell Mitzi. What he did remember with absolute clarity was the promise he'd made to her that she could always count on him, that he would always be her friend, and when he was finished with college, he'd return to Crestwood and they would get married. That promise had stopped the tears.

How pretty she'd looked with her eyes glistening with tears and hay sticking up in her hair. He'd kissed her then, and his world rocked right out from under him when she'd returned his kiss with just as much passion.

Somehow or other he'd managed to keep his pants zipped, and he'd raced home to Mitzi like the Hounds of Hell were on his heels. Mitzi had taken one long look at him and knew immediately what had happened. She'd sat him down and said in that quiet voice of hers that she used only when something was important, "This is where the rubber meets the road, Jake. Trinity is a minor, way too young for you. Later, when you're a young man with the world in front of you, you can renew those feelings, but not now."

The next day he'd been packed off to some damn camp in the Catskills, where he toiled as a camp counselor to twenty-five seven-year-olds whose mission it was to torment him till he cried "Uncle." He returned home the day before it was time for Mitzi to take him off to college. There hadn't been time to even say hello or good-bye to Trinity.

The first thing he'd done when he settled

into his dorm was to write to Trinity to tell her he meant everything he said. He'd even underlined the words *If you ever need me, I'll be there for you. I have a phone, and this is the number . . .*

With the passage of time, Trinity had faded into the background. Not wanting to go home to live in the house his mother had left in trust for him when he turned thirty, the house his father occupied, he stayed in Memphis and worked two jobs to earn enough to provide spending money during the school year. He'd become a jock, a big man on campus, with a plethora of girls throwing themselves at him. Somehow he managed to catch all of them, at which point sex and beer took over his life. Once in a while he studied, but it all came so easy he didn't have to pound the books. He'd finished college with a 4.0 GPA. Then it was on to law school, where he again graduated with little effort.

Mitzi constantly nagged him about settling down, raising a family, but he had trouble with commitment. Was it because he was still in love with Trinity? No kiss, no feeling had ever been the same as that day in the barn. Was that what he was searching for?

Son of a bitch. Just when he found his lost love, he lost her. Again.

Bullshit. He'd lost Trinity way back when. He still cringed when he thought about *that night*. He'd anguished over what happened from that day on, and while he told Mitzi everything else, he'd never told her about that night.

He, Brad Davis (his best friend), and the rest of his fraternity brothers were having a keg party. He'd gotten plastered early and had two long-legged blonde beauties practicing their lap dance techniques on him as he tried to figure out which one he could score with, when one of the brothers bellowed that he had a phone call. He'd ignored the summons until another brother brought the phone into the room and mouthed the words, "It's some chick, and she sounds upset."

In his near-drunken stupor he'd snarled words that ordinarily he would never say in front of any female, but he said them that night. Words the person on the other end of the phone could hear clearly.

He'd been so drunk it was all a blur until a

day or so later when the fraternity brother brought up the subject of the girl on the phone that night. He remembered that he'd asked who it was that called.

"Some chick with a strange name. Man, she was wailing up a storm. I figured it was some girl you'd dumped. You don't have to worry, she never called again. Got you out of that one nice and easy, Jake."

"What kind of strange name?" Jake remembered asking, his stomach starting to knot up.

"Something like . . . I don't know . . . I think it was something religious-sounding. I blew her off for you, man. You're in the clear."

"Was her name Trinity?" he'd asked.

"Yeah, yeah. That's what it was."

Jake remembered how his stomach had erupted. He'd raced back to his room at the frat house and called the Hendersons, only to be told that Trinity had run away. In a panic, he'd called Mitzi, who tearfully confirmed that Trinity had indeed run away. He'd wanted to go home, to look for her, but Mitzi said that that wasn't an option.

The knowledge that he'd failed Trinity was so terrible, he shut down completely. He stopped going to classes, didn't bathe, didn't eat, smoked and drank his head off for two full weeks. The brothers finally propped him up, arranged a meeting with the dean, and got him back on track.

Without a doubt, the worst two weeks of his life.

Jake suddenly realized that horns were blaring at him. He looked down at the speedometer and realized he was going only forty miles an hour in the fast lane. He jerked to full alert, pressed the gas pedal, and sailed down the road.

Memories like the one he'd just conjured up were not for the faint of heart.

Especially a heart like his, which was bruised and battered.

Chapter 16

Jake Forrest rubbed at the stubble on his chin as he climbed the steps to the verandah, where Mitzi was waiting for him along with her menagerie. She hugged him, squeezing him with surprising strength. "Please tell me you have good news, Jake. Please tell me what I need to hear," she whispered in his ear.

Jake sighed. "I blew it, Mitzi. She got away from me. She's on the run again. I'm sorry. You have no idea how sorry I am."

Mitzi released the stranglehold she had on her nephew and plopped down on one of the rockers. "How did that happen?" she asked hoarsely. "I was so . . . certain you were bringing good news."

Jake's voice was weary-sounding when he asked, "Does it matter, Mitzi? It was Trinity, though, I'd stake my life on it. You should have seen her, Mitzi. She's gorgeous. I could see a resemblance to Emily in her. And to Sarabess Windsor. It was her. Can you ring that bell of yours and get me a beer?"

"Of course." Mitzi was about to ring the little bell on the small wicker table when Celeste appeared with a tray holding an ice bucket loaded with Heineken. Jake inhaled the beer until there was only an inch left in the bottle.

"Look, it's not as bad as it sounds. Well, it is bad but I got this brainstorm as I drove the last seventy miles. I think, and this is just my guess, but I think she came back here. It's the last place she'd think we'd look for her. As kids, and you know this, Mitzi, Trinny was always one step ahead of us. She's here. I feel it in my bones."

"I like gut feelings and intuition, Jake. I live by my feelings. I think you might be right. However, the challenge will be to find her if it's true. You know what they say about criminals, not that Trinity is a criminal, but they always return to the scene of the crime. I can hire some private detectives to scour Crestwood. Discreetly, of course. Newcomers have a tendency to stand out, as you well know."

Jake was halfway through his second beer, his head thrown back, his eyes closed. "Put yourself in her place. Where would you go, what would you do? I was tracking her, and she had a little help." Jake explained to Mitzi about what he considered the switcheroo with BL. "She might have a little money, a good working car, and some suitcases full of clothes, but that's it. That isn't going to last very long. She'll need a job, a place to live. She might trip herself up. Yeah, Mitzi, get some investigators on it. Anything of importance happen while I was gone?"

"Do you remember my telling you about the will that your father, the night he was in his cups, told me had been made two weeks before Harold died? Well, Sarabess paid me a visit and now says that the will *was found* two weeks before Harold died. I don't believe it for a minute, but your father is going to court with it. I will, of course, challenge it. I am convinced that if there is such a document, it's a forgery. Your father was pretty pissy when he showed up here. And when she came, Her Highness was even pissier. The animals ran them both off. Sarabess said if Trinity showed up, she would demand a DNA sample. What worries me is, neither one of them appeared to be worried about Trinity herself or her well-being. It's almost as if they think she's . . . dead. I kept thinking they know something we don't know. Am I missing something, nephew?"

"Well, if you are, then I'm missing it, too. If you don't mind, I'm going to take a shower and catch a few hours' sleep. Don't let me sleep more than four hours, okay?"

Mitzi nodded and waved her hand to indicate she approved.

Jake walked into the house, Elway in his arms. He returned a moment later. "Did you find out anything about Grace Finnegan?"

"No. I came up dry. I think you need to go to New York. I'll try to find out the name of the hospital where Sarabess delivered Trinity. I'm sure I have a note or something from that time. Harold told me a lot back then. I think she met someone named Louise Amity while she was there. I seem to remember Harold mentioning her a couple of times."

Jake digested the information. "You're

probably right. But I think you should go to New York instead of me. Thirty years is a long time, Mitzi. I don't want to rain on your parade, but the likelihood of your finding someone who was there at the time can't be good."

"Run along, Jake. I'm going to sit here and think on the matter."

Jake offered up an airy salute.

Mitzi's thoughts whirled and twirled as she contemplated, then rejected a thousand different scenarios. It wasn't until the sun set that she sat bolt upright with what she considered to be a stupendous idea. *"All-righttttt,"* she muttered.

Mitzi raced into her office, her bare feet slapping furiously on the hardwood floor. She made six phone calls in rapid succession, ending each call with, "Be at my house by nine o'clock."

She knew at precisely 9:05 there would be over thirty of her peers on her front porch waiting for whatever it was she wanted them to do. All were members of Mitzi's Senior Mix & Match Club, where it was all mixing and no matching. All thirty were also members of Mitzi's Fortune Cookie Club, which dreamed up fortunes for the four Chinese restaurants in Crestwood. Not for money but for free lunches and dinners. It was a way to keep the geriatric set involved so they wouldn't sit at home atrophying. It worked for everyone. As Mitzi put it, just because there was snow on the roof, it didn't mean there wasn't a fire in the furnace. She dusted her hands dramatically before she made the seventh call. She scribbled furiously before she made her eighth.

"Darlin', I have here in my hand the confirmation number for your airline flight tomorrow morning to New York. Get a pencil." Mitzi listened to Jake sputtering on the other end of the line before she said, "Since you screwed up the first time, this is a chance to redeem yourself. Call when you get there. I have things under control here. By the time you get back I should have some news—in case your theory is right, and Trinity really is here. I don't want any arguments, Jacob. Your job is to find out what happened at that hospital in New York. In a minute, I'm going to fax you some papers that belonged to Harold and might help you. Harold did love to make notes while things were fresh in his mind. It will be up to you to make sense of it all. Some of our answers lie in that hospital. I'm sure of it, Jake, and it goes without saying that I am depending on you."

The following morning, Mitzi's geriatric club, armed with maps and newspaper listings of rentals, contemplated their leader's mission while Jake Forrest paced the airport, feeling cranky and belligerent. He was still smarting over losing Trinity back in Pennsylvania and the disappointment he read in his aunt's eyes at his failure.

To pass the time until his flight was called, he walked over to the huge plate glass window to watch the incoming and outgoing planes. He looked down at the ground at one of the smaller thirty-seven-seater planes that had just landed. He hated small planes, hated that you had to board and deplane outside, even when the weather was bad. He watched as a shaky elderly gentleman with a cane tried to maneuver his way down the metal stairway. He did a double take when he saw Betty Lou Patrewski behind the man, her gaze sweeping the surrounding area as though she were looking for someone. Well, hot damn! Who could she be looking for but Trinity Henderson, aka Lisa Summers? He looked around cautiously. Then he remembered that no one was permitted beyond the scanners.

Aha! His thoughts racing as fast as his feet, Jake galloped across the main waiting area and out to the long, narrow hallway that would take him to the scanning area. He slowed down just long enough to yank at his baseball cap, then lowered his head as he joined the gaggle of deplaning passengers from other flights, all headed toward the baggage area. He tried to see everything at once. Would Trinity be here among those waiting to greet loved ones, or would she be waiting outside? He had no idea.

What he did know for certain was she wasn't parked in front of the entrance. Since 9/11, police patrolled the road to make sure that didn't happen. He himself had parked in the long-term lot. Trinity would have parked in either the short-term lot or the hourly lot, depending on where she could find a space. Either way, it was a problem for him. He hoped and prayed BL had checked luggage. That would allow him time to drive his car from long-term to the exit of the short-term and hourly lot. They didn't know his car, so he was safe in that respect.

Jake continued to sprint toward the parking lot, his breathing ragged. So much for trying to stay in shape with visits to the gym once a week to ogle the female members.

He was gasping for breath, his body drenched in sweat when he finally made it to his car. The stifling heat made him gag. He vowed to get a new car the first chance he got, one with quality air-conditioning, unlike what was in his car now, which only worked sporadically. He floored the gas pedal and careened out of the parking lot on his way to the tollbooth, where he would pay for the ninety minutes he'd been parked.

Jake risked a quick glance at his watch. He'd used up thirteen minutes. Such an unlucky number. Two hundred feet from the tollbooth, he pulled to the side of the road and parked on the shoulder. He popped the hood and got out. An overheated car in this kind of weather wouldn't arouse anyone's suspicion. The open hood would allow him to watch for BL's Saturn, which Trinity was driving.

Jake strained to see the oncoming line of

cars, hoping he could spot the Saturn. He couldn't. He ran over to the tollbooth with his ticket, paid his fee, and explained that if he could get his car started, he would have to keep the car moving. The attendant nodded as she handed over his change. Good, now he was all set.

Jake peered at the contents under the hood of his car. What a mystery it was. Mitzi would probably know what each hose, each clamp was. All he knew about cars was that you turned the key, and either the car moved or it didn't. He risked a quick look at the line of cars behind him. He almost jumped out of his skin when he saw the Saturn. He could make out two figures behind the lightly tinted glass. The thought left him light-headed as he tried to figure out his next move. He finally decided that he would wait until Trinity paid her ticket, allow two cars to follow her, then fall in behind. He longed for a GPS system and vowed to get one. Someday. Even if he had one, he wouldn't know what to do with it. He wasn't the least electronically or mechanically inclined. Maybe Mitzi could teach him.

Jake closed the hood of his car just as Trinity pulled to a stop and handed over her money. He followed his plan and then gunned the engine and catapulted ahead. He cursed as he swiped his face with the sleeve of his shirt. The A/C vents were spewing hot air. What did it matter? He was on a roll.

He leaned back, shifted his mind into neutral and ran with his thoughts. His last thought, as he kept a good distance behind the Saturn, was how proud Mitzi was going to be and how pissed she would be when she found out he hadn't gone to New York. *You win some, you lose some,* he thought happily. All's well that ends well. At least he wouldn't miss Elway, and Elway wouldn't have to put up with Mitzi.

Mitzi clapped her hands for silence. She looked around at the members of her Senior Club and winced. All were eager for the challenge she was about to present, but were they mentally and physically up to it? She simply didn't know. All she could do was present her case and hope for the best.

Eighty-year-old Jim Watson, also known as Big Jim, waved his cane and whistled for silence. "So, Mitzi, did any of our ads get a response?" He was, of course, referring to "Mitzi's Mix & Match" newsletter that she made up as she went along, photocopied, and handed out to all the members. It had started out being a fun thing, then turned into a nightmare when the members said they were interested in hooking up with a member of the opposite sex.

"It was a good ad. I worked on it all day, Mitzi," Jim said.

Mitzi riffled through the papers in her hand. "Jim, does this ad sound like it would attract a member of the opposite sex? *'Male, 1922, high mileage, good condition, some hair, many new parts including hips, knee, cornea, several brand-new valves. Isn't in running condition, but walks well.'* No one responded, Jim."

"I was truthful. I didn't want to mislead some nice lady." The old man pouted.

Mona Richfield piped up. "That was a terrible ad, Jim. Listen to mine. *'Sexy, fashion-conscious blue-haired beauty, 80s, slim, 5'4" (used to be 5'6"), searching for sharp-looking companion. Matching white shoes and belt a plus.'* Why didn't you answer my ad, Jim?"

" 'Cause I knew it was you. Why didn't you answer mine?"

"I knew it was you, too. We need new blood in the club. Mitzi—"

"Enough!" Mitzi shouted to be heard over the din of the complaining seniors. "We can deal with the matchmaking later. I have some ideas on that, but right now we have to concentrate on the mission at hand. Can I please have your attention?"

Mitzi waited until she had everyone's ear before she riffled through the papers in her hand. "First things first. I want each and every one of you to promise, to swear to God, you will not, under any circumstance, divulge to anyone what I'm about to tell you."

Ardeth Gamble raised her pudgy hand. "I don't take swearing to God lightly, Mitzi. I think I want to know more before I agree to something that serious."

Mitzi, always astute, sensed a revolt coming. She squared her skinny shoulders and uttered the magic name. "What if I told you it has to do with Sarabess Windsor?"

The bedlam that followed made Mitzi smile. "Oh, well, that's different," Ardeth chirped. "Count me in."

Mitzi grimaced. "I thought you'd see it my way. Now, listen up. Jim, stop pouting, we're going to find you a companion one way or the other. I need your attention now."

"Aren't you serving refreshments, Mitzi?" Bertha Bainbridge grumbled.

"Not today, Bertha." Mitzi sighed as she looked upward at the ferns that were swaying in the breeze the fans created. All she needed now was for a flock of birds to swoop onto the porch, and she'd have a circus on her hands. Everyone in town knew that Helen Barnes had been attacked by a flock of blue jays when she was ten years old. It didn't matter that she was now seventy-eight, she was still petrified of anything with feathers. With that thought in mind, Mitzi hustled everyone along with their canes and walkers down the steps. She wanted to laugh at the row of golf carts lining her driveway. Most of her guests no longer had a driver's license but were still permitted to drive the carts about town. They had enough citations among them to wallpaper her giant living room. A citation was better than a traffic ticket, and no one had to buy gas. Mitzi paid the citations out of her own pocket once a month.

The golf carts cranked up, three passengers to a cart, with canes and walkers hooked onto special hitches in the back. "Let 'er rip," Jim shouted.

"You dumb cluck, we need instructions first," Ardeth Gamble said as she gripped the bar in front of her.

Mitzi blew the whistle hanging around her neck. When she had everyone's undivided attention she proceeded to enlighten her army as to what she wanted done. The brigade hooted and hollered as they made their way down the driveway and out to the open road.

Well, that was an experience, Mitzi thought as she marched back into the house just in time to pick up the ringing telephone.

"Jake! Why are you calling me? You're supposed to be over Atlanta by now on your way to New York. Where are you, nephew?"

"I'm following Trinity and her friend BL from Pennsylvania. Right now I'm on Dorchester Road about to turn onto Old Trolley Road. Ya know, I just might make a good detective after all."

"I'll be damned! All right, stay on the girls and report back. My little club is on the prowl as we speak. Does this mean you are not going to go to New York, nephew?"

Mitzi asked, her mind whirling and twirling with what Jake was telling her.

"That's what it means, Mitzi. Turn it over to a private eye. Let them do the legwork. I think I can do more in Crestwood. Detective agencies have more services at their disposal than I do. I'll call back when I see where it is the women are going. I have to be careful so I don't tip my hand. I lost her once. If she gets spooked now, it's all over."

Jake heard Mitzi mutter something that sounded like, "I don't believe all this is happening," before he ended the call.

"Guess what, Mitzi? I don't believe it, either." His eyes glued to the road, he followed the Saturn, remaining two cars behind.

Chapter 17

Sighing, BL flopped down on one of the rocking chairs on the small porch of the cottage. "This is so nice, Lisa. Perfect, actually," she said, waving her arms around to indicate the colorful flowerpots and the lush greenery that surrounded the secluded little home. "It's like a mountain retreat without the mountains. And it smells absolutely delicious. I could sit here forever."

Lisa laughed as she entered the house to fetch two soda pops. The black dog sniffed BL, then lay down between the two bright red chairs. The screen door creaked just the way a screen door is supposed to creak. "I don't think anyone can find me here. This little cottage can't be seen from the road, and it certainly is off the beaten track," she called over her shoulder.

BL shivered. Jake Forrest was like a bloodhound. There was no doubt in her mind that the young lawyer would find her friend if he suspected she'd returned to Crestwood. She wondered if she should mention her worry to Lisa. Or was she supposed to call her Trinity?

Lisa returned carrying two bottles of Dr Pepper. She held one out and offered up a toast. "To your first visit to the Lowcountry. That's what they call this area, you know. We're at sea level. I could really be happy here. I'm hoping Miss Gamble lets me stay here beyond the end of the summer."

BL looked over at her friend. "I wouldn't get too comfortable if I were you. Listen to me, Lisa, you have to . . . What you have to do is . . . is . . . lay your old ghosts to rest. You can't keep running and hiding. You've already lost fifteen years of your life. I came here to help you get back on track. So let's make a plan."

Lisa propped her feet on the porch railing. "Damn, BL, I just got here. Can't I hang out for a few days? I need to soak everything up, get my bearings, so to speak. Don't worry, I'm going to get a job so I can pay you back. And I didn't lose fifteen years. It was all by my choice. You're making it sound like I lived underground or something."

The black dog raised his head at the sharp tone of his new mistress.

"Dammit, Lisa, I'm not worried about the money. I'm worried about you. What are you going to do? Do you have a plan? What?"

Lisa slugged at the Dr Pepper. "Stop worrying about me, BL, I'm a big girl. Right this minute I don't know what I'm going to do, and no, I do not have a plan. I made some awful mistakes years ago, and I want to make sure I don't screw up this time around. Just cut me some slack. Are you sure your mom is okay with your coming here?" she asked, hoping to change the subject.

"You're trying to sidetrack me, Lisa. I told you Mom's okay with it. She's seeing someone these days and doesn't need her thirty-year-old daughter spying on her. That's how she views me being there. I don't think it's serious. He's just someone to have dinner with or go to the movies. Companionship. I really don't think they're . . . you know . . . Dammit, why do grown children think their parents shouldn't or don't have sex? Yeah, yeah, they're *doing it.*"

Lisa burst out laughing. "I wish you could

see your face, BL. You look outraged. You're just pissed off that your very own mother is having sex, and you aren't." She laughed again.

BL shrugged, chagrined that her friend had homed in on her thoughts. "We're supposed to be talking about you, my friend. So, let's get to it. I want you to talk to me and tell me everything from your earliest memories on. I won't say a word, I'll just listen. When you're finished, I'll offer to give you my opinions and advice. If you don't want to hear what I have to say, then I won't say anything. Deal?"

Lisa squirmed in her chair. "Everything?"

"Yes, everything. I'll know if you leave something out because I'm astute and used to dealing with kids, so I'm an expert at detecting evasiveness and lies. Just so you know."

Lisa squared her shoulders and took a deep breath. "I was born . . ."

As Lisa's voice droned on, Lucky got up and went off to explore the grounds. Neither young woman seemed to notice.

Jake continued down West Carolina Avenue as the Saturn made a left onto a se-

cluded gravel road. His eyebrows shot upward. Why the hell was Trinity Henderson
going to Ardeth Gamble's house? Then he
remembered the cottage at the back of the
three-acre plot of land Ardeth called home.
"Gotcha!" he chortled happily as he waited
for a break in traffic so he could make a
U-turn in the middle of the road.

Jake whizzed up the road and abruptly
made a right turn onto the gravel road. He
drove a few feet and got out of the car. It
would be nice to visit with Miss Ardeth. She
always served gingerbread and cider no
matter the time of year. Miss Ardeth loved to
chatter and was, he was convinced, Mitzi's
gossip source.

The antebellum mansion was almost
identical to Mitzi's house, the same set of
steps, the wide verandah, the same paddle
fans, wicker furniture, fiber carpets, and
glorious pots of colorful flowers. He peered
through the screen door as he rang the
doorbell. He heard it chime throughout the
house. A second later he heard a phone ring
somewhere in the back, probably in the
kitchen. Eight rings later, the caller hung up.
Obviously Miss Ardeth wasn't home.

Jake looked down when he felt something

brush at his ankle. "Elway, how'd you get out of the car?" The cat purred, then leaped onto one of the wicker rocking chairs. Out of the corner of his eye, Jake noticed a black blur bounding up the steps. Elway spotted the black blur at the same time and hissed his disapproval. Jake stood statue-still while the big dog sniffed him from every angle. Satisfied that he wasn't up to no good, the dog sat down and looked at Elway, his tail swishing furiously. To Jake's bewilderment, Elway started to purr so loudly, he immediately felt jealous.

Jake opened the porch gate, then locked it behind him so he could spy on Ardeth's new tenant without the black dog attacking him. As he wound his way around the back of the old mansion, his thoughts were going in all directions. How in the hell did Trinity get here? Did Ardeth Gamble know who she was? Not likely. Why was BL here? He slowed and dropped to a crouch behind a bushy camellia when he heard voices coming from the right. He was aware suddenly of the pine needle beds and the heady scent of the Confederate jasmine that seemed to be attacking him from all angles. The voices were louder now, and he could actually make out words. He crab-walked a few more feet and dropped down behind an azalea that was as big as an upside-down beach umbrella. He closed his eyes as he tried to recognize the person talking. Trinity. He'd know that voice anywhere. He had the presence of mind to turn off his cell phone as he settled down to eavesdrop. Mitzi was never going to believe this.

Twice Jake almost got up and ran from his hiding place, but he didn't. He felt lower than a snake's belly as he listened to Trinity recount her early life. Some of the things he heard confirmed his earlier suspicions and memories. Other things made him want to run to Windsor Hill to strangle Sarabess Windsor. His clenched fists beat into the damp pine needles, leaving a sticky residue all over his hands.

Then he heard his name mentioned. He felt himself grow hot all over as he listened to his old friend describe the despair she went through the night she'd called his fraternity, only to hear his ugly words and have him blow her off. His gut told him he was going to pay for that big-time somewhere along the way. He cringed when he thought about what Mitzi would do and say when she found out. And she would find out.

Jake was shaken to his core when he saw the big dog racing along the overgrown paths, Elway in his wake. "Shit!" he muttered under his breath as he backed out of his hiding place. When he felt he was a safe enough distance from the little cottage and the two women, he took off after Elway and managed to scoop him up. He raced to his car, literally tossing Elway onto the front seat. Snarling, Elway leaped up on the headrest and nipped his ear. The black dog was pawing the door, trying to get in. "Aw, shit, come on, big guy, back off, or you're going to get me in trouble. How the hell did you get over that gate, anyway?"

Realizing the huge dog wasn't going to budge, Jake got out and carried him up to Ardeth's front porch. He opened the screen door and pushed the dog into the house, pulling the stained glass mahogany door shut. Meanwhile Elway had gotten out of the car and started to spit and snarl as he nipped first one of Jake's ankles, then the other.

This whole thing definitely is not going as

planned. "Put a cork in it, Elway, we're going home. I need to fall back and regroup."

"If you don't slow down, Jim, I'm going to report you," Ardeth Gamble screeched, as Jim Watson swerved around a pickup that was cruising below the speed limit on the secondary road.

"All right, all right. What's wrong with you, Ardie? You look like something is bothering you. I'm only going twenty-five miles an hour," Jim lied with a straight face. "Mitzi said she'd kick my ass all the way to the Georgia border if I got another citation. What's wrong, aside from my driving?"

"Of course something is bothering me, you old coot. I thought . . . We're supposed to be a couple. Me and you. Like salt and pepper. An old shoe and an old sock. Then you go putting an ad in 'Mitzi's Mix & Match.' What am I supposed to think?"

"Aw, I was just trying to make you jealous. You know you're my honey. No one can make strawberry rhubarb pie like you. You making one today?" Jim asked slyly.

"No, I'm not baking a pie today. It's too hot to turn the oven on. Go to the grocery store and buy one. I keep looking at this drawing

Mitzi gave us all. I want to say I know this girl. At the very least, I've seen her somewhere. Does she look familiar to you, Jim? No, no, never mind, don't take your eyes off the road. Look, turn off here. I want to stop at the house for my sunglasses. Don't worry about the others; they'll figure it out."

Ardeth was right—the moment Jim turned off West Carolina, the golf cart brigade kept on going. "My door is closed. I distinctly remember leaving it open. Good grief, what if a home invasion is going on inside? My gun is upstairs. What do you think, Jim?"

Jim looked worried. "I think that old blunderbuss is so rusty, it won't even fire. You stay right here, Ardie. I'll go take a look-see." He looked around for a stick to use as a club.

Ardeth hopped out of the golf cart. "For heaven's sake, Jim, just use your cane. Your rotator cuff is healed, isn't it?"

"Well, no, but it's better than it was. I need the cane to walk, Ardie."

Ardeth yanked the cane out of Jim's hand, but not before she gently shoved him back into the golf cart. "I'll handle this, Jim. No home invader is going to intimidate me. Besides, I'm a lady."

Jim pondered Ardeth's words. "I don't think this is a time to act or worry about being a lady. This is where you kick ass and take names later. Mitzi is going to love this. I bet we'll get the front page of this month's newsletter."

Ardeth turned around on the steps to look at Jim. "Oooh, I love it when you talk tough." She waved the cane with such a flourish that Jim cowered in the golf cart.

Ardeth advanced on the stout mahogany door with its diamond-paned stained glass and tore it open. She whipped the cane in every direction as a black streak flew through the open door to barrel across the verandah and down the steps. The dog stopped just long enough to inspect Jim and the golf cart before he raced to the back of the house.

"It's okay, Jim. The dog belongs to my new tenant. My brother recommended her, and since my exchange student left, it worked out for all of us. The dog belongs to her. Come on in. We might as well have some sweet tea while we're here." Ardeth walked over to the top of the steps and tossed the cane to Jim, who caught it.

Slightly winded at the top, Jim leered at

Ardeth. "I have a racy DVD we can watch tonight if you're interested. Dinner and a movie. What do you say, Ardie?"

"How racy?" Ardeth asked coyly.

"Just racy enough to rev our engines. Pot roast would be good. I really could eat some pie, though."

"That racy, eh? All right, I'll make the pie. I guess I can take off the rest of the day and cook since I just solved Mitzi's problem. I'll prove it to you after we have our sweet tea. What's the name of the movie?" Ardeth decided her engine hadn't been revved in so long, she needed details.

Jim debated a full minute before he responded. "I think it's about a cheerleader at a football game. There are lots of pom-poms on the cover." He didn't think he should mention that the pom-poms covered strategic parts of the naked cheerleader's anatomy.

"Hey, what do you mean you solved the problem? How is that possible? Are you saying the mission is over? We didn't even get started, Ardie," Jim said fretfully. The cheerleader and her pom-poms suddenly lost all of their appeal with Ardeth's sudden declaration.

"Stop pouting, Jim, or I'll have to ask you some pointed questions about Bertha Bainbridge you'd probably rather not answer. Change your mind-set and think about how pleased Mitzi is going to be when we tell her the young lady everyone is looking for is right here in my little cottage, thanks to my veterinarian brother. I admit she looks different from that old-*timey* artist's sketch Mitzi gave us. The young lady has a fashionable hairdo now, but it's the same person. I'm sure of it. After we drink our tea, we'll meander over there for a little visit. Think positive, Jim, and put your glasses back on. You need to stop being so vain about those glasses. Everyone your age wears glasses. When I get to be your age, I'll be wearing them, too. Ten years makes a big difference," Ardeth sniped, making a reference to Bertha Bainbridge's age, which was the same as Jim's.

Jim was smart enough to pick up on Ardeth's message and took the high road. "Whatever you say, Sweet Cheeks."

Sweet Cheeks. If she'd been a peacock, Ardeth would have spread her feathers. For that little compliment, she'd add some new potatoes to the pot roast, one of Jim's favorites. Maybe some of those tiny little carrots from her garden that were sweeter than honey.

As Ardeth bustled around the kitchen getting out her grandmother's heirloom crystal glasses, ice, and the sweet tea, her thoughts drifted to the DVD she would be watching later with Big Jim. She'd never really been into football because she simply didn't understand the game. What could possibly happen in a football game that would rev her engine? Maybe it was a locker-room thing with the players in their skivvies. *Like all those sweaty bodies are going to excite me.*

"Where did you get the DVD, Jim?"

"That's the best part." Jim cackled. "Mitzi snitched it from her nephew's house. She gave it to Barney, who made six copies. Barney gave it to Sid, and he gave it to me. Barney said it will make everything stand at attention."

Ardeth felt her neck grow warm. *"Everything?"*

"Yep, that's what Barney said. Sid said he couldn't sleep for a week after he watched it. Barney said he would give it five stars. Sid said five stars plus. It doesn't get any better than five stars," Jim said, excitement ringing in his voice.

Ardeth's eyebrows shot upward, not at Jim's words but at the excitement in his voice. She hoped the copied DVD and the evening would be worthy of her pot roast and strawberry rhubarb pie. "Drink up, big guy." She leered at him. Jim didn't miss a beat, but his face turned bright red. He crossed his fingers that his engine was up to all this excitement.

They sat opposite each other at the antique claw-foot table, their thoughts on dinner and the evening ahead of them as they gulped at the sweet tea. "More tea, Jim?" Ardeth asked in a syrupy voice.

"Nope. I know my limit, Sweet Cheeks. Let's go check out the little miss so we can blow Mitzi's socks right off her feet."

"You know, Jim, I never, ever bothered my exchange students. I make a point to respect their privacy. I need a reason to go over there. I think I'll just take this pitcher of sweet tea and some of the raisin-filled cookies I baked the other day. We'll pretend we're in a hurry and are just dropping this off, sort of an official welcome. We'll stay just long enough for you to get a good look at her. If she really is Mitzi's quarry, there's no need to spook her. We won't say anything about the dog and how it got into my house. I'm going to think about that later, though. Does this all work for you, Jim?"

"Yes, ma'am, it does. Is she pretty, Ardie?"

"She certainly is. She looks like I did at her age. She would be perfect for Mitzi's nephew. It's time for him to stop catting around and settle down. Careful on the steps, Jim."

The path to the little cottage nestled in the pines was bordered by heavily scented gardenias and brilliant purple crape myrtles. Low borders of bright pink impatiens and a rainbow of Gerbera daisies cuddled with the flagstones while the Confederate jasmine and Virginia creeper curled up and around the trunks of the tall pines. It looked and smelled just the way a flower garden was supposed to look and smell, right down to the butterflies flitting about and the hummingbirds sipping at the colorful blooms.

"I just love this little place. My husband and I lived here for two whole years when we had that fire in the big house. I don't think either one of us wanted to leave when the big house was finally ready. I do ramble, don't I? Never mind. Don't say anything, just look. I'll do all the talking."

"Yoo-hoo, Miss Summers!" Ardeth called from the bottom step that led up to the little porch with the bright green and white awning. "I brought you some sweet tea and cookies."

The screen door opened and Lisa Summers and the huge dog appeared. "This is so nice of you, Miss Gamble. I haven't had time to go to the grocery store yet. This will be a wonderful breakfast. A friend of mine is here. I hope that's all right. Should I have asked you first about guests?"

"Heavens, no. I hope you enjoy the cookies. They're my grandmother's recipe. Lisa, this is a friend of mine, Jim Watson. Jim, this is my new tenant, Lisa Summers."

Jim held out a gnarled hand. Lisa shook it gently. "It's nice to meet you." Jim nodded.

"My dog isn't bothering you, is he, Miss Ardeth?"

"Not at all. I love animals. Well, we have to go. Enjoy the cookies and tea. If there's anything you need, just knock on my door."

Her hands full, the dog at her side, Lisa smiled from ear to ear. "This is so nice of you, Miss Ardeth, thank you. It was nice to meet you, Mr. Watson."

"Come along, Jim," Ardeth said, steering him down the flagstone path. She stopped a moment and called over her shoulder. "If you cut some of the Confederate jasmine and drape it over the curtain bar in your bathtub, the whole cottage will smell sweet and clean."

"I'll do that. Thank you again."

Back in the main house, her hands on her hips, Ardeth said, "Well?"

"She's a looker, all right. And you're right about something else. She'd be perfect for Jake. She looks a lot like the picture Mitzi gave us. It's the eyes. Eyes are the mirror of one's soul. You know that, Ardie. If my opinion counts, she's the girl we're looking for."

"I think so, too. I wanted a second opinion I valued. I value your opinion, Jim. Let's talk about this while I put the pot roast on. I can make the pie later. I think it will be all right to let the roast cook while we scoot back to Mitzi's. Then again, maybe that isn't such a good idea," she said, remembering that fire years ago. "I don't want to tell her something like this over the phone."

While Ardeth busied herself at the stove,

Jim leafed through the papers Mitzi had given him. "Who do you think she is, Ardie?"

"I don't have a clue, Jim. Whoever she is, she's important to Sarabess Windsor. It must be something serious for Mitzi to step in. Everyone in town, and outside of town, for that matter, knows those two women hate each other."

"She's almost as pretty as you, Sweet Cheeks."

Ardeth blushed and turned coy. "You are something else, Jim Watson. You can turn a lady's head without even trying."

Jim sighed, his thoughts going to the pom-poms on the cover of the DVD that was on his coffee table at home. He did smile, though, a sickly one when he thought about what Ardeth was going to do or say when she realized what kind of movie they were going to watch.

Chapter 18

Mitzi eyed her nephew over the rim of a coffee cup filled with organic carrot juice. The last time she'd seen Jake so agitated was the day of his mother's funeral. One second he looked like his world was coming to an end. The next second she thought she would have to peel him off the ceiling. "We need a plan, darlin'."

"Plan? Plan!" Jake said, jumping up and smacking his clenched fist into his open palm. "What kind of plan? If we show up on her doorstep, Trinity is going to say what she thinks we want to hear. And then the first chance she gets, she's going to bolt. I know this, Mitzi. We need something more than a plan. I think we should kidnap her and her friend."

Mitzi didn't bat an eye at her nephew's vehement statement. "As a lawyer you should know that kidnapping is against the law. However, I do tend to agree with you about the bolting part. What is it exactly that you're feeling, Jake?"

Jake was on his feet again, pacing the kitchen like a caged tiger. He made a snap decision and told her about the night in his fraternity house and Trinity's phone call.

Mitzi's cup slammed down on the kitchen table. Carrot juice sloshed in all directions.

Jezebel swooped across the kitchen to land on top of the refrigerator. "Big mess. Really big mess!" Jezzie screeched.

Mitzi ignored the old parrot and screeched louder than the bird. "And you're telling me this *NOW!* Well, that certainly explains a lot, nephew. I guess you know your actions were unconscionable." She stood to her full height and wagged her finger under Jake's nose. "You've always loved that girl, you failed her when she needed you the most, and now you feel guilty. That's why you can't commit to anyone. I don't believe it, Jake. How could you have?" Mitzi screeched again.

Jezebel flew across the kitchen again, expertly dodging the overhead fan to land on

Jake's shoulder. She gave his ear a vicious peck and squawked, "Bad boy, Jake!"

"Yeah, I feel guilty. Look, I was sowing my oats. I wasn't the one who took the phone call. It was a fraternity brother. That's not to say I wouldn't have blown her off myself. That's what makes me feel guilty. I simply don't know. I'm sorry. I hate myself for doing it. I feel like shit, if that's what you want to hear. If there's any way to make it up to her, to you, I'd do it in a heartbeat."

Suddenly, Jake's head jerked upright when all the animals raced through the house toward the front door. "I think you have company." He was grateful for the temporary reprieve, anything so he didn't have to see the anger and disappointment in his aunt's eyes.

"Yoo-hoo, Mitzi!" Ardeth Gamble called from the foyer. "Jim and I found the girl! She's my new renter! What do you think of that? I thought there was something familiar about the sketch you gave us. What do you want us to do? Do you want me to call the police? Oh, this is so terribly exciting. Jim and I couldn't believe it. Lovely girl, just lovely."

"That . . . That's wonderful, Ardie. Really

wonderful," Mitzi said, her mind racing. "Can you do me a favor and call the others? Right now Jake and I have some personal business we have to take care of. I can't tell you how pleased I am that you found the girl. You two could make the local detective squad. Right now, calling the police is not an option. Like I said, I will have to think about this a little more before we do something we might regret." She lowered her voice to a soft whisper. "We have to be careful right now, really careful. The situation is . . . extremely delicate, but then I don't have to tell you two that. You're very astute." She hoped she had worked up an appropriate amount of excitement and concern for the couple who were staring at her in awe.

"She has a big black dog. A nice animal. Somehow he got into my house and closed the door. He couldn't get out. Jim and I don't think she's suspicious. I took over some sweet tea and a few of my raisin-filled cookies. When are you going to tell us what this is all about?"

"Soon. I have to make a plan, Ardeth," Mitzi said, ushering the two of them to the front door. "I'll call you."

The moment Mitzi returned to the kitchen,

Jake exploded. "Great! That's just great, Mitzi! Now the whole damn town knows about Trinity. That sure as hell wasn't one of your better ideas."

"They found her, didn't they? That proves it was a good idea. You were just damn lucky you spotted Trinity's friend at the airport. Right now, this very minute, I want you to tell me the truth. Do you love Trinity? Is that why you have your Jockeys in such a knot?"

Jake looked at his aunt, his face full of misery. "Don't go there, Mitzi."

"All right, Jake. I do think you need to resolve your feelings where that young woman is concerned. Go home, think about it, and I'll do the same. Come over for breakfast in the morning, and we'll decide what our best course of action is. I don't want to spook Trinity. We can count on Ardeth and Jim. I swore them and all the others to secrecy. In case you don't know it, old people take secret-keeping seriously. Now, take that cat of yours and go home. By the way, I saw Amanda Pettijohn at my yoga class this morning. She asked about you."

"Don't go there either, Mitzi," Jake said, stomping his way out of the kitchen, Elway in his arms. He looked over his shoulder, hoping to have the last word with his know-it-all aunt. "You better be prepared to pay the late charges on that video you 'liberated' from my apartment. You're taking it back, too! I hope that kid at the video store tells everyone in town what it is you watch at night."

For the first time in her life, Mitzi was at a loss for words. When she finally got her tongue to work she shouted, "It wasn't all that good."

Jake laughed all the way home.

It was nine o'clock when Jake finished the last of his take-out. He was cranky and out of sorts. He felt like his life was unraveling right in front of his eyes. Was it just weeks ago that he was coasting along? Now, everything was upside down. He did have Elway, though, so that was one plus.

A couple of minutes later, he had changed out of his clothes and into his running outfit. He knew better than to run after a big meal, but he hadn't eaten that much. What he needed at the moment was a run so he could clear his mind of Mitzi's words, words that stung him to the quick. Now that someone had said the words aloud, he could no longer deny them.

Forty minutes later, drenched in sweat, his feet squishing in his sneakers from his run in the humidity, Jake found himself in Ardeth Gamble's backyard. He made no apologies to himself as he meandered through the dense bushes and shrubbery, hoping the black dog wouldn't pick up his scent. Pure and simple, he was turning into a Peeping Tom.

As he made his way closer to the little cottage at the rear of Ardeth's property he was stunned to see that it was pitch-black. Even a stupid person would know he wasn't going to be doing any peeping. He made sure, before heading back toward Ardeth's house, that the Saturn was parked in the space allotted to the cottage. It was. His sigh of relief was so loud, he fully expected the lights to go on in the cottage. When nothing happened, he made his way to the front of the property.

Jake looked back over his shoulder, wondering why Ardeth's house was lit up from top to bottom. He'd always heard that older people tried to conserve electricity. He mumbled something that sounded like, *Mitzi, Ardeth, and Clara Ashwood were the exception to every rule, and in the scheme of things, did it matter why Ardeth's house was lit up?* For all he knew, Ardeth Gamble had a secret life going on beyond what the public knew.

Jake probably would have laughed his head off if he could have been a fly on the wall in Ardeth Gamble's lit-up television room.

Ardeth Gamble looked straight ahead at her seventy-inch plasma television with what she hoped was clinical interest. She was embarrassed and didn't know what to do or say. If only the television was like her little fifteen-inch one in the kitchen, where everything wasn't so in your face.

"I don't think on my best day I could have done *that,*" Jim observed.

Ardeth swallowed hard. If Jim could be so blasé, then she had to follow suit. "I always watch the gymnastics when the Olympics are on, and I never saw any of the gymnasts do . . . uh . . . any of those moves." She leaned in closer. "I didn't know a person could do . . . *that.* When are they going to start playing football?" she asked innocently.

"Probably pretty soon. We've only been

watching it for ten minutes," Jim said, pretending to look everywhere but at the screen.

"This is not revving my engine, Jim. In fact, I'm not enjoying this at all. Furthermore, if my husband, God rest his soul, knew what I was doing right this minute, he would spin in his grave. So would your wife."

Jim's face registered such relief, Ardeth almost laughed out loud. She just knew he was trying to figure out how to let her down easy. "I have a suggestion. Let's turn this off and switch to cable and watch reruns of *Law & Order: SVU* to see what detectives Stabler and Benson are up to. I'll fix us each a slice of pie with some ice cream. While I'm doing that, it might be a good idea to wrap that DVD in newspaper and toss it in the trash. I wouldn't want my new tenant or one of the neighbors to see it." Ardeth reached for his gnarled hand and patted it. "It was an interesting experiment, the anticipation part, anyway. You can rev my engine in other ways, honey."

Big Jim grinned. "That's what I like about you, Ardie. You're a good sport."

In the kitchen, Ardeth leaned against the kitchen counter. Her eyeballs were at attention. *How* did *those actors do that?* As she sliced into the pie she realized she really didn't care.

As Ardeth was serving pie to her guest, her new tenants bolted out of bed when BL's phone rang, shattering the sound of the quiet night. The bedside clock said it was 10:10.

Lisa listened, her face showing concern at the panic she heard in BL's voice.

When BL got off the phone, she said, "Mom fell off the tractor mower and broke her leg in three places. She also has a concussion because her head hit a tombstone. I have to go home. That was Mom's significant other. He said he made a reservation for me on the 11:25 flight. Can we make it in time?"

Lisa stood rooted to the floor as she tried to grapple with what BL was telling her. What was happening? Finally, she managed to nod as she stripped off her nightshirt for a pair of shorts and a T-shirt. "Don't bother to pack. I'll repack all your stuff and ship it out by UPS tomorrow. Move, move!" she said to BL as she looked around for her purse and car keys and then whistled for

Lucky. "We should make it; there won't be much traffic now."

Eighteen minutes later, Lisa skidded to a stop in front of the Delta terminal. BL hit the ground running. She blew an air kiss as she barreled through the open doorway.

Lisa slipped the car into gear and inched back into the lane of slow-moving traffic that would take her to the exit. She was alone again. The urge to cry at her circumstances was great, but she fought it by biting down on her lower lip. The sharp pain made her blink away the threatened tears. She needed to do *something*.

Lucky, sensing his new mistress's distress, hopped over the seat and did his best to nuzzle her neck. Lisa did *her* best to stroke the big dog's head and still keep her eyes and left hand firmly on the steering wheel. "I have to do something, Lucky. I can't wait for tomorrow. BL's mom always says you need to take the bull by the horns and wrestle the beast to the ground." Joyce had said something else, too, something that Lisa could no longer ignore. *You can be a victim only once. After that you become a volunteer.*

"Like hell," Lisa muttered as she turned

on her signal light to pull into a Wendy's. She hopped out, ran inside, ordered a coffee for herself and a burger for Lucky. While she waited she made her way to the telephone. She yanked at the tattered phone book, which almost fell apart in her hands. It took her all of five minutes to look up the phone number and address that she wanted. When she picked up her food she asked for directions to the apartment complex where Jake Forrest lived.

Eighteen minutes later, Lisa, Lucky at her side, locked her car and looked around to get her bearings. Jake lived on the second floor. Before Lisa could decide which direction to go, Lucky raced off and galloped up the steps to the narrow porch that ran the length of the building. She didn't stop to wonder how the big dog knew exactly where to go. She followed, taking deep breaths as she climbed the steps. This, she decided, is where the rubber meets the road, a favorite expression of Mitzi Granger's.

Lisa rang the doorbell and kicked at the door at the same time. Her hands were trembling, her legs felt like wet noodles, and her heart was beating like a trip-hammer as she waited for the door to open. When it did open, she blinked. How many nights had she dreamed about this moment? Thousands. His hair on end, wearing only green plaid boxers, Jake was growling something that sounded like, "This damn well better be good."

"I heard you were looking for me! Well, Jake, here I am." Lucky raced past her into the apartment in search of his new best friend.

Lisa's clenched fist shot out and landed square on Jake's nose, making him stagger backward with the force of the blow. "That's for lying to me." She advanced and lashed out again, catching the lawyer square in his left eye. "That's for blowing me off when I needed you the most."

"Goddamn it, what the hell are you doing?" Jake squawked.

Lisa advanced farther and brought up her knee. The hard jolt drove him backward so that he fell onto the couch. "*That* was for not caring enough to find me. Say something, you miserable, lying . . . lawyer."

"Oooh, that hurt. The pain . . . the pain . . ."

"Shut up, Jake. I hate a man who whines."

"You goddamn well crippled me. My face hurts as much as my . . . Are you crazy?

You could have called me up. Do you know what time it is? What do you want?" he managed to gasp. "Your dog is on my furniture."

"Shut up, you sneak. I hate your guts, Jake Forrest. I'm here to tell you to leave me alone. You come near me again, and I'll go to the police to get a restraining order. In case you haven't figured it all out, you're fifteen years too late. You need to say something right now, Jake Forrest, or I am going to pound your ass into the ground. I can do it, too, so start talking."

"You're a real hard-ass, aren't you? Maybe when we were kids you could've *whupped* my ass. Not now. I work out. God, do you have any idea how bad this hurts?"

"I hope you die, you louse. Tell me right now that you aren't going to bother me again. Tell me you aren't going to stalk me. Tell me you aren't going to blab all over town that I'm here. That's what you lawyers do, blab and lie. Did I tell you I hate your guts? Say it, damn you, or I'm going to beat you within an inch of your life."

"Okay, okay. If that's what you really want. But if I'm going to do that, we should clear the air before you leave. Do you want something to eat or drink? Mitzi always says when someone visits you should offer refreshments." Jake groaned again. God, she was beautiful. Suddenly, he realized he had only his boxers on. "Let me put some clothes on. Don't go away, Trinny. Please."

That had to be the joke of the year, Lisa thought. Her feet were rooted to the floor. Just the mention of Mitzi's name made her insides crumble. Mitzi, the only person in the whole world who loved her. She caught sight of her reflection in the foyer mirror. She looked like a wild-eyed creature from another planet.

"C'mon in the kitchen. I'll make some tea or coffee. I'm not going to poison you. Your dog is still on my furniture," he said pointedly.

"Ask me if I care. I bet you turned out to be a shitty lawyer. I sure wouldn't hire you even if your name is Forrest."

Jake sniped back as he measured coffee into the wire basket. His groin hurt like hell as he wondered if he'd ever be able to have sex again. "You need a brain to be a lawyer, unlike someone who bakes wedding cakes. Even a stupid person can bake a cake and glop it up with that smeary stuff and then stick a ten-cent plastic bride and groom on the top."

Lisa's eyes filled with tears. Her voice was low, tortured-sounding. "Sometimes you have to do what you have to do to survive. You would have no clue about that because that gold spoon in your mouth that you were born with . . . If I ever get married, I'm not having a wedding cake. I'm having an apple pie."

If ever there was a time in his life when he was out of his depth, this was it. "Apple pie is good. I can see why you would want an apple pie. I bet hundreds of people have apple pies, pumpkin pies, or even berry pies instead of wedding cakes when they get married."

The tears were rolling down Lisa's cheeks. "Oh, yeah, name me one," she blubbered.

She had him there. Mitzi would know what to say. If she couldn't tell the truth, she'd make something up. "Okay, okay, Jeff and Alice Nevins had a blueberry pie made into a square. It was in the paper. Everyone thought it was cool. The bride spilled some on her wedding gown. That wasn't cool," Jake said, lying through his teeth. He rather thought Mitzi would be proud of him for being so quick on the uptake.

"You're lying. I hate liars. I need a tissue."

Tissue. He had hundreds of rolls of toilet paper but Mitzi's on-sale items didn't include tissues. He scampered off and returned with a roll of toilet paper. "It's really soft. Quilted, actually. Double strength."

Lisa reached for the roll of toilet paper. "I hate your guts."

"You already said that. Twice. I even understand it. Now, can we talk like the sensible adults we're supposed to be? I can even be your lawyer if you pay me a dollar. That means anything you say to me is covered by attorney-client privilege. I can never ever tell anyone what you say to me. I'll take fifty cents if you think a dollar is too much. I'm not practicing anymore. I quit a couple of weeks ago, but I can still act as your lawyer." He was babbling and knew it. Still, she seemed to be listening.

Lisa dabbed at her eyes. "You! My lawyer! I don't *think* so!"

Jake flinched. She made it sound like he was the Devil in disguise. "I'm a damn good lawyer, Trinity. So good in fact that the Montrose Institute think tank in Washington,

D.C., is after me to work for them. High six figures in salary. Really HIGH!"

"You can't impress me." Lisa sniffed. She fished around in the pocket of her shorts and came up with thirty-seven cents, the change from Wendy's that she'd shoved in there. She inched the coins across the table.

Jake snatched them up before she could change her mind. "You just hired yourself a lawyer, Trinity. I'll write you out a receipt." He felt almost giddy when he scribbled out a receipt on a sticky note. He couldn't help himself. He said, "You're even prettier than I remember."

Lisa heard him, but she asked, "What did you say?"

"Nothing important. Now, talk to me. Tell me what's going on. Why did you come back here?"

Lisa scuffed the floor with the toe of her sandal as she looked around the compact kitchen, trying to decide how she wanted to respond. "It was time. After all, I did live here for the first fifteen years of my life. It's home. I have to go now, it's late."

"But . . . How can I help you if you . . .

What do you mean you have to go home now? We need to talk. You just hired me."

"No, we don't need to talk. I hired you so you would keep your mouth shut. If you violate our agreement, I'll report you to the Bar. I hate your guts, Jake. Nothing is going to change that. Just so you know, I am not a forgiving person."

Jake's back stiffened. "You came here. I didn't invite you. You want to act like a sniveling teenager, go ahead. I thought you might have grown up. What you did was unforgivable. I didn't think Mitzi was ever going to get over it. You hurt her to the very soul. The Hendersons grieved for you. I grieved. And just to keep the record straight, Mitzi hired some of the best detectives in the country to locate you, so don't go spouting your vengeance crap on me. Right now I hate your guts, too. I guess making wedding cakes warped your mind. Go on, take your dog and go. My life is too busy to have you clutter it up with all your crap. Don't worry, I won't say anything to Mitzi, but she already knows you're here. She put her geriatric bulldogs on the case, and Ardeth Gamble turned you in. Another thing; I could charge you with assault and battery. I'm a lawyer, remember. You're still standing here. Go already!"

Lisa backed away from the table, turned, walked past Lucky, who ignored her, and headed for the front door. She opened it and waited for the big black dog, who was busy warding off Elway's flailing paws. She whistled, a puny sound. When the dog continued to ignore her, she backtracked and tried to pull him by the collar. He whimpered and cried but allowed himself to be dragged out the door. Quicker than lightning, Elway was off the sofa and zipping after the girl and dog. Jake watched, helpless, as the mangy cat leaped into the Saturn behind the black dog. He leaned over the balcony, his eyes burning unbearably.

Lisa looked up and shouted, "Animals are astute judges of character." Then she muttered, "I'll get a pet carrier and drop him off tomorrow."

Jake watched the Saturn turn around and head out of the parking lot. He felt like he'd just lost his best friend.

Chapter 19

Lisa mumbled and grumbled, chastising herself all the way back to the little cottage that was her new home. Where in the world had she gotten the chutzpah to confront Jake Forrest the way she had? What, if anything, had she accomplished by going to his apartment other than acquiring a lawyer for a retainer of thirty-seven cents? In the old days she had been a forceful kind of person. Maybe after all these years, her old personality was resurfacing. Which, she decided, probably was not a bad thing. Her instincts told her she was going to need a bushelful of guts if she intended going up against Sarabess Windsor.

As Lisa turned into Ardeth Gamble's driveway she realized she still didn't have a game plan. BL's emergency had put all that on hold. And now she had Jake Forrest's cat to contend with.

Lisa cut the engine and the lights at the same time. The night was suddenly like black velvet. She wished she had remembered to turn on the porch light. Lucky bolted from the car, Elway in hot pursuit, the moment she opened the back door. "Please don't bark," she hissed. "We don't want to wake Miz Gamble."

Inside, Lisa poured herself a glass of sweet tea and carried it out to the tiny porch. She settled herself on the rocker, the dog and cat next to her.

It was a beautiful night, the stars twinkling overhead, the fireflies flitting here and there. When she was little she used to catch them because she wanted to figure out what made them light up in the darkness. She never did figure it out, just the way she never figured out how the cicadas, just by rubbing their legs together, could make such a pleasing sound. Good old Jake had the answers, but she had refused to listen. Know-it-all Jake had the answer to everything back in their youth. Or at least she thought he did. A mighty sigh escaped her lips. Even as sleepy and disheveled as he was, Jake had looked like 180 pounds of dynamite to her. Well, she'd certainly lit his fuse. Her own, too. *Now* what was she going to do?

Lucky growled deep in his throat. Not to be outdone, Elway arched his back and spit. "Shhh, it's just a tree frog in the planter." The animals settled down, and Lisa returned to her reverie. She needed a plan. But more important, she needed to come to terms with why she'd come back to Crestwood. She'd wanted to get out from under the Kolinas. BL had told her that she was lying to herself by saying she'd returned so Jake couldn't find her. Absolutely. But she could have gone in any direction to get away from the Kolinas. She realized now that she'd come back to take back her life. She wanted to be the person she was before she'd cut and run.

So many mistakes. So much heartache. So much guilt.

There was only one person in the whole world who could help her, and it wasn't Jake Forrest. *What would the dearest, the sweetest, the kindest person in the whole world do if I showed up on her doorstep? Hug me? Boot my ass off her property?*

Suddenly, it was crucial that she find out immediately, that very minute. Mitzi never slept. Without stopping to think, Lisa enticed the animals into the house, closed the door, and made sure the screen door was also closed tightly.

Seventeen minutes later, Lisa slowed the Saturn to a full stop at the foot of the steps that led to Mitzi's front porch. Tears burned her eyes as she climbed out of the car. Her legs were rubbery as she climbed the steps to the verandah. "Hey, Mitzi, whatcha doin'?" she called out in a hoarse whisper, the same thing she'd said hundreds of times, a lifetime ago. She waited, hardly daring to breathe, for Mitzi's response.

Lisa would have recognized the voice underwater. She almost collapsed at the response.

"Just waitin' for you, darlin'."

The voice sounded older, just as hoarse as her own.

The skinny woman sitting on the rocker leaped to her feet. "God Almighty! Is that really you, Trinny?"

"It's me, Mitzi. It's really me. Oh, God, you have no idea how many times I dreamed of you, called out your name in my sleep."

Tears rolled down her cheeks as the older woman hugged her with surprising strength. Nothing in the whole world had ever felt so good. Nothing.

"Dear, sweet child. A day didn't go by that I didn't think of you. I worried myself sick over your whereabouts, had nightmares when I did manage to sleep. I want you to sit down and tell me the why, the what, the who, the whole damn ball of wax. I don't want you to leave anything out. I need to know every small detail even if you think it isn't important."

"If I do that, will you tell me why, after so many years, Jake has been looking for me? He's a little late out of the gate, in my opinion."

"Of course, but you're not being fair. Jake was in school when you left and I hired detectives to search for you. But we had no idea where to look—no clues at all. There came a time when I just had to give up. Let me get some sweet tea, then we can sit out here with the fireflies and the tree frogs, and talk till the sun comes up. The Confederate jasmine this year is so fragrant you can get drunk on the scent. We had a lot of rain,"

Mitzi said vaguely as she waved her hands about.

Lisa curled into the flowered cushions on the old swing. This was as close to home as she was ever going to get. She was asleep before the screen door, minus the screen, creaked shut.

Her nerves jumping and jangling all over the place, Mitzi walked back into the house again and out to the kitchen, where she called her nephew. She listened to his bombastic tirade for a full minute before she told him to shut up in no uncertain terms. "Listen to me, nephew. Trinny is sleeping on my porch swing. It's her, Jake. She's here. She came to see me. She was crying. I went in the house to fetch some tea and when I got back to the porch she was asleep. She's beautiful, Jake, just beautiful. Harold said she was going to turn into a beautiful swan, and she did. I'm so sorry I missed those maturing years. So very sorry."

Then Mitzi listened to Jake for a minute. "What do you mean she came to see you? How could she beat up a big, strapping fellow like you? Yes, yes, she must have been pissed off. She did not steal your cat! You're making that up! I will ask her. I can't believe

she would hire you after she beat you up.
For thirty-seven cents! You're making that
up, too. Why do you torment me like this?"

Mitzi switched the phone from one ear to
the other as she tried to talk and swig at the
tea in the frosty glass. "No, you will not
come out here. I don't want to antagonize
Trinny. If she beat you up, she had a reason.
I am not taking her side. Well, I am, but she
has no one else. What kind of representa-
tion can you give her for thirty-seven
cents?" Mitzi blinked when the phone in her
hand started to buzz. Her nephew had hung
up on her. She laughed.

Across town, Jake knew there would be
no more sleep for him. He showered,
dressed, and made coffee. While the coffee
dripped, he walked around, missing Elway
more and more with each step he took.
There was no way in hell he was giving up
his cat. No damn way in hell. When he made
his way back to the kitchen he eyed the little pile of change in the middle of the table.
Thirty-seven cents. His colleagues would
laugh their asses off if they ever found out
he took on a client with a retainer of thirty-
seven cents. It would be just like Trinny to
blab it all over town to embarrass him. Get-

ting up close and personal with one Miss Trinity Henderson was not an option at this point in time. It would probably never happen, anyway. He winced as he wondered what Mitzi was telling her about him. Nothing good, that was for sure.

"Screw it," Jake muttered as he walked around, coffee cup in one hand, his other hand picking up the plethora of cat toys that Elway played with. He tossed them all in a wicker basket, his stomach quivering with sadness at his loss. He damn well loved that cat.

Suddenly, a thought hit him. Mitzi hadn't said anything about a dog or a cat with Trinity. The way Mitzi was with animals, that would have been the first thing she mentioned, especially if Elway had been with Trinity. Being as sharp and astute as he thought he was, he surmised Trinity had probably left both animals back at the cottage. Trinity was sleeping on Mitzi's swing. Even a dumb rocket scientist could figure out his next move. A snatch and grab were definitely in order. It never once occurred to him that Elway had a mind of his own and had gone willingly with the young woman. Elway had chosen him over the other tenants. Elway loved him. And by God he wasn't giving up his cat to some girl who'd just beat the crap out of him.

Jake had to stop twice on his trek down the steps to the ground level to suck in his breath from the pain in his groin. He and Trinity were even in his eyes so from here on in, it would be strictly no rules and the Devil take the hindmost. So there, Trinity Henderson. So there.

When Jake's headlights lit up the backyard, Ardeth Gamble swung her legs over the side of the bed.

"Is your tenant having a party or something?" Big Jim asked on his sixth trip back from the bathroom.

"I don't know, Jim. This used to be such a quiet place. It's not like my new tenant is making a lot of noise, it's just cars coming and going. Young people never seem to sleep. They can go all night long and still go to work in the morning. I'll never understand that."

"I thought we were going to go all night long, too," Big Jim grumbled as he pulled on his pants. "I guess we're going to eat *again*."

Ardeth yanked at the belt of her robe. "I guess so," she sniped. "You know, Jim, I was expecting . . . hoping . . . what I mean is, I wasn't planning on serving food all night long."

"Does that mean you're going to tell the club that I couldn't get it up?"

"Jim, getting it up and being in a coma are two different things. We need to fall back and regroup. We were both too anxious. That's another way of saying our expectations were too high. At our age we have to . . . What we have to do is make allowances for . . . our age. That football movie that wasn't a football movie was a mistake. Later this week, after I choreograph it, I'll do my dance of the feathers. Peacock feathers, Jim. I'm going to give you four days to *think* about *that*. Now, what do you want to eat?"

Big Jim walked over to the back door as he tried to grapple with what Ardie had just said. No matter how you sliced it, it all came down to one word: *performance*. His blood ran cold at the thought. "It's not your tenant, Ardie. It's a man, and he's limping. What do you suppose that means?"

Ardeth clucked her tongue. Like she knew

what it meant. She scooped out pineapple-coconut ice cream in a bowl. "Maybe he had too much sex and now he wants to go to sleep. I might have to charge him rent," Ardeth snorted.

Big Jim ignored the slur, and retorted, "Are you saying he had rough-and-tumble sex, and now he's coming to see your tenant? That doesn't make sense."

"Shut up, Jim, and eat your ice cream. While you're eating it, think about those peacock feathers. If things don't go awry, you might have a chance at limping like my tenant's guest when you leave the next day. Everyone knows there is nothing about sex that makes sense."

Big Jim's hands started to shake as he turned seven shades of red.

Ardeth smirked when she thought about the peacock feathers. Tomorrow—today, actually—the minute she got rid of Jim, she was going to hightail it to Pier 1 to buy a few more feathers. Four more should do it. Then again, maybe she needed five. She also had to remember to pick up a pink-tinted light-bulb. Maybe some of that spray-on suntan lotion for a healthy glow. In the art of seduction the list of necessities was endless. If she didn't get results with Big Jim, she'd switch up and home in on Simon Jeeter, who claimed to be full of piss and vinegar. It was all in the planning. *Just win, win, win,* Ardeth thought happily.

Jim was so uncomfortable with this turn of the conversation, he left his ice cream and, saying he had a *crick* in his back, walked over to the window. He hoped Ardeth wouldn't want to massage his back. "I think our late-night visitor is leaving, Ardie," he said, grateful that he could think about something else besides sex. He might be old, but he recognized Ardie's threat even though she didn't mention Simon Jeeter by name. Everyone in the club called Simon "Mr. Blue." For the little blue pill, of course.

"It is late. He, whoever he is, should be home in bed. I won't tolerate *canoodling* by my tenants. He probably just dropped something off. Finish your ice cream before it melts, Jim."

Jim leaned closer to the window. "He didn't drop something off. He's taking something out of the house. He's carrying it. Looks like a cat to me. Oh, oh, he's taking the dog, too. A dognapper!" Jim said, his voice ringing with agitation. "No, he apparently doesn't want the dog, but it won't go back inside."

It was too much for Ardeth. She left her ice cream to look out the window. "That's Jake Forrest! Lord have mercy. What *is* he doing here?"

"I'll tell you what he's doing. He's stealing Miss Summers's dog is what he's doing! We need to stop him!"

"Well, Jim, you just go ahead and do that, but I would rethink my actions if I were you. I'm not messing with Mitzi Granger's nephew, I can tell you that! I doubt he's stealing the dog. More like he's going to take care of it because . . . well, because. Jake Forrest is a lawyer. Lawyers don't steal dogs. If you're not going to finish your ice cream, I'm throwing it out. Let's go back to bed."

"That does make sense." Suddenly, Jim was wide-awake. Getting back in bed with Ardeth was just too stressful. "I'm not sleepy. Let's sit on the front porch."

"You're no fun, Jim," Ardeth snapped.

"It's the middle of the night," Jim snapped back.

Ardeth bustled toward the front door. *Things could be worse,* she thought.

Just as Ardeth opened the front door,

Jake Forrest was facing his own dilemma. Elway was hissing and snarling in his tight grasp; the black dog was determined to get in the car with his new best friend. "Shoo, good doggie, go back in the house or sit on the porch. Elway, shut the hell up. We're going home. The dog is staying here."

As he struggled with the cat, who was fighting him like a tiger, Jake knew he was out of his depth. He looked up and saw Ardeth Gamble and Big Jim watching from the kitchen window. "Oh, shit! Mitzi will hear about this within minutes." Jake literally tossed Elway into the front seat of the car as he tried to block the big dog from hopping inside after the cat. "Listen, you have to stay here. C'mon, c'mon, I'll give you a treat."

The black dog sat on his haunches ready to pounce the moment Jake opened the car door. For all of five seconds he tried to figure out a way to trick the dog. Nothing came to mind. Even if he successfully got in the car, he knew in his gut the dog would race after it. "All right, all right, get in the damn car."

After Lucky jumped in Jake settled himself behind the wheel. Elway was purring so loud at this wonderful pairing, he had to cover his ears. "Tomorrow you are going home, dog." Elway leaped up on the headrest to nip Jake's ear. "Okay, *maybe* he's going home tomorrow. Both of you shut up so I can drive."

As Jake drove past the wide verandah he was stunned to see Ardeth and Big Jim sitting next to each other holding hands. He was perplexed when they made no move to stop him or call out to him. Then he knew. Why bother? All they had to do was call Mitzi. He muttered and mumbled to the dog and cat, who paid no attention to him at all.

Gentleman that he was, Lucky waited until Jake got out of the car, followed by Elway. He hopped to the ground, looked around, sniffed, then followed his new best friend to the second floor. Both animals waited patiently while Jake unlocked the door.

Elway leaped on the couch and started to purr. Lucky looked at Jake, at the couch, at Elway, and then leaped up, lay down, and went to sleep.

Tomorrow there would be hell to pay. From both Mitzi and Trinity Henderson.

Chapter 20

Mitzi—a cup of turnip, carrot, and boiled rhubarb juice in hand—moved from her rocker to the verandah railing to gaze out at the brand-new day confronting her. Even though it was just a few minutes past six in the morning, she could tell it was going to be the kind of summer scorcher the South was known for. In less than an hour, the sun would burn off the sparkling dew on the front lawn, at which point the sprinklers would turn on. People would get up and go to work the way they always did. The beginning of a new day where things were predictable.

Mitzi looked over her shoulder at the young woman sleeping on her porch swing. Whatever transpired with her today would definitely not be predictable. Lisa took that moment to stir and sit up. She looked around, trying to get her bearings, when she spotted Mitzi. "What time is it? I can't believe I slept so long." There was no apology in her words or tone.

"A little after six. Coffee's fresh. You know where the bathroom is."

Lisa blinked at Mitzi's cool tone. Maybe she'd made a mistake in coming. She nodded as she entered the house. She was back within minutes. "I have a dog, Mitzi. I should go back to let him out. I'll come back and bring him with me, if that's all right."

"No, that is not all right. I am not going to let you out of my sight again until I get all the answers I need. I'll call Ardeth and ask her to let the dog out. Now, I want you to sit down and think about those fifteen years you robbed me of. I'll be back as soon as I call Ardeth. Do you want a sweet roll or some toast?"

"I'm fine, Mitzi. I never eat breakfast."

Mitzi dialed Ardeth's number, explaining what she wanted. She listened, her eyebrows shooting upward at her friend's response. All Mitzi could do was sputter and squawk at the news. She made a quick call to her nephew and reamed him out royally.

"You need to bring that dog here immediately. Shame on you, Jacob. Dognapping? How unbecoming for a man of your stature."

Mitzi stomped her way back to the verandah. All she did was nod. Let the girl make of the nod whatever she wanted to make of it. "Now talk, young lady."

"I don't know where to start, Mitzi. I can tell you're angry with me. I'm so sorry. I wish I could . . . I wish so many things, but I can't undo what I did, and I can't make it better, either."

Mitzi sat down on one of the rockers and fired up a cigarette. She blew a perfect smoke ring. "What was I, chopped liver? You should have come to me instead of running away. I would have helped you. It was so cruel of you to run off like that."

Lisa kneaded her hands. "I was young. I didn't think about it like that back then. I did try to call Jake, but he . . . He was too busy to talk to me."

Mitzi watched as the young woman's back stiffened. "Go on, I'll reserve the rest of my comments until you're finished." She puffed furiously on the cigarette in her hand.

Lisa licked at her dry lips. "I always

thought . . . It felt like I was adopted. Lillian and John . . . While they took care of me, they didn't act like parents. It never felt right to me. I talked about it once to Jake, and he made fun of me. He said you couldn't pick your parents, and I just had to accept the fact that Lillian and John were not demonstrative people. I didn't bring it up again, but I never changed my mind.

"One day, when I was seven or eight, it was time for Emily Windsor's birthday party. All of us kids went up to the Hill. You know all about those command performances. Jake was there. Lillian *duded* me up in a fancy dress and black Mary Janes. Jake laughed at me, said I looked silly. I punched him good for that, too. Anyway, the party was a horror, the way all those parties were. Emily was such a snot. She was mean to all of us except Jake. She adored Jake. When the party was over, the others left, but I had to wait for Mrs. Windsor to give me a take-home bag for Lillian and John. I left but it started to rain, so I stood under the upstairs porch waiting for it to stop. Mrs. Windsor and Jake's dad, at least I think it was Mr. Forrest, came out on the porch and started to talk. They didn't know I was there. They were talking about me, so I listened.

"While I didn't fully understand what they were saying at the time, I did remember it all and put it together as the years went on. Mr. Forrest was chastising Mrs. Windsor about me. He said she was cruel and would regret it all one day. She kept saying that someday would never happen because Grace somebody and Louise somebody were long gone. Mr. Forrest said chickens always come home to roost. Later I did ask Lillian what that meant, and she gave me a cockamamie explanation that even at my young age I didn't buy for a minute. Anyway, Mrs. Windsor said I would never find out if she had anything to do with it. I guess that's when I first began to think I was adopted, and Mrs. Windsor had something to do with arranging the adoption.

"Lillian and John did a lot of whispering late at night. I tried to listen and once in a while I would hear something that didn't make sense to me. Then Mr. Windsor took a liking to me when I would come over here to be with you. He was such a nice man. I really liked him. I pretended he was my real father and you were my real mother. What I never understood was why I had to sneak around to come here and how I was never supposed to tell Lillian and John about Harold. It was a wonderful secret, so I never told.

"One day we were making up stories right here on this very verandah; Harold pretended to be a king, and I was the princess. He said one day, a long time from that day, when I was thirty, I would inherit the king's fortune. I thought that was so funny. I asked him what I should do with it, and he laughed and said I should take a broom to the Wicked Witch on the Hill and send her packing. That was even funnier. Then he said I could do whatever I wanted with all the money the king was going to bestow on me. He got real serious and said if anything happened to the princess, the Wicked Witch on the Hill would get it all.

"After Emily died, we didn't have to go up on the Hill anymore. All I had was Jake, and he started acting like I was a pest. I had such a crush on him I couldn't see straight. I thought I would die when he went off to college. He promised to write and call but . . . Well, that's not important.

"Earlier on the night I . . . left, Mrs. Windsor came down to the farm to talk to Lillian and John. I was upstairs, but I heard it all. Lillian was never one of those in-your-face people. She was quiet and hardly ever talked unless she had to. That night was different. I could tell she didn't like Mrs. Windsor, but she was always respectful. John knew he had to toe the line or she'd fire him. But that night, Lillian raised her voice.

"She was saying it was time to think about investigating colleges and to find out what it was I wanted to do with my life. She said I needed braces and they cost a lot of money. Mrs. Windsor told her that wasn't her problem. She said I could get a job at one of the shops in town. John kept telling Lillian to be quiet, but she was really wound up. She really went to bat for me, said I was an honor student and deserved a college education. Mrs. Windsor wasn't backing down.

"Then Lillian let it all out. John slapped her and she started to cry. I heard . . . Lillian said Mrs. Windsor was my mother. She said she had me for my bone marrow, so Emily could live. She said Mrs. Windsor didn't want me, she just wanted my . . . whatever it is you need bone marrow for. That's why she gave me to the Hendersons to raise. Then I understood all about Harold. You knew, too, Mitzi. Were you ever going to tell me? Was anyone ever going to tell me? That's why I picked up and ran."

Mitzi felt sick to her stomach at the anguish on the young woman's face. She looked across at Trinity's accusing eyes. Her tongue was so thick in her mouth that she wondered if she would be able to talk. "It wasn't my place to tell you. Harold . . . Harold tried. He did love you, Trinity. He left you a magnificent trust fund that I oversee. You are a very rich young lady. The king provided for his princess. You also need to know that Sarabess Windsor wants you declared dead so she can claim your trust fund. In case you haven't figured it out, Sarabess Windsor is the Wicked Witch on the Hill. Once we establish that you are Harold and Sarabess's daughter, I am bound by the laws of the State of South Carolina to transfer to you all the assets of the trust on January fifteenth, your thirtieth birthday."

"And you think I came back for *that?* I came back because I thought I could hide here, thinking it would never occur to Jake that I would return right under his nose. Everyone wants to go home. I'm home. I'm going to get a job, rent an apartment, and start my life all over again. I never want to see that woman. Give her the money, I don't care."

"It doesn't work that way, Trinity. The only way Sarabess can claim your trust fund is if you die between now and your thirtieth birthday or she somehow tries to establish that you are not her and Harold's daughter. It's yours, and your father wanted you to have it. The trust and the will are two entirely different things. His wills, both of them, were very specific, in that he left everything to you. I have to warn you, though, Sarabess is saying Harold made a later will, making the one that went through probate null and void. Jake and I both believe she forged it with his father's help. The whole mess could, in theory, be tied up in the courts forever, but since both wills specify that your trust fund reverts to you on January fifteenth, it should make no difference, and I doubt that once they know you're here they will even file the other will. As I said, Sarabess has no claim on the trust fund unless you die or are not her and Harold's daughter."

Lisa gasped. "Jake's father would be a party to something like that? He's a lawyer. Won't he get disbarred?"

Mitzi shrugged. "We can deal with that later. I want to know where you went and how you managed to elude the best detectives money could pay for."

Lisa laughed. "Pure dumb luck, I guess. I went out to the highway and started to hitchhike. A trucker picked me up. He was on his way home to Pennsylvania. He could tell I was a runaway. I told him I would go as far as he was going. I'd swiped all the cash I could find in Lillian's cookie jar. It took me a while but I paid it back, Mitzi, so don't look at me like that."

"I wasn't looking at you *like that*. I already knew about your taking the money, leaving an IOU, and paying it back two years later. Go on."

"We talked all the way to Pennsylvania. Sven took me to his house. Inga, that's his wife, welcomed me with open arms. They treated me like the daughter they never had. It was wonderful for the first few years. I suppose you want to know how I got a new identity. Sven did it. Two weeks after he picked me up, he was on a run to West Virginia. He always stops at certain truck stops, and at one they were taking up a collection for a burial in the town. A fifteen-year-old girl named Lisa Summers had been killed in a car crash. Sven managed to get a copy of her birth certificate by going to the county seat. I don't know how he got her school transcripts, but he did. I've been using her Social Security number all these years, and no one has tripped me up. She was an honor student, by the way.

"I simply settled into a new life. The Kolinas were kind, simple people. I worked my ass off for them. I had friends. I helped in the bakery. Inga made one-of-a-kind wedding cakes. She taught me how to bake. I didn't want to bake cakes as a career. I wanted to go to college. They balked, but I said I would leave. By then they depended on me. I cleaned the house, cooked, worked in the shop. Damn, I even mowed the grass.

"By the time I finished college, Inga's arthritis started to get worse, the area was depressed, business was almost nonexistent except for the summer wedding months. Sven retired from long-distance trucking. I started to hate my life and the demands they put on me. BL, that's my best friend, tried to warn me, tried to tell me they were taking advantage of me. She said I was a drone, a slave to the two of them. She was right, too, but I didn't know how to get out from under. We had just made plans to close the bakery when Jake showed up. That's my story."

Mitzi regarded the weary-looking girl and sighed. "Didn't you ever consider calling me?"

"Every damn day of my life, Mitzi. I dreamed of you, this house, this town. I dreamed of Jake the same way. But I felt so indebted to the Kolinas. How could I leave them when they were struggling to survive? Then I found out that was all a big lie, too."

"But you didn't care enough to come back," Mitzi said.

"Circumstances . . . The answer is no. I'm here now, though. I'd like to borrow some money from you," Lisa said coolly.

Mitzi raised an eyebrow. "You would? Why?"

"I want to find a way to send fifty thousand dollars to the Kolinas anonymously. I want to get rid of the guilt I feel where they're concerned. They did pay for my braces and for my college years, and they bought me a car. Yes, I worked my butt off, but I owed them that. It will take me a while to pay you back, but I will pay you back. Will you do it?"

"Of course. However, you could tap that robust trust fund and do it yourself."

"I told you, I don't want it. If you control the trust, pay yourself back from the fund. That would work, wouldn't it?"

"I suppose. What are you going to do, Trinity? I mean, where Sarabess is concerned. She said if you—she meant anyone we came up with in our search—were found, she would demand a DNA sample to prove you're not her daughter. She seemed pretty confident that you would never be found. Jake did say he would have recognized you anywhere. He said you were beautiful. Did you know he had a crush on you, too, when you were young? By the way, he told me about that episode in the barn. That's why I sent him off to be a camp counselor the very next day. That's in case you're interested."

"Well, I'm not. Interested, that is. Now you know the whole story. I have to go now. My dog is waiting for me."

Mitzi winced. This was where she should tell this beautiful young woman that Jake had her dog. She should say something. "When do you want the money?"

"Well, I was hoping your attorney could handle it so the Kolinas won't know where the money came from. What I mean is, I don't want Crestwood's postmark on the envelope. I want them to know it's from me. I need to do this, Mitzi."

"I'll take care of it, child. Jake has the address. Are we . . . Are we going to be friends, or are you cutting me out of your life?"

"Oh, no, Mitzi. My, God, no! I . . . I just have to get my Crestwood legs back. I want to put down my roots right here. I'm realistic enough to know we can't go back to the way it was. I'm grown-up now. My feelings for you have never wavered. I want you to be a part of my new life, and I want to be a part of your life. I don't know what to do about Mrs. Windsor. Part of me wants to get up close and personal with her so I can tell her what I think of her. Another part of me wants nothing to do with her. I'll figure it all out. So how much is in this robust trust fund of mine?"

"More than you can spend in two lifetimes."

Lisa's eyes twinkled. "That much, huh?"

"Yep."

"Can I really evict the Wicked Witch on the Hill?"

"Damn straight."

"Did Jake really have a crush on me, or did you make that up?"

"Now, would I do a thing like that? I don't think that crush ever went away. If you play your cards right, you just might be able to snag that bachelor nephew of mine."

Lisa laughed. She threw Mitzi's words back at her. "Now, why would I want to do something like that? See ya, Mitzi. I have to buy some groceries, or I'm going to starve," Lisa said as she gave Mitzi a bone-crushing hug. "I'll come back later today, if that's okay with you."

Mitzi nodded, tears streaming down her cheeks as the young woman drove off, gravel spurting in all directions.

Mitzi sat on the verandah for a long time as she tried to figure out what her next move should be. Should she go up on the Hill and inform Sarabess her daughter was back in town? Or should she call her brother-in-law and tell him Trinity was back and that the trust fund would be turned over to her on January 15? The truth was, she didn't have to tell either one of them any-thing. All she had to do was call the law firm Harold had hired to set up Trinity's trust fund. The law firm could call Sarabess and Rifkin. But if she did that, she wouldn't get the pleasure of seeing the look on Sarabess's face when she informed her that Trinity was back in town.

Mitzi downed the rest of the putrid mess in the cup she was holding. She'd wait to talk to Jake, then make a decision. Her day was free. She could go up to the Hill at any time. She literally danced her way into the house and back to her suite of rooms, where she showered and changed clothes. She took extra pains dressing and fixing her hair. She wanted to look her best if she de-cided to make the trip up to the Hill to the Windsor mansion. Actually, it wasn't *if* she would go up, but *when* she would make the trip. She hoped Jake would agree with her intentions. Childishly, she crossed her fin-gers.

Chapter 21

Lisa Summers, aka Trinity Henderson, swerved into Ardeth Gamble's driveway. She couldn't wait to bathe so she could put on clean clothes. She brought the Saturn to a screeching stop, got out, and ran into the house. "I'm home, Lucky!" She whistled shrilly for the big dog. It took her only heart-pounding seconds to realize her new best friend and Jake Forrest's cat were nowhere to be seen. She continued to call for the animals as she opened closet doors and looked under the bed. It took her only a moment to remember that in her state of frustration she hadn't locked the door when she made the decision to visit Mitzi. *Oh, God, how could I have been so stupid?*

All thoughts of her talk with Mitzi flew out of her mind as she tried to figure out what she should do. Lucky didn't know the area. Even though the vet had erased the old microchip and added a new one, would anyone who found the beautiful dog turn him in? Cats simply didn't allow themselves to be corralled. That meant Jake's cat was on the loose. She started to cry. Couldn't she do anything right?

Lisa knew she had to go back to Jake's apartment to tell him she lost his cat and enlist his aid in finding both animals. It was the right, decent thing to do, even though she hated the lawyer's guts.

She was out of the door in a flash and back in the Saturn. She cut a wicked right turn onto West Carolina. Within thirty seconds after she'd turned the corner, Jake Forrest took Ardeth's driveway on two wheels, river rock spiraling upward in all directions.

Ardeth, standing over the sink stuffing cantaloupe rinds down the garbage disposal, her mind wandering to her dance of the peacock feathers, gasped as she saw Jake drive up, cut the engine and open the back door of his car for the black dog and the tiger cat to emerge. He ran up the two small steps to the cottage and opened the door. The animals rushed inside. At the last second he made a snatch and grab and had the cat in his arms.

Ardeth watched, bug-eyed, as the tiger cat spit and snarled all the while, struggling in his owner's hands. She blinked when Jake jerked backward, the cat leaping out of his arms. His back arched, the cat looked at Jake with disdain and made his way to the front door, where he commenced scratching at it. A second later, the door opened and the black dog leaped onto the tiny porch and howled. *The dog must be exceptionally smart to open the door like that,* Ardeth thought. She wondered if she should take a cup of coffee out to Mitzi's handsome nephew. These young people were so impetuous and temperamental. She made a mental note to talk to Mitzi about him.

Ardeth barely heard Big Jim saying he was leaving because he had two doctor appointments. She'd had enough of Big Jim to last her till Friday. She waved airily.

She scratched the idea of taking coffee over to Jake. Besides, she had more important things to do today.

*   *   *

Dumbfounded at what was going on around him, Jake sat down on one of the two steps leading to the front porch of the cottage. Suddenly, both animals were on top of him, Elway purring, the black dog whining to be petted. He obliged both of them as he contemplated his next move. "All right, all right, I'm going to stay here till she gets back even if it takes her all day. As Mitzi would say, this is a pretty kettle of fish."

Finally, after an hour of contemplating his feet, Jake got up and entered the little cottage, where he rummaged in the cabinets for coffee. While it dripped into the pot he made himself some toast. He carried both out to the porch to settle himself in one of the creaking rockers. Both animals were asleep in a patch of sun at the top of the steps.

He was dozing off when the black dog let out an earsplitting bark. He cracked one eyelid to see the green Saturn careen to a stop next to his car. Through his partly open eyes, Jake took in the slim girl's appearance. His heartbeat kicked up a notch at her long, suntanned legs, the khaki shorts, and bright yellow shirt. He winced at her fight-ing-mad stance. "I came to get my cat."

She didn't move. "Didn't you trust me to bring him back?" she snarled.

She wasn't so pretty when she snarled, Jake thought. "Well, hell no, I didn't. I don't trust you one little bit, Trinity Henderson."

She still didn't move. "Well, guess what, Mr. Lawyer? I don't trust you, either. Get the hell off my porch unless you want to pay half the rent, and take that mangy cat with you."

Mangy! Mangy! Jake wondered if her feet were rooted to the ground. Maybe she was holding her temper in check. How well he remembered that hair-trigger temper of hers and how often he'd been the recipient of it. "Stop being so nasty. My cat is just old and . . . battle-scarred. He's not some namby-pamby pedigree like that big black lump over there. Meaning of course, your dog," Jake snapped.

He saw her feet move then, and they were moving fast. Jake leaped off the old rocker and onto the railing that ran along the porch. He was hanging on to one of the rot-ted columns that held up the canvas awning when his childhood friend thundered onto the porch. All hell broke loose when Elway screeched at the top of his lungs, the black dog jumping high enough to snag his teeth on Jake's shorts. He gave one mighty tug as Jake, the column, the awning, and the railing all gave way at the same time.

Ardeth Gamble stopped dead in her tracks as Jake's bare rump and all he held dear in front were suddenly visible to anyone who cared enough to look. She cared enough to remove her sunglasses. "Oh, my," was all she could think of to say.

"Lucky, down! Now look what you've done, Jake Forrest! I'm going to have to pay Mrs. Gamble for all this. Oh, dear, you're suddenly shy. How sweet! No, *you're* paying for all this, you . . . you . . . lawyer. I can't believe you don't wear underwear under your shorts. Everyone wears underwear. I bet you *chafe*. There's a powder for that, you know."

"Shut up, Trinity Henderson. That thirty-seven cents doesn't give you the right . . . Just shut up and get my shorts off that dog. If he rips them, you're paying for them. They're Ralph Lauren. I love those shorts. It took me *years* to break them in."

Lisa walked over to where Lucky was

happily shredding the worn material of Jake's shorts. One leg of the shorts hung in tatters, the zipper held on by a thread. She picked them up gingerly by her thumb and index finger as though handling them would actually give her the plague.

Ardeth Gamble stood behind a camellia bush, breathless with excitement as she watched the two verbal combatants. She clapped her hand over her mouth when she saw the shorts sail across the yard to land among the branches of her favorite pecan tree.

"Go get 'em, hot shot!"

Ardeth Gamble thought she was going to explode. Would he dare get up and head for the pecan tree? If he did, she would have a full frontal view for all fifty yards of his trek. She sucked in her breath.

"You witch! Get me a towel, get me something! A fig leaf will do."

"In a heartbeat." Lisa grinned. She sat down on the opposite rocker and leered at the lawyer, her eyes daring him to let go of his T-shirt, which he had stretched downward to cover his private parts. "Did I mention that I hate your guts? If I didn't, I do."

Jake grappled for something smart and

witty to say. He kept stretching his T-shirt down as far as it would go. He could see his belly button by the neckline of his shirt. "Do you know what I think, Miss-I-hate-your-guts Trinity Henderson? I think you hate what I did, but you don't hate me as a person. You never hate your friends. There are times when you don't like them for something they did or for short periods of time, but you don't really hate them because then that would make you a lousy judge of character because you picked that friend in the first place. I said I was sorry. I was caught up in the college stuff, feeling my oats, and I'm not the one who took the phone call. Mitzi would be appalled at your attitude."

"Cut the crap, Jake. That line of garbage is lawyer-speak for you were wrong and can't make it right. You're no friend. It was all a lie. Everything was a lie. I'm going to count to three, and if you aren't off this porch, I'm going to sic Lucky on you."

Ardeth Gamble, her heart about to leap out of her chest, started to count along with Lisa.

"One! Two! Three!"

Jake remained where he was.

Ardeth Gamble fell into the camellia bush.

"Lucky, chase this . . . this lawyer off the porch."

The black dog loped over to where Jake was lying under the porch railing and licked at his ears. Elway leaped onto his chest and tried to snuggle under his T-shirt. Lisa started to laugh and couldn't stop. Jake cursed under his breath as he struggled to move the section of railing with one hand, his other hand holding a death grip on his shirt.

Lisa walked over to the railing and yanked it upright. It fell into a thick azalea bush that hugged the bottom of the house. "You and your cat are free to go." She held out one hand to help him up.

Ardeth Gamble felt her tongue swell in her mouth as she watched.

Jake reached for her hand. With one mighty pull, Lisa's feet left the floor, and she was on top of him. He could feel her eyelashes against his own. Then both his hands were on her head as he brought his lips to hers.

"God, I've wanted to do that for years," Jake groaned.

Ardeth Gamble's head felt so light she had to shake it to clear her thoughts. It was the longest kiss she'd ever seen. Panting with excitement, she parted the camellia branches to see better. Good grief, where was the shirt? Up around his neck was where it was. She gasped. "Mercy," she muttered under her breath.

Jake broke the lip-lock and grinned. "Now that we settled that, will you please get me a towel before Mrs. Gamble, who is hiding in the camellia bush at precisely ten o'clock, has a heart attack. I wouldn't be a bit surprised if she doesn't ask you to relocate."

"She's been watching!"

"Uh-huh."

Lisa, her whole body twanging, forgot that she hated the man she'd just kissed. The old Trinity kicked in. "Then let's give her a really good reason to kick me out of here." A second later, her top and her shorts skittered across the little front porch. The dog and cat were on them in an instant. Clad only in a lacy bra and thong, Lisa fell on top of him again. She wiggled and mashed her body against Jake's until he moaned for mercy. "Is she still watching?"

"Uh-huh. Oops, I think she's leaving. Yep, she's leaving. Okay, let's go for it!"

Lisa rolled over. A second later she was

on her feet, towering over him. "In your dreams!"

"You look like a goddess!" Jake said. He meant every word of what he said.

"I do, don't I?" Lisa quipped.

"You liked that kiss, admit it," Jake said, chagrined at her blasé attitude.

"I like ice cream, too."

His ego bruised, Jake said, "What's that supposed to mean?"

Lisa laughed as she sashayed into the house in search of a towel. "A little goes a long way." She returned a few minutes later with a towel and wearing a mint-green sundress.

"How'd I measure up to Amanda Pettijohn?" Lisa asked nonchalantly.

Jake busied himself by wrapping the blue towel around his waist. "You're jealous, is that it? Obviously you talked to Mitzi. Mitzi needs to mind her own business. Now, let's get down to business here. We have a problem with these two animals. They want to be together, so I suggest you take them one day and I take them the next day. Since you had them overnight, it's my turn. I'll bring them back in the morning." It was hard to be authoritative dressed in a blue towel. "As for how you compare . . . Well, off the top of my head, I'd say you need to work on your . . . uh, delivery. Your performance was so-so."

"You're a buffoon. Go. I want my dog back at exactly eight o'clock tomorrow morning. One minute late, and your ass is grass, Jake Forrest. Bring back the towel, too. It belongs to Mrs. Gamble."

A *buffoon?* He'd been called a lot of things in his lifetime but never a buffoon. It rankled. He had to give back as good as he got, or she would have him over a barrel. "Yeah, well, if I'm a buffoon, you're a tease and you have *cellulite* on your butt. I *saw* it!" His horrified tone said that cellulite to him was worse than the crud, the measles, shingles, and the mumps all rolled into one. "Disgusting for someone as young as you are," Jake said, stomping his way to his car. He whistled for the dog and Elway.

"I do not have cellulite!" Lisa screeched. She could hear Jake laughing.

The minute the car was out of sight, Lisa ran into the bathroom and turned on the light. She pulled up her sundress and wiggled and squirmed to see if she did indeed have cellulite. She bent over trying to get a better look at her rear end. "Jerk!" she mumbled over and over as she straightened her dress. She did *not* have cellulite.

Ardeth Gamble picked her way out of the camellia bush, settling her sunglasses on the bridge of her nose. Her plump body twitched as she made her way to her ten-year-old Cadillac, which had seven thousand miles on it and nary a scratch or ding. Suddenly her plan to buy peacock feathers didn't seem as wonderful as it had in the early hours of the morning. She wondered how high her blood pressure was.

Lisa climbed into the Saturn. She turned on the engine and waited for the air-conditioning to kick in. Before she went back to Mitzi's house she was going out to the farm at Windsor Hill. It was time to talk to Lillian Henderson. Her heart fluttered at the thought. She hoped she didn't get emotional and end up crying. Homecomings were always stressful. At least that's what the slick magazines said. She wondered if Mitzi would approve of the visit.

Her mind continued to whirl and twirl, going in all directions. Anything so she wouldn't have to think about Jake and what happened on the little porch. Obviously she was going to have to borrow money from Mitzi to pay for the damage Jake did. That kiss didn't have to mean anything unless she wanted it to. She needed to stay focused on what was ahead of her. Thinking about Jake Forrest was like thinking about a trip to the moon. Simply out of the question.

Lisa pulled the Saturn to the side of the road that afforded her a clear view of the dirt road leading to the farmhouse she'd grown up in. How was it possible for everything to look just the same? Well, except for the trees. The old oak they'd called General Lee seemed to have grown enormously. There were no children these days to run over the fields, play in the barn, climb General Lee all the way to the top. She smiled when she remembered how she'd been the only one gutsy enough to climb to the top. She shivered at the thought. Jake had called her stupid that day.

How beautiful it all looked. The monster trees lining the sides of the rutted old road dripped with Spanish moss. They'd grown, too, since she'd left. Now they forged a canopy over the road that led to the house. It was more fragrant here than at Mrs. Gamble's house. There everything grew wild, but here Lillian and John kept everything tended and pruned. The sweet smell of jasmine was something she'd sorely missed during her time in Pennsylvania. Everything just smelled different here. She sniffed again, trying to identify what was teasing her senses. The earth. The very air. Certainly not the vibrant purple crape myrtles because they gave off no scent at all. *Something so beautiful should smell heavenly,* she thought. She sniffed again. Gardenias!

Lisa looked around. Lillian didn't have gardenias. The scent must be wafting down from Windsor Hill. Sarabess loved gardenias. There were always gardenias and jasmine in a vase in Emily's room. What a strange thing to remember.

Putting the car in gear, Lisa waited for a pickup truck to pass before she turned into the road that would take her right to the front porch of the farmhouse.

Her home. Her only home. A tear gathered in the corner of her eye. The Kolinas' house was never a home. Even though she'd stayed fifteen long years, she'd never thought of it as home. She'd known from the very beginning it was nothing more than a stopping-off place on her journey to nowhere.

From her position inside the car, Lisa could see the tidy front porch that glistened in the bright sun. Everything looked like it had just been painted. Clay pots of summer flowers sat on the steps. That was the same. Lillian loved flowers. There were ferns in white wicker baskets on the porch. That was the same, too. The old swing was still there, also boasting a new coat of Charleston green paint. The floor was painted the same color as the porch railing. A beige-and-green fiber carpet sat smack in the middle of the floor, just as in every other house in the area. On rainy days she and her friends had played Monopoly on that carpet for hours on end.

Home.

Lisa knocked on the screen door. She could smell baking bread and cinnamon. Somewhere off in the back, probably the kitchen, she could hear a radio. She opened the door and called Lillian's name but she didn't step inside. It was no longer her home. She didn't belong here. Visitors knocked.

Lillian appeared out of nowhere. "Yes, what can I do for you, miss?"

"Lillian, don't you recognize me? It's me, Trinity."

Lillian's hands flew to her cheeks. "Merciful God! Is it really you, child?"

"It's me, Lillian. Can I come in?"

"Of course, of course. I can't believe you're standing right in front of me. You are a sight, child, for these old eyes."

Trinity allowed herself to be smothered in a warm, comforting hug. Growing up, there had been no hugs. "You look the same, Lillian."

"I wish I could say the same for you, child. You left here all arms and legs, with spaces between your teeth. You're more beautiful than those models I see on television. Oh, John is going to be so surprised. When did you get back? Are you staying or is this just a visit? Would you listen to me? I'm babbling," the older woman said, wiping tears from her eyes.

"I'm here to stay. Everything looks the same, smells the same, so I guess nothing much happened while I was gone."

"I wouldn't exactly say that, Trinity," Lillian said flatly. "Come along. I'm canning peaches. I made some fresh sweet tea earlier, and I just took some bread out of the oven. Would you like a slice with some apple butter?"

"I would love some, Lillian."

As Lillian bustled about the old-fashioned kitchen, she shot off a barrage of questions. "Why did you leave, Trinity? Why didn't you call or send a postcard? Was it something John or I did? Was it because of that . . . that woman up on the Hill? I wish you had talked to me. I grieved so. Miss High-and-Mighty up there on the Hill wouldn't allow John or me to call the police. Mitzi tried to find you. She hired detectives. I did get the money you sent. I never told anyone except Mitzi, and she never asked until a few weeks ago." She wound down like a pricked balloon.

Lisa licked at her dry lips. "I didn't see that I had any other choice at the time. I know everything now, Lillian. Sarabess Windsor is my mother. Harold was my father. I want you to tell me every single thing you know. You don't have to wonder and worry about your security. I'll take care of you. I have that . . . robust trust fund, you know. Mitzi and I talked earlier today. She can fill in only so much. I need you to tell me the rest. I came here to get my records, my birth certificate, and anything else you have that says I am Trinity Henderson or Trinity Windsor, or whoever the hell I am. Will you do that for me, Lillian?"

Lillian's head bobbed up and down. "She gave me everything when it was time to register you for school. I went to the post office and made copies of everything because I knew she would want the originals back. I never even told John. I know that was wrong because you aren't supposed to keep secrets from your husband. I didn't care. I just knew that one day you would want them. I did love you, Trinity. So did John. Maybe we didn't show it the way real parents show it, but we were so afraid that she would snatch you away from us. And then our hearts would get broken. The way it all turned out was far worse."

"That was then. This is now, Lillian. Like Mitzi said, it's a whole new ball game, and I'm the one up at bat. Do you remember how I used to hit a long hard drive right down the middle of the baseball field? I'm mad enough to hit another one, only this time it will be longer and harder."

Lillian shivered at the young woman's cold tone. "I do, child, I do. John used to talk about that all the time. He said you were better than all those wimpy boys."

Lisa laughed, but there was no mirth in the sound.

Chapter 22

Jake settled each of his new roommates with a bowl of treats before he exited the apartment. His destination: Mitzi's house. He was locking the door when he heard his name called. "Yoo-hoo, Jacob!"

Jake's heart thudded. "Miss Clara! Don't tell me, you want to change your will again."

"I do, sir, and this is the last and final time. I went by the office, and they told me you don't work there anymore. Can we do it here where you live?"

"No, not really. I'll tell you what, follow me to the office, and we'll make short work of it. You know, Miss Clara, my father could change your will for you. You want to stay with the firm, don't you?"

"I suppose he could do it, but I like you better. You're my lawyer. I trust you. I don't need everyone in town knowing my business, Jacob. That's not to say your father would tell everyone. Well, he'd probably tell that . . . that person up on the Hill."

That person up on the Hill. That was what did it for Jake. "Okay, Miss Clara, I'll meet you at the office or do you want to ride in with me? I can drop you back off here to pick up your car when we're finished."

"That would be lovely, Jacob. I accept. It's rare that a young person is so considerate. Your mother and Mitzi raised a fine young man."

Jake blushed as he settled Clara into the passenger seat, then got behind the wheel. "So, what are we doing this time, Miss Clara?"

"I want to leave everything to the Seniors Club. After my funeral, I want them to take a bus trip on me. The whole works. Lodging, meals, spending money. Two weeks. Whatever is left, I want it divided among the seniors. One dollar each to my ungrateful children."

Jake blinked. "What did they do this time?"

"It's more like what they didn't do. I don't want to get into it, Jacob. You might be my lawyer, but you don't need to know my personal business. I don't mean that as an insult, Jacob."

A devil perched itself on Jake's shoulder. Everyone in town knew that Clara and Ardeth Gamble were the town criers. At the moment Ardeth might have a bead on Clara, so he wanted to even things up a bit. "You interested in a bit of gossip, Miss Clara?"

Clara pursed her lips. "Does anyone else know what you're going to tell me? Is it a scoop?"

Jake grinned as he sailed through a green light. "I think it's safe to say it's a scoop, but you can't tell anyone I'm the one who told you."

"It's a deal. Spit it out, Jacob."

"Trinity Henderson is back in town. I saw her with my own eyes not more than an hour ago. Well, maybe ninety minutes ago."

"No!"

"Yep." The devil on Jake's shoulder nudged him. "And, guess where she's staying?"

"With Mitzi?"

"No. She's staying in Ardeth Gamble's

cottage. And get this, Miss Clara, Ardeth doesn't know who she is."

"Lord love a duck. That *is* a scoop. How does the poor little thing look?"

"Like a million bucks!" Jake laughed.

"That hot, eh?" Clara cackled at her own wit. "Where does that leave Amanda Pettijohn?" she asked slyly.

Jake turned on his blinker. He drove to the end of the parking lot and parked close to the building so that Clara wouldn't have so far to walk. "I don't know, Miss Clara."

"I guess you were just using her for sex, is that it?" Clara asked smartly.

Jake thought he was going to choke on his own saliva. For some reason he found it hard to lie to old people, especially Clara, whom he adored. "Something like that."

"Tsk. Tsk," Clara said, clucking her tongue. "That's what Mitzi said. I agreed with her. Amanda Pettijohn looks like she's been steam-ironed. All the female Pettijohns look that way." Jake raised his eyebrows, not quite sure what she meant. "She always looks *wet*."

"Oh," was all Jake could think of to say.

"Well, let's get with it, young man."

Forty minutes later, Jake finished typing

up the changes in Clara's will himself. He called in the receptionist and his father's secretary to witness the changes. Clara signed the new will with a shaking hand.

"It's all done, Miss Clara. The copies are running off now. Do you want me to keep both copies or do you want one?"

"No, you keep them. My children are far too inquisitive. How much will that be?"

"No charge today, Miss Clara. I'm not really working here any longer, so I just did it as a favor to you. I don't charge for favors."

"That makes sense. Very well. I'll make you some brownies tomorrow. Will that be all right?"

"You bet." Jake lowered his voice. "I'd really like to leave, Miss Clara. I don't want to run into my father."

"I don't, either. I'm ready to leave."

Jake yanked at the papers spewing out of the copier. When he got home he would staple them and put them in a blue binder.

They'd almost made it to the parking lot when Rifkin Forrest climbed out of his car.

"Good morning, Miss Clara. Haven't seen you in a while. You look well."

"I guess that's because I am well, Rifkin. You look . . . tired."

Rifkin looked annoyed at the old woman's assessment. "It's the heat and humidity. Hello, Jacob."

"Hi, Pop." The devil repositioned himself on Jake's shoulder and danced to attention. "Did you hear the news?"

"What news is that?" Rifkin called over his shoulder.

"Trinity Henderson is back in town. I saw her a couple of hours ago. She stopped by to see Mitzi earlier in the day. I just thought you might want to know."

Rifkin's step faltered, but that was the only indication he gave as he walked away that he'd heard what his son said.

"I'm no hypocrite. I never much liked your father. When he took up with Sarabess Windsor I thought even less of him. Your mother was a lovely woman," Clara managed to say through pursed lips. "Drive fast, Jacob, so I can spread the news. I don't want your father scooping me."

Jake felt a lump in his throat. He nodded to show he'd heard and understood. He helped Clara into the car, tossed her cane into the backseat. He didn't see his father watching him through the plate glass door because the sun's glare was too bright.

Fifteen minutes later, they were back at Jake's apartment. Clara patted Jake's hand as she got out of the car, and said, "You're a good boy, Jacob. Your mama would be proud of you. I'm so glad you have Mitzi. We all need someone at times."

Jake's eyes burned. He hugged the old lady. "Anytime you need someone, Miss Clara, come to me. I'll always be here for you."

The old lady laughed. "Why do you think I keep changing my will so often? While pets are wonderful, sometimes a body just needs a hug."

That is so true, Jake thought as he helped Clara settle herself in her car. He made a mental note to send Clara a basket of summer posies for her front porch. He waited until Clara's car was out of sight before he headed to Mitzi's house.

He'd just set the wheels in motion. All he had to do was wait to see what his father and Sarabess Windsor would do.

Rifkin Forrest wasted no time by going to his office. The minute his son drove away from the firm's parking lot he was in his own car headed toward Windsor Hill. His heart was pumping furiously. What he thought would never happen had just happened.

Rifkin always admired the manicured landscaping on the road that led to the very top of the Hill, where his princess waited for him. He never quite thought of himself as a prince, but at times he felt like one, albeit a tarnished one. At the moment, all he could think about was the business at hand and where it would lead.

The instant Rifkin brought his car to a stop, Sarabess descended the steps to greet him. She was dressed in apple-green linen with no wrinkles to be seen. Looking at her outfit, he wondered if she ever sat down. As always, she was made up, every hair in place, her jewelry winking in the bright sun.

One look at her prince, and one beringed hand flew to her throat. "What is it, darling? Has something happened?"

Rifkin put his arm around Sarabess's shoulder. "You could say that. Jake was at the office this morning and said Trinity Henderson is back in town. She's staying in Ardeth Gamble's cottage. Ardeth is Donny

Gamble's sister. He's the vet in town in case you didn't know. On the way in here, I saw a strange car parked in front of the farmhouse. It wouldn't surprise me one bit to find out that Trinity is visiting the Hendersons. Jake doesn't lie, Sarabess. She's here. We have to accept that."

Sarabess didn't move. Her hand still clutched her throat. "Why now?" she whispered.

Rifkin cupped Sarabess's elbow in his hand to help her up the steps to the verandah. "She's here to claim her trust fund. I don't think she knew before she got here that Harold had died. I'm also sure that Jake told her about his passing and about the contents of his will. Yes, yes, I did what you asked. The new will has been filed, but Mitzi has her lawyers on it like fleas on a dog. Jake is going to weigh in any day now, and when he takes a definitive stand, it's going to get ugly. You need to prepare yourself. I want you to tell me one more time, Sarabess, that the new will I filed is not a forgery. If it is . . . If by some chance it is a forgery, Mitzi will make sure you're prosecuted."

Sarabess gasped. "I refuse to dignify that question with a response. If you have any doubts, why are you here? If you have doubts, why did you file the will?"

"Because I trusted you. Mitzi will have the best experts in the world going over that will. The dates . . . The dates bother me. I told you that in the beginning."

Sarabess straightened up in the rocker. She looked appalled at the wrinkles in her dress. She tried to smooth them out. "And I told you then, and I'm telling you again, Harold did come up here from time to time. He was already . . . What I mean is he had already taken up with Mitzi. The visits were not happy visits. We never spoke. He came here to take things with him. At that point we already detested one another. He locked himself in his study, and did whatever it was he did. We were still married, Rifkin. I knew Harold, and his guilt was torturing him, so he did the right thing and made a new will. It's that simple. If you don't believe me, you should leave now. I can always find an attorney in Beaufort or Columbia."

Rifkin didn't believe a word of it but he kept his own counsel. "What about Trinity?"

Sarabess let out a loud sigh. Rifkin was still with her. "What about her? Trinity Henderson is not my daughter. Now that she's here, I want you to present her with whatever it is you lawyers use to make her give a DNA sample. I'm not worried about any claim Trinity Henderson might make."

Rifkin suddenly felt sick to his stomach. He was so shocked that he did not even demand that Sarabess explain what she meant when she said that Trinity was not her daughter. "I have to go now, Sarabess. I have an appointment in half an hour."

"Will you be back for dinner? Cook is making she-crab soup." She sounded, Rifkin thought, as if she didn't care one way or another.

"I don't know. I'll call you." He walked over to the banister that ran the length of the verandah. "Come here, Sarabess. I want you to see something. See that car at the bottom of the hill? The green one parked in front of the farmhouse. I think it's Trinity's. Perhaps you should go down there and say hello to *your daughter.*"

"Dammit, Rifkin, she is not my daughter. Are you deaf? I really don't appreciate your snide humor. On second thought, it might be better if you don't come to dinner. Oh, darling, I am so sorry. I didn't mean that. Please come. Okay? It's just . . . This is so . . . stressful. I just wish Mitzi would . . . Never mind. Visiting the Hendersons is not on my calendar for today. You could, of course, drop by if you feel the need to see the young woman. I really am sorry for snapping like that, Rifkin. Say you forgive me."

Rifkin ignored his princess and got into his car. He didn't look back; nor did he wave as he usually did. He simply drove away, his thoughts skittering in all directions.

Not my daughter. For close to thirty years Trinity Henderson had been referred to in whispers in the dark of the night as *my daughter*. Now, suddenly, it was: *She's not my daughter*. Then who in the damn hell was Trinity Henderson? Was Sarabess having a meltdown? He shuddered at the arrogance he'd heard in her voice. No, Sarabess wasn't having a meltdown. If anyone had one, it would be him.

Mitzi's menagerie watched Jake from the verandah as he took the steps three at a time. He tussled with first one animal, then the other until they settled down. He looked over his shoulder at the Saturn parked in front of his own car as he tried to figure out what was going on. He opened the screen door and shouted for his aunt. Her response came from the back of the house, where she had a cluttered office.

Jezebel swooped down the hall to land on his shoulder. "Hellooooo, Jake," she squawked.

"Hi, yourself, Jezzie. What's new?" Like the parrot was really going to tell him. He doubled over laughing when the green and red bird squawked again.

"Big trouble. Little trouble." An instant later the colorful bird flew upward to land on one of the rustic beams.

"I'm in here, nephew. Trinity is here."

"Hello, Trinity," Jake said coolly.

"Hello, Jake," Trinity responded, her voice cooler. "How is my dog?"

"Your dog is fine. He torments my cat."

"Don't you mean your cat torments my dog?"

"Girls and boys, settle down. You can fight later. Jake, look what Trinity brought from the Hendersons," Mitzi said, handing over a sheaf of papers for his inspection. "Tell me how that woman did . . . all of this," she said, pointing to the papers Jake was holding.

Jake riffled through the papers. "Birth certificate, shot records for school. What's so
strange about these?"

"The name, Jake. They're forgeries. There
are no adoption papers. Lillian Henderson
never bore a child. The name is Trinity Henderson on the birth certificate. Her name is
Trinity Windsor. For one thing, there's no
baby bracelet. There is no record of where
she was born. But that's not a problem for
us. Harold told me she was born at Lenox
Hill Hospital in New York. I need you to go
up to the attic, Jake, and bring down all the
boxes labeled with Harold's name on them.
I never . . . I couldn't . . ."

"Do you know what's in the boxes?" Jake
asked.

"A record of his life. That's how Harold put
it to me. He said I might need it all someday.
I guess this is someday. He brought it all
here after Sarabess returned from New
York. Before you can ask—no, she did not
have Trinity with her when she returned.
Some nurse brought Trinity to the Hendersons a week after Sarabess got back. The
nurse dropped off the baby, then she left.
She introduced herself to Lillian as Grace
something or other. Her last name might be

in one of the boxes. Harold was meticulous in the way he kept records.

"On one of her visits here, Sarabess said if Trinity ever came back here, she would demand a DNA sample. She made my blood run cold when she said that. She was so certain . . . that Trinity would never return."

Lisa swiped at her eyes. "If I'm not Lisa Summers, Trinity Henderson, or Trinity Windsor, then who the hell am I?"

Mitzi's eyes blazed. "Honey, you are Trinity Windsor. You look just like Harold when he was young. I have photographs that will prove it to you. I also have all of Harold's medical records. I even have a lock of his hair and a lock of mine, in an antique locket that was my mother's. We can prove you are Harold's daughter. Let Sarabess spin her lies till the cows come home. In the end we'll prevail."

Jake looked at the tortured faces of the two women. He wanted to hug them both but decided it wasn't the right time. "Can you narrow my search a little, Mitzi? Where exactly are the boxes?"

"They're stacked up to the left at the top of the steps. Bring them all down."

"Yes, ma'am," Jake said, loping off to the center hallway and the wide circular staircase. He felt momentarily light-headed as he climbed the steps. Mitzi used the same kind of polish on the beautiful stairway that his mother had always used: beeswax. Right then he would have given anything to be ten years old and in the kitchen with his mom.

Jake gasped at the mountain of boxes piled up in the attic. He could carry two at a time, but it was going to take him nine trips to get them all down to Mitzi's office. *Harold must have had an impressive life to have eighteen boxes of records,* he thought.

Jake was hot and sweaty by the time he carried the last box into the office. "How do you want to do this? Should we just divide it up, six each?"

"That works for me, nephew. Divvy them up while I get us some sweet tea."

Jake dropped to his haunches. "Look, Trinny, let's call a truce, okay? We're dealing with some serious stuff here, and I don't want to spend all my time defending myself over something that happened fifteen years ago. I apologize for the cellulite remark. When we find out who you really are and get your life on track, then you can cuss me out to your heart's content; but I have to warn you, you'll have to do it long-distance because I'm leaving Crestwood. I'm going to take a job at that think tank in Washington, D.C."

He was leaving. The declaration stunned her. She felt like her insides were collapsing. She wanted to say something, but the words wouldn't come. She nodded, then looked away. She finally managed something that sounded like "Okay."

Jake tore into one of the dusty boxes, wondering why his eyes were burning so badly.

Chapter 23

Three hours into their sorting, collating, and stapling, Jake rolled over on the floor and started to beat at it with his clenched fists. "There's nothing here but business records, Mitzi. Are you sure there's something in these boxes that will help Trinny?"

Mitzi pushed her back up against her desk as she swiped a grimy hand over her face. "No, darlin', I am not sure. But when Harold said it was his entire life filed in these boxes, I assumed he meant it. Trinity was part of that life. We still have six boxes to go. I'm sure we'll come across something. Maybe we just need a break. Let's get washed up and find something to eat."

Agile as a cat, Trinity was on her feet. She extended one hand to Mitzi, who climbed to her feet. She extended her free hand to

Jake, who looked up at her, debating if she had a trick up her sleeve. At the torment he read in her face he decided to trust her. The touch of her hand sent an electric shock through his whole body. He grinned. She stared at him blankly.

He took pity on her, and said, "We'll find something. Whatever it is will probably be in the last box. Don't give up now." He reached for her hand and squeezed it. He was about to let loose of her hand when he felt her squeeze back. His heart soared. He cautioned himself not to get his hopes up where this young woman was concerned.

"I just want to know who I am. I thought . . . suspected . . . that I was Trinity Windsor. I never felt like Trinity Henderson, and while I have documentation that says I am Lisa Summers, I don't feel like her, either. I don't know what to think or feel. How in the damn hell did this happen to me? *Who am I, Jake?*" she wailed.

Jake squeezed her hand again. "If you want my opinion, and that's all it is, an opinion, I'd say the only person who can give you the answers you want is Sarabess Windsor. I think you're a Windsor because you look like a Windsor. For whatever that's worth."

"But Jake . . . If she was really my mother, why would she want me to give a DNA sample? That tells me she knows, or thinks she knows, that I am not her daughter, which is fine with me. I just want to know who I am and who my parents are. Do you really think she knows?"

"Yeah, I think she does know, and I think my father knows, too. Let's wash off some of this grime and grab something to eat. We have all day to come up with answers. I can help for the next three weeks, then I'm off to Washington. Okay?"

Trinity dropped his hand to turn left for the lavatory in the hallway. A lump the size of a lemon settled in her throat. Three weeks. Three weeks was only twenty-one days. She would need a calculator to figure out how many hours and minutes that was. *Three weeks*. Her shoulders slumped. Sometimes life just wasn't fair.

Jake shoved his way past Mitzi, his own shoulders drooping as he entered the bath off the laundry room. She'd squeezed his hand. That had to mean something. He'd thrown out his departure date hoping she'd say something. She probably hadn't even heard what he said. As he lathered his hands he wondered how he could possibly leave his old friend in the lurch and head to Washington to make a new life for himself.

Maybe he needed to call the Montrose Institute to delay his starting date. Maybe he shouldn't have agreed to take the job in the first place. Maybe a lot of things.

When Jake and Trinity returned to the kitchen, Celeste had the table set for three with colorful plastic throwaway plates.

Mitzi winked. "Celeste hates loading the dishwasher. I try to make things easier for her since she's getting up in years."

"That's a bald-faced lie, Mitzi. You bought a ton of this stuff, and we have to use it up. It was on *sale*," Celeste said sourly.

"A penny saved is a penny earned. What's for lunch?"

Celeste sniffed. "For your guests, a toasted ham-and-cheese sandwich with wild mushroom soup and a garden salad. For dessert, blackberry pie. For you, grass, weeds, and a lump of that crappy tofu you profess to love so much. You get a banana for dessert. Your guests will be drinking fresh sweet tea, and you will be consuming red beet and turnip juice, and I hope you get sick."

Mitzi threw the dish towel she was holding at her housekeeper, whom she loved almost as much as she loved the two young people sitting at her table. Life would be terribly boring without the snapping and snarling she and Celeste did with one another on a daily basis.

"Let's talk about something other than problems. Trinity, did Jake tell you he was offered a wonderful position at a very prestigious think tank in the nation's capital?"

Trinity nodded, her shoulders drooping even lower, her eyes miserable.

"I think you should buy one of those fancy houses in Georgetown, nephew. From everything I've read, Georgetown is a happening place. It's so quaint, so political. You'll have to beat the women off with a stick," she said slyly as she bit down into a chunk of tofu. She watched Trinity over the top of her reading glasses to gauge her reaction to what she'd just said. Her nephew looked embarrassed, which was just fine with her.

Jake decided to step up to the plate and give his aunt a run for her money. "Sterling idea, Mitzi. I'll e-mail a broker and tell him or her to start looking. One of those old Federal-style houses the Yankees seem to prefer. I'm going to get a new set of wheels, too. I'm thinking one of those two-seater BMWs. They have great safety features. Out with the old, in with the new. I'll invite you for Christmas."

Mitzi looked appalled. "You're not coming home for Christmas! You have to come home for Christmas. It won't be the same if you aren't here."

Trinity whatever-her-name-was looked like she was going to burst into tears at any moment.

Mitzi decided it might be a good time to backpedal. "I want to go on record as saying you're making a mistake. You're way too liberal to work in a think tank. You won't do well with all those Yankees. Besides, every Southerner worth his or her salt knows you can't trust a Yankee."

"Mitzi, the war's over. The North and South have been friendly for years. Give it up. I'm going. View it as you'll have another place to vacation as long as you call ahead."

"You are a smart-ass, Jacob Forrest. Eat!" she commanded her nephew.

"Thank you for lunch, it was very good," Trinity said, finishing the last of her soup. "I think I'll save the pie for later. If you two want to continue squabbling, I'll go back to searching through the boxes."

"I'm done, too," Jake said, pushing back his chair.

Mitzi smirked as she dug into the mess on her plate.

They walked side by side down the hall. Trinity broke the silence. "I've never been to Washington. It's on my list of places to visit after I do the Disney thing. Have you been to Disney?"

Jake laughed. "A hundred years ago. Mitzi took me once. She sat on a bench and let me run wild. I guess you can't do that these days, but back then it was an experience."

"What . . . What will we do about the animals when you leave?" Trinity asked, a catch in her voice.

Where was all that bravado she'd exhibited earlier? Her torment registered with Jake. "I don't know. A few days ago it wasn't a problem. I guess we'll have to work something out. I love that old cat. I think he likes me, too. With animals you can't always be sure." Now, where in the hell had that come from?

Trinity nodded. "I found Lucky, or maybe I should say he found me, on the way here, but we bonded. His owner died, and her daughter, who really didn't want the dog, was taking him back to Ohio and somehow he got away from her and hopped in my car. I took him to a vet, found out he was microchipped, and the rest is history. I think it's going to be a problem, Jake."

"You aren't going to cry, are you?" Jake asked anxiously.

"Now why would I do a dumb thing like that?" Trinity responded as she squatted on the floor. She yanked at a box so hard the lid flew across the room.

Jake knew when to let well enough alone. He pulled over a box and attacked it with a vengeance.

An hour later Trinity closed the box she'd been sifting through and pulled another one toward her. "You broke my heart, Jake Forrest," she muttered.

Stunned, Jake felt his jaw drop, and his eyes bugged out of his head. Had he heard what he thought he just heard, or was he daydreaming? He stunned himself further when he said, "I know, and I'm sorry."

"I had such a crush on you that I couldn't see straight. I thought when I called you that night that you'd drop everything and come home, or at the very least find a way for me to get to you."

It was Jake's turn to mumble. "I'm sorry. I wish that night had never happened. Is there anything I can do *now?*"

Trinity whirled around, her eyes full of tears. For the first time she noticed that Mitzi wasn't in the room. "I don't know what to do, Jake. This isn't like me. I react to everything. I've never been one to let the pot simmer if I can bring it to a full boil. Except maybe with the Kolinas, and I don't want to talk about them. Who the hell am I, Jake? I need to know who I am. I can't go forward until I know."

Jake scooted closer, close enough to put his arm around her shoulders. "I don't know, Trinity, but I'm more than willing to help you find out. Like I said earlier, if my opinion counts, I think you're Trinity Windsor."

Trinity sniffed. "We know for sure that I'm not Lisa Summers. I don't want to be a dead girl from West Virginia. I need to let that poor girl rest in peace. I feel so guilty having used her identity, and somehow, I have to make that right. If and when this is finally settled, I'm going to go to West Virginia and bury all . . . everything I have that has her name on it. I have to apologize to her."

Jake nodded. "We also know you are not Trinity Henderson because the Hendersons never adopted you. All they did was give you their name. That only leaves the name Windsor. Everyone knows Sarabess Windsor has her own agenda. If the real Trinity Windsor can't be found, Sarabess thinks she will get your trust fund. If you prove to be the real Trinity Windsor, you can force her out of Windsor Hill, and she has no claim on anything. That's what Harold Windsor wanted."

Jake and Trinity were so intent on what they were saying that they didn't notice Mitzi standing in the doorway. "I can verify that," she said quietly. "If either one of you wants my opinion, this is what I think you should do: I think Trinity should have her DNA tested. Then I think you should both go to talk to your father, Jake, and from there, go up to the Hill and say what's on your mind. I've engaged the services of a detective agency in New York to see if there's any trail to be found on the women Trinity heard Sarabess and your father discussing.

"Sarabess is not a person to do anything for no reason. If it's not all about her, she wants nothing to do with whatever *it* is. She extends herself for no one. The fact that she wanted to hire you, Jake, because of the attorney-client privilege tells me this is something she doesn't want anyone else to know. Possibly even your father. I'd bet a bushel of money Rifkin doesn't know anything about Grace Finnegan. If he did know, Sarabess would be using his services. My gut instinct tells me that Grace has something to do with Trinity."

Jake realized he still had his arm around Trinity's shoulders. He gave her a slight squeeze, and he rather thought she leaned in closer to him. It felt good.

"We haven't found a thing, Mitzi," Jake said. "All this stuff is Harold's old tax files, stuff for Windsor Steel, old bank records, deeds, stuff like that. There's nothing here for Emily, either. Mom kept a box of stuff that had to do with me. She saved and filed everything. Maybe it's something fathers trust mothers to do. Having said that, Mitzi, we have to rely on what you remember Harold telling you."

"Harold never mentioned that woman's name to me. I remember quite clearly that he said a nurse would be bringing the baby to the Hendersons. He never called her by name. I'm hoping the detective agency can find the records of Emily's bone marrow procedure. I'm sure whichever team of doctors did the procedure kept records. I'm not sure about this, but I don't think thirty years ago it was a standard procedure. I don't know why I say this, but at that time I think it would have been considered cutting edge and quite costly. I could be wrong, though."

"When do you expect to hear from the detective agency?" Trinity asked.

"Soon. Perhaps another day or so. I have no idea how one would go about finding records that are thirty years old. Everything would be a paper file. That means the agency has to do legwork instead of pressing buttons for an instant response. They are sending me daily updates, which until now aren't even worth reading."

Trinity put the lid back onto the box in front of her. "That's it; there's nothing in this one, either." She threw her hands up in the air in disgust. "Now what?" she asked.

"I think you should call the medical center and make arrangements to have your DNA tested," Mitzi said. "I'm totally ignorant about how that works, so give me a minute while I call my doctor. For whatever my opinion is worth, I think it is imperative you do it as soon as possible. It could take weeks or months. I saw that on television in a movie, so who knows if it's true or not."

Jake's head bobbed up and down as he closed the last box he'd been working on. "I was hoping there would be something in at least one of these boxes that could help you, Trinity. I'm sorry it didn't work out. I guess I should take all of them back to the attic."

Trinity jumped up. "I'll help you."

"Does that mean we're friends now?"

"That's what it means, Jake. I had to vent. I'm not sorry, either. I wish . . . Oh, God, I wish so many things. I want to go to sleep and wake up to find the last fifteen years were just a bad dream. I need a plan, some course of action. Something concrete I can challenge."

Jake led the way up the steps, two of the

cartons in his arms, Trinity following. His step was so buoyant he felt like he was walking on air. She was coming around. Maybe she really didn't hate his guts after all. Maybe, maybe, maybe.

Sarabess Windsor had to pry away her death grip on the telephone receiver so she could replace it in the stand. The knuckles of her hand were bone-white, and her hand was numb. Rage, unlike anything she'd ever experienced, rivered through her entire body. She knew she had to calm down before she had a stroke. What to do, where to go? In the blink of an eye, she reached for the chain on her neck that held the little gold key that would open the special lock on Emily's old room. She ran down the hallway to her daughter's room, where she fumbled with the key. The moment the door closed behind her, Sarabess threw herself onto Emily's bed. She didn't cry. She was too angry to cry.

Sarabess started to mumble and mutter as she crunched her face into the pink satin pillow. Within minutes, the sweet scent of the pillow calmed her down. She rolled over, the pillow clutched to her chest, her eyes on the spectacular painting of Emily that hung over the fireplace. How beautiful her little girl had been. She moved then to cross the room. By standing on her toes, she could reach up and touch the painting. How well she remembered the day Emily had posed for the painting. First, though, the photographer had taken pictures because he couldn't be sure that Emily would be up to sitting for long periods of time. She still had those pictures in her night table drawer. She looked at them daily. Sometimes twice.

The dress Emily had worn that day had been exquisite, white organza with two hundred pink satin rosebuds sewn onto it by hand. Tiny seed pearls circled the neck and sleeves with the same satin rosebuds. The satin sash that ended in a bow in back was pleated and hung down to the hem. A dress fit for a princess. Her princess. She still had the dress wrapped in tissue paper, but it was in shreds. Emily had thrown a tantrum right in front of the photographer and ripped and gouged at the dress, but not before he'd gotten several beautiful shots. How well she remembered her daughter's tortured screams. "Why can't I wear blue jeans like Trinity? Why can't I wear a baseball cap and sneakers like Trinity? I hate this stupid dress! Make her come up here to play with me. Do you hear me, Mama? Make her come up here. I want to play Parcheesi. Make Jake come, too. I don't want him to like Trinity more than me."

Sarabess licked at her lips. That day she'd called up Lillian Henderson and barked an order. "Send Trinity up here to the Hill. *NOW.*"

Even after so many years, Sarabess cringed at the abuse Emily had heaped on young Trinity that day. The little girl finally had enough and got up to leave. She remembered how Emily had used both hands to force Trinity back on the chair. "Finish the game, Trinity," she'd said coldly.

Agile as a cat, Trinity squirmed out from under Emily's hands and bolted. "I'm never coming back here again. Never!" she screamed at the top of her lungs.

Emily had started to wail, throwing the Parcheesi board across the room and kicking and screaming until Sarabess thought she would go out of her mind. An hour later Emily was running a 103-degree fever, and the doctor had to be called.

Later that day Harold had called and issued an edict: "Do not *ever* force that child to visit again. If you do, Sarabess, you will come to regret your actions."

Had she listened?

No, she had not.

She had never regretted her actions until now.

Chapter 24

The appointment made at the Medical Center for Trinity's DNA test was confirmed within an hour. Jake dusted off his hands dramatically as he ushered Trinity out to Mitzi's verandah. They sat together on the swing. "My father will still be at the office if you think you're up to a confrontation. If not, we can wait till tomorrow. It's your call, Trinny."

Trinity pushed with her foot so the old wicker swing would move. Jake did the same thing. "I know. Tell me about your father, Jake. Your mother, too. What's it like to have real parents who care about you? Could you see the pride in their faces when you did something they thought you couldn't do? I bet your mom hugged you a lot when you were little. Mitzi's a hugger, so it stands to reason your mother . . . Maybe we shouldn't talk about any of this. Okay, let's go see your father," Trinity said, slowing the swing so she could jump off.

Jake reached for her. "No, not yet. My mother was just like Mitzi in the love-and-affection department. She could be stern, too. Her hugs were the best. The worst thing in the whole world was seeing the disappointment in her eyes when I did something wrong. Like that day at the farm when I said you were skinny, and you said I was this and that. My mother liked you a lot. I tried to be everything she wanted me to be. I think today she would be proud of me.

"My father, now, that's a whole other story. Let's just say he wasn't father material. He's a good lawyer, I will give him that. He broke my mother's heart, so I can never, ever, forgive him for that. He knows it, too. Mitzi said he backed the wrong horse. He thought Mom's estate would go to him, and it didn't. In the end, she made him pay for what he did to her. In true Southern style, as Mitzi put it. To this day I have never been able to understand why he and Sarabess never married. Mitzi says it's because he doesn't have enough money. Sarabess was counting on the Granger fortune going to my dad, and instead it came to me. She's penniless, Trinny. Two paupers. You and I are the winners here. I don't feel like one, though, do you?"

"No, I don't feel like a winner. Maybe when I find out who I really am I'll feel differently. Maybe not even then. Are you and your father cordial? Do you hate him, Jake?"

Jake had to think about the question. "I don't *hate* hate him. I hate what he did to my mother, to me. I hate what he's still doing. I have this stupid feeling that in some crazy, cockeyed way, he's trying to make things right. I don't even know why I think that. A gut feeling is the only way I can explain it. He's like . . . like someone I know and don't much like. If your next question is, Will we ever be up close and personal?— the answer is no. I would feel too disloyal to my mother. I don't think he cares one way or another. He has his own life, such as it is. I have mine. He doesn't even know I'm moving to Washington, and I have no plans to tell him. I'm sure Mitzi will pass the word to him at some point."

There they were again, the words that

sent shivers down Trinity's spine. Jake was leaving in three weeks. She nodded to show she understood what Jake was feeling.

"BL's mother was like a mother to me. By the way, I called BL to see how Joyce was doing, and she's going to be okay. I told BL to stay there; she's needed. A daughter should take care of her mother," Trinity said, sadness ringing in her voice.

Jake bit down on his lower lip. He needed to say something reassuring to the tormented young woman sitting next to him. "Between the two of us, we're going to make this all come out right, Trinny. Mom always said everything in life, good or bad, is a learning experience. I am so sorry you didn't have a real mother growing up but, Trinny, you were loved. Mitzi and Harold loved you. So did Lillian and John Henderson. I loved you, too."

Did she just hear those whispered words? "Past tense?" Trinity asked lightly. She held her breath waiting for his response.

"We were discussing the past. When we get to the present, I'll let you know."

Trinity jumped off the swing. "I don't want to talk about this anymore. Let's go see your father. I want to see his reaction with my own eyes when he sees me."

Jake hopped off the swing and reached for her hand. "Then let's do it!"

Mitzi and Celeste watched from the foyer window. "Yessssss," Mitzi said, her clenched fist shooting in the air.

Celeste poked Mitzi on the arm. "You need to mind your own business. If something goes wrong, it will be your fault. You orchestrated this whole thing, and don't deny it."

"Why would I deny it? Those two are meant for one another. I do so love it when a plan comes together," Mitzi said, clapping her hands. "The phone is ringing, Celeste. Don't you think you should answer it?"

"Are you home?"

"Well, I'm standing here, aren't I?"

Moments later, Celeste bellowed from the kitchen that the detective agency was on the phone. Mitzi almost killed herself running to the phone. She was breathless when she said, "Hello, this is Mitzi Granger."

Mitzi listened to the voice on the other end of the wire, her face betraying no expression or emotion. When she hung up she turned to Celeste. "Her name is Grace Finnegan. Grace Tanzy now. She remarried. She was a nurse at the hospital where Sarabess gave birth to Trinity. This Grace person gave her notice a *month* after Sarabess was discharged from the hospital. Make me some coffee, Celeste. We need to talk about this. *Real* coffee."

"Are you sure you want *real* coffee? The last time you drank real coffee was after Mister Harold passed on. Are we going to smoke like we did that time, too?"

"Well, hell, yes, Celeste. I can't think without a cigarette. I don't inhale and neither do you, so that's not really smoking. Now, let's think about what this all means."

A few minutes later they were sitting at the kitchen table. Celeste coughed and sputtered, her eyes watering from the cigarette smoke. "What *do* you get out of these things?"

"Absolutely nothing. I told you, I don't inhale. It's just something for me to do with my hands. I think Sarabess paid off that woman to . . . to do something. We have to figure out what that was. We don't know if this Grace person is the one who brought the baby to the Hendersons. It was thirty years ago. I wish we had a picture of her, but the detective said there was none on file anywhere. He said he has her Social Security number and should be able to have an address by tomorrow. Think, Celeste, why is Grace important to Sarabess? Why is Sarabess trying to find her now, thirty years after the fact?"

Celeste crushed out her cigarette, got up and dumped it down the garbage disposal. She turned away from the sink and fixed her eyes on Mitzi. "Giving birth to the baby was supposed to be a secret, right?" Mitzi nodded. "The baby was born in New York. Is it possible the nurse knew someone here in Crestwood, and Sarabess was afraid her secret would get out?"

"That's pretty far-fetched. She gave birth to Trinity for her bone marrow. Maybe that's the secret. She was desperate to keep Emily alive. I imagine plenty of other mothers would have done the same thing if they were in that position. You and I have never given birth to a child, Celeste, so we don't know about mother love and the desperation when you know your child is going to die. I can't fault Sarabess for doing that. What I fault her for is denying Trinity as her child. Dammit, why can't I figure this out?"

"Because you're trying too hard. Relax,

drink the coffee, and let your mind run wild. If anyone knows Sarabess Windsor, it's you. Put yourself in her place and tell me what you would do."

Mitzi closed her eyes. She mumbled and muttered for a good ten minutes before her eyes snapped open. She bolted upright. "I just love you, Celeste. I'm going to give you another raise. You are just brilliant. Just brilliant. Follow me here, okay? Sarabess said she would demand a DNA sample from Trinity if Trinity ever showed up. She's demanding a test because she knows, or thinks she knows, that Trinity, our Trinity who just arrived, is *not* her biological daughter. Ask yourself how she could know that for sure. Because . . . because . . . Grace Finnegan switched the babies in the hospital. All she would have had to do back then was switch the bracelets on the babies' wrists. All new babies look pretty much alike for the first few weeks. I think I read that somewhere. It works. It fits. It makes sense.

"Sarabess pays off Grace for committing that dastardly deed, and Grace resigns and moves away. Sarabess and her secret are safe. A baby is brought to the Hendersons, and, of course, there are no maternal feelings for Sarabess because she knows the baby is not hers. That's why she's so adamant about a DNA sample now. That's why she wants to find Grace Finnegan so she can tell her the name of the other baby's mother."

"But the girl is the spitting image of Harold Windsor," Celeste said. "I got it! I got it! At the last minute, Grace couldn't do it. Maybe she did it at first, then got cold feet, and switched them back. She took Sarabess's money and lit out. She never told Sarabess she switched them back. It makes sense, doesn't it, Mitzi? It does make sense. What a rotten person that woman is. That poor child."

"Oh, my *Godddd!*" Mitzi wailed. "It makes perfect sense, Celeste. I'm giving you two raises. That's why she wanted a lawyer to find the woman—attorney-client privilege. She couldn't ask Rifkin to do it because she never told him what she had this Grace person do thirty years ago. I want to believe even Rifkin wouldn't condone something like that. Can you imagine living with a secret like that all these years?"

"Give me another one of those cigarettes," Celeste said. "What are we going to do? Are you going to tell Jake and Trinity?"

"And Miz Sarabess Windsor still doesn't regret what she did. She wants to find Grace and the other mother to make sure they don't spill their guts. With the real Trinity back in the picture, she loses everything. She's thinking the other baby is the one who showed up here. No Windsor DNA there. She thinks she's safe."

"I would give up those two raises you plan to give me to see that woman's face when young Trinity pays her a visit. This is so over the top, so out of the box. When the DNA test results come in, they will put Sarabess into orbit."

"Put that cigarette out, Celeste. You look as stupid as I do smoking it."

"What are you going to do, Mitzi?" Celeste asked as she followed her boss's instructions.

"Nothing until I hear from the detective agency again. This is just the two of us brainstorming. Even though it makes sense to us, it doesn't mean it happened that way. The only thing we have going for us right now is that Trinity looks like Harold. Sometimes people look like other people, and there is no relationship at all between the two parties. Waiting a few days or weeks isn't going to make all that much difference.

"I'm going to sit out on the verandah and think about all this. If I come up with any sterling ideas, I'll share them with you."

"Do you want any more coffee?"

"Hell no," Mitzi said indignantly. "That stuff will kill you. The sun's over the yardarm, so you can bring me a bourbon on the rocks and go easy on the rocks."

"Yes, ma'am," Celeste said smartly.

Jake rolled into the parking lot behind the firm's offices. As he got out to open the door for Trinity, he felt a jolt of electricity ripple up through his arms when she clasped his hands. Suddenly, he felt sick to his stomach that he'd committed to the Montrose Institute. There would be no more moments like this if he moved to Washington.

"What's wrong, Jake?"

"Nothing, why?"

Trinity sighed. "You suddenly looked like you were a million miles away. Are you sure we should . . . ? If you're uncomfortable going in to see your father, I can come back another day."

"No, no. We need to get this show on the road, and starting with my father is the first thing we need to do. His reaction will tell us a lot. I was thinking . . . about my move to D.C. Maybe I was too hasty. Then again, it's a great job offer. Don't mind me, I blow hot and cold."

"It's . . . It's hard to leave home. Make sure it's what you really want, Jake. Don't make the same mistake I did. Money isn't everything in this life. Have you ever thought about hanging out your own shingle in a storefront or something like that?"

"Yeah," Jake said, holding open the door to the lobby for Trinity to walk through. He stopped at the receptionist's desk and high-fived Jocelyn before herding Trinity down the hallway that led to his father's office. He rapped sharply. He didn't open the door until he heard his father call out, "Enter."

Rifkin Forrest was halfway across the room as Jake entered the exquisite suite of offices.

"Jake!" Rifkin said, surprised to see his son. "And who might this be?" he asked, extending his hand.

"Pop, I want you to meet Trinity Henderson."

Jake watched his father carefully to note his reaction, which was nonexistent.

"It's a pleasure to meet you, young lady," Rifkin said affably.

"You, too, sir," Trinity said sweetly.

"Can I offer you tea, coffee, a soft drink? Please, sit down." When Jake and Trinity demurred, Rifkin motioned to two comfortable-looking leather chairs before he took up his position behind the highly polished desk. "What can I do for you, Jake, or is this a social visit?" His tone of voice said he didn't really care one way or the other.

"Actually, Mr. Forrest, I'm the one who wanted to come here, not Jake. I want you to arrange a meeting with my mother. I think a neutral setting for our first meeting would be best. Also, at Mitzi's suggestion I've just made an appointment to have my DNA tested. You might want to tell that to my mother when you schedule the meeting."

Rifkin leaned back in his special ergonomic chair and made a steeple with his fingers. He was glad his son and the girl couldn't see how fast his heart was beating. It was a hell of a way to end the day. "I can suggest a meeting to Mrs. Windsor, but that doesn't guarantee she'll see you."

Jake bristled. "Why do you think that might not happen, *Pop?*"

"It's simple, Jacob. There are charlatans out there. Where money is concerned they tend to come out of the woodwork. I'm not saying this young lady is a charlatan, but the thought might occur to Mrs. Windsor. I will pass on your request. Is there anything else?"

Jake stood up, knowing he was dismissed. He reached down for Trinity's hand, but she was too quick for him.

She leaned forward and grasped the shiny desk with both hands. "Well, yes, Mr. Forrest, there is one more thing. You can tell my mother I know all about Grace and the other lady. Oh, dear, I can see by your expression that the name isn't ringing any bells for you. Well, that's certainly understandable; thirty years is a long time. People tend to forget names. It's funny, though, how that one name is embedded in my brain."

Trinity removed her hands from the edge of the desk and stood up. "It was nice to see you again, Mr. Forrest. Thank you for seeing me. I'll wait to hear from you in regard to my mother. Just call Mitzi or Jake to set up the date and the time."

Rifkin stood, his eyes blazing at his son. He said nothing as he watched Jake and the young woman at his side walk out the door.

"How'd I do?" Trinity asked in a jittery voice after they'd reached the hallway.

"Jesus, you just rocked the old man's world from under his feet. I never thought I'd live to see that happen. I think you might have tipped our hand, though. Come on, let's get out of here."

The two of them, hand in hand, ran down the hall, across the lobby, and out to the parking lot.

Settled in the car and buckled up, Trinity reached for Jake's arm. "I guess I shouldn't have mentioned Grace. He really looked like he didn't recognize the name. I can't be certain, Jake, that the man Mrs. Windsor was talking to that day I was under the porch was your father. Maybe it was Harold. Maybe it was someone none of us know. You saw him, did you think he recognized the name?"

"My father is a good poker player. Lawyers tend to show no expression in regard to anything. When it comes to Sarabess Windsor, my father will pull out all the stops. I think it's safe to say that you just ruined what's left of their day. My father will head up to Windsor Hill the minute he leaves the office. This is not something he would talk about on the phone. Neither one of them will sleep tonight, that's for sure."

"What if I'm not Trinity Windsor, Jake?"

"Mitzi says you are, and that's good enough for me. Get used to it."

Trinity watched the scenery and the passing cars as Jake hit the road, her thoughts chaotic. "But what if I'm not, Jake?"

"If that happens, which I don't think it will, we'll deal with it then."

"You won't be here, Jake, you're relocating," Trinity whispered.

Jake had never in his life made a snap decision. He made one now. His voice was airy, blasé when he said, "I'm not going. I decided the Montrose Institute is not someplace I want to be."

Trinity sat up straight and turned to look at the grinning man behind the wheel. "Really, Jake?"

"Really."

Chapter 25

Rifkin Forrest stared at the heavy teak door that his newest nightmare and his son had just walked through. He leaned back and closed his eyes. Somehow or other, Sarabess had convinced him that Trinity Henderson would never return. And if she did, it wouldn't be the real Trinity Henderson. Sarabess had been so utterly confident, so sure, he'd bought into it.

Not more than five minutes ago, the young woman who was never supposed to return had indeed done so. Sarabess's daughter had sat across from him. Even if he'd never seen her before, he would have recognized the likeness to Sarabess and Harold Windsor. She even had the same nose as young Emily. He felt unnerved when he thought of her unblinking intensity as she stared at him so defiantly.

Jake had looked so smug. So angry. How in the hell had he found the young woman after all these years?

He needed to think. To decide if Sarabess had lied to him. His insides started to crumble at the thought. Money. It always came down to money. Sarabess loved money.

He'd chosen to ignore that little quirk in his princess's personality.

Rifkin opened his eyes when he heard the faint sounds of foot traffic. The end of the day. They were all going home to their private lives. Once, a lifetime ago, he'd done that. At the end of the workday, he'd pack up his briefcase, say good night to everyone, and go home to his wife and son and a wonderful dinner. Things had changed with the speed of light when he became besotted with Sarabess Windsor to the exclusion of all else. He'd lost his wife and son's love and, worse, their respect. Yes, it had bothered him, but it hadn't lessened his feelings for Sarabess. She'd been like an addictive drug. He lived to hear the sound of her voice, to feel her hands on him. To this day, his addiction hadn't lessened one iota. The bottom line was he could deny her nothing.

He thought then of all he'd lost because of Sarabess. His wife Nola, who had looked at him with her soft, accusing eyes. Not that she'd ever said a word. She was too much of a Southern lady to admit her husband had eyes for someone other than his wife. He thought about how relieved he was that day at the cemetery when he had said his final good-bye to his son's mother.

He supposed, in a way, he was no better than Sarabess Windsor when it came to money. He'd fully expected to inherit the vast Granger fortune, which should have come to him at his wife's death, but that hadn't happened. The big house and everything else had gone to Jake. Everything. Even a percentage of the firm's revenue went to the Granger coffers. Nola's final payback for all those silent years. He busted his ass, got a salary and a bonus at the end of the year, and that was that. He knew the whole town whispered that Nola Granger might have kept her lip zipped when it came to her husband's indiscretions but in the end had the last laugh. Which, they said, was just another way to skin a roving tomcat.

Rifkin thought about his bank balance and his portfolio, neither exactly robust. As long as he kept working, drawing a salary, he could live out his days and retire in comfort. Of course he would have to downsize considerably. But didn't most people downsize when they retired? He could still keep up his membership at the club, dine out five nights a week, keep his fancy car, and make his insurance payments. He could move out of the town house he had rented when Jake kicked him out of Nola's, now Jake's, house, and get a smaller house, one in the historic district. He would, after all, have to keep up appearances. Instead of a full-time, live-in housekeeper, he would have someone come in a few days a week, or maybe just one day a week, to tidy up after him. A housekeeper was part and parcel with keeping up appearances. If worse came to worst, he could do without a housekeeper and learn to cook. If his investments took a downward turn and he had to eat in, as opposed to dining out, he could always say cooking was a secret passion. Cookbooks weren't expensive. He knew how to follow directions.

Exactly where did Sarabess Windsor fit into this scenario? She didn't. Rifkin felt sick to his stomach at the thought.

How silent the building was. Spooky, actually. He should gather up his things and leave, but he felt glued to his chair.

Rifkin's gaze settled on a pile of folders his secretary had brought in at around three thirty. He'd looked at everything and grown so light-headed he had to sit down. Mitzi and her goon squad of lawyers and accountants had been hard at work. Everything in regard to Sarabess was in a holding pattern until Mitzi's lawyers and judges gave the okay to move forward. Sarabess was not going to like this. Not one little bit. And, of course, she would blame him. He knew he'd stand there like the ninny he was and take the abuse, not because he had failed Sarabess but because Sarabess had failed him.

Rifkin walked over to the portable bar and poured himself a generous amount of whiskey. He fished a few ice cubes out of the minifridge and plunked them into the squat glass. Until then, he'd never felt the need to take a stiff belt before heading off to Windsor Hill.

As he sipped the powerful drink in his hand, he looked around the walls at all of his diplomas, his law degree, his awards, many of which were from the town council. His gaze settled on his law degree and how much it meant to him. His eyes burned, and his throat felt like it was on fire. Mitzi could, if she wanted to, complain to the Bar Association. She'd threatened it many times. This just might be the time she'd follow through on her threat. He knew if he got down on bended knee and begged her, she'd turn a deaf ear. When Mitzi Granger hated, she hated all the way. She would never believe he wasn't part of Sarabess's schemes. Never in a million years. As far as he knew, he'd broken no laws, had never abused his profession. A lawyer could do only what his client asked of him. Sarabess would never put his professional reputation in danger. Would she?

Rifkin bolted out of his chair. Would she? Until this very moment, he'd never questioned the legality of Sarabess's actions. As he'd told Sarabess, the will had bothered him from the beginning. It still bothered him.

Well, he'd know soon enough if it was a forgery because Mitzi's bloodhounds were on the case. Accordingly, the court had sent over two other folders, one about the trust fund, with a letter saying Mitzi had filed the necessary papers for Trinity Henderson to receive her trust fund in January when she turned thirty years of age. The other folder concerned Windsor Hill, and included a letter that said Mitzi had filed an eviction notice on Sarabess Windsor on behalf of Trinity Henderson Windsor.

A fax had come through from the Medical Center an hour earlier saying that one Trinity Henderson would be having her DNA processed. Mitzi's lawyers included a form asking Sarabess to give a sample of her DNA for comparison.

Rifkin laughed bitterly. Like that was really going to happen. In the end, it really wasn't going to matter, since Harold had lived with Mitzi for fifteen years. She would have samples of his DNA for comparison. He laughed again. Not only was the dark stuff going to hit the fan, it was going to splatter in all directions.

He hated clichés, but he knew there wasn't a snowball's chance in hell that

Sarabess would remain as the mistress of Windsor Hill. How was he going to tell her? How would she be able to walk away from the house in which Emily's spirit dwelled? How?

Rifkin got up to refill his glass. He added only one ice cube.

Emily.

He wasn't proud of the fact that he had detested the little girl who had such a claim on Sarabess.

How well he remembered the day Jake had dug in his heels, bellowing at the top of his lungs that he was not going to the Hill. And no amount of cajoling could shake the boy's decision. Jake had blasted both his father and Nola about Emily and Sarabess Windsor. What had he said that day to his son? Oh, yes, "That will be enough of that, young man. You need to learn compassion, and you will do as I say." Jake had told him to go to hell.

Nola, in her usual soft and gentle voice, reprimanded their son for his choice of words and the disrespect he'd shown his father. Then she looked her husband in the eye, and said, "Do not ever tell Jacob he has to go to Windsor Hill again, Rifkin. I will not have my son spit upon; nor will I have him bludgeoned with toys by that child. As you know, two weeks ago he had to have two stitches because Emily threw a tantrum. Do not ever bring the subject up again."

Sarabess had called him a wimp that day when he told her Jake wouldn't be coming to the Hill again, per his mother's orders. Or was it a twit? She'd said a lot of things that day, and he'd stood there and taken it. Secretly, he was glad that Jacob didn't have to entertain the mean, nasty child. He told himself he had to forgive Sarabess because just as he could deny her nothing, she could not deny her sick child anything.

Rifkin filled his glass for the third time. He knew he was drunk, and getting behind the wheel was not an option. He would have to order something to eat and then sleep on the couch in his office. He'd done it before on late working nights. He felt relieved that he was drunk. At least he could put off his confrontation with Sarabess until tomorrow. Maybe he'd get drunk then, too. Hell, he could turn himself into an alcoholic and never have to go to Windsor Hill again.

Rifkin held his glass aloft. "Here's to you, Mitzi, may you burn in hell for ruining our lives! No, no, I didn't mean that. May we *all* burn in hell for what we did to that little girl!" he blubbered.

Sarabess looked at the beautifully appointed table, at the candles that had burned halfway down, at the exquisite tureen that sat in the middle of the table. The salads were wilted, the delectable dinner rolls cool now and getting hard around the edges. She slid back her chair and got up. Obviously Rifkin wasn't joining her for dinner, even though she'd expected him promptly at six thirty. Cocktails on the verandah were a must when Rifkin came to dinner. Then dinner was served at seven. It was already seven thirty.

Her anger verged on rage as she left the dining room to storm down the hall to a small room in the back of the house that had once been her husband's office. She wasn't angry at the wasted food, the half-burned expensive candles, or the fact that she was wearing a new dress. She was angry that Rifkin hadn't even given her the courtesy of a phone call to say he would be late or not coming for dinner. It never once occurred to her that something might have happened to the man everyone thought she loved. Maybe

she did love him. She wasn't sure about anything lately.

Sarabess looked down at the antique
French phone. She tapped her manicured
nails on the desk as she debated calling
Rifkin. She needed to give him a piece of her
mind. First she called Rifkin's cell phone, but
there was no answer. Rifkin always answered his cell phone. At times she thought
the miserable thing was glued to his ear. She
then called the land line in his rented town
house. She didn't bother to leave a message. Her last phone call was to the office,
where Rifkin's personal line rang seventeen
times before she broke the connection.

Rifkin was never more than a phone call
away. Never. She could count on one hand
the number of times in over thirty years that
she had not been able to reach him. It finally
dawned on her that something might be
wrong.

Did she care if something was wrong with
Rifkin? Not really. Unless whatever was
wrong affected her in some way. "Rifkin, you
are becoming tiresome," she murmured.

Perhaps it would behoove her to check on
Rifkin, particularly at this point in time. It
took all of ten minutes for Sarabess to con-

vince herself she should get in the car and drive to Rifkin's new place. It, she told herself, was the decent thing to do.

It was almost dark when Sarabess parked her car in front of Rifkin's town house. It was totally dark, unlike the other houses on the block. His parking space was empty, too, so obviously he wasn't home. There was no point in getting out of the car to ring the doorbell.

Maybe he was working late. As long as she was out and about, she might as well check out the office, since it was less than five minutes from the town house. A worm of fear crawled around her stomach as she brought her Mercedes to a stop in the office parking lot. She sighed with relief when she saw Rifkin's car in his designated parking space. She got out, locked the car, and headed for the office door that she hoped would be unlocked. It was.

Sarabess entered, crossed the lobby, and headed down the hall to Rifkin's suite of offices. She smelled the alcohol as she opened the door. And there was her love, sprawled across the couch, one leg hanging drunkenly over the edge. One shoe was on, one was on the floor. He was snoring lustily.

She wrinkled her nose as she crossed the Oriental carpet to his desk. She sat down and reached for the pile of folders. Each folder had the word URGENT scrawled across the front in red ink. She looked over at Rifkin, who hadn't moved. He was still snoring loudly. Sarabess wrinkled her nose at the horrid alcohol smell. To her knowledge, Rifkin had never been drunk in his life. Once he'd said, "What's the point in drinking yourself into oblivion? The only thing you succeed in doing is losing control, and I have no intention of allowing that to happen. I am, after all, a lawyer."

Sarabess sniffed. Obviously, it *had* happened. It was also obvious that the urgent folders were what had caused him to ignore his own words and get drunk. She looked over again to see if there was any change in Rifkin's position before she opened the files. Maybe she should take them with her. It would serve him right. Yes, yes, she would take them with her. Let him wake up and wonder who had burglarized his office.

Sarabess, the folders under her arm, walked over to the couch. Rifkin stirred, but he didn't wake up. Spittle dribbled down his chin. How unmanly. How distasteful. She shuddered as she let herself out of the office.

Twenty minutes later, Sarabess Windsor was sitting on her verandah with a glass of sherry in hand. She looked out at the star-filled night and wondered how many more nights she'd be able to sit out at Windsor Hill. In front of her, as far as she could see in the velvety darkness, the fireflies glowed and made intricate patterns as they flitted from place to place. As a child, Emily had demanded she catch them for her the way the other kids did at night while she watched from the upstairs verandah. She'd obliged, and when the little creatures didn't light up in the daytime, Emily had squashed them, spewing words of hatred at everything and anything.

The sudden, crazy urge to run about the garden to catch the tiny insects was so powerful, Sarabess found herself digging her heels into the fiber carpet to still the impulse.

Trolling for past memories was so painful. So very painful. Harold had seen Emily squash the fireflies and gave her a swat on her rear end. He'd called her heartless and

mean-spirited. Emily had pitched a hysteri-
cal fit, but Harold hadn't backed down. To
add insult to injury, he'd grabbed Sarabess's arm and dragged her out to the hallway, where he gave her a blistering tongue-
lashing. They'd both said so many hateful
things to one another that day. Things that
could never be unsaid, things that stayed
with both of them.

Of course, immediately after Emily's tantrum, she'd started to run a fever, which
peaked at an alarming 105 degrees, thus demanding hospitalization. Harold had weighed
in one more time by saying it was her punishment and Emily's as well for what she'd done.
More hateful words had been said and in her
heart of hearts, Sarabess knew her husband
was right, but she would never admit it, not
even for all the gold in the world.

A lone tear of self-pity rolled down Sarabess's cheek when she remembered Harold's
last words that night as he left the hospital:
"You're responsible for what that child has
become. You single-handedly turned her into
a little monster. You, Sarabess, you did that.
Mark my words, the day will come when you
rue what you've done to that child. God will

make you pay for Trinity, too. That's the legacy I'm leaving you."

Another tear rolled down Sarabess's cheek. She sniffed. Harold Windsor was dead, and she was alive.

Sarabess sniffed again as she rose from the wicker chair and went indoors. She had some reading to do that couldn't wait.

"I never did love you, Harold Windsor," she whispered to the quiet house. "I did love all the money that came with you, though."

Chapter 26

Jake rapped sharply on the door of the little cottage. He could hear Lucky barking as the door flew open. "Right on time, Jake!" Trinity trilled, happy to see her old friend.

Damn, she looks good, Jake thought. And she was wearing his favorite color—yellow. He wondered how she thought he looked. He decided he didn't want to know. "Well, today is *the day.* You've had a whole week to think about this trip up to Windsor Hill. Are you sure you still want to go up there to confront your mother?"

Trinity held the screen door wide-open. Elway streaked toward him and started to purr. "Want some coffee? I just made it."

Jake would have agreed to anything to be in her company. "Sure. Black. I think this guy misses me. I sure miss him."

Trinity reached up to the cupboard for a cup. "I know what you mean. I miss Lucky when he's with you. We're going to have to come up with some kind of plan where these two animals are concerned. It's becoming stressful."

"I know. We'll work on it. I don't suppose the DNA report came back, did it?"

"Not to me. I suppose, knowing Mitzi, she might have them send her the report. It's only been a little over a week. Have you heard anything from your father?"

"No, not a word." Jake looked around and sniffed. On the windowsill was a clear glass with several sprays of Confederate jasmine. "My mother always kept a jar of jasmine in the kitchen and in all the bathrooms. I like it. When Mitzi visits she fills up a jar, then I forget about it." It was all such meaningless talk when he really wanted to ask Trinity if she had feelings for him. He wondered if he asked her outright what she would say. A second later he stunned himself by giving voice to the thought.

Trinity blinked. Then blinked again. "Isn't that kind of like asking a girl if it's okay to kiss her?"

"I don't know, I never asked a girl first. I just kissed her."

Trinity smiled. "Well, there you go."

Jake felt stupid. "Is that a yes or a no?"

Trinity laughed again, then turned serious. "We have a lot of stuff to wade through, Jake. I don't think this is the time to let emotions cloud what's going on. Let's just say we liked one another a lot when we were kids, and right now we're exploring . . . looking into . . . thinking about . . . considering . . ."

"And . . ." Jake said, although he rather thought he had his answer. "I wonder how many coats of paint are on this table. This stuff is really old," he said, looking around the kitchen. "Old means a musty smell. Maybe that's the reason for putting Confederate jasmine all over the house. Mitzi says old means character. I think old just means smelly. I like modern stuff."

"I like comfortable. I don't care if it's old or new as long as it's comfortable. But to answer your question, I think there might be eight or nine coats of paint on this table. We're just jabbering here because . . . (a) we don't want to talk about us or (b) we are putting off our visit to Windsor Hill as long as we can."

All Jake heard was the word *us.* He felt hot all over. He saw that she was waiting for his response. "Probably a little of both." Jake was saved from saying anything further when Elway jumped up on his lap.

"What are you doing this evening, Trinity?"

"Nothing, why?"

"Would you like to go with me to the PBA carnival on the grounds of the YMCA?"

"Oh, do they still do that? Lillian and John used to take me. Yes, I would love to go," Trinity said, excitement ringing in her voice. "Do they still do the potluck supper first?"

"If you want to eat, you have to bring something made from scratch. I always take a string bean casserole. I got the recipe off a can of dried onion rings. One of Mitzi's coupon specials. I have canned string beans and onion rings stacked up from the floor to the ceiling. Takes ten minutes. What are you going to take? I think the rule of thumb is you pretty much eat what you bring and pay ten bucks for the privilege."

Trinity giggled. "Guess some things don't really change except the price of admission.

I'll stop at the grocery store on the way back from Windsor Hill. I think we've procrastinated long enough. Let's go and get it over with. How do I look, Jake?"

"You look like a million bucks. And, you look just like Harold Windsor's daughter. Does that answer your question?"

Trinity's head bobbed up and down. "I'm nervous. I've dreamed of this day for years and years. In that dream I was always mean and spiteful. I always told Mrs. Windsor off, told her what I thought of her. Told her about how mean Emily was. In my dreams I always wanted her to cry, to say she was sorry. She never did. In the dreams she always stared through me. Even though they were dreams, I knew she was comparing me to Emily, and I came up short. When I woke up, I was always crying. Maybe I shouldn't go there. You can handle all the legalities. I might make matters worse by confronting her. Sarabess Windsor might be my biological mother, but she's not my mother. Does that make sense, Jake?"

"Absolutely." They were both on their feet, no more than an inch apart. Jake wanted to kiss her so much that his lips went numb with the thought. Instead, he hugged her.

She smelled all summery and powdery. If he waited one more minute, he knew things would get out of control. "Let's go. If you change your mind on the way, I'll simply turn the car around."

"Okay. What if she refuses to see us? Won't I look like a fool if that happens?"

"It will never happen. Trust me, that woman is more curious than you are. Maybe *curious* isn't the right word. We'll never know if we don't give it a shot. Do you want to stop by Mitzi's for some moral support?"

Trinity sighed. "Yes, let's do that. Maybe she won't want me to go up to the Hill. She didn't seem too keen on the idea when I first mentioned it."

"I think that might have changed. I know she's had several run-ins with my father since you got back. It's that damn will he tried to push through probate, the one Sarabess says she found at the eleventh hour. Mitzi's hired on a whole team of hand-writing experts from all over the country to prove that the will is a forgery. By now she might have something concrete from all those private detectives she hired."

Trinity settled herself in the car. "Why is Mitzi doing all this, Jake?"

Jake turned the key in the ignition. He waited for a squirrel to scurry across the gravel road before he inched forward. "She has to do it. She said if it turned out to be true that Harold made a later will, then her whole life was a lie perpetrated by Harold. I don't think Mitzi, tough as she is, could handle that. She'd have a major meltdown. I think I would, too. She's going on what Harold said, when he said it. They both loved you. She's doing her best to do what Harold asked of her." He turned to look at her. "How do you feel knowing Emily was your sister?"

"Knowing doesn't change who she was. I often wondered if somehow she knew about me. Maybe that's why she was so mean and hateful to me. Grown-ups aren't always as careful as they should be when they talk with young children in the background. I have to think that Mrs. Windsor and Harold had conversations about me. Emily, as you know, was a bit of a sneak. She was just unpleasant with you and the others. To me she was absolutely hateful. That had to come from somewhere, so my guess would be she knew. In her later years, before her death, I can picture her throwing me in her mother's face. I'm just rambling here, trying to make myself feel better. Yes, Jake, I have feelings for you," she blurted.

Shazam! He grinned from ear to ear as he maneuvered his car to the entrance of Mitzi's property. "We'll talk about that later, okay?"

"Okay, Jake," Trinity said in a shaky voice. "Okay," she repeated.

Jake laughed. He reached for her hand and squeezed it.

Mitzi was waiting on the front porch. Something tugged at her heartstrings when she saw the two people she loved most in the world clasp hands and race to the porch.

"I have news!" she said.

"We're going to Windsor Hill. Does your news have anything to do with our going there?" Jake asked. "Did the DNA results come back?"

"No to the DNA. Sit down, sit down." She bellowed for Celeste to bring some sweet tea. The words were no sooner out of her mouth when Celeste appeared with a tray holding a cut glass pitcher of tea with matching glasses filled with ice.

Celeste sniffed. "The heat index is 104 today, so drink the tea before the ice melts."

Mitzi rolled her eyes but did gulp at the sweet tea, as did Trinity and Jake.

"Tell us what your news is," Jake said.

"It seems that the agency I hired is not the only agency looking for Grace Finnegan. Just for the record, Grace Finnegan remarried—a man named Gerald Tanzy. She never went back to work, so that's the main reason we weren't able to find her until now. Way back when I tried to find Trinity, I asked the agency to locate the nurses who were in attendance at Trinity's birth, but nothing showed up anywhere. That's for starters."

"Is it my father who's hired them?" Jake asked.

"No, it's Sarabess Windsor herself. It seems she got herself a lawyer in Columbia when you turned her down. The law firm, in turn, hired an investigative agency to try and locate the same woman we're looking for. Neither detective divulged any details to the other, or so I've been told. The thing is, they keep bumping into one another. My guy wants to know what he should do. Here's something else to think about. Sarabess Windsor pawned a whole sack of jewelry in Columbia. She needed cash, I guess."

Jake grimaced. "And you know this . . . how?"

Mitzi preened with importance. "Emma Lannigan's sister-in-law's cousin's best friend's next-door neighbor works in the estate jewelry section of some big store up there. What do you think of that?"

Jake shrugged. Trinity just looked blank.

"It means Sarabess still doesn't want anyone to know what she's up to. In order to hire that lawyer in Columbia, she needed cash for a retainer. Since I won't give her any, as per Harold's instructions, she had no other choice but to sell off some of her jewelry. Harold always said she had a ton of it. Every time something went wrong on the Hill, the only way he could keep peace was to show up with some kind of bauble. She still thinks everything is a big secret. Your father hasn't been up to the Hill in over a week. That's my news. What's yours? Celeste!" she bellowed.

Celeste appeared with the ice bucket, plopped it down on the table, and left. Mitzi refilled the three glasses. "Speak, nephew!"

"I'm taking Trinity up to Windsor Hill. She

wants to meet her mother. I will be acting as Trinity's attorney in case . . . just in case. If you have anything to say, say it now, Mitzi. By the way, are you going to the carnival tonight?"

"Go for it, nephew. Of course I'll be there. I'm taking my tofu, bean sprout, goat cheese casserole."

"Uh-huh," Jake said.

Trinity took the high ground. "I bet people fight over it, Mitzi."

"Yeah." Jake guffawed. "They fight to get out of the way so no one puts it on their plate. Mitzi and the police chief eat it all. The chief is sweet on Mitzi." Jake roared again.

Mitzi flushed a bright pink. "Go!" she said imperiously.

As the couple scampered down the steps, Jake said, "I love to throw Mitzi for a loop once in a while. I wish she'd give the chief the time of day. He's a really nice guy, a widower, and he truly does like Mitzi. I think she's playing it cool."

"And you're playing Cupid, is that it?" Trinity giggled.

"If anyone deserves happiness, it's Mitzi. I hope it happens for her sake. If it's meant to be, it will be. It's that simple, so it doesn't matter what I want. It has to be what Mitzi wants. Just pay attention tonight at the carnival, and you'll see what I mean. The whole town turns out."

"Even Sarabess?" Trinity asked.

"Usually. She meets up with my father once she gets there. But she arrives alone and drives off alone. Whatever the hell that means."

"You have to let it go, Jake. You can't move forward unless you do."

"I will when this is all resolved. I promise."

Sarabess Windsor felt as if her heart was going to leap right out of her chest. She stared at the phone in her hand as though it were a rattlesnake. She shuddered and dropped it. She didn't bother to pick it up. Finally, when she was able to control her chaotic thoughts, she moved quickly to her bedroom, where she gathered up her purse and car keys. She was on her way to the door when she stopped and headed back to the bedroom, where she dumped out the contents of her jewelry box into a black velvet bag. She rummaged in her lingerie drawer for the small packet of money that was left from the jewelry she'd sold weeks earlier. It wasn't much, fifteen thousand, but it would have to do. With the jewelry, surely it would be enough.

Her destination: Charlotte, North Carolina, where Grace Finnegan, now Grace Tanzy, lived. Time, the agency said, was all-important because another detective agency was searching for the same person.

She'd asked all the right questions. Did the subject know anyone was looking for her? The agency she'd hired had guaranteed secrecy but couldn't vouch for the rival agency. She'd scribbled directions to the small lakeside community.

All Sarabess Windsor could think was that finally, finally, she was one step ahead of Mitzi Granger. How it was all going to turn out was anyone's guess. If nothing else, she had time on her side even though the clock was ticking. If she could just get to Grace before Mitzi did, she was confident she could make the whole situation work for her. She had to make it work for her. She had no other options.

Sarabess looked down at her watch. If she drove five miles over the speed limit, she could be in Charlotte in three hours, three and a half at the most.

UP CLOSE AND PERSONAL   425

Mitzi, she knew, would be at the Police Benevolent Association's carnival that evening, where she would reign supreme. Hours. She had hours.

If things worked out, she could make arrangements with Grace, get in her car, and be back home before Mitzi sicced her bloodhounds on the former nurse.

With nothing to do but think, Sarabess let her thoughts go to Rifkin and the strained relationship that had developed over the past week. He hadn't come up to the Hill, but he had called. Each message was more derisive than the last. The weird thing was, he'd never asked about or accused her of taking the files from his office. That he did not accuse her was probably a bad thing, but she refused to dwell on it. Rifkin was expendable.

She shuddered when she thought about the last thing he'd said to her earlier that morning: "You aren't going to like living in that clapboard house in Hilton Head, Sarabess. The roof leaks, the plumbing needs to be replaced, and the wiring is ancient. There won't be a gardener or a cook. No one to pick up after you. There is no garage, so where will you store all Emily's treasures? The furniture is old and smells like mildew. The front steps need to be replaced. There's also a termite problem. I told you years ago to take care of the house, but you didn't want to spend the money. We're talking a hundred thousand easily. And that's just to get it into *livable* shape. This is what you're looking at if you forged Harold's will, assuming you aren't in jail. Are you listening to me, Sarabess?"

Oh, she'd listened all right. And then she'd lost her breakfast. These things couldn't be happening to her. They just couldn't.

She hadn't forged Harold's will. She'd simply traced his signature. Tracing a signature was different from forgery. Way different.

As she turned onto the interstate, she thought about something she'd either read or seen on television. No person ever signed their name the same way twice. If they didn't have the original signature, they wouldn't have anything to compare it to. She remembered clearly tearing up the letter Harold had written to the newspaper complaining about something or other but never got around to mailing. She'd torn the paper into hundreds of little pieces and flushed them down the toilet. Down the toilet in Harold's old bathroom. Would they take the pipes apart? She chastised herself at the silly thought.

But if Mitzi found Grace Tanzy before she did, everything would come to a screeching halt.

Like she was really going to live in that ramshackle house in Hilton Head with all those nasty golfers hitting balls through people's windows. It was out of the question. Simply out of the question.

Sarabess turned on the car radio. The soft music soothed her frazzled nerves.

As Sarabess tooled along listening to golden oldies, Trinity Henderson and Jake Forrest were ringing her doorbell, only to be told the mistress of the house had left and didn't say when she would return.

"I guess it's true, since her car is gone," Jake said.

"We'll come back tomorrow then," Trinity said, relief ringing in her voice.

Chapter 27

Jake Forrest looked down at the string bean casserole with satisfaction. All he had to do was sprinkle a little shredded cheddar cheese on top, and voilà! He slid the glass dish into the oven, adjusted the temperature, and dusted his hands with glee. Trinity was going to be so impressed with his culinary expertise. Twelve minutes, and his creation would be ready for delivery. He popped a beer and carried it over to the kitchen window. For the first time he realized how dark it was and that it was raining.

Rain, if it continued, would force the evening's festivities indoors. The carnival rides for the children would have to shut down, and all the scheduled races would likely be cancelled. The event would still be a success, though. The whole town turned out for the Police Benevolent Association because it was such a worthy cause. Somehow or other Mitzi had enticed Hootie and the Blowfish to perform, guaranteeing a sellout for the PBA.

Jake continued to watch the heavy rain batter his kitchen window. He told himself that it could just be a typical summer thunderstorm, and things would clear up by six o'clock. The field would be a little muddy, but so what. The electricity to the rides would be grounded, and they would operate safely. Hootie would play in the gym. The games of chance each had their own little canopies. He crossed his fingers the way he had when he was a child that the rain would let up for the evening. He wanted to walk around the fairgrounds with Trinity. He wanted to throw the baseballs and win her a big prize. He wanted to do all the things with her that he'd dreamed of doing when he was a kid.

The timer on the stove pinged. Jake swigged the last of his beer before he tossed the bottle into the recycle bin. He felt like beating his chest when he withdrew his casserole from the oven. The cheese and onion rings were a rich golden bronze, and the cheese was still bubbling. Perfection.

Jake looked at the clock. He had forty-five minutes until it was time to leave to pick up Trinity. Enough time to shower, shave, dress, and feed the animals.

A half hour later Jake was dressed in new khakis, a white Nautica shirt, and Docksiders. Looking in the mirror, he winced and flinched as he smacked aftershave onto his cheeks before combing his wet, unruly hair, which, when dry, went in all directions. His mother once said his hair was the very bane of her existence. He looked at the array of men's cologne on his vanity, all compliments of Mitzi. She said women liked men to smell as good as they did. Mitzi was usually right, he thought grudgingly. He opened a bottle that guaranteed he would smell like a woodsy glen, whatever the hell that was. He did smell, though, so that was a plus. He sailed down the hallway to the kitchen, where he settled his contribution to the potluck dinner in a cardboard carton.

Jake turned on the TV to the Disney Channel for the animals, handed out treats, and was good to go. Outside, he was delighted to see that the rain had let up. Things might be soggy, but at least the carnival would go on. Happier than he'd been in a long time, Jake settled the box with his casserole on the passenger seat. Trinity would have to hold it on her lap for the short drive to the YMCA.

Ten minutes later, Jake whipped around the corner and into Ardeth Gamble's driveway, where he cruised around back. She was waiting for him on the little porch, wearing pumpkin-colored capri pants with a matching top. She carried a pair of sneakers, but straw sandals with little pumpkin flowers were on her feet. Elway would love them. Jake knew all about capri pants because one day Mitzi had been wearing a pair, and he'd busted her chops by laughing and asking if the manufacturer had run out of material. He'd gotten a fashion lesson on the spot.

Trinity looked beautiful.

Breathtaking.

Gorgeous.

Stunning.

His love.

Maybe.

Maybe by the end of the evening he'd be

able to think of them as a couple. He wondered what she thought of him when he got out of the car to open the door for her. He didn't have long to wait.

"Hmmm, you smell good, Jake."

Damn, Mitzi was right. "Do I smell like a woodsy glen?"

"Huh?"

"Never mind. You smell pretty good yourself."

Trinity burst out laughing. "It's called Sensi by Giorgio Armani. BL gave it to me for Christmas last year. She said it was guaranteed to reduce men to hopeless, lovesick fools."

"I think I'll stick with smelling like a woodsy glen. The earth, you know," Jake said breezily. "How is BL's mother?"

"I called her a little while ago, and she said she's doing quite well. Joyce is really a nice lady. I'm glad she has a companion these days. With BL going off to Philadelphia, she won't be alone. I really miss them both. They just included me in their lives and made me feel like family."

"It happens like that sometimes. I guess you don't miss the Kolinas?"

"Not one little bit. I know that sounds terrible, but that's the way it is."

"I understand. Are you looking forward to the evening?"

"Oh, I can't wait. Lillian always used to bring me. She'd bake two sweet potato pies. She'd carry one and let me carry the other. I felt so important."

"In case you don't know, Mitzi arranges the whole affair. I think she runs the police department. That's why I think she and the chief are sweet on one another, even though she denies it. She outfits and oversees the K9 Division. She just bought them a new cruiser when the other one conked out. She got the department to allow the seniors to use their golf carts on the secondary roads. She knows every family in the department. You should see the Christmas party she throws for them. It's a real wingding. I guess you can tell how much I love her. I probably don't tell her that often enough."

"You should tell her every day. Just think what it would be like if you had no one to say that to, like me."

"Oh, jeez, I didn't mean . . . I'm sorry . . ."

Trinity smiled. "It's okay, Jake. Listen, do you remember the year Mrs. Windsor brought Emily to the PBA in her wheel-chair? She brought these exquisite little cakes with frosting umbrellas. They were all different colors, and she put them in the middle of one of the long tables. Then she made an announcement saying Emily had helped the cook make them. I wanted one so bad, but Lillian wouldn't let me take one. Did you get one?"

Jake listened to Trinity's tone of voice more than the words. He remembered the night very well. Even at that age he'd had a hate on for Sarabess Windsor and her whiny daughter. He knew his answer was important to Trinity. "My mother said I could have one later, but I never did get it. I remember Emily pitching one of her fits and her mother taking her home. I don't ever remember seeing them there again. Mitzi told me that in later years, after my mother passed away, Sarabess would still see my father. Hell, everyone in town knew what was going on."

"It was so strange," Trinity said. "No one ate them. They were such perfect confections. At the end of the evening when Lillian was helping to clean up, they were still sitting in the middle of the table. No one knew what to do with them. I'm not sure, but I think they threw them away."

Jake let out a loud sigh. Obviously, he'd given the right answer. He sighed again. "For a lot of years I searched my heart and soul in regard to Emily. This is weird, but a few months ago, I was playing golf with Dave Dougherty and he brought up Emily. He asked me if we were rotten kids with no compassion in regard to Emily. Then we met up with Dina and Zack for a burger, and we got to talking about Emily again. The consensus is . . . was that if Mrs. Windsor wasn't hovering around, Emily was okay. She only pitched those fits when her mother was there. Too bad we never figured that out when we were kids. If we had, all of our lives, including Emily's, would have been a lot happier. You and I were her direct targets. You know that, right?"

Trinity's head bobbed up and down. "I think she knew, Jake. I really do," she whispered.

Jake reached out to take Trinity's hand in his. "It would certainly explain her attitude where you and I were concerned. Think about it, Trinny. There we were, rough-and-tumble kids, climbing trees, going a mile a minute day after day, swimming, riding our bikes, always together, and all she could do was watch and ride around in that fancy pony cart. She used to kick that poor little pony."

"I don't want to talk about this anymore, Jake. Ohhh, valet parking! How grand."

Jake climbed out of the car, relieved that the conversation about Emily Windsor was over. He opened the door for Trinity before he turned his car keys over to a young kid whose jeans were so baggy they were about to drop to his ankles any minute.

Holding their potluck contributions, Jake and Trinity crossed the parking lot, where games of chance already had long lines of customers who couldn't wait to try their luck. They climbed the steps to the main door that one of the seniors held open for them, pointing toward the gymnasium where the potluck dinner was being held.

"Ohhhh, it's just like I remember. There's so much food. Everything looks so good. I wonder if Lillian will be here. Oh, look, there's Mitzi. My, she looks . . . resplendent in that . . . that dress. She fixed her hair, too." She winked at Jake. "You might be right about the chief. She hates getting dressed up. Be sure to tell her how beautiful she looks."

Mitzi swooped down on them, hugged them, and waved around the gym. She was wearing a powder blue linen dress that hugged her bony frame. "The seniors decorated it. Aren't the crape myrtles gorgeous?"

Jake looked around at the spectacular blooms in the heavy urns, borrowed, he was sure, from Dyle's Funeral Home. The tablecloths matched the blooms to perfection.

Conversation was at an all-time high as the citizenry of Crestwood mingled and ate, and children whined as they tugged at their parents to go out to the parking lot so they could buy their tickets for the carnival rides.

"You look great, Mitzi. The chief will be after you all night."

"You stop that 'chief' business right now, darlin', or I will swat you right here in front of everyone. Help yourselves. The food all looks wonderful. Joe Lewis donated all the colored plates and utensils. Actually, all the paper products. Being mentioned in the

PBA Newsletter is still as important as it was twenty years ago. Just so you know, my offering is all gone." She cackled.

"Uh-huh," Jake said as he heaped his plate with Trinity's cheesy bake. He watched as she took a like amount from his casserole. "Aren't you eating, Mitzi?"

Mitzi looked around at all the food. "Darlin', I can hear arteries snapping shut right and left. I ate some of my own food. You two are entering the sack race, aren't you?"

"Yep, got a new partner this year. She's a pro. I think we might win this year." He turned to Trinity, and said, "I came in second three years in a row. Never been first."

"What's the prize this year?"

"A twenty-five-dollar gift certificate to Enderlin's Pharmacy. For sundries, not prescriptions. So that's twelve-fifty for you and twelve-fifty for me," Jake said to Trinity.

She giggled as she dumped her empty plate into the trash bin.

"Oh, look, there's Fernando!" Jake lowered his voice to a bare hiss. "I swear that guy *trains* for this event. He's not eating. That's it, that's it. We just stuffed ourselves and look at him. Lean and fit. See that smirk! I'm telling you, he *trains!*"

"Get serious, Jake. No one trains for a sack race," Trinity retorted, laughing.

"He does. I know it. The winner gets his picture on the front page. Above the fold. What better advertising could you want? And it's free. Freddie sells cars." He turned to Mitzi. "Who's his partner?"

"Why are you asking me, nephew?"

"Because you know everything, that's why. Who is it?"

"Some female," Mitzi responded vaguely, her gaze sweeping the room.

"A name. I need a name, Mitzi."

Mitzi whirled around. "All right, all right, his partner is Amanda Pettijohn."

Trinity's eyes narrowed at the mention of Amanda Pettijohn. Emily Windsor wasn't the only one who had tormented Trinity's childhood. Amanda had made fun of her clothes and her hair, and called her Bugs in front of the other kids because of her protruding teeth. Amanda Pettijohn, the prettiest girl in class, the best-dressed girl, the girl with the most spending money. The girl all the boys fawned over. *That* Amanda Pettijohn.

"Really," Trinity said sweetly. "Well, then, Jake, we'll have to get serious and kick some ass. I want that prize." Then she smiled.

Jake thought it was the most evil smile he'd ever seen in his life.

"You better get going; Arnie Wilson is calling the race. You have to sign up and pay your money. I have fifty bucks riding on you two, so don't shame me. Go! Go!"

Jake reached for Trinity's hand. Together they galloped out of the building and across the parking lot to the field where the sack race was being held. "Are you any good at sack racing, Trinny?"

"Does the pope pray? Every year at the end of the school semester, BL's school held a Teacher-Student Day. I always sack-raced with BL, and we always won."

"I don't know, Trinny. Freddie's pretty good. He probably gets a bonus if he wins. Amanda has those long legs. Jeez, I didn't mean that the way it sounded. What I meant is they are both long-legged, and they'll make a good team. But . . . she can be a bit of a klutz. For whatever that's worth," he mumbled under his breath.

"They just want to win to show us up. I'm

making this personal," Trinity said, smiling at Jake.

It was that same evil smile he'd seen earlier. Jake shivered as he plunked down his money and signed their names to the entry forms. Trinity accepted the sack and moved off.

Jake ran after his partner. He looked around at the gathering crowd. The Adult Sack Race was the stellar event of the evening. He felt jittery as he looked around at his competition. It looked like this was the biggest year yet as far as entries went.

Arnie Wilson, a melon ball of a man wearing a baseball cap, brought his golf cart to a stop at the starting line. On the seat next to him were a megaphone, a high-beam searchlight, and an air gun. He took his job seriously and brooked no nonsense from the contestants. He hopped out of the golf cart, a sheaf of papers in his hands. He handed out sticky-backed numbers to the contestants, which they plastered on their chests. Jake accepted his #5 and looked around to see where Fernando was. Ah, #8.

"There are forty-two entries this year. I want to wish you all luck. Listen up, everyone. This year the race is a little different due in part to the weather conditions. We've added two new obstacles. Nature provided the third obstacle, and you'll just have to deal with it. There will be a three-foot-high scaling fence. It's slatted for footholds. There is also a scaling wall, which will be the major obstacle. As I said, nature provided the third obstacle. It's a huge hole filled with water. The rain managed to fill it up. You cannot go around it, and you can't jump it, either. If you lose your sack at any point, you are automatically disqualified. Raise your hand if you understand all these new instructions." Eighty-four hands shot upward.

Mitzi appeared. "You can win this, Jake! I'm counting on you! The seniors are betting on you, too."

Jake panicked. "All of them?"

"Yep. Five hundred dollars total. You can't let them down!"

The gathering seniors let out a collective whoop of encouragement.

"Just what I need, Freddie and the pressure of the seniors."

Trinity looked at her partner. Her face was grim, her jaw determined. "I don't think you heard me back there. I said I want to win this race. If we lose because of you, I'm going to kick your butt all the way to the Georgia border. Read my lips, Jake. We have to win this race!"

"I hear you," Jake said, stepping into the sack. "Do your part, and I'll do mine. Freddie is the only one we have to worry about. Tomorrow I'm going to start *training.* I think he looks worried. Yeah, yeah, he looks worried."

"You talk too much, Jake. We're talking performance here."

Jake cringed. If there was one word that men all over the world dreaded hearing, *performance* was it, and it didn't matter in what context. He looked over at Trinity. There was that evil smile again. He took a second to wonder if she practiced in front of a mirror. Jake knew that there was more riding on this race than the twenty-five-dollar gift certificate to Enderlin's Pharmacy. He also knew his ass would be grass if they didn't win. He squared his shoulders and stiffened his right leg.

Arnie held up his air gun, the megaphone to his lips.

"On the count of three. One! Two! Three!" The air gun popped. And the race was on.

A shout of "Go! Go! Go!" filled the air.

"Freddie is going to hop. I know his MO."

"Stop worrying about Freddie and worry about me. You and I are evenly matched leg-wise. We can run if we do it in sync. We can win this thing. We have to act as one. You listening to me, Jake?"

"Yeah, yeah. Let's do it!"

Amid the cheers and catcalls as the citizenry of Crestwood rooted for their favorite couple, the contestants raced off. "It's okay to fall or trip, you just can't lose the sack," Jake gasped as he tried to see where his archrival was. Way ahead of him. He groaned.

"You wimping out on me, Jake?" Trinity snarled.

"Hell, no. I'm trying to catch up to Freddie. Listen, I want to win this thing as much as you do. We have five hundred bucks riding on us. Mitzi will strangle me if we lose. Can't you go any faster?"

"No, I can't go any faster, the mud is slowing us down. It's caking up on the sack, and that makes it heavier to drag. Do you want to try hopping for a while? Two couples are down, there goes your friend Freddie," Trinity gasped.

Arnie's high-beam light circled Freddie and Amanda as they struggled to get to their feet, the sack intact. The delay allowed Jake and Trinity to forge ahead.

"Oh, my God, it's starting to rain," Trinity squealed. "Will they call it off?"

"Do pigs fly? The short answer is no."

Mud splattered upward and hit Jake square in the face. He used his free hand to wipe it away but it was a losing battle. They slogged on, Arnie's light guiding them, as the rain started to come down in torrents.

The mud-soaked sack was so heavy, it was like dragging a bag of rocks. Jake felt so winded, he tripped and went facedown in the mud, but his grip on the sack was tight.

"Get up! Get up, Jake. There's the fence. We have to get over it."

Jake tried to rub the mud away from his eyes. He held his face up to the rain to wash it away. He saw Freddie's long legs hovering over him, then he was gone. He struggled to his feet, dragging Trinity with him. "He's got a lead on us. We climb the fence and do a backflip. Don't lose the sack. Amanda won't be able to work in sync with Freddie. Like I told you, she's a klutz."

He was wrong. Amanda and Freddie scaled the fence like Olympic champions.

"Oops, there goes Pete, he lost his sack. Bernie is still in the race. He's good, too. He sells insurance. He wants that photo above the fold. We can do this, Trinny. We got out of sync there for a few minutes. I guess Amanda trained with Freddie. We're gonna win, stop worrying." He wished he felt as confident as his words sounded.

They were right alongside Freddie and Amanda when Arnie Wilson's searchlight lit up the scaling wall. Jake heard Trinity gasp. He could feel her shaking next to him. "What? What?"

"I . . . I don't think I can do that. I don't have any upper-body strength. All my power is in my legs and thighs. I can see the toeholds, but I don't think I can climb, hold the sack, and hang on with one hand. I can't do it, Jake. I'm sorry. I didn't think it was so high."

Jake was stunned, Trinity admitting she couldn't conquer something. "The hell you can't. I'll hold the sack so that will give you two hands to hold on to the top. We back-flip the way we did with the fence. Now do it!"

Trinity gave it everything she had, but her hands were slick with mud, preventing her from getting a firm grip on the top of the wall.

With the driving rain, Jake couldn't see Freddie and Amanda, but he could hear them moaning and groaning as they fell into the mud at the base of the wall. He and Trinity joined them a moment later. "You have to do it this time, Trinny. I'm getting tired. This damn sack feels like it weighs fifty pounds."

Tears burned Trinity's eyes as she struggled to her feet. She'd never been a quitter, and this sure wasn't the place to take a hit. She gritted her teeth, found the toeholds, and reached the top, Jake encouraging her. She struggled for a death grip with both hands. She looked over to see Jake grinning at her. "They're right next to us. Sync, we're in sync, so focus and go over, I'm right beside you. Now!"

They were on the ground, the sack around their ankles, but they hadn't lost it. Arnie's searchlight lit up the area to reveal Freddie and Amanda dropping to the ground.

"Hey, Arnie, how many are still in the race?" Jake shouted to be heard over the driving rain.

"Todd Mitchell is coming over the wall now. Tony Malfi is right behind him. Here comes Donny Gamble. You're in the lead, Jake. Well, you were in the lead," Arnie said, as Freddie and Amanda took off, hopping ahead like jackrabbits.

"You just had to chitchat, didn't you? We had the lead and you decide to have a gabfest! We lost *seconds.* Next year I'm getting a new partner," Trinity snarled.

"Oh, yeah, who couldn't make up her mind to scale the wall? It sure wasn't me. We lost *minutes* while you dithered around," Jake snarled in return. "We can do this. We still have a chance. Now we run. Freddie is hopping. Todd, Tony, and Donny are no threat. Anything goes, right?"

"Yeah. Yeah, do you have a plan?"

"Let's startle them. Throw them off balance. We're almost abreast of them. You take Amanda, and I'll take Freddie. Think of something to yell that will make them falter. You got it, Trinny?"

"Yep."

Jake was so busy listening to Trinny yelling about false eyelashes that were hanging down Amanda's nose and the hair extensions that were coming loose he forgot what he was going to say to Freddie. It didn't matter because Amanda Pettijohn let go of the sack to check out her eyelashes and hair extensions, and both of them went down fifteen yards from the finish line.

Jake could see Mitzi and the seniors in the light from Arnie's searchlight. The geriatric set were whistling and clapping as they crossed the finish line.

Jake and Trinity dropped to the ground and rolled over and over in the mud and rain. Both of them were laughing so hard they couldn't stop.

"We did it, Jake. We won! We get our picture in the paper tomorrow. I think you're going to have to help me get up."

Jake reached out for her hand to pull her to her feet.

"Great race, Jake. I'll get you next year," Freddie said, holding out his hand.

"Not a chance. I'm going to *train.*"

Amanda weighed in. "Didn't think you had it in you, *Bugs.*"

"What did you say, Amanda?"

Jake sucked in his breath as he stepped backward while Trinity advanced a step.

"I said I didn't think you had it in you, Bugs."

"Hey, Freddie, you might want to take a step backward. You're about to see some serious attitude," Jake said, as Trinity pushed him out of the way with her elbow.

"I thought that's what you said," Trinity said sweetly, the evil smile in place. "Do you remember on November 12, 1987, I told you what I would do to you if you ever called me Bugs again?" Amanda Pettijohn looked blank, then fearful. "Well, that time has arrived."

Mitzi, the seniors and the rest of Crestwood watched in awe as Trinity's fist shot forward to land squarely on Amanda's nose. Freddie caught his partner as she reeled backward. "Call me that again, and I'll give your dentist a nightmare. Send me the bill for your nose job."

Jake watched in awe as his love smacked her muddy hands together and advanced toward him. "You know what, Jake Forrest? I think I'm in the mood for . . ." She leaned over to whisper in his ear.

Jake's eyes almost bugged out of his head at what he was hearing. "Well . . . I . . . Hey, I'm up for . . . *Let's go.*"

Jake did his best to wink at Mitzi, but his face was caked with mud as he dragged his partner toward his car amid cheers and loud clapping.

"Hey, darlin', you forgot your prize!" Mitzi shouted as she waved an Enderlin's Pharmacy gift certificate in a ziplock bag and caught up to them.

"I have my prize," he yelled, pointing to Trinity.

"So I see, nephew. So I see," Mitzi whispered.

Chapter 28

A light mist was falling when Sarabess turned off the paved highway to a shale road that led to Tall Pine Lakes, where Grace Tanzy lived. She switched on her fog lights to better see through the mist.

A quarter of a mile down the road, Sarabess turned off her fog lights and coasted to the side of the bumpy road. She'd stopped for gas five miles back and asked for a map. The young gas station attendant had gotten her one, and she hadn't even gotten out of the car. She hoped he wouldn't remember her if anyone came around asking about strangers in the area. He might not remember her, but he would remember the car because he had commented on it. She wasn't going to worry about that, though. She turned on the map light to see the lake area on the map better. It looked to be one big circle, with maybe a hundred homes surrounding the lake. All the homeowners would have an unobstructed view of the water. Sailboats, power boats, and canoes would be more plentiful than cars.

Grace Tanzy lived at 62 Lake Drive. Sarabess folded the map and stuck it in the glove compartment. Her fog lights back on, she drove slowly as she strained to see the numbered mailboxes. It was eerie, she thought, with the sodium-vapor lamps casting halos of light around the monster lake. *Why,* she wondered, *would someone want to live in a place like this?* She just knew the house would smell like marshland, and, undoubtedly, mildew would be a problem.

Sarabess switched to high beams to see the mailboxes. There it was, #62, sandwiched right between #60 and #64. She cut the ignition and got out of the car.

Where were the night sounds? The tree frogs, the crickets, the evening birds, the children? Maybe this was a retirement area. How desolate, how strange. Where were all the people who lived there? It was still early in the evening. Was it the fine mist soaking

everything that was keeping people indoors? Not that she cared. Still, it would be
better for her if no one saw her.

Sarabess stood at the end of a flagstone
walkway littered with pine needles. She
could smell them. She reminded herself that
pine needles were slippery when wet and
moved accordingly.

Grace had said her husband wanted a
lakeside cottage. This one looked like a normal house in a residential development.
Sarabess looked around the large front
porch, which was covered with colorful
plants and trailing vines that worked their
way around the pillars holding up the roof.
There was a swing with colored cushions at
one end of the porch. The other end of the
porch held a glider, two chairs, and a wicker
table.

The front door was wide-open, the screen
door showing a lighted hallway, indicating
that someone was home. Sarabess looked
around for a doorbell, found it across from
the handle on the screen door. She pressed
it with her thumb.

She heard a voice call out over the sound
of a television game show. Suddenly, the
volume was lowered, and the porch light

came on, bathing Sarabess in a golden glow.

They stared at one another through the fine mesh of the screen door. Grace's hands flew to her chest. "You!"

"Aren't you going to invite me in, Grace? I've come some distance to find you, and it is rather wet out here. I don't think you want your neighbors to know your business. Voices do carry in the night, you know."

Grace made no move to open the screen door. "What . . . What do you want?"

She hasn't aged well, Sarabess thought. The sacklike dress did nothing to hide the weight Grace had put on over the years. Her hair was gray and pinned back with bobby pins, something that startled Sarabess. She didn't know they still made bobby pins. She could see scruffy slippers on the woman's bare feet. "I want to talk to you about something, Grace. Will you please unlatch the door?"

"You . . . You said we would never see each other again. What do you want to talk to me about?"

"Something important. Don't make me take other measures, Grace. Now, please, open the door."

Grace Tanzy reached up to unlatch the screen door. Sarabess opened it and quickly stepped inside, where her nostrils flared at the scent of cinnamon and Bengay. It was humid in the house, the outside marsh smell invading the room. And yet people loved living lakeside. Well, they could have it.

As Sarabess walked past her hostess she got a whiff of the woman's body odor. She started to breathe through her mouth. With any luck she would be gone in fifteen minutes, sooner, if she could manage it.

There was no offer of refreshments, and if there had been, Sarabess would have declined. She perched gingerly on the edge of a sofa that had seen better days. Grace lowered herself into a recliner. "I kept my end of the bargain, so why are you here? How did you find me?"

"I hired a detective agency. I didn't know you had remarried. Did your husband get to . . . enjoy this little section of paradise? Your children, did they all finish at those fine Ivy League colleges, and are they settled in good jobs?"

"My first husband died, and yes, he loved it here. My second husband died, too. My children graduated and have families. We visit from time to time."

"That's nice, Grace. I'm so glad I was able to help. Now, I need *your* help. I want you to consider it part and parcel of our original deal. Tell me, dear, that you understand what I just said."

"I'm not an idiot, Mrs. Windsor. You want me to do something. What is it?"

"If anyone comes around asking questions, I don't want you to talk to them. Just say you have nothing to say, and you know nothing. I don't want you to give up any information."

"Why?" Grace asked bluntly.

Sarabess bristled at the woman's defiant tone. "Because I said so, Grace. By the way, where is Louise Amity?"

Grace Tanzy's head jerked upright, her shoulders stiffening. "Now, how would I know that? I didn't even know the woman. If you remember correctly, she was a patient, not a friend." Her tone was cold enough to chill butter.

Is that attitude I'm seeing here? "Oh, I think you do, Grace. I think you kept track of Mrs. Amity because you worried that one day I would show up on your doorstep.

Well, that day has come, and I'm here. I want to know where my daughter is. My *real* daughter. In the interests of keeping you abreast of what's going on in my life, some imposter has shown up on *my* doorstep claiming to be *my* daughter. She wants to claim her inheritance. Now, we both know that's impossible, don't we, Grace? Now, I'm asking you nicely, where is my real daughter? I'm willing to pay for the information."

Grace finally found her tongue. "So, this is . . . was always about money. You must be a very heartless woman, Mrs. Windsor. The word *inheritance* leads me to think there must be a great deal of money at stake. Are *you* following *me,* Mrs. Windsor? How much?"

"I don't think that's any of your concern, Grace. I'm prepared to pay you fifteen thousand dollars for information as to how I can find Louise Amity. Otherwise . . ."

"You'll tell my family and my neighbors, is that it? I don't think so. You don't want me to talk to anyone about that time. You want me to keep your secret. If there's one thing I learned in this life, it is that you never make a threat unless you're prepared to carry through on that threat. We both know you don't want anyone to know about your dirty little secret."

"*Our* secret, Grace. You're the one who switched the babies, not me. It's your word against mine."

"You paid me to do it."

"In cash. Cash cannot be traced. I'll say you blackmailed me."

"Now, that's a stupid statement if I ever heard one," Grace sputtered. "Why would I blackmail you?"

Why indeed? Grace was right, it was a stupid statement. "I'll think of something. I always travel with a lot of cash. You could have stolen it. Who do you think the authorities will believe? Now, where is Louise Amity?"

Grace Tanzy pursed her lips into a thin, tight line as she looked around the cluttered living room, which was filled to overflowing with garage sale treasures. Fifteen thousand dollars would go a long way to supplement her Social Security payments. She might eventually even buy some things for her grandchildren if they turned into more loving kids, which was unlikely. *All the more for me,* she thought. "It's not nearly enough, Mrs. Windsor," she said coldly.

"How much is enough, Grace? Give me a number."

"Two hundred thousand," Grace whipped out, her eyes cold and hard.

Sarabess didn't blink an eye. "Fine, but you'll have to take it in jewelry. I don't carry that much cash around with me. Is that acceptable? I have it with me in the trunk of my car. Do we have a deal?"

Grace felt her shoulders sag. *Why not?* She'd taken money from this woman once before, even though she hadn't done anything wrong except to lie. With the money and the jewelry she could move into a nice condominium in town if she wanted to, get away from the white trash that lived at the lake. She could sell the dump to some dumb Yankee whose idea of retirement was living lakeside. Still, she hesitated. But then her greed finally won out. "All right, Mrs. Windsor, we have a deal."

"If you go back on your word, I will press charges. At that point, I really won't care. Do we understand each other?"

"Yes, we do. I take the money and jewels, and if anyone comes around asking questions, I say nothing. Or, am I supposed to say something you want me to say?"

"All you say is you delivered the baby to the Hendersons. Your husband was ill, and you wanted to move here because it was what he wanted, and it's cheaper to live in the South. Now where is Louise Amity?"

"Show me the money and the jewels. While you're getting it out of your car, I'll look for her address."

Sarabess was so light-headed she thought she was going to faint. The trip had been worthwhile after all. She nodded as she got up off the couch. When she reached the front porch she saw that it was raining harder. She would be drenched in minutes. But it wasn't like she had a choice. She called out, "Do you have an umbrella, Grace?" She heard the woman laugh. She took the woman's response as a no.

She was back in the house within minutes. This time she let herself into the house and walked toward the shabby living room. She wondered if the house in Hilton Head that Rifkin had referred to looked and smelled like this one. She perched on the end of the sofa and opened the velvet sack in her hands. The packet of money came out first, then four diamond bracelets, followed by three pairs of earrings and one ring. She lined everything up on the glass-topped coffee table.

Sarabess looked up when Grace returned to the room with a ragged slip of paper clutched in her hand.

"How do I know this jewelry is real?" Grace demanded.

"Because I wouldn't be caught dead wearing costume jewelry."

Grace reached for one of the diamond bracelets and scratched the glass on the coffee table. Satisfied, she scooped up the jewelry and the money. She dropped the slip of paper in Sarabess's lap. "You can go now, Mrs. Windsor."

"How do I know Mrs. Amity still lives at this address? Don't try giving me a pig in a poke, Grace, because if you do, I will be back. I found you this time, and even if you move I will find you again."

"She sends me a Christmas card every year. She's lived there for a very long time."

Sarabess flew out of the house but not before she looked down at the address on the paper, committing it to memory. Louise

Amity lived at 187 First Street in Perth Amboy, New Jersey.

Grace Tanzy stood in the doorway watching the expensive Mercedes drive away. Then she started to laugh until she couldn't catch her breath. What a kick in the pants this visit was. She had two hundred thousand dollars sitting on her coffee table and she hadn't given up *her* secret. Now *that* was a pig in a poke. She started to laugh again.

"Yes, Mrs. Windsor, I switched babies just the way you told me to, but then I felt so guilty, and Louise Amity was such a fine person, I simply couldn't do that to her, so I switched them back. I suspect, Mrs. Windsor, the imposter on your doorstep is your very own flesh-and-blood daughter, and you don't even know it."

Grace Tanzy moved then as fast as she was capable of moving. She packed two huge suitcases and carried them out to her battered SUV, where she stowed them in the cargo hold. She'd have to think about purchasing a new vehicle one of these days. When she left in the morning her neighbors would think she was simply going out to run an errand. If they even bothered to wonder.

She tidied up her house, unplugged all the appliances, and dumped the contents of her refrigerator into the trash can at the curb. She felt pleased that the trash company would pick up the trash in the morning. One of her neighbors would return the can to the backyard. If not, oh, well, trash simply wasn't on her list of things to worry about.

Next, she called her four sons and told each of them she was taking a trip up North to visit friends and an aging aunt who was in a nursing home. Not that they would care. She knew they hated their obligatory monthly visits as much as their children hated coming to the lake. They should only know where she'd gotten the money for those fancy college educations she'd provided them. Well, she couldn't cry over spilled milk.

When she got settled, she'd send each of the grandchildren fifty dollars—maybe.

In the morning she would call the power company, the water department, and the phone company to turn everything off. She'd send each company a check, and if she ended up with a credit, so be it. She'd stop at the post office and ask them to hold her mail until she returned. Things like her life insurance, her car insurance, and her single credit card could be dealt with when she was settled. That left her automatic deposit at the local bank for Social Security. She could also take care of that with a phone call.

The last thing she did before crawling into bed was to tear all of Louise Amity's correspondence into tiny pieces. She flushed them down the toilet.

In the morning she would head west to Gilbert, Arizona, to visit a childhood friend she'd stayed in touch with over the years. She'd leave a note tacked to her front door saying something like, BE BACK IN JANUARY.

The neighbors she was semifriendly with would be talkative to anyone who came around asking questions. She'd always talked longingly and lovingly of New York and her life there before the move to the lake, so it would be logical for them to assume that was where she had gone. If those detectives came looking for her, they would probably be told she was going North.

Grace's last conscious thought before drifting off to sleep was to remind herself to make the bed in the morning. She wanted to leave her house neat and tidy. Rather like a mystery novel, where the main character leaves a neat, tidy house behind before she disappears off the face of the earth. She shed all her years of guilt as she fell into a deep, dreamless sleep. A sleep that was finally peaceful.

It was noon of the following day when Sarabess Windsor turned on the ignition of her rental car. The map the agency had given her was spread out on the passenger seat. The agent had said it was twenty or so miles to Perth Amboy. All she had to do was get onto Route 1 and follow it. The agent had advised her to stop at a gas station in Perth Amboy to ask for directions to the house she wanted to go to. It sounded simple enough. She was allowing anywhere from thirty minutes to an hour for the visit, another half hour for the trip back to Newark Airport in time for her flight back to Charleston at five o'clock. She'd be back on Windsor Hill by nine this evening—with no one the wiser about her travels.

Nervous with all the eighteen-wheelers on the highway, Sarabess stayed in the right lane, her thoughts all over the place. Was she doing the right thing? Would she somehow be found out? Would she have to go to plan B? She choked up when she realized she didn't have a plan B.

Had Grace Tanzy called Louise Amity? She wished she knew the answer to that question. Maybe she should call Rifkin. To say what? She wished she wasn't so tired, so jittery. Even though she'd gone to bed at one in the morning, she really hadn't slept. She didn't feel as sharp and alert as she usually felt in the morning.

Maybe what was bothering her was the note her housekeeper had left on her night table saying a young man and a young lady had stopped by the house right after she'd left. Young people never made it up to the Hill. It had to be Jake Forrest and Trinity Henderson. She wondered if Rifkin knew, and if he did know, would he tell her? She'd been stunned that he hadn't called at all yesterday. What did his silence mean?

Twenty minutes later, Sarabess left the turnpike, following the directions on the map. She stopped at the first Shell station she saw to ask for directions. She repeated the directions twice to make sure she wouldn't get lost.

As she drove down Smith Street she realized the town couldn't compare to picturesque Crestwood in any way. She wrinkled her nose at the industrial smell. Paying careful attention to the street signs, she turned right on Elm Street, then left on Market. She slowed till she came to First Street, where she made a right-hand turn. She slowed even more, crossed Gordon, then pulled to the curb and parked. She got out of the car before she could change her mind and walked across the street to #187.

It was a two-story brick house with a big front porch. She was surprised to see the wooden ramp alongside the steps. The wood on the ramp looked new. There were no paddle fans, and no hanging plants, no flowers in clay pots to greet visitors. *How depressing,* she thought. *I can hardly wait to leave this place.*

There was no doorbell, only a lion's-head door knocker. She raised it and let it fall. The sound was so loud, she jumped backward. A moment later, the door opened. A pleasant-looking woman with wire-rimmed glasses looked at her curiously.

"Yes, can I help you?"

"I'm looking for Louise Amity." As she said

this, two young boys zipped down the sidewalk on their bikes, screaming and yelling at one another. A huge black dog raced after them, barking his head off.

"Well, you found her. I'm Louise Amity. What can I do for you? I should warn you, if you're selling something, I'm not buying it."

Sarabess forced a smile to her lips. "I'm not selling anything, Mrs. Amity. My name is Sarabess Windsor. You and I were in the same maternity ward in New York. I was talking to Grace Tanzy the other day, and she said you lived here. I'm on my way to New York and thought . . . I don't know what I thought," she finished lamely.

"Well, for heaven's sake, come in, Sarabess. Would you like a glass of ice tea or some coffee?"

Sarabess felt relieved because obviously Grace had not called Louise about her impending visit. "That would be so nice, thank you. I just wanted to say hello. I don't have much time. I . . . I rarely do . . . spontaneous things like this. How is your child? Was it a boy or a girl?"

"A girl. Her name is Marion. You had a girl, too, as I recall."

Sarabess trailed behind the woman through

a cluster of rooms that were neat, tidy, and clean, to a pleasant kitchen of red brick, green plants, and stainless-steel appliances. The round table looked to be antique oak. A white ceramic bowl full of pink and white peaches sat in the center. "This is a lovely kitchen."

"I like to cook. I retired a year ago, and it's become my hobby. It's just my daughter and me these days. My sons live in New York, and my husband passed away five years ago."

"Your daughter lives with you? That must be comforting."

Louise Amity was still an attractive woman with curly hair and a slim figure. Her eyes were a deep, serene blue behind the wire-rimmed glasses.

She lowered her voice, and said, "Not really. My daughter was in a terrible car accident two years ago. She's wheelchair-bound. I wasn't . . . what I mean is . . . I didn't anticipate this happening. I had plans to travel and enjoy my retirement. That isn't possible now. Marion works from home on her computer for a bank. I'm just so glad they didn't abandon her. She has a caregiver who comes by twice a day but I still have to be here. How is your daughter?"

The young woman is a cripple. "I'm so sorry. My daughter is fine. I'd like to meet your daughter. Is that possible?"

"Of course." Louise looked up at the kitchen clock. "I'm running a little late today. It's lunchtime. Ah, I hear her coming."

Sarabess was glad she was sitting down when the wheelchair whirred into the room. She was so shocked at the young woman's appearance she had to grip the edge of the old oak table with both hands. She fought to keep herself under control.

Introductions were made. Marion was gracious, Sarabess polite and formal.

This isn't my daughter. Not this red-haired, blue-eyed girl who is a replica of her mother. She has the same nose, the same chin, the same eyes. There is no way on this earth that Louise Amity could deny this young woman is her offspring.

Sarabess felt sick to her stomach. She struggled for something to say. "Do your brothers have red hair, too?" she asked inanely.

"Do they ever!" the young woman responded cheerfully. "We all look like each other. When we were younger, people thought we were triplets. We're all just a year apart.

Mom, where's that picture of the three of us you took on Easter?"

"Right here on the fridge." Louise reached for the photograph and handed it to Sarabess.

The young woman was right. They did look like triplets. "Where . . . Does red hair run in your family?"

The wheelchair moved toward the refrigerator. Marion opened the door and withdrew a bowl of tuna fish. "From my dad. Everyone in my dad's family had red hair. What's even funnier is all three of us have the same birthmark in the same place. Isn't that amazing?"

Sarabess swallowed hard. "Yes, it is amazing."

The young woman rambled on. "Dad always used to tease Mom by saying she could never sell us off to the gypsies because of our red hair and identical birthmarks."

Sarabess forced a sound she hoped would pass as amused. "I guess you'll never have to have a DNA sample to prove your identity."

Louise waved her hand airily. "Oh, we already did all that. After Marion's accident, when the doctors thought she might need a bone marrow donor, all those tests were done on all of us. In the end she didn't need to have it, thank God. I understand it's painful."

She's not my daughter. Where is my daughter? I have to get out of here.

Sarabess looked down at her watch. "I really have to leave. I hope I haven't held up your lunch. It was so nice to meet you, Marion, and to see you again, Louise. No, no, don't get up, I can see myself out."

Outside in the bright sunshine, rage coursed through Sarabess. *You bitch! You living, lying bitch. You never switched those babies at all. You took my money and lied to me. Last night you lied to me again,* she seethed.

The reality of her situation finally hit Sarabess as she got into the rental car and drove away. Trinity Henderson really was her flesh-and-blood daughter. The daughter she'd borne so Emily could live. For fifteen years she'd lived right under Sarabess's nose. She was right there, down the hill from the big house all those years! "And I never knew, never suspected," she muttered to herself. No wonder Mitzi Granger didn't have a problem with the girl's providing her DNA. It also explained Rifkin's sudden change of attitude.

The daughter she'd never loved, the daughter she'd given away, the daughter she'd denied was back in town and soon to be in control of the Windsor fortune.

Chapter 29

The Honorable Judge Malcolm Collins looked at the man sitting across from him at the luncheon table. He hated meetings like this one because they always ended on a note of sadness or anger. Today, he suspected, he would see both emotions. He was still trying to figure out why he had personally arranged this luncheon. He didn't particularly like Rifkin Forrest as a person, but he respected his capabilities on the golf course and in the courtroom. He liked the young buck, Jake, who had some piss and vinegar to him. At the core of his dislike for Rifkin Forrest was Sarabess Windsor.

Back in what he called the old days, he'd counted Harold Windsor a friend. Not just a friend but a special friend. Even then he knew there was trouble in Harold's marriage. He'd done his best to counsel his friend without stepping over the line. Harold's passing had left a void in his life.

Judge Collins knew he was treading a fine line, possibly even breaking the law. With just five months to retirement, he knew he had to be careful. He looked at the bourbon in his glass, then at the Perrier in Rifkin's glass. He downed the bourbon in two long swallows. He told himself he needed to fortify himself for what was to come.

He thought about the late-night visit from Mitzi Granger. They'd sat on his front porch watching the fireflies until well after two in the morning. He'd listened raptly to her tale, most of which he knew. The recent events had left him speechless. So speechless, he'd had no trouble promising her he would talk to Rifkin today. And here he was.

"Nice day," Rifkin said. "We should be on the golf course."

The judge nodded. He toyed with the knife on his bread plate. "I invited you to lunch to give you a heads-up, Rifkin. I know I'm stepping over the line, but I don't want to see you . . . go to prison for something you didn't do. Now, if you did do something, I wouldn't lift a finger to help you. I want to believe that you've been acting ethically in regard to your client. I'm speaking of Sarabess Windsor.

"I suppose you're wondering how I come by my knowledge. Everything I know I got from Mitzi Granger. For whatever her reasons, she didn't want to talk to you and asked me to do it. I said I would. I cancelled my court this morning to verify everything she told me, which I am about to share with you. Do I have your full attention, Rifkin?"

"You do, Your Honor," Rifkin said coolly.

"It seems that the young girl named Trinity Henderson is Harold and Sarabess's biological daughter. She had a DNA sample taken. It matched up with her parents. By parents I mean Sarabess and Harold Windsor. The will you filed for probate is not authentic. Mitzi hired the best handwriting experts in the country. The signature was traced onto the will. I don't know the intricacies of how it all works, but what I gathered was that there were small, infinitesimal breaks in the signature. Meaning it wasn't a free-flowing signature. My question to you is: Did you know about this or did you act in good faith when you filed that will?"

"I acted in good faith, Your Honor. I won't

say I didn't have a suspicion or two. My client said it was authentic, and I had no reason to believe otherwise. Sarabess and I, as you know, have a history."

The judge buttered his roll and popped it in his mouth. He looked up when the waiter set down a plate with a delicious-looking fillet of red snapper, sweet potato curls, and a corn mango relish. He nodded to acknowledge Rifkin's words.

Rifkin looked at his own plate, wondering if he would be able to choke down the food. "What do you want me to do, Your Honor?"

"For starters, I think you need to speak with your client. Tell her she's standing in some seriously muddy water. Withdraw the will from probate and let the other will stand. I can take care of that end of it with a few colleagues' help. Mistakes happen all the time. As to the young lady, I don't know what to tell you other than she will take possession of her trust fund sometime in January. In the end, Harold took care of things.

"In addition, Rifkin, this is just some personal advice, not from a judge but from an old man who is a father and a grandfather. Make things right with Mitzi and your son. Do the right thing, but first take off your blinders. You won't be the first nor will you be the last person to have gone that route. Life is simply too short to be on the wrong end of the stick."

Rifkin Forrest felt his stomach start to cramp. His mouth was so dry he knew he couldn't eat the flaky fish on his plate. He'd be damn lucky if he could ever eat again. He gulped at the Perrier in his glass and felt it dribble down his chin. He dabbed at it with his linen napkin.

"I hear Jake and the Windsor daughter won the sack race at the PBA carnival last night. Saw their picture in the paper this morning. Young Trinity is the spittin' image of Harold, don't you think?"

Rifkin didn't respond. He gulped again at the water. He hadn't looked at the morning paper because he'd been too nervous about this command performance luncheon. He raised his eyes to stare across at the judge, who had just speared a chunk of the red snapper onto his fork. He managed a nod.

"I think we can keep this all quiet if you do what you have to do, Rifkin. I'll speak to Mitzi and tell her you're going to take care of things. Unless you want to tell her yourself."

Rifkin shook his head. "I don't mind stopping by and having a glass of sweet tea with her. I like that old house of hers. It's so full of animals that it makes you wonder how she has room for herself. Mitzi is one of a kind. Over the years you should have come to realize she doesn't make a good enemy. I guess you already know that, or else Sarabess Windsor blinded you."

Rifkin was stunned when the judge leaned across the table, his voice a bare whisper. "Man to man, Rifkin, I want you to listen to me. That Windsor woman has your dick in the wringer. Cut yourself loose before it's too late. I understand you probably have a lot of things to take care of, so go right ahead. I'll just finish my lunch and head on over to Mitzi's house." His fork in one hand, the knife in the other, the judge waved Rifkin away.

Rifkin stood up, looked down at Judge Collins, nodded, and made his way out of the restaurant. His mind was whirling and twirling like a windmill in a tornado.

Mitzi's front porch looked like a summer social, with her guests sipping beverages and fanning themselves with linen napkins.

The fans overhead whirred quietly, causing the fern fronds to dance in the breeze. The scent of the new-blooming gardenia plants at the base of the verandah wafted upward, the scent intoxicating.

The police chief, resplendent in his summer uniform, was sipping sweet tea in a rocker next to Judge Collins, who was on his third bourbon and branch water. Mitzi was sucking on a lemon ice pop when Jake and Trinity arrived, their faces wreathed in smiles, Lucky and Elway scampering up the steps ahead of them.

Mitzi gave the little bell on the table a vigorous shake. Celeste appeared like magic because she'd been listening inside the door. "I'll have a beer, Celeste." Jake looked over at Trinity who nodded. "Two beers, Celeste."

Mitzi eyed her nephew and said, "We have good news and some news that isn't all so good. But not devastating. The DNA is back, and you, my dear Trinity, now have undeniable proof that you are a Windsor. More specifically, you are Sarabess and Harold's daughter. I'm not sure what your name is, but I don't think that's something we have to worry about right now. You'll always be Trinity to me, my dear."

"What's the news that isn't all that good?" Jake asked as he tried to figure out if the chief was just visiting or if he really had designs on his aunt. He decided he would ask at some point. *Someone has to look after Mitzi,* he told himself.

Mitzi then sat down on a rocker next to the chief. "The private detective I hired called early this morning and said Grace Tanzy is gone. Obviously, the firm Sarabess hired got to Grace before my people did. The neighbors didn't know anything to shed light on the situation, but then my man did say they're an older, close-mouthed bunch. There was a note on the door that said she would be back in January."

Trinity reached out to touch Jake's hands, tears rolling down her cheeks. "I'm a person, Jake! I have a name! I can give Lisa Summers back her identity. Now I can finally go there and bury all . . . everything, where she's buried."

"Absolutely."

"I think this might be a good time to leave," the judge said. "If you give me a ride, Chief, I might be able to get in a few holes of golf."

The good-byes were brief and loud.

Trinity was still crying quietly. "I can't believe all this."

"Let me make it as real as I can. Wait right here," Mitzi said. She was back within minutes, a copy of Harold Windsor's will in her hands. She handed it to Trinity, who took it with trembling hands. "You need to read and understand what your father wanted, dear.

"Come along, Jake, let's give Trinity some privacy. Besides, I can use your help in the kitchen."

Jake recognized a ruse when he heard one. He followed his aunt into the kitchen. "Well, what do you think she's going to do?"

Mitzi shrugged. "For starters, I hope she boots Sarabess's elegant ass off the Hill. That's what Harold told her to do when she was a child. Not in so many words, but the meaning was clear. So clear, she remembers it with a great deal of precision. It's going to take a tremendous toll on her, Jake. Right now she's overwhelmed."

"I know, Mitzi. I think she can handle it. Let's talk about you and the chief."

"Let's not," Mitzi snapped.

"Is that your final word?"

"It is. What are you going to do about your father, Jake?"

"Dammit, Mitzi, what do you want me to do? He was never there for me. He betrayed Mom. He fought you tooth and nail and never gave you anything but grief. 'I don't know' is the best answer I can give you right now."

"The judge had lunch with your father today. As a favor to me to give him a heads-up on the will and the DNA. He said his opinion is that Rifkin didn't know the will wasn't real. He said he seemed stunned and didn't stay to eat. Sarabess duped him, too, Jake. I think I can almost understand your father these days. He feels for Sarabess the way I felt about Harold. Some people just love once in their lives. I think Rifkin and I have that in common. Does that answer your question about the chief?"

"He's a nice man, Mitzi. Don't deprive yourself of his company if you enjoy being with him. You're not getting any younger, you know."

"When did you get so smart, darlin'?" Mitzi sniffed.

"That night when you finally fell asleep ten years ago." Jake guffawed. "I think I'll go see how my girl is doing. She might need me."

"Ha!" Mitzi snorted. A moment later she looked up to see Jake standing in the doorway. "What?"

"She's gone. She took the car. I guess she took the will with her because it isn't out there. She went up to Windsor Hill, didn't she, Mitzi?"

"That would be my guess, Jake."

"I was supposed to go with her. I am her attorney."

"Jake, look at me. That child doesn't need an attorney for whatever she's going to do. I could be wrong, but I think this is something she needs to do alone. Don't be surprised if she never talks about it when she gets back."

"What if . . . ?"

"There are no what-ifs, Jacob. Now, feed all the animals while I go about my business. I have to get my newsletter ready for the seniors."

"Yes, ma'am," Jake said, saluting smartly as he got up and whistled for the animals, who came on the run. It was a zoo, but he welcomed the commotion to still his run-away thoughts.

Rifkin Forrest, briefcase in hand, rang the doorbell at the house on Windsor Hill, only to be told the mistress was in the garden clipping flowers for Miss Emily's room. "Now, why doesn't that surprise me," Rifkin muttered as he dropped his heavy briefcase onto a chair.

He descended the steps and walked around to the garden area. He saw her then and it was like a still from a magazine ad. His longtime love was wearing a straw hat with satin streamers billowing out behind her, the streamers matching the teal blue linen dress she was wearing with matching linen shoes. She picked and clipped, adding the blooms to a wicker basket. He observed her for a few minutes, peering over the top of his sunglasses. His heart kicked up a beat as he listened to her humming under her breath. She was acting as if she didn't have a care in the world. Damn, it was all so surreal.

Once, this fine-looking woman had been everything to him. He'd betrayed his wife and lost his son's love for her. In turn, she had never promised him anything, not even her love. He thought about the judge's words, his advice, and knew the aging jurist had meant well. *How could she do this to me? How? She did it because I allowed it to happen.*

Rifkin cleared his throat. Sarabess turned around, her face lighting up in a huge smile. "Darling Rifkin, I wasn't expecting you. It's too late for lunch and too early for dinner. Tea?"

"Business, Sarabess. Rather urgent, as a matter of fact." He couldn't help but wonder once more if he'd ever want to eat again.

"Well, in that case, I can finish this later. Like you always say, business is business, and it has to be taken care of. Do you want to conduct *business* in the study or on the porch?" Sarabess linked her arm with Rifkin's and smiled up at him. "I think the study then, it's becoming so humid out here one literally wilts. You look terrible, darling. Is something wrong?"

Rifkin didn't trust himself to speak. Instead, he freed his arm from Sarabess's arm to remove his sunglasses, which he stuck in his breast pocket. All the while Judge Collins's words kept ricocheting inside his head as he headed for the entrance to the back door, an indication that business would be conducted indoors.

"You certainly are surly this afternoon, darling. I don't see or hear from you in over a week, then when you do show up, you're cranky and out of sorts. Are you having trouble with Mitzi again? I wish that woman would just die and be done with it so she stops tormenting us."

They were in Harold's study. A comfortable room, a man's room. Rifkin wondered if Harold had hidden out in this very room to avoid Sarabess. He looked over at the door and had his answer. The solid mahogany door had what he knew was a titanium lock, the best and safest that money could buy. Yes, Harold had come to the study and locked himself in.

Sarabess let her impatience show. "Well, Rifkin, what is it?"

Rifkin excused himself to walk out to the porch to retrieve his briefcase. He was back within minutes. He busied himself by opening the case and pulling out papers, some of them bound in blue, others simply stapled. He stacked them into a neat pile and dropped them in Sarabess's lap. "How could you, Sarabess? How could you have used me like that?

"Malcolm Collins invited me to lunch to give me a heads-up. He's promised to keep things quiet if you withdraw the will from probate, saying you made a mistake. I hate to be so blunt, but they have you dead to rights. You could go to prison for doing what you did. All the handwriting experts' reports are in your hands. You traced Harold's signature. You would have been better off simply forging it. In addition to that, the DNA report came back on the young lady. Trinity Henderson *is* your daughter. You lose the estate and you lose your claim on your daughter's trust fund. The bottom line is you have to leave here. Unless your daughter is in a generous mood and allows you to stay on— something I don't think is going to happen. Mitzi will continue to pay you a monthly allowance per Harold's instructions."

"That was not what I wanted to hear, Rifkin. Why didn't you do something? Couldn't you have paid someone off? That's what you lawyers do all the time, isn't it? If that young woman is my daughter, then she will take care of me. After all, I am her mother. Daughters don't turn their backs on their mothers."

Rifkin threw his head back and laughed. "I think I can guarantee your daughter has a hate on for you that will simply not permit such generosity on her part. Didn't you turn your back on her? Didn't you throw her away? Did you lift a finger to find her when she ran away? Oh, yes, you gave birth to her, but you did so for all the wrong reasons. She knows because I'm sure Mitzi told her everything. There will be no forgiveness there, my dear. In case you've forgotten, Mitzi is writing her memoirs. I would imagine your name is mentioned in every chapter."

"So you say. Mitzi this, Mitzi that. I am sick to death of that woman," Sarabess snarled.

Rifkin ignored the woman screeching at him like a fishwife. "If you want me to take you to Hilton Head, give me a call. You need to make arrangements very soon, Sarabess. Your days of being Queen of the Hill are over. All your daughter has to do is call the authorities, and—do I need to remind you?—Mitzi basically runs the police department. They will be here in a heartbeat and personally carry you out. They will stretch that ugly yellow tape around the premises, and you won't be permitted to set foot on this property. You could be taken to jail, then on to prison."

"And you would allow that to happen?" Sarabess shrilled.

"It's out of my hands, Sarabess. You might want to give some thought to that shrine you maintain upstairs." Rifkin turned and walked to the door with the titanium lock.

"Where are you going? You come back here right this instant, Rifkin Forrest. Go to that . . . that young woman and beg her. Do whatever it takes to let me live here."

"I told you, it's out of my hands, Sarabess." Rifkin turned in the doorway, and said, "You backed the wrong horse, my dear. I think your daughter turned out to be a wonderful person. She's going to marry my son, if I'm not mistaken. They'll have children. You're going to miss out on all of that, but I have no intention of joining you. I'm going to beg my son and that young lady to allow me to be part of their lives. If I have to grovel, I will."

"Now why doesn't that surprise me? The next thing you're going to tell me is you and

Mitzi Granger are bosom buddies. Well, who needs you? Go on, leave. I never want to see you again."

Rifkin chewed on his lower lip. How bitter the words sounded. He felt like she'd gouged out a slice of his heart. "The address to the house in Hilton Head is in that pile of papers you're holding. Good-bye, Sarabess."

Sarabess looked around, panic flooding her body. She'd never been alone in her life. She clarified the thought to herself. She'd never been without a man in her life until that minute.

She lashed out, kicking her husband's desk. A yelp of pain spewed from her mouth as she started to wreck the office. "This is all your fault, you bastard!" she cried, shaking her fist at Harold's picture, which hung on the wall. When her late husband's sanctuary was in a total shambles, she left the room to run down the hall to her sanctuary, Emily's room.

Tears rolled down her cheeks as she fumbled with the little gold key in her hand.

She would stay in the room forever if she had to.

Forever and ever.

Chapter 30

Trinity, that's how she had finally come to think of herself, parked the car in front of the Hendersons' house. Lillian was sitting on the porch snapping green beans into a colander. Trinity had seen her doing the same thing hundreds of times when she was a little girl. She wondered if the beans were for dinner or if they were to be canned.

Lillian set aside the colander and walked down the steps and over to the car. "What's wrong, child?"

Trinity swallowed hard. She pointed to Harold Windsor's will on the passenger seat. "That's a copy of my father's will," she said, pointing to the sheaf of papers bound in blue. "Mitzi gave it to me a little while ago."

"I see."

"Do you, Lillian? See, I mean."

The older woman's head bobbed up and down. "You're going to go up to the Hill and confront your mother. Do you want me to go with you, Trinity?"

Did she? Of course she did. If she had a choice, she'd prefer to take an army with her. "I appreciate the offer but this is something I have to do alone. I'm nervous about it, Lillian."

Lillian wrapped her plump arms around the trembling young woman. "That's understandable. Confrontations are never pleasant. She's just a person, Trinity. She has no control over you. If I'm right about what I think is in Mr. Harold's will, then you are the one in control. She can't hurt you anymore, honey. I saw Mr. Forrest go up to the Hill a short while ago. He sure didn't stay long. He zoomed down the hill like someone was after him. He hasn't been here for over a week. That in itself is strange because he's here most every day, sometimes twice. Do you want to tell me what's going on?"

"The DNA came back, and I am Trinity Windsor. I want a copy of my birth certificate. I want to see it with my own eyes. As of today, I think I'm in a position to demand it. I read my . . . father's will. He left everything to me, Lillian. Everything. I'm . . . I'm overwhelmed. I'm not sure if I'm reacting to the will, the DNA, or if I'm just piss-ass mad. I waited so long to find out who I really am. I decided I couldn't wait another minute. Do you think I'm wrong?"

"No, child, you're not wrong. Just do what your heart tells you. Maybe Mr. Forrest told Mrs. Windsor what to expect, and that was the reason for his visit. He is her lawyer. She's probably expecting you."

"Oh, I doubt that, Lillian. What if she won't see me?"

"I thought you just told me you owned everything, but I suspect that woman already knows that. Doesn't Windsor Hill belong to you? You are within your rights to demand entrance to the house. If you encounter opposition, call the police. I'll go out to the barn to get John, and we'll both watch from the porch. If you need us, we can be there in five minutes. That woman is tetched in the head."

"Okay. I'm going to go up there now. I've had nightmares about this day for years when I just *suspected* she might be my mother. Now that I'm certain, it seems different somehow."

"Honey, you don't owe that woman anything. She owes you more than she could ever repay in a lifetime. Go along now. As John would say, 'You're all grown-up now, Little Miss. You can handle this.'"

Trinity laughed. "He would say that, wouldn't he?"

"Yes, he would."

Trinity stretched out her arms. "Lillian, if I wasn't always . . ."

"Shhh, no words are necessary. We did love you, child. I want you to know that."

Trinity stepped out of the older woman's embrace. "Time to beard the dragon lady." She could hear Lillian laugh as she made her way to the car.

The short drive seemed even longer than it had when she was a child and forced to climb the hill. Back then she walked as slowly as she could to postpone the inevitable. Now, though, BL's car ate up the road to the top of the hill as she gave herself a pep talk until it was time to turn off the engine.

Outside in the humidity, Trinity brushed her damp hair back from her forehead. She mounted the steps and rang the doorbell with a steady hand. The housekeeper or maid, wearing a neat, tidy uniform, looked at her questioningly.

"Please tell my mother I'd like to see her. My name is Trinity Windsor."

The woman's eyelashes fluttered. "Did you say your mother? Mrs. Windsor doesn't have a daughter. Well, she did, but she passed away some years ago."

"Yes, my sister Emily. Please, tell my mother I'm here, and I want to see her right now. As in *right now*."

Clearly, the maid was flustered. "Uh . . . Mrs. Windsor is . . . She's in Emily's room, and we are never to disturb her when she is in there."

"In that case, I'll disturb her myself. Please don't make this difficult. This is my house now, and I know exactly where Emily's room is. It's really hot, so why don't you get a cool drink and go about your business?"

"But . . . I . . . Mrs. . . . ."

"Go!" Trinity said, her voice ringing with steel. The maid scurried to the back of the house as Trinity made her way up the stairs to the second floor.

Nothing had changed since those long-ago days when she'd come to play with Emily, protesting every step of the way.

And then she was standing in front of the door. Before she could change her mind, she brought her hand up and knocked loudly.

The voice was muffled, but Trinity could make out the words. "I told you never to interrupt me when I'm in here. This is cause for discharge. Go away."

"Open the door . . . *Mother*. If you don't, I'll call John and have him break this door down." When there was no response, Trinity turned on her heel and was halfway down the hall when the door opened.

"What do *you* want? How dare you come here! How dare you!"

Trinity made her way back to her sister's old room to stand opposite her mother. "I'd like my birth certificate, please."

"I don't much care what you want. Get out of my house."

"That's my line, *Mother*. This is *my* house," Trinity said, shouldering her way into Emily's old room. She made her way to the bed and leaped up on it, then did a little bounce. "My bed down at the farm was really hard. The sheets were rough, the blankets rougher. This is really nice."

"Get off that bed! Get off this instant!"

Trinity yanked at the fancy coverlet to fluff up the pillows before she settled them behind her head. "It's mine. Why should I get off? You can't give me orders, *Mother*."

"Don't call me that," Sarabess screeched.

"You certainly don't deserve the title. I can call you Mrs. Windsor if you like," Trinity sing-songed.

"I want you out of this house. You have no business here. You never liked Emily. None of you snotty-nosed children liked that dear, sweet girl."

Trinity swung her legs over the side of the bed. "That's true, but it was your fault, not Emily's. I want to know why you threw me away. After I saved dear, sweet Emily's life."

"She died, so you really weren't the miracle I was led to believe would save her. I didn't throw you away. Whoever told you that lied to you."

"So, Mommie Dearest, what you're saying is that Grace Tanzy lied and Louise Amity lied and you're the one telling the truth. Even a fool can figure out what happened. You paid off that Grace person to change babies with Louise Amity's but she got an attack of conscience and switched us back. I imagine for a good many years you really thought I was Louise Amity's child. Surely you had to suspect when I started to grow into myself and resemble my father. But you're an expert at deluding yourself, I've been told.

"Harold . . . my father, used to tell me stories. As I got older I began to realize the stories weren't make-believe at all. It was his way of telling me who I was. You tried to destroy all that. Why? I just want to know why."

"If I tell you, will you leave?"

"No promises, Mrs. Windsor. I want my birth certificate. I want my baby bracelet. I want my life, and I need those things. Now, tell me why," Trinity said coldly. She was stunned at how calm she felt.

"There's nothing to tell. I gave birth to a child who was . . . ill. I blamed myself for her frail life. She was everything to me. Everything. I never thought I could love a human being the way I loved that child. I would have died for her. It's called mother love. I never loved Harold. I never loved Rifkin, either. I did love Harold's *money* because it allowed me to do what I had to do for Emily. I don't expect you to understand, but I knew I could never love you, so it made sense to me at the time to give you up. You served a purpose, no more, no less. I didn't want any reminders of you. It's that simple, so don't try to read something into what I said that isn't there."

Trinity felt like she'd been punched in the stomach. She knew in her heart of hearts she'd been hungering for a kind word, something that would make sense of her life. "You brought me into this world so Emily could live. You didn't care if I lived or died. You tossed me away like an old shoe and never gave another thought to me until it was time for the trust fund to come to me. Does that pretty much sum it up?"

Sarabess screwed her face into a tight grimace. "Yes."

"That doesn't quite track, Mrs. Windsor. By the age of fifteen I really did resemble Harold. You must have noticed. You had to be afraid somehow or other Mitzi or someone would start delving into my background. Harold knew and tried to tell me in a hundred little ways. To prepare me, I guess. You came to the farm that day and caused a ruckus with Lillian and John. You knew I was upstairs and would hear them talking. You knew how headstrong I was. You knew I would bolt, didn't you?"

"Yes, damn you, I did."

Trinity squared her shoulders. "I'll take my birth certificate now, please."

Sarabess laughed, a ghoulish sound. "What a foolish young woman you are. I hated you. I hate you even more today for upsetting my world. Why would I save your birth certificate? I burned it and that stupid bracelet."

Trinity thought she was going to faint. She reached out to grasp the bedpost until the feeling left her. She needed her birth certificate. She needed to see it, to hold it in her hand, to know she was real. "You're lying. I needed a birth certificate to register for school."

Sarabess laughed again, the same ghoulish sound. "The birth certificate Lillian presented to the school was one I had made up. I did have some interesting friends back then."

"The same friends who traced Harold's name on that bogus will? I'm leaving now. I'm serving you notice, Mrs. Windsor. You have exactly thirty days to leave this house. I understand that Mr. Forrest has the key to the house in Hilton Head that Harold left to you. I'm going to turn this monster house into a home for displaced and handicapped children. I'm going to staff it with the brightest, the finest people I can find. That's what I'm going to use Harold's money for. I think he would like that. He told me once he would love to see the Hill alive with children running about."

"You're insane," Sarabess screeched. "You can't expect me to live in that . . . that hovel. The roof leaks."

Trinity shrugged as she made her way to the door. "Thirty days, Mrs. Windsor. One day longer, and the police will be here to evict you. I'll have Jake call his father to tell him my decision. I'm sure he'll help you."

Sarabess ignored her as she started to smooth back the exquisite coverlet on Emily's bed. Trinity knew her mind was someplace else.

"Mrs. Windsor . . . Look at me." Sarabess turned, her face full of hate. The look stunned Trinity. "If you had said just one kind word to me, if you had said just one nice thing, I would have moved heaven and earth to help you. I would have given you anything you wanted. You gave birth to me so Emily could live. I understand that."

"You understand nothing. It didn't work. Emily died. *She died!* In the end you couldn't save her."

"That's not my fault."

"Yes, it is your fault. Get out of here. I can't bear to look at you another second."

Her eyes bright with unshed tears, Trinity felt her shoulders slump as she made her way down the hall to the wide circular staircase. At the bottom, she turned to look up at the railing that ran along the hallway. She fully expected to see Sarabess Windsor but she wasn't there.

So be it.

Five minutes later, tears streaming down her cheeks, Trinity ran to the Hendersons, who were waiting for her with open arms. They hugged her, squeezed her, crooned to her. As she sobbed against their breasts she at last knew what it was like to feel so loved. These kind, hardworking people *did* love her. They did. She cried harder as the couple led her into the house and out to the kitchen, where she finally calmed down enough to tell them of her encounter with Sarabess Windsor.

Trinity looked up at John Henderson and was stunned to see how wet his eyes were. Lillian was openly crying. She handed out dish towels to everyone to wipe their eyes before she poured frosty glasses of sweet tea. A carrot cake sat in the middle of the table. Not bothering to cut it, Lillian tore off chunks and handed them out. John laughed, and Trinity giggled as she stuffed her mouth.

"Well, it's all over and done with. I gave Mrs. Windsor thirty days to pack up and move out. I'm going to turn the Hill into a school, a home, whatever you want to call it, for displaced and handicapped children. I'd like you both to stay on at double your salary. This house will be yours; I'll see to deeding it over to you. If you would rather move to that gated community Mitzi and I talked about, I'll understand. I think the kids who come here will need some mothering, Lillian. The boys will want to learn how to throw a baseball and I know you can teach them how to shinny up a tree, John, just the way you showed me and Jake. You don't have to give me your answer right now.

Think about it and let me know. And know this: you won't offend me at all if you decide to move out."

John twinkled down at Trinity. "We don't have to think about it, Little Miss. Just let us know when you're ready for us. It's a new beginning for all of us, and it's been a long time in coming."

Trinity burst into tears again. "It was all so wrong. I had parents and a sister that I never got to love. I don't think I'm ever going to understand any of this."

"Shhh," Lillian said, holding her close. "John said it best. It's a new beginning for all of us. Let's hold on to that thought. Don't you have a young man waiting for you?"

Trinity wiped her eyes on the sleeve of her shirt. "I do. Listen, I'll be back, okay? I have a whole bunch of stuff I have to take care of before . . . before we start that new life that looks so promising."

"Anytime, Little Miss. We'll be here waiting for you," John said gruffly.

There were more warm hugs and wet kisses, and more tears.

Trinity looked back at John and Lillian standing in the drive. They were both waving wildly. She gave her horn three sharp blasts. Her little family. John, Lillian, Mitzi, Jake, and BL. A wonderful little family. "And they're all mine."

It was time to call BL, who picked up on the first ring. Trinity babbled nonstop for ten minutes, ending with, "I gave her thirty days to leave. I'm going to hire a contractor to update and refurbish the house in Hilton Head. A nice modern kitchen, one of those sunken garden tubs. A nice deck in the back. All new furniture. She'll be more than comfortable. Do you believe Jake and I won the sack race? So, your mom is okay? Will you come down and help me run the new operation? Can you cancel your contract? Do you believe this, BL? Say something!"

Trinity listened to the laughter on the other end of the phone. "Girlfriend, you were so busy telling me things I wanted to hear, I didn't want to interrupt. Yes to everything. I never really wanted to go to Philly. I just wanted out of this town. When do you want me to come down?"

"As soon as you can. Fly down. Take my car back to the Kolinas and leave it in the drive in back. I had Mitzi send them a big check. I think we're all squared off now. There's just one more thing I have to do before I start my new life. Two things, actually. I have to get in touch with the Bureau of Vital Statistics to get a copy of my real birth certificate, then I have to go to West Virginia. Then, look out, world, I'm going to hit the ground running."

"Woohoo!" BL laughed. "I'll see you sometime next week. I'll call ahead to give you the flight information."

Trinity wore a smile all the way to Mitzi's house, where the animals welcomed her with joyous barks and growls of pleasure. Best of all, though, was seeing the two people she loved most in the world, who were standing at the top of the steps to welcome her with open arms.

Her eyes welling again with tears, Trinity looked at Mitzi and Jake, and said, "We'll talk about this sometime but not right now, okay?"

"You got it, darlin'," Mitzi said.

"Don't you have something to do, Mitzi?" Jake asked.

Mitzi laughed. "As a matter of fact, I do. I'm going to check on Ardeth and Jim. They've been looking really *peekid* this past week. All Ardeth can talk about is all those stupid peacock feathers she bought. I have no idea what *that's* all about, but I plan to get to the bottom of it. Jim seems to be in some kind of daze this whole past week."

Jake and Trinity both burst out laughing. "Mitzi, I think this is one time you really need to mind your own business. Neither Big Jim nor Ardeth will thank you. Trust me, old girl."

"What are . . . Are you saying . . . Ardeth and . . . Jim? Oh, my God!" Mitzi said, her cheeks turning a rosy pink. "Well, now I understand about the peacock feathers," she mumbled, making her way indoors.

"I love it when I can one-up Mitzi," Jake said.

"How about one-upping me, Mr. Forrest?"

"I thought you'd never ask."

Arm in arm, Lucky and Elway alongside, they walked down the steps to the car.

"So, when do you want to get married?" Jake asked.

"February. I always wanted a Valentine's Day wedding. I want your father and John to give me away. The mother of the bride and groom will be Lillian for me and Mitzi for you. Does that work for you, Jake?"

"Yeah, yeah, it does. I want to make a stop before we go back to my apartment. I need to talk to my father. Does that work for you, Trinny?"

"It does, Jake. I want us all to start our new lives with a clean slate."

"Then we better get moving. February isn't that far away."

"Are you happy, Jake?"

"Absolutely. How about you?"

"Never happier."

Epilogue

Seven months later

The January day was cold and overcast, thick gray clouds scudding across the sky at the speed of light. Before long it would rain or snow. More likely sleet. Trinity hoped it would be a cleansing rain. A low, damp fog seemed to be creeping across the cemetery. She strained to see her rental car but finally gave up when the sky opened up. She made no move to get up. She wasn't finished here. Here was the Bluefield Memorial Park Cemetery, where the real Lisa Summers lay at rest. The stone was simple and stark. White granite with the words BELOVED DAUGHTER. Underneath were the dates of her birth and death. Beloved daughter. Taken from this earth way too soon.

Trinity looked down at the patch of dried, frozen grass she'd pried up with a trowel she'd bought in a hardware store a mile from the cemetery. She'd buried her driver's license, the copy of Lisa's birth certificate Sven had gotten for her, Lisa's high school diploma, and the college diploma BL had secured for her. They belonged here.

Tears dripped down Trinity's cheeks and mixed with the freezing rain. "This can't make it right, but I don't know what else to do. I want to think you gave me a life and now I can return it to you. I graduated high school in the top three percent of my class and in the top five percent in my college class. The honors belong to you.

"I wish I had known you. I want to believe we could have been friends if we had met. I came here today to thank you for allowing me to use your identity even though there is no way you could know what Sven and I did. I don't think a day went by that I didn't wonder what you were like. I led almost fifteen years of my life knowing I could never do anything wrong, never shame your name in any way. I want you to know that.

"I don't . . . What I mean is . . . I've never been to a cemetery to . . . to visit someone.

I've never been to a funeral. I don't know if there is a protocol for coming here. I told you about my life when I first got here, about BL and how her mom tends the cemetery back in Northern Cambria. I have to go now. She's waiting for me back home with my new little family . . . They're all waiting for me, so I have to say good-bye and thank you for providing a life for me for fifteen years. Good-bye, Lisa Summers, rest in peace."

Trinity squished her way across the sodden cemetery to where her car was parked. She almost fainted when she saw a car parked next to hers. Frantically, she looked around to see who else was here on such a horrible day. She saw him then.

"Jake!"

"Yeah, it's me. I didn't want to interfere. I was on the same plane. I didn't want you to have to do this all alone. Are you okay?"

"I am now. It was a little dicey there for a while. Thank you for coming."

"We have to stay the night. The airport is going to close because of the storm and the fog. This is just the beginning of the storm. I got us rooms at a motel. Follow me, and we'll settle in for the evening."

"Oh, no, Jake. I have to get back. We're dedicating the school in two days. I can't afford to lose a whole day. What if we can't get out tomorrow? This is terrible. I knew I should have come here last month, but I kept putting it off. I wanted to start the year off right by coming in January and now look what's happened. What about driving?"

"Not a chance. Neither one of us knows these roads, and the fog is going to get worse. If the flights are delayed in the morning, then we can think about driving. Things are under control. BL and Mitzi will keep things running smoothly. Now, guess what?"

"What?"

"Guess who drove me to the airport?"

"Who?" Trinity asked, settling herself in her car.

"My father. We talked more on the ride to the airport than we've talked in the last fifteen years. It was okay. He said he was going to stop by Mitzi's house on his way home. He's taking her a sack of animal food as a peace offering. She'll say all the right things, as will he. In time . . . perhaps we'll see some genuine affection. If it doesn't happen, we'll just have to live with it. I don't know if you want to hear this or not, but he said Sarabess has settled into the renovated house. She was stunned when that moving truck showed up with the contents of Emily's room. He didn't say if she was happy or not, and I didn't ask." He got into his car. "Stay close, Trinny, the fog is terrible. I don't want either one of us to have an accident."

"Don't worry, darlin'," Trinity said in her best imitation of Mitzi's voice. She knew Jake would laugh all the way to the motel.

The day was clear and crisp, the sun shining brightly. Windsor Hill looked like a fairy castle in the golden sunshine. Trinity gasped the way she always did when she drove up to the Hill. Four months of renovations and she was now looking at what she considered her father's legacy. The unveiling of the name of the new school that so far she'd managed to keep secret was about to occur.

The mayor was standing at a makeshift podium, flanked by other town dignitaries. A bright red ribbon ran across the front door. She was supposed to cut it with a pair of shears donated by Little's hardware store. Off to the left were sixteen children who were staring bug-eyed at their new home and school. Tears flooded Trinity's eyes. This was such a good thing. Everyone said so.

The carved sign over the door was still covered. Later, possibly tomorrow, another sign would be erected at the bottom of the hill.

Eight-year-old Timmy Bartlett kicked his wheelchair into high gear and tried to do a wheelie. BL was on him like white on rice. Trinity listened as BL patiently explained that Friday was Pop a Wheelie Day, not today, and he didn't have his harness and helmet on.

Trinity nudged Jake, who was grinning from ear to ear. "She's really good with kids, and they all seem to love her. The mayor looks impatient. He must have a tee time, and we're holding him up. Let's get to it."

Trinity marched up to the podium, nodded to the town fathers and the mayor that it was time for the two-minute speech she'd allotted him.

Mitzi and the seniors clapped and whistled. The police chief handed Trinity the shears to cut the bright red ribbon. A shout of happiness went up from the small crowd.

Trinity's stomach muscles crunched up. She licked at her dry lips as she got ready to remove the covering to the name of her new school. She wondered if the small audience would clap or boo her. Maybe this was wrong, maybe she hadn't thought it through. Too late. She yanked at the covering to reveal the plaque above the entrance:

THE LISA SUMMERS & EMILY WINDSOR
SPECIAL NEEDS SCHOOL

Trinity waited, hardly daring to breathe as she waited for the reaction to the sign.

When it came, she almost fainted with relief. Jake looked at her. She could see pride in his eyes. Mitzi hugged her, and said, "I'm proud of you, darlin'. I had a gut feeling you were going to do this. Perfect, just perfect."

Rifkin Forrest approached. "I'd like to volunteer for anything the children might need." He extended his hand, but Trinity ignored it and hugged him instead.

"Don't think we won't be calling on you, because we will. We have our work cut out for us. We even have a waiting list to get in here. We're going to have to think seriously about building an addition pretty soon. I'd like you to send Mrs. Windsor a picture of our new school. I don't know if it will mean anything to her or not, but I'd still like you to do it," Trinity said in a shaky voice.

"Consider it done. Is there anything I can do right now?"

"Well, hell yes, Pop," Jake answered. "You can help me with all the gear that belongs to these kids. Your golf days are just memories from here on in."

Rifkin clapped his son on the back as he heaved to.

Tears burning her eyes, Trinity turned around to Mitzi. "It's going to work, Mitzi. I feel it in my gut. We're not all warm and fuzzy yet, but I think with a lot of hard work on everyone's part, we might become a *real* family at some point. I hate to ask you this but do you think you could . . . ?"

"Darlin', I invited Rifkin for dinner on Sunday. You and Jake are also invited. He said yes. It's a start. Now, do you think we can head on back to my house so we can go over some of those wedding plans? Time is going by so quickly. Before you know it, Valentine's Day will be here. Looks to me like your fella is trying to get your attention."

Trinity looked upward to the porch where

Jake was blowing her kisses. She blew one back before she galloped up the steps. Jake picked her up and swung her around until she squealed for mercy.

"We did good, Jake. I couldn't have done it without you."

"We're a team, and don't you ever forget it."

"I won't, Jake."

Arm in arm, they walked into the special needs school to applause from the seniors, who were laughing and singing as they revved up their golf carts.

"It's a helluva family we got out there," Jake laughed.

"It's all about family, Jake. It was always about family. It will always be that way if I have anything to say about it."

"Hear! Hear!" Jake said.